# WONDER GIRLS

17/12/18

CHE

Please renew or return items by the date
shown on your receipt

**www.hertsdirect.org/libraries**

Renewals and enquiries:  0300 123 4049
Textphone for hearing or  0300 123 4041
speech impaired users:

L32

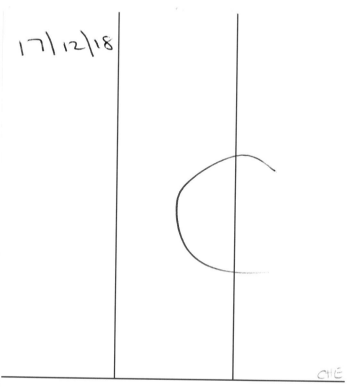

# WONDER GIRLS

Catherine Jones

**WINDSOR**
**PARAGON**

First published 2012
by Simon & Schuster UK Ltd
This Large Print edition published 2012
by AudioGO Ltd
by arrangement with
Simon & Schuster UK Ltd

Hardcover     ISBN: 978 1 4713 0149 0
Softcover     ISBN: 978 1 4713 0150 6

British Library Cataloguing in Publication Data available

Printed and bound in Great Britain by
MPG Books Group Limited

'I suppose there is one friend in the life of each of us who seems not a separate person, however dear and beloved, but an expansion, an interpretation, of one's self, the very meaning of one's soul.'

EDITH WHARTON

'Far away there in the sunshine are my highest aspirations. I may not reach them, but I can look up and see their beauty, believe in them, and try to follow where they lead.'

LOUISA MAY ALCOTT

# PROLOGUE

November 1937

At the dead of night you could peep into another half-lit world.

Every door in the clinic had a little round window, so when the comings and goings of the day were over, when Matron was gone and the lamps were dimmed, and the road outside was as quiet as darkness falling, you could see the babies born to the richest women in the land.

Cecily Stirling stood in the vast redbrick maternity hospital on a quiet London square, looking at her favourite baby lying in a crib at the bottom of his mother's bed. Every so often, she glanced both ways down the corridor as she wiped the pinprick beads of her breath from the glass.

She'd seen him being born, this one. There was a little window in the door of the operating theatre too, and she'd watched as he was pulled out feet first from his mother's belly. She'd heard them talking because she always listened—a Caesarean section, they called it—and she'd repeated it all shift. *Caesarean section.* Cecily liked words. Her teacher at school had said she was good with them.

It had been such a thing to see the surgeon's hand run down the mother's painted purple belly and then out came this little baby from that great big bump. A pause while everyone held their breath for him to take his own first gasp, and then the wail, a great long mewl that ripped through the air like a cut through skin. *Hallelujah! A child is*

vii

*born!*

Cecily thought of the park across the road, the palm trees by the bandstand like green chimneysweep brushes, perhaps a rustle in the undergrowth, and the cold, clear, clinging night air, while here was the special baby, as safe and sound as Jesus in His manger.

He was a boy baby, she was sure, coming into the world so importantly like that. He would grow up in a house in Belgravia with a black door and a lion's head for a knocker; he would become the Prime Minister of England and never let the country go to war again.

It was midnight, more or less, the between time when Cecily finished her shift cleaning the long dark halls and rooms, all the bits shed by people busily bringing babies into being. There was sticky drool to mop, there was sometimes blood pooling by a new mother's bed, or puddles of vomit—'I want every speck wiped,' Matron would say—or a white feather strayed from a pillow.

She should be taking her mop and bucket to the cupboard, but Sister had told her to stand outside the special baby's room.

Footsteps tapped by on the pavement outside. The girl heard the metal thump of a trolley hit a door somewhere beyond the end of the corridor. Cecily blew on her hands. It was cold staying put, even with her coat on. She went to the little window again, looked at the baby and the mother as still as the crocodile suitcase set on the floor by the bed. She'd been in the room once and touched that case. Dark and shiny it was, as smooth as the skin of a proper lady.

She waited, wondering what was to happen.

There had been talk that the mother might die and that a new lady would come and take the baby away. Earlier, Cecily had heard Sister say words like *paperwork* and *discretion* and *night-time* to Matron, who had nodded and said it all seemed in hand.

'What will happen to the baby if the mother should die?' Cecily had asked when it was just Sister and her two nights ago. 'And what does discretion mean?'

'You ask a lot of questions,' Sister had replied, and after that Cecily kept quiet. Nobody argued with Sister, not even Matron—and she was no pussycat. But then much later, Sister had come and found her in the linen cupboard and said how Cecily might help the poorly mother and her baby, but she must tell nobody because the lady was very important. Cecily felt very important herself then.

She'd stay here all night if Sister wanted her to, standing with her hand on her mop, like a shepherdess with her crook, in this endless corridor in this great big building, with its staircases and landings and rooms with distant ceilings, and a London Transport omnibus going by below. Cecily didn't usually go home in any case. The large cupboard where the sheets and blankets were kept was better than another telling-off from her father, or laying the fire at home each morning so silvery flecks of ash flew up her nose. There was food here too, in the kitchen, where Cook gave her a cup of warm milk and a crust with jam and a sit-down in front of the range.

'Discretion means keeping quiet about things,' Sister had said. 'Not saying a word.'

Cecily had been worried she'd be told to leave,

what with the linen cupboard and food and asking too many questions, but Sister hadn't seemed to mind. She'd even put her hand on Cecily's shoulder and said she could call her Sissie, not Sister, if nobody else was about. 'We can be Sissie and Ceci,' she'd said. 'Our little secret,' and that had been that.

The names stuck and Cecily didn't ask too many questions.

Watching the special baby's visitors, hoping to see his father, Cecily had kept the corridor spotless, going back and forth. The husband would be an important person, she was sure. He would wear a suit, have long legs and hair swept off a sloping forehead. He would arrive from his office and his polished shoes would tap importantly into the room to admire their pink-cheeked baby. He would bend and kiss his fashionable wife.

But the only man who came was old and fat and hairy; he smelled of tobacco and kept his hands in the pockets of a big dark coat. There had been lots of ladies instead. The first night, there was an odd one, a neither here nor there one, who wasn't old or young, with black hair parted by a white line and a bosom that bounced as she came clumsily down the corridor, but then she'd smiled and seemed to Cecily like a lady. But that other one, the second night, she was like a scarecrow in a long black dress, with sleeves like flappy triangles and shoes that came tap-tap-tapping like an impatient fingernail along the corridor.

Cecily had been standing outside with her mop when that lady came out of the room. You couldn't expect someone like her to say anything to someone like Cecily, but the woman had put spiky white fingers on her arm and said, 'I am to have a baby.' Cecily had panicked and thought she meant there and then, but the lady wasn't fat enough and had blue jelly veins sticking up on the backs of her hands. Cecily had given a little curtsey and been glad when that lady swept off.

Knowing the mother might die, she started to think of these women as mourners at a funeral, not visitors to a birth. It was strange because there was something dark and flitting about them that reminded her of her own mother being buried, and her father in a suit borrowed from his brother quickly throwing soil on the coffin in a hole in the ground.

The door at the end of the corridor opened and two figures—*please let one of them be Sissie*—were coming towards her. The corridor seemed to have a silent hum to it—that was queer as well, as though it was waiting, like Cecily, for something to happen.

It was Sissie and a lady in a black hat with a veil over her face, and a dark coat like all the nurses wore that almost hid her feet.

'Stay here, Cecily,' Sissie told her sternly when she opened the door to the poorly mother's room, and Cecily stood back for the lady to go inside. She couldn't help but look at her. Something was wrong. The woman seemed uneasy, the way her head and her eyes were still under the veil. She reminded Cecily of the new mothers who sat up straight in bed pretending to be comfortable for visitors when everyone knew that really they would prefer to lie down and sleep. She was putting on a show, Cecily was sure.

The door clicked shut. Was that it now? Was she

to leave? Cecily wondered if the lady wearing a black veil meant the mother had died. It frightened her, the idea of a dead body beyond the door before her, but that little window . . . where was the harm in just one look? She was a curious child, fourteen years of age, with a brain the teachers said could have taken her far if she hadn't needed to get out and work for her keep. 'This is a private clinic, and private means *private*,' Matron had said when she'd last caught her looking through windows. Cecily knew she was pushing her luck.

There were voices through the door. Cecily lifted the cold metal handle of her bucket and took the wooden mop in her other hand. She'd pretend she was just moving off and had happened to look through the window.

Sissie was lifting the baby from the crib. The two women were talking, their heads bobbing about, then Sister looked towards the door. Quick as anything—she was good at getting out of her father's firing line back home—Cecily moved to one side, worrying about the tell-tale fading circle her breath had left on the glass. Nothing happened. She waited, felt her heart beat, then stepped back for another look and oh, she almost had a turn! She was face to face with Sissie, each of them looking at the other through the window in the door.

Cecily moved to one side. The door opened. She had a hopeful half-smile on her face as she looked at the roll of blanket in Sissie's arms.

'Ceci,' said Sister in a stern voice, 'as you know, the baby's mother is very poorly and this lady has come to help give the baby a safe home.'

Cecily nodded. She wished she had brought her

mop and bucket away from the door.

'Remember I said you might help the poorly mother too?'

She nodded again. Perhaps she wasn't dead. Perhaps Ceci might help save the baby's mother.

'Well, here.' Sissie was holding the baby to her.

Cecily couldn't speak. Any words were jammed in the top of her throat like a knot of rope. She was thinking about the lady in the room. The baby's mother must be dead. Her own mother was dead too.

Sister said, 'This lady will meet you outside. We just have to fill in some paperwork for Matron and the doctors and some other important people who know that I am giving you the baby.'

Cecily looked at the woman in the veil. She could see the whites of her eyes flicking between the two of them. The lady had her hands clasped in front of her as though she was trying not to grab at the baby and Cecily saw that she didn't wear nail polish as a lady might—and that her fingers were rough and red.

'Take the baby,' Sissie said. Her voice was urgent but firm. 'Take the baby out the back way, and wait for me at the top of the stairs.'

'What about the mother?' Cecily thought of the woman in the bed, her pale face, the way she hadn't moved when Sissie and the lady were taking her baby.

'The baby's mother is very, very poorly.'

Cecily had heard this kind of talk before, when her mother, who had glorious shining hair the colour of conkers, had stayed more and more in her chair in the corner.

'Is she . . . will she . . . ?' She couldn't take the

baby from his mother.

Sissie shook her head as though there was nothing more to be said.

'Cecily, I am asking you now to take the baby.'

The girl stretched her hands out and Sissie stepped towards her. She felt the weight of the child in her arms, as heavy and light as a fresh egg, and she couldn't let go.

Sister said, 'No more questions now, Ceci. It is down to you.'

Cecily knew then what to do, and as she turned away from the door and the little window and the lady who was saying nothing, the baby's weight settled against her, as good as a pat on the shoulder.

She watched the two of them, Sissie and the lady, walk off down the corridor, and at the door Sister turned and waved, and then the door closed and it was Cecily and the baby alone in the dark.

With her palm on the baby's back, she walked, following in Sissie's footsteps, opening the door with one hand and easing the two of them, herself and the baby, through, across the landing and—a push with her shoulder—through a second door, along another dark corridor.

'Wait out the back for me,' Sissie had said. At the end of the hall, Cecily opened the door and stepped carefully onto the rear stairs, thick with black, pitted paint and shiny dark in the faint light from the lamp on the street corner.

Her heart was drumming crazily in her chest. She couldn't think straight. Into her mind came the memory of a day she'd spent with her mother not long before she died. It was summer, they were in the park, and a crowd was gathered round a man doing card tricks on a small wooden box. 'Find the Lady,' he'd cried, winking at her mother, which Cecily hadn't liked. Her mother had laughed and bet a penny she could say which card was the Queen—and then he'd turned the three cards face down on the box, and moved them around here and there, back and forth, until Cecily pulled on her mother's hand and said, 'Tell the man to stop.'

Cecily stood at the top of the stairs for she didn't know how long, before she slid her hands under the baby's warm, thumb-sized armpits and lifted its face to hers. Find the Lady, she thought, wondering at what had happened just now in the hospital. The way all the ladies had been in and out of this little baby's room had her head in a spin. Her mother hadn't guessed right that day in the park, but the man had given back her penny, saying a lady should never pay. Lots of people had called her mother a lady, though she washed her own floors, stripped the weekly roast to the bone, and didn't have the money for her prescription before she died.

The girl's breath clouded fiercely into the icy air and then she heard the voice.

'Ceci,' it said. 'Ceci. Ceci. Ceci.' The sound of her name seemed to lash frantically at her through the darkness, over and over, like a circus master's whip encouraging an animal to perform.

# PART ONE

PART ONE

# CECILY 2009

I liked the way the girl asked if she could call me Ceci. It wasn't Mrs this or Miss that or, heaven help us, Ms something else entirely. I must be half a century older than her, but she wanted to call me Ceci.

Forget pumping needles full of poison in your forehead to fill out the wrinkles—not that I'm young enough to go in for that kind of thing—but it knocked years off me in an instant, her expecting us to be equal like that.

'Well, I'm Sarah,' she said, 'and would it be OK if I call you Ceci?'

'Yes, I'd like that,' I told her. I'm not one of those who complain about call-centre staff using Christian names. No need for titles where I come from, but I didn't say that.

The first time, I was cutting the laurel in front of the house, struggling to get the branches of sturdy leaves in the council recycling bags, when she came round the corner with her dog. She said my hedge had lovely bright berries, and didn't the combination of red and green remind me of Christmas. I felt the pause after she'd spoken and later, I wondered if it was a question but it wasn't. It was just the right amount of time for me to see she didn't think Christmas was always a happy occasion.

Usually I'm not anywhere near so chatty, but by the time we finished we'd covered allotments and knitting, egg cosies, bee-keeping, and the council wanting to get rid of the lido on the seafront.

3

'I love that white, curvy garage from the 1920s on the road out of town,' she told me.

'It's like a grubby old wedding cake,' I replied, and she laughed.

We didn't stop. People were walking by us—off to fetch a newspaper or a bar of chocolate or repeat prescription—and then those same people were coming back and there we still were, on the pavement outside the house, talking. The girl was so full of things to say I did wonder if she might be throwing out ideas to find what best would work with me, but I soon felt shame for questioning whether she wasn't being her real self. I saw I'd been spending too much time with the women at the old age get-togethers in the community centre. If anyone under fifty talks to them, they think they're after their money.

'I often come this way with the dog,' she said, 'so if we get on your nerves, you can tell us to walk on by.'

After that first day, with spring coming, I started going out the front more and more. Since Freda died, I'd let the garden go. I wasn't keen on being outside, a sitting duck for the small talk of passers-by wondering how I was coping now my 'companion' had 'passed on', but soon after meeting the girl, I told myself it was time to smarten the place up. It looked such a mess, last summer's plants shrivelled and caught up with dead papery leaves, and dandelion heads standing like lollipops between the tiles on the path.

It's a quaint enough set-up, one of a square of redbrick Victorian mansions around a church in an orchard, but when Freda bought us this house, the terrace was going down. Now it's going up. My neighbours have cars with three rows of seats. They get their food delivered in vans from fancy supermarkets. Their back gardens are like theme parks with trampolines and tree houses for the children. I am the old woman in the shoe lowering the tone.

If the weather was fine, I'd start the morning by opening the front door and putting my tools in the porch, just in case she came by when I was having the first cup of tea of the day out the back. Then I started finding it difficult to relax with that cuppa, wondering if I'd miss her, so I took a chair to the front and perched there sipping, as though I'd opened an outdoor café. It wasn't all sitting about like a dummy. I weeded, I thinned out the geraniums, I snipped off dead daffodil heads, I turned over the soil, all the while going back and forth to top up the fire while keeping an ear out for her voice. I took it slowly—I had to. At my age you don't bend over knowing for certain you'll come back up again.

'Ceci?' she'd call, saying my name like a question over the hedge, as though if I didn't reply she'd move on and not mind.

I looked forward to seeing her standing at my gate in her brown tweed coat, flecked with yellow and pink, and her little knitted hat, and the way the dog pulled on his lead up the path towards me, as though I was a family member. Mungo, his name is, a great yellow lump of a thing, walking about the place like King of the Road in a big manly collar with studs.

'That's me,' I'd say, hoisting myself up from digging.

When she saw all the new patches of empty soil,

she carried round a tray of foxgloves—three for two at the garden centre!—and said, 'Let me plant them for you, Ceci, if your hips are bad.'

I didn't like to say how I've always thought of foxgloves as not weeds exactly, but roadside flowers, let's say, like poppies or those big daisies—but in they went and they should come up nice and tall this year.

'Did you know that bees like blue and purple flowers?' she asked when she saw they'd gone in. I could tell she was worried she'd forced them on me and I saw her pleasure at the grouping of green leaves lifting from a sprinkling of compost.

'No, I didn't know that,' I said, 'but I do now.'

I was starting to see the way she looked at things, and they were usually things people don't notice, things with a bit of colour that come free. I'd have thought at her age she'd be all for the bells and whistles, the fancy cars and frocks, but she seemed content to sit and stare. Soon enough, I found out she had a husband working long hours as a lawyer in London, that she read a lot, and that she was down here having a break in her parents' house while they did up a place in Spain. I was determined to get it all out of her, just as soon as she left me a gap long enough to ask.

With her, it was always a dive straight in to something else, usually to do with the past. I suspected she thought I'd had a rather different upbringing to the one I did have. Not all old ladies wore floral-patterned frocks on camomile lawns, I wanted to say, but I enjoyed answering her questions as best I could. Every so often I tried to tell her something bleak and real in the hope she'd see my life wasn't all chandeliers and Shim Sham bands—well, none of it was—but she gobbled up every little detail about powdered egg in the war as though I was handing out spoonfuls of caviar.

'You're thirty-four,' I told her. 'You shouldn't be talking about rations.'

'I'm not talking, I'm listening,' she replied.

'You and me will get on like a house on fire then,' I said, because the amount I was chopsing I must have been making up for the years I'd kept quiet.

'I like people with memories,' she told me one day. 'I always get teary watching those brave old men marching on Remembrance Day.'

'What's the matter with you?' I asked, though I had an idea. 'You need to get out a bit more.'

When Sarah first came in the house, she marvelled at the length of the hall, at the height of the ceiling, at the mosaic of tiles on the floor, at the picture rail, the cornices. Look at the banister, she said. Think of the hands over the years that have burnished this to such a shade of ginger.

'I've got a romantic on my hands, have I?' I said, leading her into the room where I spend most of my time.

'I wish,' she replied quietly, and I thought, Full marks for putting your foot in it, Ceci, because by then I suspected something was up with her marriage; thereafter I resolved not to go interfering in her life just because I hadn't much of a one left myself.

After Freda died, I went for days without speaking to anyone. I only ventured out in the dark, walking the pavements and looking in at front rooms, wondering how it would feel to be part of the family framed in the bay window beneath a big paper lampshade.

I enjoyed those walks, the way the darkness turned down the volume on the day's glare. Everyone was inside. In summer you could always tell a Sunday night by the soap suds around the tyres of squeaky-clean cars and the faint peppery whiff of garden fires. You might spot a fox, looking so spindly and prehistoric, rush across the road, or curtains being drawn just as you walked by. I started to see why Freda went on her night-time treks, though the two of us used to row something chronic about her going off without saying. Even in winter she'd be away for a couple of hours, coming back through the door with cold skin and eyes so red they looked peeled. I never went with her. People aren't together all the time, she'd tell me. Stop following me from room to room. I used to think it was the walking that finished her off and I'd wish she had listened to me.

That's what I used to think.

'We're having a bit of space from each other,' Sarah said, when I couldn't help dropping in whether her husband would be down at the weekend. She gave me a look as though I wouldn't understand and she didn't want to explain.

'Oh,' I said. 'Well, that's a precious form of loving, isn't it? Giving each other the space to be.'

It's a heck of a shaky balance, I thought to myself, working away at making sure both of you are happy in a marriage—or a friendship, for that matter—without upsetting the applecart, though I didn't say anything. Not then anyway.

She was the first in a long time to come inside my control centre, where I have my computer on a desk pushed up to the window, and a real fire in the grate to warm my back. There's not much beyond that, just two easy chairs tilted towards the telly in the corner, a small table and a Welsh dresser on the side wall—*How lovely, Ceci, the original one!*—filled with my books because I've done a bit of studying in my time.

That first March afternoon it was dark—I see now I was silly not to have got a good desk lamp, though the doctor says that wouldn't have made a difference—but the room was as warm as a car left all day in the sun. I felt such a fool when I tripped and almost went over.

'Oh, and a step down into the room, doesn't that make it cosy?' Sarah said, as I straightened myself up before she got close enough to give me a hand.

'Yes,' I replied. 'To keep me on my toes.'

One thing I will say is the girl didn't like to come empty-handed. That's a nice attribute to have, I think, always arriving with something in your hands. You don't see many people wear gloves these days either, so I noticed hers straight away— duck-egg blue wool with a navy velvet trim around the wrist—and I remember thinking we had a bit of a lady here, on the quiet.

The first time she brought biscuits she asked, 'You don't mind if I dunk, do you?' We looked at the biscuit as it came back up out of her tea.

'See it quivering, Ceci?' she said.

When Freda died I thought I'd never smile again.

'Down the hatch!' I replied, dipping my own. I liked the way she shed her gloves and dug her nail into the plastic packet to split open the biscuits. There was no hesitation.

'I hope you're getting some goodness down you

9

too,' I told her one day, because that's all we seemed to be doing, eating the biscuits and cakes she was making and carrying round in a tin with an ice-skating scene on its lid.

'Oh yes, Ceci,' she told me. 'There are apples and broad beans and carrots and all sorts of other things on the horizon. Why don't you come and see my vegetable patch?'

'Sounds like you're bedding in for good.'

'I'm looking forward to having apples with leaves on their stems in the fruit bowl.'

'Never mind the fruit bowl,' I replied. 'You make sure you get up to London to see that husband of yours before you forget what he looks like.'

The girl—it took me a while to call her Sarah, but she called me Ceci all the time—thought this place was one of those funny little seaside towns that'd seen better days, the kind of faded resort with cafés serving ice-cream sundaes in long thick glasses, a place where nothing ever happened. I had a smile at that.

What are you talking about, I'd say to her. Look at the fairy-lit seafront and all these streets busy with trees and Blue Lias houses, and that quaint railway station that hasn't changed in years. Look at the beach with its giant firefly circles of light at night from the fishermen's lamps—you won't get that in your city, and we'd both laugh. It isn't the best by day, I agree. Lots of pebbles and mucky-looking water when the tide is up, and a rusting pier that's like a lot of the town's inhabitants—on its last legs.

'Think of that lovely library with its clock tower,' I said once, and that became another of our jokes.

10

'You and your library,' she replied. 'Come out with me if you think this place is so great. Let's go out on the town.'

I was horrified. I'm in my eighties. 'Get off,' I said. 'Where were you thinking?'

'Let's go for a pizza at the Italian place on the front.'

So one evening she picked me up in the car and we motored down to the prom. I'd run an iron over my best white blouse and wore it with black slacks. I put the amber bead necklace Freda gave me for my seventieth to my neck but I couldn't fasten the catch and left it behind on the dressing table.

The place was packed, but we got a table by the window, just the road between us and the sea which was high that night and seemed almost to lap onto the pier. The water can come up onto the pavement—something to do with the moon and the tides, I've been told—and if you're there to see it, then it looks so strange and frightening: all these great waves of dirty, salty water heaving over the promenade railings and lunging at the café windows.

Don't let the pier and the ice-cream seller, nor the restaurants and the Yacht Club fool you. That stretch of water has the second highest tidal range in the world and it ain't shy of taking lives.

That night—we've been twice since—we had a pizza between us and talked about I don't know what: post-natally depressed women being put in asylums, biscuits only coming in tins at Christmas and whether Cadbury's Old Jamaica was still going.

I remember Sarah looking round at the tables of families with kids and saying in a sad sort of voice,

11

'Think of the children going home and being tucked up in little attic rooms with cosy sloping ceilings.' She talked as though everyone lived in a tall thin house straight out of *Mary Poppins*.

'You've got all that to come,' I said, and left it at that because she didn't reply, though her appetite for questions never let up. *What's a tea dance, Ceci? Did you play hopscotch when you were a child? Was there ever a hat shop in the town?*

So I can't say I didn't know that when I put out the photo on the Welsh dresser, it would be the first thing she noticed the next time she came round. I set it just back from the corner too, and in any case it's the kind of picture that stands out, not least because it's the only one in the house. I haven't got that many bits—Freda hated things lying about—just a bowl of onyx eggs I used to collect and warm in my hands when we were watching the telly. I still find it so relaxing.

'Who's this, if you don't mind me asking?' Sarah said, as I knew she would. The girl didn't disappoint, she went straight for it, like a rat to a bin bag.

'I love her long-legged bathing suit, not like today's skimpies.' She picked it up to pore over. 'Is it you, Ceci?'

I tried imagining what Sarah was seeing. She'd got me going a bit with her pointing at things, with all of her questions and wanting answers, always after a touch of something else and more. I told myself I was putting it out for her as much as anything. I could tell the girl was lonely and looking for something to take her mind off things.

Well, I knew she'd see that it was an old photo, that much was obvious, being black-and-white and

12

so grainy, and it doubtless looked far older to her than it did to me. And what about the young girl in it wearing a bathing suit, one of those old-fashioned styles that look so sturdy and prim now swimwear is no bigger than a thumbprint? Sarah would look at the costume, I was sure, with her interest in clothes and hats and tippets and brooches and going to jumble sales and charity shops and picking things out of skips on the road.

I reckoned she'd like the bathing suit, all-in-one with long legs to it, like shorts that come down over the thigh, and big thick straps at the top to be sure everything's safely up and in. I've seen similar outfits in films with girls and boys running from a row of brightly coloured beach huts, and I've a fancy this kind of costume might have been popular in white and navy stripes, perhaps with a little red bow on the collar . . . but anyway, I'm starting to sound like Sarah.

This girl's outfit is black and the rubber swimming cap hanging from her hand is white—cream, maybe, you can't tell with the old photos. She looks stout enough, her bare feet on a beach of grey pebbles with what looks like the side of a cliff in the background. Her hair is dark, in a bob that comes to a point on either side of her mouth, she has a pretty, curvy face and dark eyes, as milky brown as chocolate pennies, I'd say, though that might be a bit of poetic what-have-you.

It's an old image from an age gone by, but the funny thing is I've seen black-and-white shots just like it in the fancy greetings cards shop in town. They made me stop and stare and pick them quickly from the shelf, I can tell you, but it's never been the same girl as this one. Of course not. This

13

one's been all but wiped off the face of the earth. I've a feeling that happens to a number of women ahead of their time.

Anyway, I did ask the woman in the card shop what's all this then, with all the old things coming back in fashion? Retro-chic, she told me. Oh, I said, I'm old—does that make *me* retro-chic? She didn't even crack her face and out I went, thinking, It may take me five minutes to get off the bus but I'm more with-it than you, dear. The birthday cards they had in there ended at seventy too.

'No, it isn't me,' I told Sarah, picking one of the dog's hairs off my slacks pointedly, as if I was removing the topic from the conversation. 'That dog's hairs get everywhere.'

I regretted putting the photo out now. What possessed me? Beyond an urge to come clean, I was in something of a hurry and got carried away wondering where the girl's appetite for information might lead.

'She's very pretty,' Sarah said. 'A swimmer. Is that our beach in the background? I wonder if she was meant to look at the camera.'

It had taken me a while to work out what I made of her expression, the girl in the photo, not least because these days I need to look twice at anything to get much of a picture. She's not smiling, this young girl, and you'd expect a girl to smile, having a photo taken back then when it was such a novelty, wouldn't you? I'd say it's almost as though she doesn't know the camera is there, that she's off somewhere else with that faraway look.

'Perhaps she had her own ideas about things,' I said. Then, quickly, 'That's enough of your questions. That dog looks as though he could do

14

with a walk.'

I must have sounded like Freda, with my gruffness. Freda wasn't one for questions, or answers. Too much gossip in this place, she'd say. Small-town mentality, she'd call it—but then she did spend a lot of time away and it must have been awfully difficult coming back here after all she had done and all she had been through.

## 1

Ida Gaze was the only swimmer waiting at the pool for the first race to begin.

As the townsfolk poured through the turnstiles for the 1928 Annual Gala, red, white and blue pennants crisscrossing the turquoise waters of the seafront lido fluttered noisily in the salty breeze.

On normal summer days, the pool was scattered with splashing bodies as though they'd been tipped, kicking like newborns, from a giant's sack, but today it was empty, stretching before Ida like a vast tray of blue jewels rippling and glinting.

The cement edge was cool and gritty beneath her feet. Her black Wolsey costume felt as snug as the submarine cap on her head.

When a small cloud slid onto the high white-gold sun, two tiny points appeared on her chest and Ida folded her arms. Her tanned skin was covered in goose bumps.

'Golf balls,' she mouthed at Freda who was sitting on her left, and the two of them laughed. No doubt someone in the crowd was watching, just as they'd probably seen Ida squat clumsily so she could yank at her new bathing suit riding up between her legs. People didn't miss a trick in this town, according to her father, but nobody would know what golf balls meant, only Freda.

On both sides, the packed benches bobbed with cloches, flat caps, Homburgs, and straw boaters trimmed with stripy silver bands picked out by the June sun. There was even a bowler hat.

The town's galas were always an occasion, but

the lido was a spectacle in itself. With its curved white walls and blue railings, it was as handsome as a grand ocean liner docked for good on the headland of this small seaside town.

It was the largest, bluest pool in Wales with the sky stretching forever as its ceiling. It took your breath away, it really did, a great spearmint oblong that smelled of chlorine though the water was pumped in from the sea. There were rows of changing rooms for ladies and gentlemen that arched each side like white crescent moons, and a small paddling area for the children with a stone dolphin in the middle, its mouth spouting water.

The Girls' 50 Yards couldn't be far off starting, but the others were still standing on the grassy slope, looking over at Ida with their hands to their mouths, no doubt discussing what Maeve Cawley, the Ladies' Swimming Club captain, had just said.

'Your swimming could take you far,' she'd told Ida as the girls filed out of the cubicles.

'How far?' Ida asked, tightening the strap on her cap. She knew she was in good shape. Enough people had commented on how she didn't stay out of the water, swimming every night after school until dusk.

'What year were you born?'

'Nineteen hundred and twelve.'

'That's the year Irene Steer, who came from Cardiff, won a gold medal at the Olympics in Stockholm.'

The others had been limbering up, shaking out firm arms and legs the sun had turned a healthy milky caramel, but listening all the same.

'Where's Stockholm?' asked Ida. 'I was thinking more of Weston-super-Mare.'

18

She'd meant it as a joke, and though Maeve had smiled, some of the girls looked at each other as if to say who was Ida Gaze to think she might swim the Bristol Channel.

Ida looked beyond the lido's railings, at the dangerous grey waters which separated Wales from England. Men with muscles like prize marrows were always trying to swim from the town's beach to Weston and being hauled out of overpowering currents halfway. Nobody had done it and nobody thought anyone—let alone a girl—would ever get to the other side.

She turned back to the pool. The crowd was clapping the Gala Committee chairman, who held a loudspeaker and a starting gun. The others moved to their lanes around her.

'Go for it,' Freda had whispered, before she went to sit down. She'd stopped going in the water some time ago because she wouldn't wear a bathing costume.

'Why?' Ida asked her.

'Because of these,' Freda said, pointing at her breasts. 'They're growths. I loathe them, they're like golf balls.'

'We're nearly sixteen. There'd be something wrong if we didn't have them.'

'People would think there was something wrong with me,' Freda replied, 'however I was.'

Sometimes there was no point in arguing with Freda. She was touchy, that's the word people used about her. Oddball was another, but Ida would always be friends with Freda. She noticed things, and understood things nobody else did. She loved animals and birds and wearing baggy trousers, and hated housecraft lessons as much as Ida did. None

19

of the other girls seemed to think it a waste of time cleaning windows with newspaper dipped in vinegar, but Freda had thrown her sodden ball at the wall and run off, saying she felt sick.

Ida dropped her head, toes curving over the edge of the pool, braced for the quiet then the start gun. All that mattered was the crack and they were off! It was the same every time she went in the water, her desire to get to the end as fast as she could.

She would win for her parents, who hadn't turned up, and for Freda who helped her train, sitting on the beach with a stopwatch every night, shouting out the time it took Ida to swim between the pier and the Yacht Club causeway.

At the pool's end, Ida turned from left to right as the other heads came in behind. She had done it. Freda stood with two fingers in her mouth and let out a whistle as loud as a shrieking train.

After her last race, there were cheers and shouts as she raised herself from the pool. Pulling off her hat, Ida felt a hand on her back and heard the words, 'Well done.' She had come first in everything and was to be crowned the Gala Princess.

'It's down to Freda Voyle,' she told the crowd after the chairman handed over her medal, a silver disc engraved with the words *Gala Princess* 1928.

As she held the small chrome circle in the air, Ida's towel slipped from her shoulders and there was a flash like sunlight hitting a looking glass as the town's photographer took a shot of the winner.

'If it wasn't for Freda coming to the beach with me every night,' she shouted, 'I don't think I'd have done this. Thank you, Freddie!'

The wind was getting up. People had hands on their hats as they turned to look at Freda, who was rolling her eyes.

'What's the matter with you today?' Freda mouthed. 'Can't you keep your mouth shut?'

But Ida thought she seemed secretly pleased and clapped her all the more, and then everyone started applauding Ida again until she bent to pick up her towel and bowed off the small stage erected at the side of the pool.

The Gala finale was a synchronised display by the Ladies' Swimming Club. 'Ladies and gentlemen!' the captain shouted at each pose the girls struck in the water. 'We give you the Submarine! The Porpoise! The Swan!'

As it came to a close, the girls formed a circle, holding hands and frantically treading water, with Ida in the centre. She looked around at the wide faces, narrow faces, eyelashes stuck with water, black straps on bronzed clavicles, all coming towards her, until the next thing she knew, she was being raised in the air by a mass of hands.

'Ladies and gentlemen!' called Maeve Cawley to the applauding crowd. 'We give you the Gala Princess!'

Later, as the girls filed down the aisle between the two rows of changing rooms, Maeve called for quiet.

'I know the club was formed with the competitive spirit in mind,' she said, 'but I am pleased to see a sporting atmosphere has prevailed and you are all keen to congratulate Ida on her success.'

'Three cheers for the Gala Princess,' a voice shouted.

'Hear, hear, hip hip,' said another.

As the group chorused 'hooray' three times, Ida blushed. They were such a nice lot.

Maeve turned to Ida. 'What's next?' she said. 'The Channel?'

'Oh, I don't know about that,' Ida replied, hearing the quiet around her. One of the girls rubbed her arm. In the shade of the changing rooms it could seem suddenly chilly.

'I do.' It was Freda, coming round the end of the row in grubby white trousers and a pale blue fine-knit top.

'Of course you will swim the Channel,' Freda went on as the girls moved off, caps swinging from the straps in their hands.

'Oddball,' a voice said as wooden slatted doors swung open and closed—bang bang bang—and everyone disappeared into their favourite cubicles.

Inside the changing room, Freda plonked herself on the small bench at the back and handed Ida her towel.

'What did you have to go and say that for?' Ida asked, stepping out of her bathing suit.

Freda was studying her sand-shoes as Ida rubbed herself down.

'Just because of the way people are,' Freda replied. 'Giving those looks as though we're making things up.'

'Living in cloud-cuckoo-land,' said Ida, trying to take off her father, but it was Freda who was the mimic. She could do all the teachers. Once she'd called across the quadrangle to the Headmistress in the Scottish accent of the history teacher. 'Och, Miss Casling dear, you have your skirt tucked into your slip and we have a pretty picture-postcard

22

view of your wee undergarments.'

Ida put a finger to her lips. 'Sssh,' she whispered. 'Listen.'

From the gap above and below the saloon doors came voices.

'I think Ida Gaze will swim the Channel,' said Ivy Gerrish.

'She will be the first ever,' called Nellie Marsh.

'The newspapers will come from London,' Ivy replied.

'That's because they don't believe a girl can do it,' Nellie yelled. 'And I for one hope Ida Gaze does.'

Freda grimaced. 'Why do people do that?' she asked. 'Talk as though we're not there? My Aunt Sylvia is the same, always coming round asking my mother what I'm doing with myself as though I'm not in the room.'

'Oh heck,' said Ida, as several pairs of bare feet appeared outside their cubicle and the doors were pushed open. Bella Pertwee, her least favourite member of the Swimming Club, put her head through the gap.

'Well?' she said. 'Is it true?'

'Is what true?' Ida asked, holding her towel in front of her naked body with the bottom covering her feet.

'Keep your beak out,' said Freda, pushing her foot at the door. 'Literally.'

'It's you that said it, Freda Voyle.' Bella's voice was friendly enough, the kind of teasing it would be easy to say was joshing if the club captain appeared.

'Then why do you doubt it?' Freda's temper flared quickly if she thought people were being

23

tricky and unkind.

Ida heard herself say, 'If you're on about me swimming the Channel, then of course it's true.'

'Well, I hope you'll be putting your costume on to do it,' Bella replied, before disappearing. As the cubicle doors swung back together, Freda kicked her foot out angrily.

'Leave it, Freddie,' Ida said. 'They're only having a bit of fun.'

'Only a bit of fun,' came Bella's fading voice. 'Is that what they call it?'

Shaking her head, Freda pulled a paper bag of coconut strips from her pocket and offered it to Ida.

'You're not really going to swim the Channel, are you?' she asked.

There were endless stories of lives taken by the Severn Sea. Seven people in a pilot boat from Somerset swamped. Sixty soldiers drowned. Men who failed to swim it talked of being lucky to come away with their lives.

'I'll have to now,' Ida replied, 'or they really will think we're always making things up.'

\*　　　\*　　　\*

The place was empty by the time Ida and Freda emerged from the changing rooms.

As they stood at the pool's edge, Freda reached for Ida's hand. The day had grown long enough for the water to seem cold and uninviting and the lido far less sparkling.

Beyond the railings, the Channel stretched eleven miles to England. In the middle of the water, there was an island, Flat Holm, from where the first wireless communication across water was transmitted in 1897.

'Do you remember that lesson about Marconi and his message?' Ida asked, as they pushed through the turnstile. It was queer to think school would be over for good soon enough.

' "Are you ready?"—That's what it was.'

'I'm ready,' Freda replied, but Ida was gazing at the perilous waters. I've done it now, she was thinking. Or rather, that's just it—I haven't done it yet.

## 2

Though the results of the Gala had yet to be published in the town's newspaper, word had already reached the Gaze household that Ida intended to swim the Channel.

Back from the lido, Ida stood in the half-light of the hallway listening to her parents in the front room.

'What's wrong with her,' Mrs Gaze asked, 'in the water all the time like that? Where's she got this from now, about swimming the Channel?'

'Cloud-cuckoo-land,' Mr Gaze replied. 'The girl's living in cloud-cuckoo-land and still no sign of a job.'

If Mother mentions Gladys Baker, I may have to say something, Ida thought. Gladys's family was stumping up twenty-five pounds for her to become an apprentice hairdresser. She would be paid half a crown a week, and fifteen shillings when she became an improver, which meant you had someone else do the shampooing.

The Gazes' terrace was on a hill overlooking the Docks where ships brought tea and sugar and bananas from the other side of the world, but the house always seemed so weary and disappointed, as though it had held its breath for something to happen and nothing had.

Beyond the open front door, the late-summer evening seemed a mile wide with possibility. On the pavement, children jumped over a rope they had tied to a lamp-post. A hopscotch pebble skittled across the flagstones and the *sssht* of small feet quickened.

'I see Gladys Baker is turning into a proper little lady and has got herself set up as a hairdresser,' said Mrs Gaze.

Oblivious to her daughter standing at the door with her arms folded, Ida's mother caught up her pink knitting which never grew wider than a finger width. She hadn't been the same since Ida's baby sister, Maud, died of a fever five years ago and was taken away in a hearse pulled by two black horses with white frills on their feet.

'And then there's that Freda girl,' she went on. 'I say girl, but . . . I'm amazed at her parents letting her go about the place like that, in those trousers, with that wild streak to her, and always so dirty.'

Mr Gaze looked up from his book, one of the Everyman Classics collection he'd bought from a door-to-door salesman who'd told him the covers were leather when they weren't.

'Shall I have a word with the girl's parents?' he said.

Ida's father knew that Freda, who was being taught golf by her Uncle Jack, was picking up golf balls in the fields next to the club and selling them back to the original owners. Walter Gaze needed two members of the club to nominate him for membership.

'She's a queer one, that's what she is, and turning Ida the same way too.'

'Winifred!' Mr Gaze said, sounding as though he was trying to restrain a belch. Her mother looked up as Ida walked in.

'I want a word with you, young lady,' her father said.

'Young lady,' Mrs Gaze murmured. 'Where?'

Both her parents were quick-witted, but not in an amusing way. Having a go at Ida seemed to be the only time they talked to each other. She'd come to think of the two of them as a pair of brackets with nothing in between.

'Hello, Mother, I won all my heats and was given a medal. I'm the Gala Princess.'

Mrs Gaze's face was aghast as Ida held up the disc. Thanks to the salty pool water, her daughter's long dark curls had expanded to a vast triangle.

'Where's your locket?' she asked. Ida had been given it last birthday, a locket with a lock of her dead sister's hair locked inside, and it had bounced up and down on the bone in Ida's chest as she took the Corpus Christi Walk.

'Upstairs, safe under my pillow,' Ida replied, and her heart shrank a little at her mother's face sagging with relief and despair. She worried in case Mrs Gaze thought she didn't care, that she carried on with her life, swimming and winning things, as though Maud didn't matter; but Ida missed the baby's packed jelly limbs and her tiny seashell nails, and the way her head topped her body like a big rosy apple she wanted to smell and kiss all the time. Mr Gaze had told her she wasn't allowed to say so.

Her father cleared his throat. 'This swimming business,' he said. 'It's getting out of hand.'

'I'd like to know who told you when I don't really know myself,' Ida replied.

'I don't know where this girl's come from,' Mrs Gaze murmured. 'Why can't she be more like Gladys Baker?'

'About my Channel swim, Father,' Ida said. 'Who was it?'

'Gladys comes from such a nice musical family,' Mrs Gaze went on.

Gladys was a member of Madame Treharne's Temperance Choir, an army of children who travelled to Crystal Palace by coach to sing in formation.

'She's certainly got the hump tonight,' said Mr Gaze, looking straight ahead at the picture of *The Holy Sepulchre* hanging over the empty fireplace. The other two hanging on the dark green walls were *The Mount of Olives* and *Nazareth*.

'As if I want to flap a large white handkerchief around while I sing "Nymphs and Shepherds",' Ida said. 'Don't you think I might be a little old for all that, Mother? I leave school soon. I might even get wed!'

'I'd like to know who to.' Mrs Gaze pulled one of her faces.

'Ida, that's enough,' said Mr Gaze, but his wife was off again, her needles clicking crossly in time to the clock on the mantel set between two brass shells from the war.

'They're a nice harmonious family, the Bakers,'

28

she said.

'Her father sits in the corner playing his violin while Gladys and her brother blow on paper wrapped round combs,' Ida replied.

Walter Gaze stood from the table.

'Right, that's it.' He sounded nervous but firm. 'I've had enough of this. You're off down west.'

'But, Father, I need to practise for my swim.'

Ida already had her training planned. Back and forth on the beach until dusk, and an hour or so before school at the lake in the grounds of the old house that belonged to a ship owner who'd died. The place was empty after the rest of the family had gone to live in Jamaica.

'I'll give you swim,' said Mr Gaze. 'I want you out of your mother's hair. Two weeks with your Aunt Bess.' He cocked a thumb up at the ceiling. 'But for now, up to your room.'

There was no point in arguing. She was off to West Wales. Every birthday was the same, as though it didn't mark Ida being a year older, but was a reminder Maud was another year gone. It was this time of year she had died.

'And I don't want to hear another word about that Channel,' he called, as Ida went up the stairs. 'It's time you grew up and got yourself a living, my girl, or you'll end up like that crone with her feet in the water.'

Ida knew who he meant. There was an old woman who washed in the canal and was known as She-Him because she'd never married, wore men's old suit trousers and had hairs all over her chin.

On the landing, Ida glanced across at her parents' room where on top of the wardrobe squatted the black hat with a trail of black ribbons that her mother had worn the day her sister was buried. Just because poor Maud died doesn't mean you shouldn't have a life. That's what Freda said, but Freda never accepted adults knew better.

Ida went straight to her bedroom window, hoisted up the sash and climbed out. She half-clung, half-slid down the drainpipe. Then it was onto the side wall, up onto the roof of the coal shed and over the back wall into the alley.

'Open sesame!' she called when she knocked on the Voyles' front door, and Freda's father shouted, 'Password, please!'

In the hall, Mr Voyle gave a small bow as Banjo the dog barked from the back room.

'In you come, little mermaid,' he said. 'The menace is up in her room.'

'You took your time,' Freda said from the bed when Ida knocked and went in. The place reeked of cigarettes.

'You're right about this town,' Ida said, stretching out alongside her. 'Everyone already knows I'm doing the swim.'

'I don't know about that.' Freda was holding a cigarette over a small plate on her bedside cabinet. Smoking was her new hobby.

'What do you mean?'

'I expect everyone knows you won't.'

'Freddie! Thanks for the support.'

'What I mean is,' Freda said, 'they think they know a girl can't do it.'

Ida was hoping Freda would say that though the toughest of fishermen called the Channel cruel and treacherous, and though people were always drowning when their boats turned over in the currents, Ida would succeed in swimming it.

30

'I thought we could train on the beach every night and go to our lake every morning—a bit more private, you know, with the Bathing House,' Ida said.

She knew Freda loved it when they lay on the floor of the Bathing House, an old peeling building you reached by way of a line of huge boulders that stretched from the bank of the lake to the island in its middle. The two of them went there on summer nights, crossing the stepping stones with a lantern held high. There was a glass dome through which you could see the sky. It was one of their favourite things, lying listening to the owls' cries with the tall green-black trees around them, the abandoned house beyond, and Ida imagining aloud all the people who had hung their clothing on the hooks that ran along one of the painted tongue and groove walls.

'Will you help me, Freddie?'

Freda wiggled into the bed, like a hand settling into clay to make a firm print. As she pushed her hand under Ida's neck, the candle on the bedside cabinet flickered as though fighting a sigh. Freda blew out a mouthful of smoke.

'I wasn't aware I had a choice,' she replied, turning away to stub out the cigarette.

'What happens if your mother comes in?' Ida asked.

'What happens if she doesn't?'

The room was dark and warm and safe from the silence brooding outside in the streets and houses of the small town. They were close, they were the best of friends, but Ida worried that Freda thought they felt exactly the same about things when perhaps they didn't.

31

Freda turned back so they were ear to ear on the pillow.

'I've got something to ask you too,' she said, her voice suddenly full of seriousness.

'What's that?' Ida looked at her uneasily. The tips of their noses were touching.

'Why can't you be more like Gladys Baker?'

Freda had Mrs Gaze's voice to a tee and Ida laughed so hard they had to pull the covers over them in case Freda's parents should hear, though Mrs Voyle was very fond of Ida and said she kept her daughter on the straight and narrow.

*      *      *

'You know the drill,' Ida said. It was sweltering. The day had reached a crusty stage, like the bubbling surface of a creamy pudding already burned around the edges. Each blade of grass on the little front lawn curved like a sigh. A bird's late-afternoon lullaby sounded sweet and sad.

Freda nodded. Every Sunday she stood lookout, but she knew things would change. With school nearly over, Freda's form mistress, Mrs Button, had told her she could make something of her life despite everything. You're bright enough to become a nurse, Freda Voyle, she said. You won't make a doctor, but you are perfectly capable of being a nurse.

I don't have to do anything just because someone tells me I must, Freda kept saying.

Ida liked English and history lessons and telling stories, but when she wasn't able to point out Persia on his new globe, Mr Gaze had said she'd be lucky to get something in a sweet shop.

32

Freda waited on the pavement under the shade of the tree, standing with her two long feet together, her bare arms pink in the heat, her fists clenched.

Inside the house, Ida looked through the gap between the open door and the frame of her father's new study. Mr Gaze had returned from his club barely able to walk and his wife was no doubt upstairs having her usual lie-down.

She moved slowly, telling herself that if she didn't tread on the darker bits of the floorboards, where the sun wasn't shining, her father wouldn't wake.

The desk, the books, his newspapers were as warm and dry as the dust that danced in the sunlight like bubbles in Sarsaparilla, but Walter Gaze was like a man dipped in beer and laid out to dry. Moist air blew from his perfectly round nostrils. His jacket seemed to crouch on the floor, its grey lining darker round the armpits. His stomach rose and fell.

Moving quickly, Ida pincered her fingers into the loop of his trouser pocket and pulled at a key fob, like a leathery old earlobe.

The key in her hand, she backed from the room, and as she ran from the house giving Freda a thumbs-up, a seagull cried—a plaintive line of fading dots in the high sky.

'Step on it, Princess,' Freda said, pushing her palms under her thighs on the sun-warmed passenger seat of Mr Gaze's new Renault.

Ida pulled the choke out, started the engine and put her foot down so the car lurched forward and they were off.

As Mr Gaze dozed, they cruised through the

33

town, along dusty roads beneath vast shredded umbrellas of lime leaves, past the Salter Rooms, where young ladies in gem-coloured dresses took tiny pencils to mark down each partner in the Cinderella Dances every Saturday night.

'I'm going away tomorrow,' said Ida. 'Two weeks with Aunt Bess down the Wild West.'

'Surely they can't make you.'

Freda's parents were different from Mr and Mrs Gaze. They let her say what she liked, mostly, though there was a line. Freda had a younger brother and sister who tied cotton to door knockers and then hid behind hedges to pull it. When any Voyle opened their front door, callers usually got the dog barking through the gap and a small burst of bedlam from beyond.

Freda folded her arms. 'I bet they've done it to try and put the mockers on your swim,' she said.

'No chance.' Ida stared at the road ahead. 'I'll carry on training without you and I'll be back soon enough anyway.'

Down the hill, so steep it was a wonder the car didn't run away with them, they passed the pier where families were promenading. As they took the road up to the headland, Freda turned to watch the town below get smaller, upright figures like black sticks, waves like white lines, and above them all the sky an arch of blue.

'We could always just carry on in the car as we are,' Freda said. 'Get away from here and never come back.'

Nobody batted an eyelid as the car glided by with barely the crown of a head to show for a driver. But everything was noted. It was a small town. People talked.

## 3

For Ida's sixteenth birthday, Aunt Bess laid on a spread fit for a princess on the small wooden table in the back room of her harbourside home.

Later, after her swim—it wasn't training as such without Freda and the stopwatch—Ida planned to get Bess saying more about the men who once used lanterns to lure ships onto the sands so they could loot the holds. You could talk about anything with her. There were no boundaries and things to steer clear of, and she never blamed Ida for anything, even when she poured away green liquid by the sink and it had been Bess saving the water she'd cooked the greens in because she said it was full of goodness.

With both hands behind her back, Bess asked, 'Want your gifts?'

'Yes, please,' Ida replied. She was missing Freda, the way she'd turn up at the door with Banjo, and not give a damn about people looking as they went through town aiming gobstoppers in each other's mouths.

Aunt Bess, Ida's father's only sister, had little to do with Mr Gaze beyond having Ida for two weeks each summer. She thought her brother a bit of a bully and a bore and a drunk to boot, but she'd never tell the girl that.

'Ta da!' Bess went, producing two hangers, one in each hand like a scale. On one hung a pale green dress with cream lace around the neck, from the other a pair of trousers which Ida made a grab at. They unfolded to show pleats and a high waist, just like the ones Freda had.

'Try them on,' said Bess. 'Don't think we don't get the fashions down here, young lady.'

Bess was an excellent seamstress. Everyone in the village carried round butter or bananas in exchange for sewing jobs which Ida's aunt completed on a black machine against the wall opposite the fire.

The front door slammed. It was Gwynnie, Bess's best friend, a tall dark woman with eyebrows flying off her face who treated the place like home.

'Best not tell your mam about those trousers,' Bess said, as Ida pulled them on, 'or else she'll say we're stopping you being a lady.'

Bess knew about Ida's mother. Once, she'd said little Maud dying had turned poor Winifred Gaze a bit touched.

'Thank you so much for my presents,' Ida replied, watching Gwynnie kiss Aunt Bess on the forehead. Gwynnie's coat was behind the front door. She knew how to sharpen the kitchen knife against an iron rod like a giant knitting needle, and she cut logs for the fire with an axe which leaned in the back porch. She seemed to do all but sleep there, and only left when the two of them had one of their tiffs.

'Very nice,' said Bess, seeing her niece waiting for approval in her new trousers before the three of them sat at the table which had in its centre a white iced Victoria sponge topped with a glacé cherry. Freda called glacé cherries the devil's nipples. She could make you laugh after a funeral, the things she came out with.

'Happy birthday, Ida!' Gwynnie said, raising a slice of cake.

36

On her top half, Ida wore a black bathing suit, the thick straps crossed on her small tanned back.

'And best of luck with your Channel swim!' Bess cried, raising a glass of home-brewed Dandelion & Burdock, which involved quite a palaver with boiling pans.

The trio munched in harmony until the soft tap of rain started on the corrugated lean-to roof.

'Thank you for a lovely tea,' Ida said. 'But I'd better get on and swim.'

'Don't go in the water for at least an hour after you've eaten,' Bess called, as Ida went out of the door with a towel under her arm. 'Or you'll sink to the bottom of the sea.'

It was a short walk along the harbour road to the path over the sand dunes and the beach where she swam back and forth for hours.

What was that? A few minutes into a length and Ida brought up her head. A noise, not a boat's engine under the water, but the whir of bicycle wheels above her, growing louder and louder. She raised her face to the warm misty sky which hummed and rattled and spat rain in her eyes, and took a shocked breath when a plane came out of the clouds like a giant iron dragonfly, with the noise of a million bees.

Ida watched it curve up and away. It was orange with wings of gold and seemed like a flame suddenly whipped up in the sky. Back it came, heading for the water, dropping smoothly as though it followed a sloping line until it was as low as could be without touching the sea. Ida looked back at the land. The plane was going to crash, she was sure of it.

'It will sink!' she shouted, but three men

working on the rail track nearby had their heads down.

As the spray from the plane touching the water hit her, the current caught Ida's body like a gently sweeping hand. She took her fingers from her eyes. She was a strong enough swimmer to save the pilot if she got to the cockpit before it went under.

But the plane wasn't going down. It was floating like a boat. It was topping the surface of the water like a decoration on a cake.

'It sails!' she shouted. The men on the railway still didn't look up. A handful of crossbills, feathery little balls as orange as the plane, flitted by on their way to the conifer forest beyond the bay.

'He's alive!' Ida yelled, when a figure appeared at a door in the middle of the plane and jumped down onto the long paddles—was everyone half-asleep?—and then a voice called from the beach, 'What the . . .'

She swung round in the water. People were pouring down the dunes like an apocalyptic flood. A man on the beach was waving his jacket in the air.

'Get out!' he shouted at Ida, jumping up and down. 'Get out of the way!'

Raindrops were running down Bess and Gwynnie's faces as she came out of the water.

'I could have rescued him,' she said.

'*Uffern Dafydd*!' Bess replied. She often blasphemed in Welsh. 'Thank the Lord you're safe from his clutches.'

'Him?' the man told Ida. 'There's three of them on there. Now clear off out of it.'

Ida turned and counted the figures on the wing

38

of the plane.

'Heck-alive-oh,' said Gwynnie, which was another of their phrases. 'The man's right.'

It seemed forever before a boat rounded the point and the trio climbed into it.

'I'm sure that one's a girl,' Ida said, pulling her towel round her shoulders.

A boy shook his head. 'Don't be daft,' he replied. 'How can it be a girl in a plane?'

When a policeman moved his hands up and down to shush them, the crowd went quiet. His jacket buttons moved as he took a breath full of historic importance.

'The girl's name is Miss Amelia Earhart,' he said, 'and she is the first lady to cross the Atlantic. That plane has been in the air more than twenty hours, with the three of them inside all that way.'

'Told you,' Ida said. 'It is a girl.'

'There's excitement!' Bess shouted. 'Let's catch the boat coming in.'

They were off, everyone running back up the dunes in their coats and hats and Ida in her bathing suit with her cap swinging from her hand and her hair streaming behind her like a banshee's scream.

As the boat neared the harbour wall, the rain gathered pace and the crowd swarmed to estimate the boat's destination.

When the girl stepped onto the quayside, Ida stared at her white-and-brown headscarf, her bony face, her clothes like a man's, her laced boots. When she grinned and said, 'I have done it,' it seemed to Ida that the flier had spoken only to her.

'Hip hip!' shouted Bess, and the rest of them called back hooray, shyly the first time, but by the third they were yelling so hard, raindrops hit their tongues.

The woman was being gently jostled away from the crowd by a policeman. She walked on politely, one hand behind her back and the other free. Ida ducked between the bodies and shot forward, and just as she gripped the flier's hand, a camera bulb snapped, and then the woman was gone, slipping away in a circle of policemen.

Though the rain became heavier, everyone stayed to watch the plane being pulled into the harbour, bringing a slick of seawater to their feet.

'Look,' Ida said. 'Look at the writing on the side. The plane is called *Friendship.*'

'Now there's an important thing,' Bess replied. 'Friendship.'

\*     \*     \*

The next day, half of Wales was there to see the plane take off for Southampton, which was where it should have landed in the first place. Ida watched until it was less than a pinprick in the sky, then crossed the field to the town and bought the local paper. She wore a cloth cap, smelling of Gwynnie, that she'd taken from a hook in the hall, pulled over her head with her hair tucked up inside because she liked the feel of air on her neck.

'Here you are, son,' said the newsagent, who didn't realise Ida, aged sixteen and one day, was pictured in her bathing suit on the front page holding the hand of Amelia Earhart.

*Western Mail. Tuesday, 19 June 1928*
*GIRL FLIES ATLANTIC*

40

Freda was waiting outside the Gazes' when Ida returned from Bess's, her case on her lap in the front seat of her father's car.

'Not that girl,' said Mr Gaze in a slightly fearful voice, when he saw Freda jump off the Gazes' front wall and blow cigarette smoke into the close, summer afternoon air. Ida had spent the half-crown Aunt Bess had pressed into her hand on a silver cigarette case for Freda.

'Take my case, would you please, Father?' Ida said, opening the car door as he pulled in.

'You stay where you are and take those trousers off,' replied Mr Gaze.

'I can't, Father. It's the middle of the street, and in any case I need to see Freda about my swim. She's helping me train.'

Mr Gaze pushed his head forward like a tortoise as he looked over the suitcase through the open car door at his daughter on the pavement.

'Just you wait until you get inside the house,' he said. 'What have I told you about that swim?'

'Nothing, Father. In any case, I think actions speak louder than words, don't you? See you later.'

'I haven't finished with you,' he said.

At the end of the road, the two girls paused from running to look back at Mr Gaze parking. Sometimes he took as long as ten minutes to line the wheels up with the edge of the pavement, and people would watch from their windows.

As they strolled through the town, past the bakery and Freda's father's saddler's shop, past the

41

library and coal company and grocer's, and over the railway bridge to their blackberry field, Freda said, 'What's all that you've got?'

Ida clutched Freda's package and the newspaper showing her shaking Amelia Earhart's hand.

'I met the American woman who flew from America in a plane called *Friendship*.'

Freda took the newspaper and spent a moment marvelling at the front-page photograph.

'Now people really can say you're never out of your bathers,' she said. Then she pointed at Ida's new trousers. 'We're like twins. Your mother will have one of her episodes when she sees you.'

'She'll have one of her episodes anyway.'

Their favourite field was like a square of paradise on a hill with a glimpse of the sea through the five-bar gate. There was birdsong and the biscuity scent of dry grass under the oak tree. Soon blackberries would decorate the hedges like red-black jewels.

'Don't you think it's amazing a girl flew all that way when nobody thought she would do it?' Ida asked, once they were sitting against the sturdy trunk.

'I do,' Freda replied, pulling a fist from her trouser pocket. 'Close your eyes.'

'What's this in aid of?' Ida asked.

'Happy birthday,' Freda said, dropping a silver tube into Ida's waiting palm. 'You didn't think I'd forget, did you?'

The present was a red lipstick in a small case etched with a beach scene—a woman throwing a ball into row upon row of wavy lines.

'Those squiggles are supposed to be the sea,' Freda said. 'Seeing as you love it so much.'

42

'Thank you, it's wonderful. Here's your present.'

'Don't go away again,' Freda said, unwrapping the cigarette case. 'This is very smart, thank you, but please let that be my next present, you not going away. Aunt Sylvia's been insufferable, on all the time about what I'm going to do with my life.'

'Take no notice,' Ida replied. 'That's what you're always telling me.'

'It's not as if anyone expects anything,' Freda went on. 'Why can't people just leave people be? Why is everyone always on about something?'

'I suppose it's an idea to try and make something of our lives, isn't it, Freddie? You know, not just staying put, being told what to do all the time.'

Freda lit a cigarette before pulling her legs up to her chin and blowing out smoke.

'Are you still intent on doing that swim?' she asked.

'Of course. More so, if anything.'

Ida had read about Amelia taking her first flying lesson, swooping over sweet-smelling citrus groves in Los Angeles, and pink and white and pale green buildings by the sea. She remembered what Amelia had told reporters who asked if she'd ever thought of backing out of the flight. *I love life and all it has to offer*, she had said. *I want every opportunity and adventure it can give.*

'Nobody thought a woman would cross the Atlantic and Amelia Earhart did—so why shouldn't I cross the water to another country?'

Freda rearranged herself so her head was in Ida's lap. To Ida, it felt the same kind of weight as Maud when she'd been allowed to hold her baby sister on her knee.

43

'I expect your father could give you any number of reasons,' Freda said.

They could be like this for hours, talking or silent, feeling happy and calm and away from parents who told them to behave like Gladys Baker.

Ida gently moved about and sighed. The stubbly grass was pricking through the cotton of her trousers and it seemed to darken and cool quickly once the sun had gone down. She pictured her mother in her chair back home, like the ginger cat that sat on next door's wall waiting for dogs to pass so it could leap on their back.

'Things will change now, won't they, Freddie, with us leaving school? I wonder what will become of us.'

'As long as we're together we'll be all right.'

'Don't you ever feel as though there's a world beyond this town? Exciting jobs and money to buy nice clothes, and things like that?'

Ida hadn't mentioned she'd been into the town's newspaper office to ask for a reporting job and been told by the woman behind the counter that the editor only took boys. They may well have fancy lady reporters in London, she'd remarked to Ida, but we don't go in for that here.

'I don't know what I'll do,' Ida went on. 'My father says I'm not having anything more from them, now I can earn my own keep.'

'Stop fretting, you'll find something,' Freda said. 'You're getting as bad as your mother for making a performance out of things.'

Most of the girls had something lined up. One was going to study medicine, but she had always been clever. Everyone knew this because her

44

father was a doctor for the town's grandest families. Freda had told her parents she was happy with her job as a paper boy. I like it, she kept saying. Going out and about when nobody else is there. Suits me.

Ida said, 'I want adventure, to go here and there, and meet new people.'

Freda opened her eyes and sat up. 'I think people are the problem,' she replied. 'Most of them anyway.'

Ida stood and started brushing herself down. 'I should be training really,' she said.

As they walked back through the town, Bella Pertwee and two other girls came towards them.

'Oh no, not her again,' Freda said. 'I can't stand her voice.'

'Do you like *anyone*?' Ida asked. Braced for Bella and her cronies, Ida had a nervous, fixed smile on her face.

Freda turned to her. 'Like? No, not really.'

'I didn't know you were back,' Bella said, when they stopped outside the town's new cinema. 'Did you have a good break in that back-of-beyond place you keep disappearing to?'

'Yes, thanks.' Ida heard herself talking in her best voice. Bella scared her a bit. Her name was down for a secretarial training course in a basement in Cardiff run by a woman called Miss Chivers who used a silver lorgnette with a handle like a teaspoon.

'It was terribly exciting actually,' she went on. 'I met the girl who flew from America.'

She felt Freda's elbow as she handed Bella the picture of her shaking Amelia's hand. Freda maintained it was best to keep your business to

45

yourself. *Say as little as possible to the police or anyone else*. That was one of Mr Voyle's sayings.

'Is that you?' Bella tipped her head about. 'You're all hair.'

One of the girls sniggered and said, 'It looks like a ghost or a girl with no face.'

The bell in the library tower chimed its eighth stroke.

'It's the camera flash,' Freda told them. 'But it is Ida.'

'I don't doubt it,' Bella replied. 'I expect you'll be in your cossie in the paper again, doing that swim. Is that still on or was it all talk?'

'Oh yes,' Ida said, folding up the newspaper. 'It's full steam ahead.'

The girl who'd sniggered giggled again.

'What did I tell you?' Freda said, after the others walked off. 'Nobody thinks you will do it. Even when it's on the front page of a newspaper they don't believe it. Look how they were then with you and your flier. There it was in black and white but they still weren't having it.'

'Perhaps I should tell the *Times* I'm doing my swim,' Ida replied. 'That would make it official.'

Freda took Ida's hand. It was late evening, the light sort of dark that made the high street's buildings seem more shadowy than real. A dog's bark came from the back garden of one of the terraces behind them.

'There's no need for a rotten newspaper in this town,' Freda said. 'You need only tell Mrs Gates in the chemist's and the smallest thing goes round like wildfire. Bloody people. I might just give them something to damn well gossip about.'

'I promise you,' Ida replied. 'They will have

46

something very soon.'

'And I promise *you*,' Freda said. 'It's not you who decides what they talk about.'

## CECILY 2009

It wasn't all that long ago a curt response came so easily to me. I'd be in the post office queue—more than likely snaking out of the door with me on the pavement—or sitting watching the pigeons in the outdoor café in town, and someone would come out with, 'Fine today, isn't it?' 'That's a matter of opinion,' I'd tell them in a voice that could shred lemon rind. It generally did the trick.

I feel so ashamed. I wasn't the world's most social butterfly when Freda was taken from me. One month a cough, the next a coffin. It really was that quick.

Funny to think that not so long ago I took pride in starting a fight over the weather, and now here I was, thinking of spilling my guts to Sarah, dressed in one of her bright little cardigans the colour of wine gums.

The girl talks so nicely. Her father is a retired architect, her mother a teacher and she's got a brother who flits about the world taking photos for magazines. She grew up a bit of a tomboy, she told me—had to, in a way, because that brother of hers would sit on her face and break wind when she was young.

'Hope that hasn't made you think that's all you're fit for,' I said.

'Oh no, Ceci,' she told me. 'I'll be going back to

work.'

She used to have a job at a housing charity finding homes for the unlucky, and she's not long started volunteering to mentor young offenders, all those naughty boys a pencil line away from being locked up. There's a thing to be doing if you're trying to patch up your marriage, I thought to myself, but I didn't say anything.

'Will you tell me today, Ceci, about the girl in the old-fashioned bathing suit?' she asked.

The girl didn't give up. I liked that. Nor did Pat down the road, who didn't stop until I agreed to the old age meetings. Either I was underestimating these people's stamina or I'd got to liking a bit of company again. I'm grateful to them really, showing how nice it can be to have a chat, with all this time to kill rattling about in a house the size of a hotel and nobody in any of the rooms but me.

'Let's talk about you,' I said. 'I'm worried about you living in the past on your own all the time. You'll turn a bit funny if you don't mix a bit more.'

What cheek I had. I only started leaving the house again six months ago when I discovered that photo, and then it was just as far as the library in daylight and the town's pavements when darkness fell.

'Shouldn't you be thinking of going back to London?' I went on.

Sarah started chewing at the corner of her mouth. I was holding some shortbread she'd made with its crumbly, sugary surface prodded all over with holes from a fork.

'I'm sorry,' I said. 'I shouldn't be so forward.'

'It's not that, Ceci, it's just difficult. I'm not sure I'm ready, that's all.'

'All these years between us and we've got one thing in common at least then,' I continued. 'Not being ready.'

'All of us might be different on the outside but inside I think we feel the same sorts of things, don't you?' she replied. 'We could always swap stories, Ceci. What do you say to that?'

The two of us looked at each other and laughed. After Freda died, I didn't think I'd share a joke with anyone again. I closed down, tucked myself into a ball leaving only my spikes on show, and now here I was, knocking my head back like the guffawing clown that used to sit in a glass case on the end of the pier. One shilling it cost, to get him to crack his face.

I watched her take up the photo from the dresser, saw a young woman from one age sizing up another. I wondered what Sarah and that imagination of hers were cooking up. Did she see the girl in the old-fashioned bathing suit laughing and joking with friends as they swam to a sun-baked wooden platform floating off the beach? Or running from the water, shaking her hair, slipping on the short-skirted fashion of the day, and skipping home to a house with a garden that sloped to a river quivering with dragonflies?

Because with her little Flapper hairdo, the girl in the photo might look like a pin-up for the fancy side of the 1920s, but there's another story too, beyond the glamour and the love affairs, the silk frocks and parties in grand houses. Yes, there's guts and there's go-getting, there's headlines and cinema shows, there's newspaper offices and taxis and bars filled with smoke. There's all that and more, but even then that's only half of the picture.

'When was it taken?' she asked.

Oh, it could all have come rushing out of me so easily, like one of those rivers you see bursting their banks on the TV news.

'1928,' I replied, feeling my voice give.

It happened such a long time ago now, but the girl in bathers feels like family, or is that saying too much? I'd spent so long not asking questions, I didn't know how to start answering them either, and with so much of it wrapped in darkness all these years, it's been like a secret shrouded in sheets in the attic.

Yes, I know time is running out for me, it's running out for all of us every time the second hand does another lap around the clock. And then you do wonder if it isn't just better to leave things be. At least I did think that, until this new girl, with her taste for questions and for pulling the past into the present, turned up.

If I was fanciful, which I'm not (or at least I hadn't been in a long time), I might think Sarah, who should have been out on the town or in having dinner parties but who wanted instead to sit and hear me talk, was sent so I could tell my story and see what came of it.

I looked at the girl sitting there with her big eyes on that picture and her ears almost to points with curiosity. Her there like that put me in mind of the mad old bat at the old age pow-wows who's always on about angels. They're all about us, all the time, they look like the rest of us, I tell you, she'll say when we're sitting at the table waiting to see what they bring us for dinner. I keep finding their little white feathers in my room left like messages, she'll whisper, as she pushes her teacup forward for a

50

top-up. Well, I'm not an angel, that's for sure, I say to her, and I'll bet your pillows aren't stuffed with foam either.

'Is she a relative, Ceci?' Sarah asked, though I could see she knew by now not to push it.

I should have kept the photo upstairs, in the bottom of the chest of drawers where it'd been all that time. It was safer that way. Otherwise I could start talking and not be sure when I would stop, or what Sarah would think of what I told her. I couldn't bear to see her face harden into a tolerant smile. Yes, yes, Ceci, time for another tablet, Ceci, is how it would be. As you get older, the joke about men in white coats doesn't get any funnier.

'Best get on,' I said, heading for the kitchen. I couldn't let her see my face. She hadn't known me long enough for her to see me cry, though I'll tell you something. It's anything goes, down the old age club. Those oldies don't seem to care who's about when a photo or a letter sets them off. They'll sit pushing tissues in their eyes and then you'll have to think of something that'll cheer them up, something they'll want to hear. Someone popping their clogs usually does the trick. That stops them sniffling and gets them sitting up straight soon enough. If ever anyone's flush enough to leave a newspaper lying round, there's always a scramble for the obits page.

Sarah didn't stay long after that.

'Never mind, Ceci, I'm a bit much with my questions, aren't I?' she said. 'You should tell me to shut up.'

'Nothing wrong with questions,' I replied, but five minutes later she was off with the dog pulling so hard she might have been on water-skis.

51

I worried all evening I'd upset her with my ways. Old habits die hard. I ended up giving myself a headache thinking about whether she'd be put out and sitting alone in her parents' house thinking me an ungrateful old grump who stuffed all her biscuits, stuck my nose in her business, wouldn't tell her mine, and then sent her packing.

Coming up to nine o'clock I'd had enough of myself and thought the best place for me, so I couldn't spoil anything else, was bed. I switched everything off and shuffled down the hall.

I only noticed the picture-postcard on the floor tiles when I went to pull the curtain across the front door to stop the draught. Since when did spring stay so damn cold? I was longing for the weather to warm up, to hold my face to the sun and feel it seep under my skin, but Freda was always one for the winter. She said the cold was as cleansing as water. She liked rain too. Gets all the rabble off the streets, she'd say, but she'd still wait until darkness to go off on one of her walks. I always knew she'd been down to the seafront because she came back smelling of air.

The card was a view of an outdoor swimming pool, not this one we've got on the headland here, but one with a similar look to it, with people splashing about in outdated costumes. An old black-and-white photo. I'd received a retro-chic postcard and I was old enough to be in the picture!

I rushed to find my magnifying glass which kept slipping down the side of the chair and was a devil to get out again.

*Hi Ceci*, she'd put. *Listen to Radio 4 tonight at 8 p.m. There's a documentary about our vanishing lidos. I'll look forward to hearing your thoughts.*

*Sarah x.*

Well, I hurried over to Freda's old Bush radio but the programme was just ending, playing out with a voice pointing out the irony of all these old pools being filled in, and fancy apartments being put on top, when global warming means we'll probably end up building more.

I stood there feeling so grateful for Sarah's little card, which I balanced next to the photo, and so sorry to have missed that programme. I should have known she wouldn't take offence at me giving her short shrift. She's probably got a touchy old bugger in her family somewhere—most families have. Or maybe that ninny who believes in angels is right and they *are* all around us, marching round the corner in a cloche hat when you're cutting back your laurel.

*         *         *

Not long after Freda went so suddenly, more than a year ago now, I was told my eyes would go gradually. The consultant said it would be the sight in the centre of the visual field that would disappear completely.

'What's that in plain English?' I asked him, not meaning for it to come out sounding so sharp. He's a nice enough young man and it couldn't be easy telling people their eyes were on the blink, if you'll excuse the expression. Until I posed the question, I didn't think I, Ceci, the girl who used to know to carry a mop and bucket as quiet as a mouse past the surgeons, had the nerve to talk like that. Thinking back now to that appointment in the doctor's office, I saw that I was right to worry

53

about coming clean to Sarah or to anyone else. You can speak and it comes out wrong. Go with your gut reaction, I thought. Know what you did when you were that fourteen-year-old cleaner, Ceci, and keep your mouth shut.

Anyway, my doctor chappie had a framed photograph on his desk, and when he pushed it round to face me, I saw a woman grinning at the camera.

'Is that your better half?' I asked, wondering what this girl had to do with me and whether the doctor was so annoyed at my cheek just now that he planned on ignoring my question. He nodded. Then I said, hoping to smooth things over, 'Isn't she pretty and smiling.'

I felt guilty thinking I'd upset him, with his serious face, looking like a schoolboy in a shirt and tie.

'This is what you see now.' Then he gave me a thick piece of card. It was the same picture as before, but with a blur where his wife's face had been.

'And that is what you will end up seeing.' He paused before adding, 'Or rather *not* seeing.'

'A girl with no face?' I asked. I didn't know what to be most put out about, the fact I wouldn't see faces or that he was using his wife's picture to explain it to people like me.

'That's one way of putting it,' he replied.

He told me it would become difficult or impossible for me to recognise faces. He said macular degeneration was one of the downsides of old age and the major cause of blindness in the over-fifties. He said it affected 30 per cent of the seventy-five to eighty-five age group.

'Phew, I'm too old to qualify then,' I said, trying to make up for before, and in a way I was glad it had taken till now, and not fifty, to show itself.

The doc went on about blood vessels growing behind detached retinas and blind spots and central scotomas and my condition being too advanced for medication that might have stopped the growth. I'm ashamed to say all his science talk about wet forms went over my head. I did wonder if it was because I didn't really understand what he was saying or because I didn't want to. He told me time was running out, that there was nothing he could do about it, and yet here we still were, an hour or so in, with me looking at his sideburns and the shining whites of his eyes, thinking, Well, I don't know about you, but I've got things I could be getting on with.

I got the impression he thought it wasn't sinking in. If he'd said as much, I would have told him that I lived through the war with an eight-foot unexploded bomb in the back garden and didn't tend to get in a flap so easily after that.

'Don't think it will be here one day and gone tomorrow,' he went on. 'You've got between one and three years. It will be gradual.' I should say so, I thought. I've been stuck here for seventy-five minutes. Whatever happened to the hard-pressed NHS and being rushed through appointments?

After my visits to the hospital, I'd started taking the bus into Cardiff before going home. I usually got lost trying to leave the ophthalmology department, and when I finally shook the place off I was mindful of taking my pleasures where I could see them. I like town best on a weekday when everyone is at work. At least it used to be like that,

55

but nowadays people seem to be on this flexi-time lark. They're on the go so much more. One Sunday, Sarah took me to the garden centre for some lavender plants to run along the front path, and the roads were heaving.

'What's everyone *doing*?' I said, realising I sounded like Freda but I didn't mean it that way. Good old Ceci, guaranteed to put her foot in it. It was so much easier when I kept quiet. At least I didn't spend half the night worrying about what I'd said and whether it had come out the wrong way.

'The same as you and me, Ceci,' Sarah replied. I'd found out that scarce husband of hers was in 'human rights'. Civil liberties—it's not company law or anything grasping like that, she'd added, and I thought to myself, Yes, I can see how the two of you might fit together, always ready to do money down and with a defence for everyone, even if you can't stay five minutes in the same room together—but I didn't say anything. He still hadn't been down from London, and the last time I raised it she said she wasn't going back up there. So far I'd managed to keep schtoom on that one too.

Sarah seemed amused by me having such an attitude, but I hadn't meant that people shouldn't be out and about, I said to her. I just couldn't see what was so urgent for so many people on a Sunday afternoon when they could be at home with a cup of tea.

Anyway, in town, I head for my favourite department-store caff to mull over bits and pieces. I like the idea that everyone else is at work, making the world go round, stacked in office blocks, at a desk, on the phone, or shut in rooms with blinds having meetings, and there I am, sitting sipping my

56

drink watching the world go by.

I'm partial to department-store cafés. I like the mini stainless-steel pots, the sugar sachets and those seats they fit in corners that mean you can have your favourite cubbyhole. It's like a little doll's house for the old-age end of life, though they've revved it up a bit recently with fancy Italian sandwiches that have to be heated and can't be taken straight on your tray. That spoils it no end, and it would have put Freda out on our trips into town. With good reason. I used to like carrying our full tray to the table, knowing we wouldn't be bothered with the to-do of raising an arm when a voice shouted, 'Toasted teacake!'

Freda was one for her cup of tea and a sandwich in town, but she had no patience with those little milk cartons. It was always me trying to peel off the top. 'You do know you're supposed to pick at the little flap,' she'd tell me.

And then one of the girls who came out with the cooked food that people had ordered would linger by our table and say, 'You two would starve on a plane.'

'Why's that?' I asked. We went through this carry-on every time she was on shift, and in those days, I had to do the talking. Freda mostly ignored people, assuming what they said would be nonsense.

'All the food comes in airtight trays with plastic lids on. If you haven't got the knack, you go hungry. I can never do it without spilling it.'

'Is that so?' I'd say, knowing Freda would be rolling her eyes or worse, start tutting. I saw that this girl only really wanted to tell us about all the places she'd been—self-catering in Ibiza, an all-in

57

hotel in Tenerife, back-packing round Thailand—and I would have liked to listen, but Freda could have made Hitler nervous, biting the way she did into her thick wilting sandwich.

When the girl went, my tea was usually cold. 'She's coming round with that wet cloth and yet the tables are still as sticky as old Sellotape,' Freda would go, pouring herself another cup.

I do miss her ways. Freda was good to me, buying us this house and paying for everything with her pension. I still have one of her old shampoo bottles, lidless, under my pillow. I like to catch the faint sweet herby whiff of her hair in the middle of the night. You'd think it would be uncomfortable, a plastic bottle under my pillow, like that tale about the princess and the pea, but I ain't no princess. Bit of a madam sometimes, or so Freda would say, but no princess.

One occasion, I remember, she got very rattled after I cleared out the drawer of her sideboard in the sitting room and asked about a shiny disc engraved *Gala Princess* 1928 inside a silver cigarette case. 'Stop being such a fusspot about the house,' she told me. 'It's not a palace, it's our home. There are no prizes for keeping the place spotless,' she said, 'nor for prying, if it comes to that.'

## 4

It was the last day of term, ever. There would be no more sitting in small square rooms with high windows and dark desks and black holes for inkwells. No more crowding round the woodburner in the porter's lodge to dry clothes after rain or stepping round the man rubbing the assembly hall floor with teak oil that stayed in your nostrils all day.

'No more housecraft lessons,' Freda said. 'Thank the Lord for His mercy.'

In one session, Freda had taken a wicker beater used for banging out dust from the Headmistress's rugs to lash at the back of Bella Pertwee's legs when she complained Freda wasn't pulling her weight. Aged six, Freda had broken up her toy wash tub, saying she didn't see how girls were expected to play at scrubbing when their mothers found it a rotten chore.

'Come to the blackberry field,' Freda urged. 'Let's not bother with the goodbye assembly.'

'I've just got something I need to do,' Ida replied.

They were walking through the park that sloped down to the sea. The sun had burned away the Channel's muddy tint, and the sky was high and blue above them. Ida sniffed the nutty scent from a clutch of firs rustling in the breeze.

'You've been in a funny mood for a while now,' Freda said. 'What are you up to?'

Ida handed a rolled-up towel to Freda, with her costume and cap in its middle.

'Never you mind,' she replied. 'See you at the Bathing House at midday.'

Ida watched Freda lope off. She had shot up as tall as her father and started arguing with her brother, Josh, about wanting to borrow his clothes.

Outside the newspaper's office, a paper banner announced the local *Times* had a circulation of three thousand. Inside, the woman sitting at the wooden counter didn't look up when Ida pushed through the door.

'Excuse me,' Ida said. The woman's head was bowed over a pile of coins and a wad of notes she was flicking through with a finger capped with a rubber thimble. Her tongue clicked as she counted and Ida listened to her intakes of breaths.

'You again,' the woman said, when she finally looked up. 'I thought I told you, he says no girls.' She reached for a cigarette resting in an ashtray and put it in her mouth.

'I have a story for you,' Ida said.

'Have you now?' The woman narrowed her eyes as she pushed smoke dramatically from her mouth. She was probably used to people coming in telling stories. Mr Gaze was fond of saying the townspeople needed oxygen and other people's business to live.

There were footsteps coming down the stairs behind the counter. Quickly, Ida told her she was sixteen and planned to be the first person to swim the Channel. Surely the editor couldn't decide only boys were allowed to do that too.

'Blasted boys,' said the man coming through the door. 'Teach 'em everything they think they need to know and they're off. Evelyn, my sweet, I'm going to need you to put another advert in the window.'

'Certainly, Mr King.' The woman turned to Ida with a bored expression. 'Are you serious?' she asked.

Ida nodded. The man carried on talking.

'He reckoned he'd turn the place around but I told him, I said, you young guns might think you

60

know what sells papers, but let me tell you, circulation has dropped since you got here, young man.'

'I didn't like him myself,' the woman replied. 'While you're down, Mr King, we've got a Channel swimmer here.'

'The damned know-all has dropped me right in it,' he said.

They looked at Ida. The woman took another drag on her cigarette, but she didn't seem quite so hostile. The girl was known to be down in the water every evening. Drinkers at the Yacht Club, standing on the bar's first-floor balcony, were guessing Ida's time on each lap and mouthing it silently at each other the moment Freda looked up from her stopwatch to shout from the beach.

'I will be the first ever to swim the Channel,' said Ida. 'Now what do you think *that* will do to your circulation?'

The man was short, with a face as round as a clock and strands of grey hair splayed across the top of his head like a chicken's foot. He flatted his palms on the dark wooden counter, fat hands with a small gold ring on his little finger and black smudges round his nails.

'I am sure you are aware of Amelia Earhart,' Ida went on. 'Well, I am to do the same as her—cross the water to another country, only swimming, not flying.'

Ida had amassed quite a library of cuttings, including *Miss Earhart's Rousing Reception in Southampton*, with a photo of Amelia in a white shirt, red tie and breeches, and the Lady Mayor of Southampton, Mrs Louise M. Foster Welch, announcing, *She is the first woman who can say I*

61

*have crossed the ocean by air . . .*

*TO YOU THE FIRST WOMAN SUCCESSFULLY TO SPAN THE NORTH ATLANTIC BY AIR THE GREAT ADMIRATION OF MYSELF AND THE UNITED STATES*, said a telegram from President Coolidge.

'The town's answer to Amelia Earhart, eh?' Mr King said, glad he'd come down to get the ball rolling on a new reporter to find this dark-eyed little madam talking big. He liked the idea of a good-looking girl in her bathers down on the seafront. It would be like something they'd have at one of those fancy French resorts like Nice or Deauville.

'That little friend of yours isn't keeping you company then?' he asked.

'No,' Ida replied. 'It will be a solo swim. I am the girl who walks alone.' She'd read this in one of the papers. It had been Amelia Earhart's yearbook caption at Hyde Park School. *AE—the girl in brown who walks alone*.

His interest was piqued. He liked a girl with guts who could coin a phrase, and girls were more versatile than boys. Girls made tea and wouldn't turn their nose up at covering a cookery demonstration.

'Young lady, you look as though you have an eye for what makes the news,' he said. 'And what do you plan on doing when you leave school?'

'I have just this minute left the County School and I intend to make news.' Ida thought for a second and added, 'I would like to become a high-flier.'

The man laughed, though he had a paper to get out and with one man down he was over a barrel. The girl seemed to have inherited her father's gift

62

of the gab.

'No harm in that,' said the woman, and she smiled at Ida.

'You might do nicely,' Mr King said thoughtfully. 'People would let you in because you don't look like trouble, but they might end up regretting it. It just so happens I'm looking for a junior reporter. You're a County girl so I take it you can spell.'

Ida's gaze was steady.

'You'd be covering the Boy Scouts, town council, church notes. Making calls to the police station to find out who's been a naughty boy. Majors exposing themselves, motorists jumping pedestrian crossings or parking on the wrong side of the promenade, who's in court for being on the pop— that kind of thing.'

Ida dropped her head, thinking of Mr Gaze staggering back from the Con Club, with his customers pretending they hadn't seen him and not returning his wave.

Mr King tapped at a paper on the counter. 'Here,' he said. 'You talk a good game. Let's hear your reading.'

Ida read from the newspaper in a high sweet voice: '*MR ARTHUR PEARSON'S application yesterday for a temporary four-week licence for musical concerts on Sundays in the new Pier Pavilion was granted.*'

And: '*MISS LILLIAN HART, the town's dancer, who has been indisposed for three months, is now faced with the edict that she must have her tonsils removed.*'

'Good job she's a dancer, not a singer,' added Ida.

Mr King laughed. 'Good job?' he said. 'I think

63

*you'll* do a very good job.'

'What do you mean?' Ida asked.

'Never mind your swim,' he told her. 'You said you want to make news. I'm giving you a trial run as cub reporter on the *Times. The Voice of This Town.*'

\*       \*       \*

Ida could barely get home quick enough to coat her mouth in the lipstick Freda had given her. She hoped her mother was there to tell, but Winifred Gaze was under the clothes on her bed, with the curtains pulled. Ida knew to leave her alone.

She turned her face from side to side in the bathroom looking glass, seeing the way the red made her lips so big and shiny. She was a grown-up, a working girl, and she would tell her father she'd got herself a job. Things might even pick up at home.

On her way to Mr Gaze's garage, Ida thought about her new boss laughing when she told him he was getting double value—for not only would she write the news, she would make it by doing the swim. She hadn't known if he thought her humorous or deluded, but either way she'd show him. That woman she'd thought peevish had turned out to be nice, after all. 'Good for you,' she'd said as Ida was leaving. 'You'll be the first girl reporter and the first person to swim the Channel.'

Mr Gaze's new garage, a large curve of concrete with two coats of white paint, situated on the main road out of the town, was finished. It was widely acknowledged that despite a taste for the whisky

64

he'd done all right for himself, working his way up from the pit as a mechanic to parading about with clean hands in a three-piece suit from Mr Wilson's men's outfitters.

There were two cars in the shade on the forecourt. All Ida could see in the reflection in the polished showroom window was her lips. She ran a hand up her neck to lift her hair, which seemed as heavy as a rug, and thought of Amelia's short cut, so couldn't-care-less and good-looking. There'd been a picture in the *Daily Trumpet* showing her lean body, her trousers falling over slim hips, her cheekbones, heavy-lidded eyes with pale lashes that gave her the look of a boy in sandshoes just come up from the beach. Ida hadn't realised it before, but Amelia Earhart looked like Freda.

'What the hell have you got on your face, girl?' said her father, emerging from his office, which had a brass nameplate on the door.

'I have something monumental to tell you, Father.'

'Who is he?' asked Mr Gaze, in a thick voice, looking her up and down.

'There is no he,' said Ida, her jaw jutting a little.

'Freda?' Mr Gaze tipped his head forward. From behind, his neck bulged over his shirt collar, and sometimes he gave a nod that wasn't one, as if to release something caught in the fold.

'I've got myself a job.'

'What? Stood on a corner down the Docks?'

Ida wasn't sure what her father meant but she knew by his expression and the way he pulled a handkerchief from his trouser pocket it wasn't good.

'Wipe that mess off your face now before you

65

see the back of my hand.'

He pushed the handkerchief at her face but Ida folded her arms. A man stood not far from them peering through the windscreen of one of the cars.

'Am I talking to myself?' He glanced to his side at the man, who was lifting his hand as though he wanted attention.

'I'm going to be a reporter.'

Mr Gaze drew back the handkerchief.

'And I'm Mary Queen of Scots,' he said. 'Now go home this minute with your stories.'

Her father's eyes were slipping away from her, to the man who was clearing his throat, and then back to Ida's lips.

She said, 'And they are going to cover me swimming the Channel.'

People would have to believe her now.

'Think of it, Father. Our names will be in the newspaper.'

Mr Gaze allowed *gaze's garage* in lights to flash briefly in his mind. The new place would look smashing in a photo in the *Times,* but adverts cost the earth.

'And I said go home this minute,' he said. 'Do as you're told now or you'll be back up that street so fast your feet won't touch the ground.'

'Good,' Ida replied. 'Then I'll be the first person to fly.'

She walked off with her head held high but then, further along the pavement towards town, a child with his mother pointed at her mouth and screamed. Pagan Red, the lipstick was called. In the heat of the day it felt greasy and glamorous, but people were looking as she walked past shops. Mr Jennings the grocer, laying out vegetables on a trestle table, turned and glared. Had Miss Webster looked up from her desk in the Imperial Coal Company and put a hand to her mouth? Mrs Gates in the chemist's definitely shook her head. Freda said people singled out anyone who was different. Even Amelia Earhart got picked on. The editor of an American magazine had complained that she was getting a lot of fuss for doing very little. She'd only been a passenger on that transatlantic flight, after all, and why did such a feat arouse any particular comment in these days of sex-equality?

Piqued, Amelia Earhart, sitting between Lady Astor and Winston Churchill at a luncheon hosted by the Women's Section of the Air League of the British Empire, said such flights helped other women to think. *The woman who can create her own job is the woman who will win fame and fortune*, she had said.

Ida walked the rest of the way to meet Freda with a hand over her mouth. She suspected her father hadn't heard a word she'd said.

*     *     *

Freda sat on the flattest boulder halfway between the bank of the lake and the island, with her knees to her chin, as still as a statue so she didn't knock the heavy, silver-rimmed stopwatch into the water. Ida's things were in the Bathing House, hanging on one of the giant brass hooks, with two brown paper bags of sweets from the newsagent's for after her swim. Ida was late.

It was calm and quiet and warm. Small brown fish darted here and there, and tiny see-through flies made join-the-dots patterns on the surface of the water. Every so often a fresh scent, like newly cut grass, filled her nostrils.

A kingfisher was hanging sideways from one of the velvety brown bulrushes at the lake's edge. Freda watched the bird watching the water. Once or twice, she thought it would swoop but it stayed as still as she was, biding its time. She wanted to see it make its move. The bird was so colourful and compact you knew it was skilled at its game. It was entrancing.

'Newsflash!' Ida shouted from the bank.

Freda turned and put a finger to her lips.

But it was too late. The kingfisher whooped off, a flit of turquoise so quick it seemed as small as a dragonfly, almost as though it had never been there at all. Freda stood.

The only sound was the tap of Ida's black barred shoes as she came towards her over the stones. Months of training had made her limbs as sinewy as frogs' legs.

'Nice lipstick,' Freda said.

'Guess what, I'm going to be a reporter.'

'A reporter?' Freda followed her into the Bathing House.

'You know, writing stories. For the *Times*.'

'How so?'

'I went in to tell them about my swim,' Ida said. 'And the editor himself came down and offered me a job.'

Freda looked away as Ida stepped into her costume.

'Don't be like that, Freddie.'

'I'm not being like anything. Congratulations.'

'Come on,' Ida said. 'Let's get cracking. The deadline approaches.'

'You'll make the news, I'll deliver it.'

'Very clever, Freddie.' Ida left her clothes on the floor and ran to the water, tucking her hair under her cap. *'En garde!'* she called. 'Let's see if I can beat my record.'

Freda watched Ida wade into the deepest part of the lake and fling her arms before her. She wore one of her old suits, faded blue with a white trim still bright enough to highlight the darkness of her skin. Round and round she went, circling the island and stopping every few laps to hear her time. When she swam out of sight, behind the Bathing House, Freda listened to the splash of her arms turning like pistons. Ida stayed in so long the lake darkened like the sky.

'Isn't that enough now?' Freda called, when Ida raised her head to signal the start of another lap. But round she went a couple more times and came out looking cross about stopping.

They lay for ages on the floor of the Bathing House, staring at the night sky through the glass ceiling. The air was hot and dry.

'If it wasn't for the sea washing it away, I'd wear your lipstick for my swim,' Ida said, running a finger thoughtfully round her lips. 'The editor says I'm to have my picture taken.'

Freda didn't reply. She hadn't noticed before but there was a small hole in one of the ceiling's panes, circular, as though a bird high in the sky had dropped a tiny pebble that went like a bullet through the glass.

Ida turned to her, propped on her elbow, so a trail of dark fluffed hair slipped over her shoulder and hung touching the floor. Her toes were cold as she prodded Freda's leg, bare below her shorts.

69

'I hope you're not going to go all funny on me,' Ida said. 'Now we're on the home straight.'

The whites of Ida's eyes came and went as she blinked. Her lips were a fleshy smudge in the darkness. Freda looked back at the navy sky, her own mouth dry from sucking on pear drops. It was so peaceful, the silence of closed lips.

Ida said, 'Isn't it exciting?'

'Exciting isn't the word Harold Simons is using,' Freda replied. Harold was the Men's Swimming Club captain. He'd been into her father's place listing off the Olympian swimmers who had failed to cross the Channel. One was thwarted by twenty-foot waves, another by a south-westerly wind. The tide had swept a third too far down to cross-current in time, and a fifteen-stone stevedore who claimed he'd swum fifty miles one Bank Holiday was brought down by a violent attack of sea sickness and cramp in both legs and shoulders.

'Harold probably just wants one of his boys to be the first,' Ida replied. Freda was right. Nobody did think a girl could do it. Ida let out a terrific sigh.

'Oh, I know it's terribly dangerous,' she said, 'and the currents have pulled people down, and I'm frightened—of course I am—but there's no giving up now, is there?'

Her voice broke as she said, 'I do hope I do it.'

'So do I,' Freda replied.

An owl called, not a gentle hoot but a wild, searching cry to its mate. Hunting. Freda moved about. The bare wooden boards felt splintery under her back.

'You never know, it might be the start of something,' Ida said. 'Showing people what we can do instead of being told what we can't.'

70

## 5

Mr Gaze hadn't wanted any daughter of his making an exhibition of herself on the seafront, but he'd had a think and there could be something in it for him. Whether or not the girl swam the Channel or was dragged out five minutes into the whole charade, her antics were the talk of the town. People were calling her brave. Foolhardy would be his choice of words, but never let it be said Walter Arnold Gaze hadn't an eye for the main chance.

Once he'd visualised the potential benefits of a double-page spread in the *Times*, Mr Gaze swung into action. He organised a small boat to trail his daughter in the water and spoke to a man who knew a ship-owner in one of the grand stone houses on Victoria Parade. Ida was to ride to the seafront in a pink Rolls-Royce, courtesy of Algernon Fear Esquire, who owned a dozen ships and thought Ida's caper a show of great vim.

Walter was in his element telling his pals at the club that he had a bit of sway at the *Times*. The editor himself would cover the swim, and journalists from London were coming too. Furthermore, his photographer pal was going to record the event, which meant that a fancy reel of Ida would be shown at the local cinema. Goodness knows who all would be there, he said, and now more and more of them were asking to come along in the boat for a laugh. They could take a few bottles of whisky and a banjo. It would be jolly if the weather held out.

'You'll be up on the big screen at the picture house, boys,' he'd told them.

'Your little girl will certainly be a star if she gets across that water,' said Seth Myers. 'It took Billy from us and he'd been fishing that estuary fifty years.'

'Good luck to her, I say,' put in another man. 'Because she's going to need it when those freezing North Atlantic waters come rolling in over her head.'

'The silly season,' the club steward said. 'A sixteen-year-old girl trying to swim the Channel. If there's any film at all, it will show the child being pulled from the water like a half-drowned rat.'

There was one other slightly sour moment when a man forced to buy ten golf balls back off Freda, who knew he always hit long on the fourteenth hole, said, 'I'm amazed that loopy friend of hers, Freda Voyle, hasn't gone in for that lark. Don't those two do everything together—joined at the hip or the mouth or whatever it is they say?'

Mr Gaze had gone quiet then. He wanted positive publicity in the *Times*, not a story about his daughter and that madcap Voyle girl making fools of all of them.

'You do know they're in and out of that lake at Jackson's old place, don't you?' Mervyn White told him. 'Good job his lot have gone to Jamaica or they'd have something to say about them disappearing into that hut in the middle of the water.'

'They're down on the front all hours too,' came another voice.

Evening strollers on the prom had taken to leaning over the bright blue cast-iron railings to

72

watch for Ida's head in the water. Further and further she swam, getting closer and closer to the shipping lane from Cardiff's Docks, then back again, over and over, until out she came up the pebbles to Freda, waiting with a towel.

Nobody told Walter Gaze he should put a stop to it, but that's what they were saying. If the current didn't take her, one of the ships leaving harbour carrying two thousand tons of coal would. Rain or shine, those two girls were out there, and once in an electric storm.

Walter was standing in the kitchen drinking a glass of water when his daughter returned from work.

'Skiving, is it?' he said, watching her empty a bag.

'I was allowed to leave early on account of tomorrow's historic swim,' Ida replied, placing two jars of Bovril, a packet of rusks, two bars of chocolate and a tub of lanolin on the kitchen table. The first three were to feed her during the swim. The fourth was to grease her, to help keep her warm, before she dropped into the water.

'Freda will do it,' she told him with her hand on top of the lanolin. No, she damn well won't, Mr Gaze thought. There was already enough talk in the town.

Ida could hear movements above and water trickling into the drain outside from the bathroom. She wondered if her mother was getting ready for the swim, whether she would leave the house in her black hat with its thick band of white grosgrain ribbon.

'See you later, Father.' Upstairs, her bathing suit was laid over the back of her bedroom chair ready

73

for tomorrow. 'I've got things to do.'

The last job on the list was a trip to Regina's hair salon on the high street.

Mr Gaze looked after her, walking down the hall in a new pair of pantaloons from Mrs Dixie's dress shop. 'Pantaloons from a dress shop?' Mrs Gaze had said that morning, sitting up in bed eating Bassett's Liquorice Allsorts. 'The world's gone mad!'

'It could be worse,' Ida replied. 'Mr Wilson's men's outfitters could be selling frocks.'

*  *  *

Outside, newly written in gold paint, were the words *Regina's for Making Waves*. It was all the rage. Ida had stood outside often enough looking at women wincing when the irons, warmed on a gas burner, singed their scalp, but at least they came out with a head of curls.

The little salon was painted lilac inside. There were brushes, hairpins and magazines on the counter in front of a row of three red chairs which faced oval mirrors. A life-size clay model of a head had a hairnet pulled over its eyes with a card balanced against it saying *Net profits! Get your cover here!*.

'Hello, young lady,' said Gina. 'Sit yourself down.'

Once Ida was settled, Gina approached with a pair of scissors. There were women in the two other seats being attended by Gina's assistant. All of them were quiet, looking at Ida's trousers.

Gina said, 'Now then, are you sure your parents know what I am going to do to you?'

Ida nodded. 'It's my decision in any case,' she said, as Gina gathered her hair with both hands, raking her fingers through it, then gripping it tight as she reached for the scissors.

'Here we go,' Gina said. 'No going back.'

'I know all about that.' Ida couldn't deny she was nervous. Someone had told her about a 300-foot drop in the water just past one of the islands, but there was no backing out now.

'I'm swimming the Channel tomorrow,' she said.

It was all fixed, with the tides right. The Ladies' Swimming Club captain had organised a team to accompany her in a boat; she'd have pacers to keep her pecker up; and the man from the Welsh Amateur Swimming Association was coming to make it all official.

'I know that, young lady. You're the talk of the town.'

Ida felt a slight tug as Gina worked the scissors through.

The hair that came away looked like a horse's tail when it was held in front of Ida's eyes.

'Want this as a keepsake?' the woman asked and Ida shook her head.

'Hair always seems so much nicer on the head than off,' remarked one of the women. Her new curls were being combed out and Ida watched them spring back into light brown silky coils.

'I think it is definitely nicer *off* the head than on,' said Ida, tipping her head about. It felt as though she had lost half her body weight.

All the women looked when there was a knock at the salon window and the oldest tutted. Tut-tut-tut she went at Freda who stood flapping her hands back and forth as though she was trying to stop

75

traffic.

'What does *she* want?' said Gina.

'Is it all right if she comes in?' Ida asked.

'Not really,' Gina replied, but Freda was already through the door, bringing with her the scent of cigarettes. She didn't look at Ida's new shorter hair, but at the hair in the salon-owner's hand.

'I'll have that,' Freda said in that voice she sometimes had, which sounded as though people should do what she told them.

Gina looked at Ida, who had her head cocked at her reflection. It wasn't quite Amelia Earhart but she was getting there. She'd read about the Atlantic flier saying she used to cut small bits off her hair every few weeks and keep it pinned up at home so her mother didn't notice. *They, all of them, can't see beyond a girl having long hair,* Amelia had told a reporter.

'Is she to have it?' Gina asked, tapping Ida on the shoulder.

'What? Oh yes, though I can't see what for.'

Ida watched Freda take it carefully, as though it was slippery like a skein of liver. Her own hair was scrappily pulled back in a ponytail. Freda really did have the same kind of dips and bony bits to her face as Amelia Earhart.

Gina cleared her throat. 'Best get on if you've a swim to do,' she said, and Freda went to sit on a chair, turning the hair in her hands.

'You and your swimming,' Gina continued to the looking glass. Ida was catching eyes with Freda in the mirror but the rest of them were looking straight ahead. 'You ought to watch you don't get out of your depth.'

When they left the salon, Gina came to the door

and said, 'At least you'll look nice for your pictures.' It was clear nobody thought she would get to the other side.

It was late evening. On the hill to Ida's house, they passed the French onion man's bicycle with its pedal jammed down on the edge of the pavement.

Outside the gate, Ida stopped and looked at the hair still wrapped round Freda's wrist.

'What on earth do you want that for? It's like my mother keeping Maudie's hair in an envelope in her dressing-table drawer. People are right about you. You are an odd duck.'

She kissed Freda's cheek. Ida's lips were dry from always being in salt water.

'Takes one to know one,' Freda called, as she walked off with her hand to her face. 'Only a crackpot would swim that Channel tomorrow. Sweet dreams.'

'What was all that commotion and silliness with the Voyle girl outside?' said Mrs Gaze from the front room when Ida stepped into the hall and closed the front door. 'You should be careful, you should. Getting the gossips going when it's not as if your father doesn't give them enough to pick over.'

Ida took a breath and walked into the room. Winifred Gaze put a cupped hand to her mouth. 'In the name of all that is good and holy,' she said. 'I knew it. People will think you're a boy.'

\*       \*       \*

She didn't care what her father thought, in the driving seat up front. People could say they were too old for that kind of thing, but really, she didn't care. If a current took her, the last thing Ida would

77

think was that she had held Freda's hand in the back of the borrowed Rolls-Royce.

As they wound down the hill to the beach, dawn's yellow-white light seeping through the tree branches curving over the road, raindrops bounced like buttons on the roof of the car.

'You'll do it,' Freda whispered. 'I know you will.'

When the two girls stepped out onto the prom, Ida glanced at Freda and the two of them pushed out their cheeks with their tongues at the size of the crowd, all along the front and up the hill, like a giant tide line.

'And it's raining,' noted Freda. 'Some people will watch anything.'

Despite her nerves, Ida giggled. In the half-light, the sea looked cold and grey, waves here and there tipped with white, like sharp little shards of ice. A ferry juddered along the distant horizon. Ida ran her eyes over the faces. She knew what people were saying.

'Ida, lovely!' Two shapes larger than the rest broke from the line of onlookers being kept in check by a policeman. 'Good luck!' came the same shrill, determined voice.

'Auntie Bess!' Ida cried. 'And Gwynnie too!'

The pair came towards her, elbowing off the officer, Aunt Bess with a wide-brimmed hat tied under her chin with a huge pink ribbon bow and Gwynnie in a rust corduroy waistcoat holding out a bar of chocolate. Mr Gaze shook his head.

'Here,' Gwynnie said gruffly. 'Sugar. It's what those men take up the mountains to keep them going in the cold.'

'Thank you,' Ida replied, embracing Aunt Bess who smelled of cooking bowls and fire and soap-flakes.

'Break it up, will you,' Mr Gaze said into the warm, wet air. The last thing he needed was that up-the-pole sister of his spoiling things.

'Come and have your picture taken, sweetheart!' shouted one of the London photographers.

Bess gave Walter a filthy look and caught hold of Gwynnie's elbow before the two of them stepped back into the crowd.

The rain eased and there was such a clamour for photographs Ida reluctantly agreed to change on the beach, wobbling about on the pebbles.

'Can't you wait until I am dressed?' she asked Mr Gaze's photographer friend, who'd set up shop as though it was his studio in town. Ida refused to look at him when he clucked his teeth as though she was a performing pet, but she kept her cap off for as long as she could so he could capture her hair.

When one of the London reporters approached, handsome and dapper in plus-fours and a waistcoat, with a notebook and pen, Ida pulled her towel tighter.

'Frank Shankly,' he said. 'Reporter with the *Daily Trumpet*.'

She could almost smell the difference in him, the scent of another world settled confidently in the folds of his clothing. Ida smiled and ran a hand behind her ear. She could practically hear the clatter of typewriters bouncing back and forth in streets of tall office buildings, the hooting of cabs and omnibuses, elegant women tapping hurriedly along halls of vast houses with marble mantelpieces carved with cherubs and grapes.

Mr Gaze was always telling Ida she had a

vivid imagination—and it wasn't meant as a compliment.

'Miss Gaze,' the reporter said. 'I wonder if you might spare a few moments to tell us how you feel before your swim.'

'Oh,' she replied, dark eyes widening back at him. 'You may call me Ida.'

'Time is getting on. Has the girl been greased yet?' shouted the man from the Swimming Association. 'Someone grease the girl quickly.'

'Here,' said Freda, appearing from behind Ida's father, who was holding the tub of lanolin. 'I'll do it.'

Mr Gaze ignored Freda. The fair-haired reporter took a step back.

'Turn to face me, girl,' Mr Gaze said.

'I said *I'll* do it.' Freda reached for the tub.

Ida put a hand to her face as Freda tried to tug the tin from her father's hands. Through her fingers she felt a camera flash. All those months of training in freezing water, bloodshot eyes, skin shrivelling like a burst party balloon, and now this.

'Get off, girl,' said Mr Gaze to Freda. 'You're mad, you are.'

'No, you get off,' Freda replied. 'Why shouldn't it be me? Why should it be you?'

'Please, Freddie, leave it,' Ida said quietly, and Freda reluctantly dropped her hands.

Ida watched her father unscrew the lid and the lanolin made a sucking noise as he scooped his hand inside. He slapped it against her knee and she felt his hand travelling up her leg. The fine rain made the grease seem greasier. Ida looked out to sea thinking, Please let this be over.

'That's enough, Father.' She pulled away. 'I'll do

80

the rest.'

'I'll do it,' said Freda.

Mr Gaze looked at her. '*You?*' he said.

'Who else?' Freda replied, looking about her as though searching for the queue.

A camera flashed again. Mr Gaze let go of the tub. A howling dog was shushed. The crowd waited. The sea was a million pinpricks of tiny raindrops. Ida's mother was going on a boat to Weston to greet her when she got there, and more people again would be here when she returned from the other side in the boat laid on by Mr King.

'I will do it,' said Freda—which was the last thing Ida said too, five minutes later when she stepped into the water, after blowing Freda a kiss.

'Ladies and gentlemen, children and animals,' said the man from the Swimming Association. 'Miss Ida Gaze attempts to cross the Channel.'

'Fat chance,' said a voice, a man in the crowd, nobody she knew.

'I trust you're not a betting man,' yelled the lady from *The Vote*, the newspaper of the Women's Freedom League. 'Give the girl a chance.'

*THE QUESTION THE WHOLE TOWN IS ASKING!*
*DID BRAVE LITTLE IDA MASTER THE MONSTER*
*SEVERN SEA?*
**By Orson King, the Editor**

No gentlemen's drinking institution worth its sea salt has ignored it. In Jenning's, the grocer's, they speak of nothing else. All have been debating the single most pressing issue

81

of the year—nay, century!

Not the price of coal or beer, nor the diet of the Suffragettes, the delay in the erection of the Pier Pavilion, or the likelihood of Maxfield Amos becoming the town's new Mayor.

The question on everyone's lips—not least Harold Simons', the Men's Swimming Club captain, who has made no secret of being sure of the answer—was this: would Miss Ida Gaze—five feet one inch tall, seven stone three pounds in weight, and aged just sixteen—swim the Bristol Channel?

Bets taken at Davey Brown's suggested not. Customers at Gina's hair salon agreed it was nigh on impossible for anyone, let alone a woman—especially a girl not long departed from the genteel County School—to take on the treacherous currents and come out on top.

Let us get to the point. In truth, there is not one sane man in the town who did not at heart believe that Miss Gaze's high hopes were destined to sink like a stone.

The omens were certainly ill—heavy rain and poor visibility—when she set out on her reckless quest.

Waved off by hundreds of people, gathered in a mood of unfounded optimism to give the girl the enthusiastic send-off she deserved, Miss Gaze waded into the water at 4.25 a.m. accompanied by a small rowing boat containing Mr Benjamin Porter, the pilot, and three pacers.

Mr Walter Gaze, her father, and Mr J. T.

Cackett, representing the Welsh Amateur Swimming Association, were in a launch, which also held press snappers, and the town's prestigious photographer, Mr Redvers Dare, who planned to host an exhibition of pictures at his studio after showing a reel of the attempted swim at the Kinema.

What good would come of such an enterprise? Certainly, those standing in the drizzle of an August dawn were convinced of the outcome. But quiet, you Doubting Thomases! Before you damn her to certain failure and a nasty bout of pneumonia, give the girl a chance!

Upon being greased by her father before entering the water, Miss Gaze struck out with her favourite stroke, the trudgen, and made good progress, passing the West Cardiff buoy at 5.30 a.m.

There was a light rain and the girl fought with all her might for two and a half hours when she hit an unusually strong south current and made little progress.

At 5.45 she was fed with beef tea, but it seemed we would never pass the Holm Islands. At seven o'clock, Mr Morgan Tyne, the first pacer, entered the water and he too battled hard against the current and neither swimmer covered much ground.

Here there were some anxious moments. Few on the launch expected Miss Gaze to retain her energy and cheerfulness when it seemed a racing certainty she was doomed to failure. At 7.45 Mr Tyne was relieved by Mr Bert Farthing who stopped in the water for over an hour.

Gradually the tide was changing and a little distance was covered. Slowly we steered through the Holms, where the tides are mighty and strong currents run in odd directions. By 12.15 Miss Gaze had overcome the most difficult and trying part of her swim, or so it seemed.

Around came the feeding hour and our plucky swimmer, recently crowned this year's Gala Princess, was again given necessary nourishment. The Weston coast was now clearly visible and our swimmer saw it with a start of delight and not a little wonder.

Those fine men on the boat, minds addled by the heave of the waves, talked darkly of miracles and beginner's luck and flashes in the pan. Certainly, one or two embarrassed themselves by leaning overboard to relieve their sickened states.

Until now, Miss Gaze had been in the best of spirits and was always smiling. Her stimulants consisted of Bovril, rusks and chocolate, and they appeared to have kept her 'tip top' as she never complained of any physical trouble.

At three miles from the other side, everyone now breathing freely with the Holm Islands passed, our swimmer was enthusiastically cheered on from the launch.

The weather conditions cleared and what a welcome it was to see friend Sol appear over the horizon. Was this a sign the gods were smiling on our fearless mermaid? The pleasure steamers, which continually overtook the swimmer, blew their sirens while their many passengers waved merrily.

Weston was now one and a half miles away, and much to the sorrow of the people in the launch, Mr Cackett, riding in the rowing boat, took out his banjo and gave the swimmer a few encouraging tunes ('Muddy Waters', 'Ole Man River', 'One More River to Weston' etc).

Still Miss Gaze kept on. When half a mile from the bay she showed signs of slight exhaustion, and her strokes became slower but still quite determined, Mr Stanley Dummer entered the water and offered encouragement on the last lap.

Success in her grasp, would she sink at the final hurdle?

We heard the distant splash of a speedboat and before long a boat full of cheery and happy faces was alongside the launch. Mr Gaze jumped aboard it and was taken to the Old Pier at Weston so all arrangements could be made by the time the swimmer arrived.

Well-wishers were gathered on St Thomas's Head, Weston, and when Miss Gaze landed at 43 minutes, 22 seconds past midday, three long cheers arose.

The good news had already spread through the West Country town, and hundreds of people were waiting to welcome the Wonder Girl.

Lest anyone be in any doubt, here is the outcome. Miss Ida Gaze is the first person to swim the Bristol Channel, one of the most dangerous and difficult stretches of water imaginable, in eight hours, eighteen minutes and twenty-two seconds.

On arrival at the beach she was plied with questions from waiting reporters before being presented with a beautiful bouquet of flowers and embraced by her mother who had remained silent with tender distress.

'I have done it,' the girl declared, adding she was following in the footsteps of her heroine, Miss Amelia Earhart, who had uttered the same such words after crossing the Atlantic in an aeroplane, the first woman to do so.

It should be no surprise the girl seemed barely able to breathe. Indeed, many on the beach were close to choking as the truth dawned: a woman had crossed the Bristol Channel and was indeed the first person to do so.

The swim is a meritorious triumph, one of the most remarkable feats of endurance and courage ever witnessed.

'There were times when it felt as though I was taking two strokes back for every one forward,' Miss Gaze told us. 'My heart is banging urgently in my chest. My limbs feel as weak as melting wax. This crowd is overwhelming.'

'Never mind your fancy talk, let's check your heart-rate,' announced her father. The rest of us can only imagine the fear and anxiety with which he and his lady wife were gripped as they watched their precious daughter's uncertain path to victory.

Miss Gaze was conveyed by car to a

Weston hotel where she was refreshed, cleaned and dressed.

The big fight over, the successful swimmer enjoyed a well-earned rest. At four o'clock the merry party motored to the pier to board the *Princess* steamer which was specially decorated with flags for the trip back across the Channel.

The return to the Swimming Town was a veritable pageant. It might have been a Royal Reception. Miss Elizabeth Gaze, the swimmer's aunt, had made a special trip from the west to see her niece crowned the Mistress of the Channel. All the town's swimmers, young and old, turned out to receive their heroine as the *Princess* drew in, and they cheered loudly, planted kisses on her cheeks, and lifted her onto their shoulders.

Mr J. T. Cackett, of the Welsh Amateur Swimming Association, said this was the finest swimming effort he had ever seen and was deserving of a commemorative tablet on the town's pier, which he would endeavour to secure for her.

The three-hour battle off the Holms spoke well for the girl's endurance and courage. He said Miss Gaze, of 23 Cliff View, must have covered a distance of twenty-two and a half miles.

'A more plucky swim I have never seen,' he said. 'There may be people present who think there is little in such a feat, but I can assure you I wouldn't even like to row it. We can, I am certain, expect great things of this young lady.'

*The feat was all the more pleasing as Miss Gaze is a reporter with this newspaper.*

## 6

*KINEMA EXCLUSIVE*
*For One Night Only*
*SPECIAL UNIQUE FILM*
*of the Wonder Girl, Miss Ida Gaze*
*SWIMMING the BRISTOL CHANNEL*
*This will be the ONLY film in the Country showing all the Incidents of this Remarkable Swim*

It had all been going so well. The turn-out for Ida's reel was touching. Three hundred (plus the projection man and the rewinding boy) watched her swim from their bristly red velvet seats in the town's cinema. Mrs Gaze even smiled when people walking out of the foyer congratulated her on Ida, though Freda was watching too and described it as more of a wince.

But when everyone filed into Mr Dare's photographic studio to see the pictures, things took a decided turn for the worse.

There had been one large portrait of Ida on the beach set on an easel as though Mr Dare had painted it, and lots of smaller copies of the same image propped on cardboard flaps around the room.

'It's like a shrine,' Freda had said loudly. 'He's just like the rest of them, never thought you would do it.'

'Please,' Ida had said, glancing at her father who

88

was chums with Mr Dare. 'Look how many people have come to support me, please don't start,' but Freda was off, pointing at the back of the pictures: on every one was written *Ida Gaze Attempts to Swim the Channel,* 1928.

'Look, I'm right,' she was saying, 'he still won't credit you with having done the swim. Nobody in this place wants to accept that girls can do whatever they please.'

Now, seated at her desk with the breeze ruffling her hair and the wood pigeon doing its usual urgent coo-cooing through the open window, the townspeople leaving Mr Dare's with faces like stone was all Ida could think about. That, and how short and tubby she'd looked up on the big screen wading out of the water in her black one-piece.

When that reporter, Frank Shankly, had appeared at her side with his notebook, someone in the audience had shouted, 'Give her a kiss!' She'd blushed at that and Freda had elbowed her hard.

A week on and she could tell people were being funny with her. On the way to the office, Mr Jennings, the grocer, had run back in the shop, and Miss Webster in the window of the Imperial Coal Company had bitten her bottom lip. Only Evelyn downstairs was the same as usual, looking up from the front counter to give one of her conspiratorial winks when Ida came through the door. Were the rest of them cross about Freda's scene at Mr Dare's, or was it Ida herself who needed taking down a peg or two?

'Still with us then, Wonder Girl?' Mr King said, when she arrived a few minutes after nine several days on the trot. 'Half-day again?'

89

'Late shifts in London, is it, Miss Gaze?' asked David, the senior reporter, continuing to type. 'At least that's what I've heard.'

People must think she'd been fast with the reporter when he took her off down the prom to ask questions. That, or perhaps Freda was right about people picking on anyone different.

Her mother wasn't speaking to her and all Mr Gaze kept saying was she would get herself into trouble, the way she was going. He'd been up early for a round of golf and saw her sheets smooth on the bed the morning after the swim, and then caught Ida coming up the path at dawn with a blackberry stain on her new white trousers.

Would it be worse or better to say she hadn't spent the night with that London reporter but with Freda under the oak in their field?

Frank the reporter was spot on when he told her that Wales was the back of beyond, and Freda was right too. The town was a nest of gossips.

Banging at her typewriter, Ida wondered how she hadn't realised it before. It was so obvious. London, a place far enough away, a great smoky mass of stone and offices and shops and turning wheels and traffic horns, was clearly the answer to her prayers.

How many times had people said she should go to London? There was Frank Shankly, that old man at the Kinema. She imagined London, all jaggedy buildings and omnibuses and skylines and dashing, shimmery people, and Frank in an office with telephones going, and here she was with the flip-flip-flip of Maisie, the Editor's daughter, leafing through unsold newspapers, and David ripping a sheet of paper from his typewriter and

90

screwing it up in a mood.

At ten to eleven, she would say she had too much work to fetch the buns for the tea-break and could Maisie go instead. David would have left for court and Mr King was attending a Rotary Club lunch and always disappeared early for those. She would be on her own in the office and she would call that reporter.

She waited to be connected—*Hello, would you hold . . . Shanks, lady on the line for you*—and then Frank's voice. Ida was breathless with nerves.

'You sound like you've done another swim,' he said and she laughed.

'I want to come and work in London.'

He'd told her about travelling to work on the Underground and emerging up the steps heading for Fleet Street. There was silence.

'Are you still there?' Ida asked.

'You're a little young for that, aren't you?' he replied. 'I hope you're not coming on my say-so.'

'But it was you who told me I should. I can look older and I've got reporting experience. Will you find me a job, do you think?'

'I'm busy on a story but I'll try and have a word.'

'I've got to speak to someone too,' said Ida, and she put the phone down just as David came into the office shaking his head.

'Some boy up for making a bit of noise,' David said. 'Driving a motor cycle with an inefficient silencer,' he added in the stuck-up voice of the magistrate. 'He made the cycle from parts himself. Ordered to pay thirty shillings and there's no way he can afford it. Poor lad.'

Ida smiled, not sure what response he wanted. She thought he had her down as a silly girl after she came in one day wearing the lipstick and quickly went to the lavatory to wipe it off when nobody would look at her face if she spoke.

That afternoon, Ida finished banging out a filler for page seven.

*Can ladies bowl?* she wrote. *On Friday Mrs Widdowson replied emphatically with 17 'touchers' on 22 heads.*

'Mr King?' she asked. The Editor didn't look up or speak.

'Mr King, I wondered if I might write about Amelia Earhart.'

'Old news,' he said, still not raising his eyes from a magazine propped on his typewriter. 'We did a small piece on it at the time.'

'I mean her effect on young women. You know, the way she inspired me to do my swim and how other girls in the town might feel the same way.'

'Not local interest. Our bread and butter.'

Who? What? When? Where? Why? Mr King was always saying. That's what the readers want to know. Ida had been so excited when she started the job, repeating back all she was learning to Freda as they sat under the pier. Who? What? When? Where? Why?

Sounds like the chant of everyone living in this town, Freda had replied.

Ida said, 'Well, she did land in Wales.' It was so depressing, this obsession with wedding pictures and people up in court. That's why people bought papers, the Editor had told her, not to read about fashion or girls flying high.

'Hardly the *Times*' circulation area, is it?' Mr King took a gulp from the whisky bottle he kept in his desk drawer, and said croakily, 'Do me one thousand words on the Presbyterian Church Bazaar.'

He threw the magazine on the floor and started tapping at his typewriter, but she heard him well enough when he mumbled, 'I think everyone's had their fill of high-flying ideas for now.'

Ida couldn't bear it. She really couldn't stand this any more, wondering what people meant—and that was if they said anything in the first place. Why had everyone turned so? Was it the lipstick?

'Girl like you should go to London,' that's what that old man in the Kinema foyer had said. 'Guts and a pretty face. Nobody never said no to that in the Big Smoke.' What was she doing here?

When Ida finally backed out of the room at five, she ran down the hill to the beach, the pavement seeming to come up through her legs, so hard did she slap down her feet. Freda was under the pier, a bowed shape, her head between her knees.

'Are you ill?' Ida asked. Freda didn't look up as she slipped across the pebbles.

'People are so hellish.' Freda's voice sounded thick, as though she was holding her nose. Ida sensed she was crying and sat a respectful distance away. She threw a stone into the water that frilled up and away, over and over, not far from their feet.

'Want to tell me?' she asked.

'Nothing to tell,' Freda replied. 'It's so petty and nasty that if I say it it doubles it. That's the problem with this place. Everyone repeats things to make them worse.'

Ida ran through what might have happened. Freda had her paper round first thing and got home around nine o'clock. She helped her mother in the house, spent time with her father in the

93

shop, and sometimes went to fetch her brother from a friend's. Ida knew her Aunt Sylvia was round at the house a lot, sticking her oar in.

'Listen, I've got a plan,' said Ida.

'I'll bet you have.' Freda still didn't look up but her voice sounded clearer, less bent over.

Above their heads, fishermen called—there was cod and whiting and eels to be had off the pier—and children ran back and forth.

'No—look, please listen,' Ida said. 'I—we—need to get away from this town. I'll tell you, but you have to let me treat you to baked beans on toast.'

It was Freda's favourite in the Italian ice-cream parlour on the front. She got paid so little for her paper round and yet she was always bringing sweets for Ida after work. Toffee dabs. Fairy chips. Gobstoppers. Coconut strips.

'We?' Freda looked at her.

'Into the caff, now.' Ida held out a hand for Freda to grab and be pulled up. They always had to be careful doing this. If Freda let Ida try to pull all her weight, the two of them would go over like skittles.

'Why don't we go to London—you know, for good?' Ida said when they were sitting at the table with two plates of beans on toast. Freda had cut her slice into four pieces and was on the third.

She was obviously hungry. Ida could imagine her up in her room all day not going down to the kitchen because Sylvia was there. Ida was using her knife and fork, with little appetite.

'What, with our possessions tied in a handkerchief on a stick? I hear the pavements be paved with gold,' said Freda in the kind of voice they'd laughed about when they went over to

94

Weston for the day on the paddle steamer. Freda was so good at accents or noticing people's tics, noticing anything really. She gave Ida's life such detail.

'I'm serious,' Ida said.

'So am I,' Freda replied. 'I can't go to London.'

'Why not?' Ida was used to Freda making broad, final statements like, 'Rice pudding is the devil's vomit,' or, 'This town was put by the sea so it should drown.'

'I like it here well enough.'

'You're all right,' Ida said. 'Your parents leave you alone.'

'Aunt Sylvia doesn't.'

'But don't you think it would be fun, Freddie?'

Ida imagined grand white buildings and grey statues, shop mannequins in elegant clothing and theatre doors bursting open with music and laughter, and couples kissing in squares. Frank had told her about nail-thin debutantes descending glittering staircases at the Queen Charlotte's Ball.

'I don't want to go to grimy old London with omnibuses puffing out fumes,' Freda replied. She thought of the Bathing House. They hadn't been there together since Ida did her swim.

'And buildings like cliffs either side so you can't see the sky when you go down the street,' she added.

Ida moved the glass sugar-shaker from the centre of the table and reached across for her hand but Freda folded her arms. Ida had the same look she'd had when talking about the swim. It reminded Freda of her dog when he had a long stick in his mouth and barged past people on the narrow footpath that ran along the canal.

95

'Nor would you like it, if I know you as well as I think I do,' Freda said. 'There's no sea in London.'

Ida thought of the currents pulling at her, the standing still even though she fought with all her might, strands of seaweed trailing below the surface of the water like the ribbons on her mother's funeral hat, and the sugary warm taste of chocolate handed from the boat just when she thought she would go under.

'You don't even go in the water,' Ida said.

'You do,' Freda replied. 'How will you stand it? You won't be able to swan down the prom in a bathing suit in London, you know.'

Ida stretched her arms under the table. She knew what Freda was getting at.

'I just think we need to get away from here,' she said. 'I can't bear all this silly gossip and people looking at us when we walk round the town.'

'Take no notice,' Freda replied. 'They haven't got anything else.'

'There you are then. You've just said it. We want more.'

She'd seen that Freda responded to positives. The best way to say it wasn't that she didn't fit in here: it was that she would fit in somewhere else. If ever Ida talked about the two of them having a good time, Freda was all ears.

'How on earth would I earn a living in London?' Freda asked.

'What about nursing?' Ida hesitated but she said, 'Mrs Button said you could.'

'Mrs Button said I wouldn't make a doctor.'

'And she said you would make a nurse. Why are you listening to her anyway? You could be brilliant at anything you wanted, Freddie.'

96

Freda sighed and it came out then, about how Aunt Sylvia had been saying she would come to less than nothing if she stayed at home. Her husband, the doctor, had a brother who was something big in a London hospital. For ages, they'd been on about her going as a nurse. Freda's uncle may not have saved Maud's life, but he was said to know people with influence in the medical world. Freda repeated this last bit to Ida in a sarcastic, apologetic voice.

'Go on, Freddie. You'd make a brilliant nurse.'

'What would you do?' Freda asked. 'Would you work?'

'Of course,' Ida said. 'I will be a reporter.'

Freda's eyes narrowed. 'With minus ten?' It was what she called Frank Shankly in his plus-fours.

'Don't start that again. I've told you, nothing happened on the prom. He just asked me some questions, that's all. In any case, this is about you and me, Freddie. Girls doing what we want, like you said at Mr Dare's.'

Although the image of Freda bouncing off the walls of the photographer's studio made Ida flush with embarrassment, she kept her eyes on Freda's.

'What will you do if we stay here?' Ida said. 'You'll have your fill of that paper round soon enough and Aunt Sylvia stirring back at the house.'

She leaned across and flicked the end of Freda's nose.

'Just think, you'll be Free-da!' she said. 'Ha, we'll go about holding hands without anyone talking.'

Freda looked out of the window at the sea.

'People are no different wherever you go,' she said. 'You'll see.'

'They're different in London,' Ida replied. 'Like us, so we'll fit in. Frank says.'

Freda gently kicked her under the table.

'I don't have to fit in,' she said. 'Why would I want to fit in with people who have nothing better to do than talk about who is holding hands with whom?'

Ida sensed things had been said that Freda wasn't telling her.

'I'll always walk shoulder to shoulder with you,' she said seriously. 'You will come, won't you, Freddie?'

'Shoulder to shoulder?' asked Freda, leaning across to take one of Ida's baked beans. 'More like your shoulder to my hip.'

'Wait till I get myself some new shoes for the city with heels so I'm as tall as you,' Ida whispered. 'Red ones, with silk ribbons that crisscross up my legs, or green velvet ones with diamond brooches on the front . . .'

Freda listened, an awkward smile on her face as Ida detailed the clothes she would buy as though she'd already made a list in her head.

'A darling little sequined skullcap,' she said. 'And a peach crêpe and black satin peignoir trimmed with ivory lace . . . A pair of T-bar shoes in gold leather with the most charming bronze rosebud buttons to make you walk with a wiggle . . .'

Ida's voice rose and a man on a high chair at the counter turned to look.

'And a black chiffon evening gown with a beaded bodice and splits to the thigh that will make any man tell you he loves you.'

'I'm not going,' Freda said suddenly.

98

'You mean to London?'

Freda nodded. 'It's not that I won't,' she said. 'It's that I don't want to.'

'But, Freddie, why not? It won't be the same without you. Please.'

Ida strung the last word out so it sounded as shrill as a child's cry, but Freda shook her head.

'If you want to go and wear all your fancy outfits and fit in with all your different people,' Freda said, getting up from the table, 'please yourself.'

'I will,' Ida said, following her. 'I will, you know, if I say I will.'

'Well, I won't,' Freda replied at the door.

They walked back up the hill, apart and silent. At the top, instead of going to their blackberry field, Freda said she had to dig the garden for her father because his back was bad.

'I expect I'll see you before you leave,' she said.

'Don't be horrible,' Ida replied, adjusting her navy beret which she had to the side because that's how the papers said a French designer wore hers.


## CECILY 2009

Sarah was wearing a dress she had found in the charity shop up town. It was white with tiny pink flowers and twirly green leaves, and she wanted me to tell her how old I thought it was. All I could think, looking at her holding the skirt out so I could see the pleats unfolding, was—with her accent and her upbringing, her education and her tastes—what a world apart she was from secretive old Ceci.

99

I stood there, fingers to my lips, and the thought popped into my head that Sarah, her auburn hair pinned with diamanté clips, would have been the kind of woman who came in to have a baby at that clinic in London all those years ago, with me clanking by with my mop.

'Thank you for the card about the wireless programme,' I said. 'I'm sorry I missed it.'

'That radio documentary, Ceci? You know you can listen to it on your computer, don't you?'

'Can I? I thought I'd missed the boat.'

Sarah went over to my desk and gestured for me to sit in the chair. I watched the blur of her fingers on the keyboard, the plastic clatter so much swifter than my laborious prodding.

'See?' she said. 'Or rather listen.'

There was a snatch of old news and then the *beep beep beep* of a moment gone forever before on it came, the programme I thought I'd never hear. I find myself so much more aware of what I'm missing these days. The clock on my bedside cabinet ticks so loudly it's a wonder I ever get to sleep.

'Well,' I said. 'I don't know what all these computers can do. To think I reckoned I was on top of it with Google.'

Sarah went through it again, slowly. I'll make a note of it, she told me, and when I looked at what she'd put, it was in great big capitals. I've only done it that way because of my awful handwriting, she said. Yes, I thought, and I've got X-ray vision. The girl didn't miss much.

'Oh,' she said, picking up a sheet off my desk. 'Another girl in an old-fashioned bathing suit.'

'Just some old research,' I replied gruffly,

100

missing when I made a grab for the page.

'On Google, I'll bet.' She handed it over.

'Yes,' I replied, in such a voice Sarah knew to drop it. I must have learned that off Freda.

'Shall we go out the back?' she asked.

The day was sunny and I'd been moaning about getting the rear garden into shape. I stood and told her, 'You're wearing me out with your ways.'

Sarah turned back at the door to the kitchen. I hadn't meant it to come out the way she took it.

'Really, Ceci?' she said. 'I'm sorry if I'm a bit much. I don't mean to be a pest.'

I wobbled a little as Mungo pushed past me. I loved the warm weight of his body against my old legs, even if it was touch and go as to whether he'd knock me off balance.

'Don't be daft,' I told her, flapping my hand for her to move on. 'Where would I be without you and your questions?'

There were so many little things Sarah did to help me on the quiet. Putting the recycling out, carrying in letters and leaflets dropped through the door. When I'd told her there were bags of clutter waiting six months to come downstairs, she told me, don't worry, Ceci, if there's any lifting to be done I can take it in the car to the charity shop. Well, I said, you better check for pussy-bow blouses and geometric-patterned vases and all the rest of your fads first. Oh, she replied, that wasn't what I meant, and I smiled at her young, thin skin. I know that, I told her, because she was the last girl in the world to be a taker. You don't take any notice of me and my talk, I said.

'You say that, Ceci, but I'm all ears about the girl in the old-fashioned bathing suit,' Sarah replied as she yanked at the back door, which took ages to open because it had warped over winter. 'However many of them there are.'

I wish you showed the same stick with your marriage as you do with old-fashioned bathing suits, I wanted to tell her, but I thought that might come out wrong too.

'All in good time,' I said, though in truth I didn't know how much of a future there was. I didn't tell Sarah I was thinking of going to the estate agent about putting a price on the home Freda and I had shared for nigh on sixty years. There was always talk at the old age place about retirement flats, new buildings of small rooms stacked on top of each other going up around town like towers of Tupperware containers. I knew I had to go from this place with its cast-iron ribbed radiators that took an age to heat up come winter, and sash windows that vibrated in the wind. Whatever the time of year, it was always cold inside.

Outside, the early-summer air was so still the birdsong had the clearness of a perfectly tuned concert on the wireless—or the computer if you missed it first time round. I was so grateful for what Sarah had shown me because I often forgot to tune in to all sorts I'd remembered to circle in the *Radio Times*.

The girl was halfway down the overgrown lawn when I blurted out, 'They were saying at the old age about a biddy on her own falling down a well at the bottom of the garden. They only found her when next door went to power-wash their patio and couldn't get the pipe down the well.'

Sarah turned back. 'Let that be a warning to us both then,' she said. 'Now stop being depressing.

102

What's this for?'

She was tapping an old piece of string hanging from the buddleia. Always asking questions, seeing things I couldn't. Every time she left, I missed her company and used to sit wishing for another heart beating in the space left behind.

'Oh, that's where Freda used to hang fat balls for the birds,' I said, watching her count the one, then two, three, four pieces, all hanging, looking a bit pathetic with nothing at the end of them now the jackdaws had ripped off the little green net pouches long ago emptied of fat. To think Freda's hands had been on them and I hadn't noticed they were there.

'You must have had a lot of birds in your garden, or else they were very well fed,' she replied. She never asked too much about Freda. She just let me talk about her when I could.

'A bit of both,' I said, and then I told her how Freda would tie string round the bottom of the netting because otherwise it would burst and spill its contents. Rats, she'd say, we'll attract rats. Freda got very animated about rats. One of the few times I caught her listening to what anyone was saying was when we had the vermin man round from the council. He was one of those chatty types who liked his job, ready for a cuppa the moment he got through the door, and full of stories. He told us he'd been to one house where a rat was living the life of Riley in an oven, eating fruit cakes and all sorts else cooked and cooling in it, with everybody in the house blaming everyone else for polishing off cakes before they even got to the plate. What happened, Freda wanted to know. Let's just say one day the smell of cooking wasn't a plum pudding, he told us. It was very rare for Freda to ask questions—or answer them, for that matter—and she'd mention this sleeping rat roasting in the oven for days afterwards.

'Freda was a great one for feeding the birds,' I said.

One afternoon, I'd come downstairs to find out what all the banging was about, and there she was, bouncing apples in the hall. What's the racket for, I asked. It was usually Freda who liked her quiet. Sarah listened to me rambling on, about how Freda had said the apples were for the blackbirds and that they liked them best bruised.

Then, once she had counted out all these bits of string, the girl was on about putting out more food for the birds.

'It's not just in winter they need building up, is it, Ceci?' she said. 'They've got their chicks now, haven't they?'

Oh, the way she said it made me feel so old and small and useless in this big, empty house with its loose bits of string hanging, doors that wouldn't open, and a garden like a jungle. The rhododendron turned yellow not long after Freda went. The soil's too limey here, they like it acid, she used to say, putting a tablespoon of sulphur powder round the base of the bush so the leaves stayed green and vital.

I looked at Sarah, wondering when she might get back with that husband of hers, and if they'd start a family and when, and if I was still here . . . whether she might bring a little one to see me. I remembered having a baby around the house, squealing and creating, little arms waving semaphore from the cot for some attention and

104

what the Welsh call *maldod*.

'What about you?' I asked. 'Are you one for babies then?' Call it a nudge if you like. It was so forward of me, but I was seeing that when you get to my age there isn't much point pussy-footing about. She glanced at me—I'd seen that look in my time, a kind of calculation of what to say—and she came down on the side of coming clean.

'Oh Ceci,' she replied. 'We tried for such a long time, but it was so difficult . . .'

It came out then that they'd been doing this IVF business, three lots of it, and still nothing, and that was the start of the rift. Her husband, Tom, was always working, never there to give her the injections in her backside. Over time she became tired, felt hopeless and resentful, and finally came back here to take stock when he said this wanting a baby was coming between them.

I was taken aback. Moments earlier I'd been thinking of the girl as the mother of a new baby and now here she was telling me—an old woman with one of them long gone—that she couldn't have a child. I started to see why Sarah might pause when she mentioned Christmas, that it might not be a barrel of laughs if you're imagining setting out presents under the tree for a child, or even a husband, who isn't there.

'Even when things are difficult you have to keep up hope, don't you?' I said. 'And if you love each other, you don't just drop everything at the first sign of trouble, do you?'

Sarah gave me a look as if she knew I was saying something more than I had. She'd told me she spent a lot of time with her grandparents and as such knew the value of keeping warm, a crossword

105

dictionary, and cuttings from other people's gardens. The girl was probably used to old know-alls pushing platitudes too.

Back inside, I sent her to sit down while I stayed in the kitchen boiling the kettle and putting a few slices of Battenberg on a plate. I was getting to know what tickled her. Look at the cake, she'd say. Look at this little china plate with its flowers and gold rim. It took me a while, I'll admit, to see she wasn't putting a frill on everything for the sake of it, and that she really did get pleasure from the old red spotty fairy-cake cases I'd thrown in the bin, or the rusty green watering-can standing out the back.

I took the tray through and set it on the table I'd brought in from the front room for our tea. I fell back so easily into setting out two of everything. Being a tidy type, I surprised myself by wanting to leave the two cups and saucers and plates on the drainer. They started staying there until bedtime, with me enjoying the idea they were waiting to be put away and fetched out again the following day.

The dog was on the rug in front of the fire, dropped down flat like a little collapsible table. Sarah had let slip he slept on her bed. I like animals but I don't agree with that sort of thing and I couldn't imagine it went down well with the husband either. Oh no, she told me when I'd hinted as much, he was like our baby, and she gave me a sad sort of smile.

'He's got a good set-up here, hasn't he?' I said, and Sarah nodded. The dog banged his tail. 'Better make the most it,' I told him. 'Last fire of the year.'

Sarah kept inviting me round to her place—I often wondered at each of us alone in our houses of an evening, in one room and the rest of them

106

empty—but I told her: why change a good thing? I didn't fancy it, to be honest. The parents might come back from Andalusia and wonder how they'd got themselves an elderly squatter.

'It's strange the dog seems so at home here,' Sarah said. 'Usually he's wary of new doorways, won't go down people's halls. He thinks it's a trap, that he's going to be taken away just as he's calling somewhere home.'

Sarah described him as a rescue dog who'd been given a home by the sea. That dog and me have a lot in common and I'd noticed he liked the same things I did—a bit of scone and butter, Madeira cake without the cherry, or a shortcake finger—so I said, 'That dog is yellow and he likes to eat anything yellow.'

She loved that.

'You are clever, Ceci,' she said. I don't know what took me back more, Sarah thinking I had something to say or her laugh zigzagging merrily into the room. She gave me such a look of delight and it brought back so many memories. Her saying I was clever—I thought a lot about that later. I started counting up the other nice little things people had told me over the years, but I puzzled for ages when it came to Freda. She was that type, Freda, that if ever she did say that sort of thing, you felt you'd been given the sun on a plate.

'You're spot on, Ceci,' Sarah said. 'He loves chips too.'

Now I will say that dog is always shedding—even in the colder weather he was doing it—but I've stopped Hoovering up the cream hairs on the rug. They've got thicker by the day.

I reckon it might be my downfall, that big patch

107

of hairs before the fire. If anyone from the old age comes round to check on me, they'll put me down as a dirty mare who's letting things slide, and say I should go straight to a home not my own.

I've always kept things straight, see, and the fur used to bother me until I realised it was a sign of life, of company not long gone, like the dent in a pillow or the warmth of a bed just left.

\*     \*     \*

If they hadn't kept putting those plastic charity sacks through my door, things might have stayed just the way they were, or thereabouts.

If some busybody hadn't gone posting bags asking for old bric-à-brac, Freda's clothes would have been left in the chest of drawers until I went too and some poor bugger was obliged to come and take away a couple of old biddies' lifetime possessions.

Funny, isn't it? If some overpaid do-gooder brainstorming in a charity HQ off the London orbital hadn't suggested they target this town, I would never have discovered that photo and so much more besides.

It was a while after Freda died, and six months or so before I met Sarah, when I saw the first folded white plastic package in the hall. We'd been warned down at the old age that fraudsters were posing as charity collectors. The police officer, looking as usual like a giant baby in fancy dress, told us our donations did not go to children in war-torn countries. They were collected by chancers in trucks who sold the stuff on and pocketed the takings.

I picked up the bag, not knowing if it was a good or bad idea, but I did think that if I was having a big clear-out, wasn't it better to put it in a faceless sack to be left outside the door and taken to somewhere else completely, war zone or not?

The one thing that had stopped me opening anything containing Freda's clothes was the thought I'd have to take the lot into one of the charity shops in town, and there are plenty of them doing a good trade. I couldn't and still can't see who it is that takes a dead loved one's possessions to the local charity shop so that they might walk past the window a few days later, on their way for half a dozen sausages or a packet of Nice biscuits, and see a familiar jumper hanging lifeless on a headless model. Or a pair of empty shoes with a price tag on the strap they once bent to fasten when their sweetheart put their back out.

I had a wry smile taking the bags upstairs, thinking about how it was asking for bric-à-brac and how much Freda hated having things—knick-knacks, she called them—lying around. If we ever went to someone's house (which wasn't that often), she'd come back complaining about a cabinet of figurines or a row of brass horse's heads hanging on a black leather strap. 'What are they *for*?' she'd say in real earnest. Freda liked things to have a reason, to be in a straight line and for there to be no extras. If I tucked a hankie under the puffed sleeve of a summer top, she'd call me Popeye until I took it away.

I started stacking up her clothes on the bed, taking them from their neat piles in the bottom set of drawers that she'd said a long time ago she'd like for herself. It was to be just her gear, and all

109

my kit was to go next door. She did have her fussy side, Freda, always closing the lav door, not eating anything I offered if I'd taken a bite from it. She wouldn't have alcohol in the house and I only ever saw her have the one, when we went to an anniversary do, but she took one sip and left the drink on the trestle table in favour of a cigarette on the steps at the back of the hall.

Freda wasn't a chore to live with, by any means. We had our moments, and little jokes too. She had this thing about me saving food. I'd always put a plate over a spoonful of tinned salmon left behind in a bowl, saying, 'You'll be glad of that in a sandwich.' Or every time I made home-made soup—it was a good show, full of tomatoes and celery and onions and all sorts of leftovers—I'd put a bowl before her, saying, 'It's a meal in itself.' So it would be, 'You'll be glad of that in a sandwich,' if either of us left something behind on our plate, even a fishbone, or I'd be opening a tin of soup and Freda would pass me, lightly touching my shoulder or giving my neck a kiss, and say, 'It's a meal in itself.'

That day I tried to make a start on the sorting out, the square was silent, the trees already stripped for last winter. A car went by, startling me, whooshing past below as if to say 'Ha-ha-ha, silly Ceci, don't you know that moments can't be held on to, so no good you clutching at those pullovers . . .'

Ain't you a daft ha'p'orth, I thought to myself, wondering what Freda would think of me unfolding each of her tops and holding them to my face. It would have been far quicker to shove the lot in the bag and put her old Dunlop slippers from

110

the *cwtch* under the stairs in there too. That would have been the Freda way of doing things.

The photo was between two jumpers, her red cable and her navy Fair Isle. The first thing I noticed was the fancy frame—very OTT for Freda, who wasn't one for show. I looked at it for a while, trying to think if there was a swimmer in her family. They're all gone now, of course, nobody left to ask.

I did ponder who this girl was, standing there looking so strong with her sturdy legs and arms on show, but I didn't think to take the photo out of its frame for a few days.

In that time, this young face from the past played on my mind, and seeing her in a swimming costume, I did wonder if I'd found the Gala Princess who belonged to the silver disc in the sideboard.

I must have caught Freda crouching at that bottom drawer in her bedroom three or four times in the days before she died. I'd go to help, because its sticking used to annoy her terribly, but she'd tell me to leave her be. She was barely able to walk but she'd say she could manage on her own. Freda had an independent side, but it could break your heart, her habit of going it alone, when all you wanted was to stroke her hair or hold her long, cold fingers and tell her you'd give your life to save hers.

## 7

'I don't know what you think you're playing at,'
Mr Gaze said from the hallway, looking up at Ida
bumping her case down each step of the stairs.

She had dressed quickly in a navy-blue dress
with matching jacket and a new black cloche hat
from Mrs Dixie's. On her feet she wore brown
shoes that fastened with dark blue crystal buttons.
Ida paused to look through the transom above the
front door and saw the white winter morning
beyond.

'I'm old enough to know my own mind, Father.
I've told you, I'm going to make a name for myself
in London.'

Before coming down, she had made her bed,
straightened the eiderdown, and glanced out of the
window at the coal shed she used to climb over the
wall to go and see Freda.

'Make a name for yourself?' her father said. 'I
can guess what kind of name that will be. Look at
you, made up like a chorus girl.'

Mr Gaze was wearing a new grey overcoat as he
reached to take his hat off one of the hooks that
ran like thin brass thumbs along the hall wall.

'Leaving your mother like this,' he went on,
when Ida got to the bottom. His hair seemed
longer than usual and the ends of his moustache
curved onto his lips. Her father's nose was redder
than ever.

They looked through the doorway at Mrs Gaze
in her chair in the sitting room with her knitting on
her lap. The house was dark bar the fire in the

grate spitting because the coal was wet. There's no point continuing to try and explain, Ida thought. They'll never understand.

'I'll let you know how I'm getting on,' she said, before kissing each of their cheeks. Her father's skin was smooth and scented. He wore a new cologne that smelled of the sea and which he kept in its blue box on the shelf in the bathroom.

'Poor Maud up in heaven and you carrying on like this,' her mother said. 'You're no daughter of mine, leaving me here with *him*.'

In the gloomy morning light, Mr Gaze looked intently at his daughter as his wife's needles started up. Every night after work he said he went to his club.

'Don't think we'll be here waiting with open arms when it all goes belly-up,' he called as Ida walked off down the path, the freezing air hardening her lipstick and the woman opposite watching from the front-room window.

The sky was low and dark with snow. At the station, a man waiting on the platform lifted Ida's suitcase onto the train.

'Oh thank you,' she said, as he blew into his hands.

'My pleasure,' the man replied, tipping his hat, and when she turned round as she climbed into the train, he was staring at her legs in silk stockings that had cost a small fortune.

She thought she would feel light and excited to be leaving, but pushing her case down the corridor, Ida was as tense as a clenched fist. She'd waited until the last minute to board in case Freda came to see her off. The two of them had parted the night before, Freda saying she was off home and wouldn't come to the seafront for one more look at the water. You won't change your mind, will you, Ida had pleaded. You could always change yours, was all Freda ever replied.

'Enjoy yourself!' Mr Baker called from the platform to his daughter, Gladys, who had a day off from her salon apprenticeship and was going into Cardiff with her mother for afternoon tea at the Angel Hotel.

'So long, Father, see you later,' replied Gladys, in a new emerald-green coat.

On the bridge over the track that cut through the town, Freda paused, looking down at the train waiting to depart.

The guard peered along the platform. Sitting, Ida felt an iron bolt of sadness go through her at leaving Freda.

Inside the station's arched hall, the man in the ticket office watched as a figure appeared at the open double doors lit either side by fancy flamed lanterns. There was always one who tried cutting it fine, but rules dictated that should the King of England pitch up now, he'd be told to sling his hook too.

Suddenly exhausted with all the silences and creeping about she'd been doing at home in the days leading up to her going, Ida concentrated on her reflection in the train window.

The guard was making his way along the carriages, flapping his hand to move people away from the track. When the train jolted, as though its elbows had slipped off the edge of a table, everyone gave a little whoop of surprise.

Ida heard a door slam, then another. People waved and blew kisses from gloved hands as the train gave off noisy clouds of steam. It lurched again. This was like watching the tide come closer to driftwood. You thought it would go with one wave but it was another three or four before it was eventually pulled into the water to be carried out to sea.

Ida was finally leaving town and couldn't understand why she was crying.

'Oi!' the guard shouted. 'Oi, you! What's your game?'

Ida watched him drop his flag. The stationmaster, Mr Higgins, who drank at Mr Gaze's club, emerged from his office with his hands to the lapels of his uniform. She rose to see what the fuss was about, half-expecting to see her father coming along the platform to drag her off the train. A metallic noise like bolts being pulled sounded close by, and then a door slammed. Mr Higgins shook his head.

'Good riddance!' Ida heard, in a high, desperate voice, sounding neither outside nor in. As the train moved off, she felt bewilderment and relief. At a rap on the compartment window, she looked, hoping it wasn't that man who had lifted her case onto the train giving her another of his funny looks.

Through the glass, Freda was staring back at her with a watery, frantic gaze.

'Oh Freddie!' Ida pulled the door back and saw a case on the floor of the corridor. 'Are you coming after all?'

Freda was breathing so hard the top half of her body moved in and out. Though it was cold, her face was red and sweaty. She couldn't speak. The train was slowly going faster.

'Come on in,' Ida whispered.

Freda lifted both of their cases onto the netting above the seat opposite before she sat and said, 'At least we've got the place to ourselves.'

'Oh Freddie. I can't believe it. I'm so glad you're here.'

'Are you?' Freda ran a hand over her eyes. 'Are you *really*?'

'Of course!' Ida leaned and kissed her forehead, which was hot and damp, and dropped down next to her.

'Your parents know though, don't they?' she asked.

Freda didn't trust her voice to come out sounding normal; instead she nodded. Then she said, 'My mother's over the moon with you.'

'Oh heck, not another one.'

'No, seriously. They think you've got "go" and that you're good for me.'

Freda glanced at Ida but she was fiddling with her gloves.

'They've put me down for nursing,' Freda went on. 'Mother's hoping it will be the making of me.'

She closed her eyes, remembering the scene with Aunt Sylvia saying she didn't know why she was getting involved but would pull some strings anyway. Her aunt had given her three months tops and claimed they were more likely to see Freda's picture captioned *Wanted* in connection with a bank robbery than witness her knuckling down to nursing.

'Oh Freddie, that's marvellous news.'

'I don't know that they think I'll stick it.'

How quick her father had been to put his hand in his pocket for her training.

'What about you?' Freda asked. 'Are you sure minus ten doesn't work at this news agency you're going to?'

Ida let out an exaggerated sigh. 'How many times have I told you?' she said. 'He works on a newspaper. The agency is something different, but it's still journalism.'

'Just so long as that's the case.'

'Think of the fun we'll have with nobody telling us what to do,' Ida replied.

Freda stood to pull down the blinds on the compartment door.

'I just hope London isn't teeming with people,' she said.

'Don't be daft, Freddie. That's what the Big Smoke is all about. People.'

As the train built up speed, they passed fields white with the faintest sprinkling of January snow.

'Just imagine,' Freda said. 'Our lake will ice over for skating.'

Ida dropped her head onto Freda's shoulder and Freda tipped her head against hers so the two of them were propped together as though to stop each other falling. It was warmer that way too.

'Oh Freddie, that's old news. Soon it will be streets of grand houses and shops full of all sorts to buy. Look out, London. Here we come!'

Every so often the view from the window was a flash of stone as they went under a bridge.

Whether it was the emotion of being back together or the anticipation of what lay ahead, they fell asleep quickly, with Ida's hat on the floor, their hair tangled and their hands clasped.

The chocolate and cream carriages rumbled on, cutting between curving hills until gradually a plume of smoke appeared here and a tall building there, and finally there was no more green or white, only grey and black with spires stretching to the sky.

When Freda opened her eyes, she nudged Ida. 'Look,' she said, as the train pulled under a vast canopy ribbed with steel like the skeleton of an upside-down boat. 'It's your Big Smoke!'

\*     \*     \*

Standards were definitely slipping, Matron thought, eyeing the new intake lined up in the hospital corridor. You might expect the odd lapse in selection, but there were at least a couple here who in her opinion—and she'd been doing it for long enough to know—wouldn't last the course.

The tallest one, who stuck out from the others like an organ knob at full blast, she'd already pinned as a piece of work, but Matron would sort her out. Matron had grown up on a farm in Somerset and aged nine had her small hands down a cow's bottom to help pull out calves the right way up. A girl planning on playing the fool in her hospital was always a walk in the park.

'I expect,' Matron started up again, 'to see your uniforms immaculate. No caps skew-whiff, no shoelaces untied . . .'

'I thought we were here to tend the sick, not for a fashion parade,' Freda whispered to the girl next to her. Edna her name was, from Yorkshire. She had a mad, purple look about the eyes and a black bob with a fringe cut into it.

Matron's voice rang out. Her hearing wasn't as good as it had been, but she'd seen that tall one's

118

lips going.

'Nurse Voyle,' she said, 'though I hesitate to jump to conclusions as you have yet to prove your ability to become a valued member of the medical community, I would remind you that it is the doctors and consultants who are here to hold forth—and not the likes of you.'

'Yes, Matron,' Freda replied, in a heavy Scottish accent though Matron could have sworn the girl was from Wales. It was surprising what got through the net sometimes, but you couldn't say anything if the family connection was a bigwig.

When the girl next to Freda sniggered, Matron, proceeding back down the row of trainee nurses, turned on her heels.

'Was that an expression of mirth, Nurse Simms?' she said, her swinging elbows giving off a waft of carbolic soap.

'No, Matron,' Edna replied. 'I have a slight tickle in my throat, Matron, that's all.'

'Have you now?' she said, eyeing the girl. 'Which brings me to another point. I am glad you mention ailments, for I will not tolerate ill health on my wards.'

Freda blinked in what might have been an amused fashion or it could have been something in her eye.

'And for that reason,' Matron went on, 'I reiterate that there are to be no late nights. This is not school. This is a hospital. There is to be no carousing.'

Freda's mind wandered onto what Ida would be doing at the news agency. Frank 'minus ten' Shankly had got her a job typing up shift rotas and making pots of tea when Ida had thought she was

119

going as a reporter. Is that all he thought her fit for? Freda hadn't said anything—yet—but she hoped Ida would find something as a journalist soon enough. It was what she wanted very much—to write about fashion, actresses in Hollywood, and all that hoopla.

'You are all,' Matron was saying, 'to be in your rooms by ten o'clock each and every night. Guests beyond that time will not be tolerated. I repeat, there are to be no high jinks.'

At the sound of a loud snigger which turned into a cough, Matron looked at Freda but she was standing to attention, thinking about getting over to Ida's little attic flat which had its own bathroom, and a hob with a green kettle that whistled as loud as the trains pulling into the nearby station. Freda's room was in the nursing school, a series of buildings around a small quadrangle which had four benches looking onto a dried-up piece of lawn.

'Do you hear me, Nurse Voyle?' Matron was saying.

'Sorry, Matron,' Freda said, shaking her head frantically. 'I think I may have my ears blocked with this cold.'

'My, my,' Matron replied. 'What a sickly lot you are, and here expecting to be fit to make others better too.'

As they were filing off, muted shoe shuffling the only sound, Matron put a hand on Freda's shoulder. The woman had a round red face and a hint of grey hair from beneath her headdress.

'There's always a joker in the pack,' she said, 'and I've got my eye on you.'

'Yes, Matron,' Freda replied, before giving her a

120

hand salute, clicking her heels, and walking away with her back unnaturally straight. In the pocket of her new nurse's cape she had Ida's favourite mint toffees. They could lie in bed, up in that flat with the door closed and nobody to harass them, and they could do what they damn well pleased.

*     *     *

'I know this has been billed as a West End production, but cocktails aren't my cup of tea,' Freda said, raising her fourth White Lady, knowing her tongue had loosened and there was nothing she could do about it.

This wasn't Freda's kind of place—the grand hotel lounge or losing control to alcohol that came with tiny cherries speared on paper umbrellas—but Ida liked things like this, the waiters in black-and-white bringing drinks to your table on silver trays, and men and women in fancy outfits hawing away.

The cocktails were pricy and Freda felt shame at thinking of her father working his fingers to the bone to bankroll her getting blotto. She had been reared on the maxim: *Annual income twenty pounds, annual expenditure nineteen pounds nineteen and six, result happiness. Annual income twenty pounds, annual expenditure twenty pounds ought and six, result misery.* For ages, Ida had thought it was Freda's father who'd made it up until Freda told her it was Charles Dickens and showed her the passage in *David Copperfield*.

For the past ten minutes or so, they'd been talking gibberish to fill the silence as they stared around them. Then a man at the white grand piano struck up a tune and a woman in a black lace dress started moving her palms around like a Flapper.

'This is probably the absolute most opposite you could get to the Bathing House, isn't it?' Ida murmured, raising her glass. 'Remember how you'd sit there and time me going round the lake, Freddie? What a friend you were.'

'Were?' They should probably stop drinking now, Freda thought, while they could still walk, but she heard herself saying, 'I used to love it, us lying there side by side. I'd go swimming in that lake, you know, when nobody was about, to see the golf balls.'

'You and your golf balls,' Ida replied.

She leaned to put her empty glass down heavily on the apricot-mirrored table and was quiet then, as though brooding about something, just like her mother who could sit in her chair for ages saying nothing.

'All that going round in circles,' she said eventually.

'You weren't going round in circles. You were training to become the Wonder Girl.'

'How important it seemed, to cross that Channel and get to another country. And now look at me, with a job I loathe and . . . and . . .'

'Have you seen that reporter lately?' Freda asked.

'As if. Every time I've been to his offices he's always busy, or out. I've been so often the man on reception knows my name without me saying. I won't go again. It's embarrassing. I'm quite sure he's trying to avoid me.'

'Sorry I asked.' From what Freda remembered of Frank Shankly, he was depressingly cocksure

122

and Ida was having a lucky escape. She didn't want to hear about him anyway.

'Shall we have another one?' Ida asked.

When the bill arrived, she didn't seem appropriately bothered that the cocktails cost half Freda's weekly allowance and the rest of Ida's wage too, but it sobered Freda up.

'Come on,' she said, stubbing out her cigarette. 'Let's pay up and get going.'

'We could always make a run for it,' Ida said, and she giggled.

Freda considered it—they could leg it down the hall, even in those shoes of Ida's, before anyone got wind of their game—but she thought of Matron, and what she'd have to say if one of her trainees was caught scattering from a hotel.

'As if,' Freda said.

The walk home through the cold night air was silent, aside from the occasional taxi coming through the smog with headlamps like glimmering marbles.

At the door of her flat, Ida said, 'I was just thinking . . . you asking about that reporter and, well, it makes you think, doesn't it—about how things might change. How we might meet other people now we're here.'

'That's a threat, is it?' Freda asked, but Ida didn't laugh, and just shook her head sadly.

'I can't bear to think of it,' she said. 'I'll always want to know you, Freddie, but . . .'

'Come on,' Freda replied, though she felt uneasy. 'We're both as drunk as your father coming back from one of his clubs.'

'He hasn't got back either,' Ida said as they lurched up the stairs. She'd sent letters to her

123

parents, and job requests with cuttings to every newspaper in London, and not had one reply except for a black-and-white postcard from her mother showing St Joseph's Church with the message *May God help you* written in capitals on the back.

Up in the room, Freda took off Mrs Gaze going berserk about them staying out so late, but Ida's laugh was short.

In bed, she turned away from their usual night-time gossip saying she was tired.

'I don't know I can stick that agency for much longer,' she said. 'And the pay is rotten.' So much for the Wonder Girl, that's what she'd started saying.

'Nor me with this nursing lark,' Freda replied. 'It's like bloody housecraft lessons, with Matron on all the time about this and that.'

But Ida was making little heavy breathing noises that Freda felt sure she was putting on so she lay on her back listening to how quiet the city became once everyone had gone to their bed. She could smell Ida's new scent, like soft pink roses.

8

How had it come to this? After endlessly rushing about trying to see editors, and returning to her attic day after day, exhausted from filing and general drudgery at that agency, and nothing ever coming of anything, now here Ida was standing with Frank outside his flat and the taxi about to draw away.

Even Leonard, the freelance journalist in the flat downstairs, had said he'd put a word in for her, but that seemed to have fizzled out. No wonder Freda found her company depressing and was spending more time in her hospital room. Ida felt shamefully grateful for Frank's presence, but she was on her toes too.

Coming back with him wasn't the plan when she'd pushed through the crowds at the hacks' club and tapped him on the shoulder. She'd felt such a fool wondering if he'd remember her name after all this time, and then standing there waiting to plead for a job, eking out the drink he'd bought her in a round for his colleagues.

'Would you please help me find something on a newspaper?' she'd asked, though Ida wasn't sure he'd heard. The club was noisy and smoky, and people had kept coming up and slapping Frank on the back. He had a new role at the paper and everyone seemed to want to know him.

Frank turned to Ida. They were on a street like any other she saw on Sundays, row after row of them, if she walked the city when Freda was working. When she'd finally shouted in Frank's ear that she needed to speak to him urgently, he'd said come on then, it'll be quiet back at my flat.

'Not so urgent any more, is it?' Frank said, seeming amused. 'Are you coming up or not?' He started counting down from ten, looking at the cab revving puffs of exhaust into the night air as the driver prepared to leave. 'Seven, six, five . . .'

As the taxi pulled off Ida stood, wary but determined to say her piece. She thought of Leonard and his articles on adventurers for that magazine which never got back to her, and laughed. All she wanted was a chance to prove herself. This was hardly Dr Livingstone territory.

'What's the joke?' Frank asked. He looked just as fair and handsome, but there was a new air about him too, the way he'd hailed the cab, as though people should know who he was.

'Nothing,' she replied. 'I was just thinking of that time you covered my swim and invited me back to your hotel room.'

'You've got a good memory. And a taste for the cold. Are you coming up, or will you freeze out here on your own?'

Summer seemed to have come and gone. She'd enjoyed a few months of getting excited about clothes she couldn't afford and going to the park with Freda—where there were always masses of people which Freda didn't like so they'd go back to Ida's room—and now it was winter again. Nothing changed. Leonard was still downstairs banging away on his typewriter and Ida wore her old cloche hat to bed in the cold.

It was only Freda making her laugh that made things bearable, though she was coming round less now nursing was taking so much of her time. More and more, Freda stayed on when her shift had finished, to comfort a feverish child, say, crying after its parents were told it was best if they left. By contrast, Ida couldn't wait to leave the office. All heads would turn when she walked across the room on the dot of five carrying a bit of shopping she'd done at lunchtime.

She followed Frank up the path, in through the front door and up the greasy-looking stair carpet. In his room, the light came from a bare bulb in a lamp on the bedside table. Frank put his mackintosh over a hook on the back of the closed door and sat heavily on the bed. There wasn't much furniture. The room smelled brown and dusty, as though the open curtains would give off powdery puffs if you pulled them. She'd thought he would live somewhere a bit better than this.

Standing against the wall, Ida said, 'So you've been promoted, have you?'

Frank pulled off his tie so quickly it sounded like a whip in the air.

'Yes,' he said. 'Now are you coming over here to tell me what it is you want, or are you still as shy as you were coming out of that water? You certainly don't look it—you're quite the little London madam.'

Ida wasn't sure how that was meant so she said nothing. If she was going to make a fool of herself, she'd do it without whining about him not having kept in touch. Why didn't a dignified way to behave come effortlessly to her as it did to Freda? She seemed to be giving nursing her best shot, which made Ida proud as well as a little envious.

Frank patted the eiderdown. 'Come on,' he said. 'What's up? Tell Uncle Frank.'

'I'm fed up,' she replied, staying where she was. 'That agency—well, I'm grateful to you for helping me get started and everything, but it's reporting I want to do.'

'Oh, that's what all this is about, is it?' Frank sighed and laid himself out on the bed. There was a bang as he pushed each of his shoes off. Ida couldn't help but stare at his feet in black socks but then he tucked the pillow up behind his head and looked again at her. She blushed, thinking of being in a room with Frank, when for so long—in the

127

safety of her bed when Freda was on nights—she'd played out such a scenario.

'I was a reporter before, you know,' she said. 'And, well, you did say I should come to London and . . . I just want to be a reporter, that's all, and I wondered if there might be something at the paper. I'll do anything, make tea and things like that if it means I'm back in a newsroom.'

'Want, want, want,' Frank replied, eyeing the ceiling and sounding like Freda when Ida had mentioned a cross-cut summer dress with banjo sleeves in shocking-pink silk she'd seen for three times her weekly pay. 'You can't always get what you want, little mermaid.'

With Frank stretched out, she could look at him properly. Even in this light she noticed that the ends of his long white fingers were covered in newsprint. His body was long too, and slim—and from the side, the cut of his jaw was sharp and determined. Frank was going places, she could see that by the way people at the club had been with him. He would probably marry a beautiful blonde woman who'd attend his company functions in a navy satin dress and a two-line choker of pearls.

Frank said, 'May I speak frankly, Ida?'

She gave a spiky little laugh, sensing something unpleasant coming. There was laughter from another part of the house too and a door slammed. People made life look so easy, having jobs they liked and friends and family and plenty of money for buying gifts at Christmas. Ida felt suddenly apart from things, that she and Freda going about together was somehow out of a circle where everyone else behaved as they should. And then there was Leonard downstairs saying, 'Even if a

128

boyfriend isn't your thing,' in a funny voice that made Ida look twice at him. She and Freda being such friends made them different, she was starting to see that. Ida put her hands behind her back and leaned against the wall.

'Well, if anyone should speak frankly, it's you, Frank,' she said, surprised at her flirty tone.

He gave her a quick on-off smile.

'I don't think you're cut out for reporting. You need to be tough.'

'Tough? You mean I need to wear a mackintosh and not stop drinking? Is that what you mean?' That's how his colleagues had been at the club.

'Don't be insolent,' Frank replied, but he laughed and looked at her as though thinking afresh about her.

'Anyway,' Ida said, 'I am tough. I still have the discipline of an Olympic swimmer.'

'I'm serious. I don't see you interested in news. You're not cut out for it.'

'How do you know, if I've not been given the chance?'

'Do you know what the Kellogg-Briand Pact is?'

It was Ida's turn to laugh.

'I was thinking more of the women's pages,' she said. 'Writing about girls going places.'

'See? You're just not interested in what matters.' He beckoned to her. 'Come over here and tell me the name of the Foreign Secretary. You won't get on, not knowing that.'

Ida was silent as she went over. On the street, the lamp went out. She perched sideways on the bed looking at the black oblongs of window with curtains either side. Being closer to Frank made her body fizz a little, not unpleasantly, more like a

129

sense she had of something out there she very much wanted. Outside, a car engine revved.

Frank said, 'Or understanding the implications of . . . or the possibility of . . . another war.'

'Please don't talk about war.' Ida felt she might easily lie down beside him. War was one of those words, like mass unemployment, financial crisis and Depression, which made her feel instantly low and ill-informed. She liked hats and screen icons and hearing about yachts and nightclubs and glamorous goings-on.

'See what I mean?' Frank's voice was kinder. 'Give it a couple more years, Ida. Get some experience first.'

A couple of years? That snapped her out of it. She turned to look down at him and asked, 'How do I get experience if nobody will give me a job?'

Frank laughed again and put his hand lightly on her arm.

He said, 'Come here if you like and I'll tell you.'

Ida could feel the warmth and energy of his body and the way Frank's voice sounded solicitous but she stood, remembering Freda's dark hints about women who came to the hospital after trying to abort babies. There was no doubt in her head that leaving without what you wanted was better than leaving with something you didn't.

She saw Frank's expression of surprise and disappointment, like a child having a toy suddenly snatched away, and felt an unexpected moment of power, and a touch of sympathy even, for him not getting what he'd hoped for either.

'Thanks for the advice, Frank,' she said. 'And now I'd better get going.'

He stood too. 'Ida, sweetheart. Don't rush off,

let me hail you a cab.'

'No. No, thank you. I'll be fine on my own, honestly. I have to get on.'

But when he kissed her on the lips, she stayed where she was, for several seconds and more, until he'd taken his hands away from her arms.

'You smell as sweet as roses,' he said as she headed for the door. Frank had smelled salty and industrious.

'Are you sure you're all right on your own?' he asked.

'Yes,' Ida replied, 'thank you very much. You've no need to worry. I'll be all right on my own.'

She walked off up the street feeling guilty and confused and sad. With that kiss had come a hungry flutter at the top of her legs. Ida felt a stab of regret at leaving Frank and then started convincing herself she had just escaped something terrible, like being squashed or split open or all the other things she'd imagined might happen. Then she made herself feel better again by thinking how glad Freda would be that she had left. If only Ida could talk over things like this with Freda, without feeling disloyal and cruel, or that she might somehow be rubbing salt into wounds.


9


'Is she coming or not?' Freda asked Edna, who stood at the door of one of the hospital's examination rooms.

'I can hear someone,' Edna replied. 'Hold on in there. She's getting on my wick. We'll have her

131

now.'

As the sound of footsteps grew louder, Edna stepped behind the door and Freda lay back flat on the high narrow bed, pulling a sheet on top of her.

So when Nurse Mullins, who was a bit of a goody-two-shoes and thick to boot—though her worst crime was having told on Edna for not turning the bed casters inwards—rounded the corner with a copy of *Picturegoer* magazine, it was a hell of a shock when a white figure rose wailing from the bed in the rarely used room where she went for her break.

Vera Mullins let out a shriek as piercing as one of the female patients in maternity and knocked a metal tray of instruments off a table as she fled the room.

Things moved quickly then. Further down the dimly lit corridor, Matron came from her office to find Nurse Mullins running towards her with a hand over her mouth.

'What in the name of God is going on?' she asked, and Mullins pointed back down the corridor.

'That's us for it,' Freda said, stepping back quickly as Matron looked in their direction. It was the same sinking feeling she'd had back at the County School when she and Ida had been called before the Head for sticking a row of rose thorns on their noses for housecraft lesson. Actually, this was far worse, because Freda had started to enjoy nursing. Helping people who couldn't help themselves was rewarding. It was the pushy people, the narrow-eyed, pinch-mouthed ones in life, the ones always looking and pointing and having something to say about you that Freda didn't mind

132

not helping.

Five minutes later, Freda was back on the ward, about to place a thermometer in the mouth of a patient, when Nurse Mullins appeared at her side and said in a loud voice, 'Matron wants to see you.'

'Very well,' said Freda, handing her the thermometer. The patient watched them.

'You up before the beak then?' he asked Freda.

'It certainly looks that way,' she replied. Freda hadn't realised how much she would enjoy chatting to the patients, what she might have written off before as 'waste talk'. This old man had taken to her, telling her about his daughter working in a button factory and how fathers always worried for their daughters. Freda was starting to understand that people, like parents for example, looked at things differently, and not always because they wanted to make trouble.

'Ah, Nurse Voyle.' Matron looked up from her empty desk. Someone had discovered that her first name was Enid, which for some reason had made them all laugh. 'Something has come to my attention.'

'Yes, Matron,' Freda said, regretting trying to put on a bit of a performance for Edna. She'd been showing off really because she liked Edna's violet eyes and the way the ends of her bob caught each side of her mouth, but only off duty. On shift, Edna's hair was drawn off her face but Freda liked that too because it showed her broad, round forehead which was smooth and tanned.

Matron said, 'I already have your number and know you to be a girl—not dissimilar to myself, it has to be said—who does not like being told what to do.'

Freda scrutinised Matron. Her voice sounded softer, not at all geared up for a final sort of telling-off.

'So,' she said, 'it is with a heavy heart—for it is not my way to ask any nurse, qualified or not, anything, for I am in a position to tell, not ask, do you understand?'

Freda nodded. She was as serious as anything, and felt herself starting to split at the idea she might be told to leave for a stupid prank. What a clown she was.

'I'm very sorry,' she interrupted. 'It was a stupid thing to do. Please don't make me leave. It won't happen again.'

Matron raised her hand as though she was preparing to speak on oath.

'I have no idea what you are speaking about, but do not interrupt while I am doing the talking.'

Freda looked down at her shoes, noticing a lace undone.

'I'll keep this short and sweet,' Matron said, 'which is possibly the polar opposite of you. But Nurse Voyle, take it as a compliment that I am bothered enough to call you in and ask why it is you have this urge to be silly.'

Freda couldn't look up. Matron, for all her appearing suddenly round corners and watching you for you didn't know how long when you glanced up from something you were doing, was right.

'This urge you have to be silly,' Matron said. 'Don't let it spoil your life.'

\*      \*      \*

Later, after the shift was finished, there was a knock at Freda's door. She knew it couldn't be Ida who'd said she was attending a drinks get-together after work, which sounded suspicious as she'd never shown any interest in spending time with her agency colleagues. She had been quite excited, calling it an opportunity to make contacts, which had sent a shiver of wariness and faint despair through Freda. Ida rarely came to her room in the nurses' quarters anyway. She said all the different rooms off one narrow hallway made the place feel like cells in a prison.

'Who is it and what do yer want?' Freda called to the door, in a Yorkshire accent. She'd been thinking about what Matron had said and how difficult it was to be sensible all the time. Nursing was hard work, but off shift, once she'd shed her uniform and the smells of other people's bodily fluids, Freda was ready to start up again. Mrs Voyle used to call it 'looking for it' as though Freda was forever walking about rubbing her hands saying, 'Let's see where we can cause a bit of trouble now.' She supposed that was what Matron referred to as 'this urge to be silly'.

Nobody came through the door but she could hear giggling.

'Come on, let's be 'avin' you,' she said. Freda was bored—she intended to learn the name of every bone in the body, and all the veins and arteries that ran this way and that—but she'd welcome a diversion.

'Are you taking me off?' asked Edna, falling into the room laughing. 'How did you know it was me?' Freda thought what a difference there was to girls in their uniforms and then in their civvies. Edna

135

wore a pale pink sweater and black trousers tucked into brown calf-length boots trimmed with cream fur. She looked like a little aviator.

'Ee, us Yorkshire girls,' said Freda smiling. Underneath she was thinking Matron had a point but she still said, 'People think we don't know nowt about owt, but we do.'

'You're awful, you are,' Edna replied, coming to sit on the bed. Freda noticed her eyes were glittering with enjoyment. She liked making people laugh, and if people were happy they tended to leave her alone with their judgements.

Edna said, 'Do Matron on about the casters again.'

Freda shook her head. 'I'm not a performing monkey,' she replied. Then seeing Edna's disappointed face, she got off the bed, thrust her stomach forward like Matron, put her hands on her hips, and said, 'All casterrrs are to be turr-ned inwards to prevent anyone tray-pin and go-in overrr.'

But as she flung herself back down she thought, That's the last time I'm doing that, not least because I don't want to make fun of Matron any more.

After a few seconds, Edna's laugh turned to a smile and she stroked the green silk eiderdown brought from home, all the while not taking her eyes from Freda's.

'I'm glad we've palled up,' she said. They had spent quite a few evenings together, testing each other on blood types and disease symptoms, and eating together in the canteen. Sometimes they did the two things at once. Neither was squeamish. What Freda liked about Edna was her straight-

136

down-the-line attitude, though she had a caring side too. After one week Freda had spent complaining about the food they were given on nights—in tubes it came, like torpedoes of the devil's slops—Edna stayed up late to bring her a round of cheese sandwiches.

'Who says we've palled up?' Freda asked. If she liked someone, she tried to antagonise them as much as if she didn't, just to see the measure of them in battle, but also too it was partly the hope they would walk away and leave her alone without the need to wonder at how she should be with them.

For a moment, Edna looked upset and then she rallied.

'You'd be lucky to have me as a friend, Nurse Voyle,' she said, pushing at Freda's side so she could lie beside her on the bed. 'You being the joker in the pack.'

Edna had never forgotten Matron saying that to Freda on their first day of training. She waited for Freda to laugh, but Freda was thinking about how she'd thought she knew it all, like having her own room here seeming a relief at first—without her brother running in accusing her of taking his jacket, or her sister saying the dog needed walking—and now, how Edna throwing herself down beside her made her miss so much.

From outside the door came the chatter of nurses off to the pictures. Freda had shaken her head when invited and then wondered if she was getting a reputation as an oddball when they'd looked at each other as if to say, 'What did I tell you?'

The others in Freda's year displayed photos of

family or pets but Freda's walls were bare. All she had in the room besides her bed and uniform, a case of clothes and a towel and wash bag hanging on the back of the door, was a pile of medical books, borrowed from the library after her talk with Matron.

'Do you still miss home?' Edna asked. They were both lying flat, looking up at the ceiling.

'I don't get a chance,' Freda said. 'My mother won't stop sending me Welsh cakes.'

Edna hitched herself up on her elbow to look at her. It was dark outside but the radiator was on. Freda hoped she hadn't felt the fancy photo-frame under her pillow. Though she kept Ida's picture there, they didn't see each other anywhere near as much as they used to.

'Go on, tell me what it is you miss,' Edna said.

Freda turned to her. On her last trip home, her brother and sister had hung off her in the hallway as she was leaving, and her father had given a little speech about how they were all very proud she still hadn't been sent packing from London. Mrs Voyle enclosed brief notes with the parcels that arrived at the porter's lodge in brown paper tied with the thick plaited string her father sold in the saddlery. The last message read *Sylvia at loose end with you making a go of it.*

'No,' Freda said, 'there's nothing I miss so much any more.'

Edna cocked her head to one side before she thumped herself back down on the bed, closer again to Freda. Edna's parents had not long moved to India. Her father worked in government intelligence and her mother sent letters about watching elephants wash in the river.

138

'I don't know that you're telling the truth,' Edna said, 'but I know one thing. I miss things less since I became friends with you. Are we friends, Nurse Voyle?'

'Depends what you call friends,' Freda replied, leaving her eyes shut longer and longer each time she blinked. 'Let's see how we go.'

If she didn't think about Ida and all the lovely things they had done, it was easier to start again from the black space that came up in her head when she closed her eyes.

Freda felt a moment of confusion, that suddenly she didn't mind swapping Ida for another girl, but nursing—all these people in and out, and here and there in wheelchairs and trolleys and, best of all, walking free themselves from the ward when they were better—was making Freda see there was more to life than what had gone before.

There was something to this nursing lark. Making a good fist of it was becoming less about disappointing Aunt Sylvia, though for a while that had been a huge incentive. You could do things to help people and they weren't always on at you.

'Can I have a go?' Edna said, looking across at Freda blowing smoke into the warm silence, and when she handed her the cigarette Freda didn't look away when Edna put it slowly between her lips.

\*    \*    \*

On the one hand you had Matron going on about being clean and pristine, and on the other you were expected to tend wounds that leaked all sorts of things. Patients' coughs could go right through

139

you, and sometimes they came out with terrible stories about being estranged from their families so nobody came to visit, and then you'd sit with them in the middle of the night or hold their hand, even though the morphine probably stopped them knowing you were there.

So when Ida, seeing blood dripping from a carcass on the butcher's stall at the Saturday market, felt faint and needed to be supported to the pavement edge to sit down, Freda said, without thinking, 'You really ought to toughen up a bit, you know, not be so soft about things.'

Ida had been down all morning. She'd said nothing had come of the works do, though she'd met an interesting man who owned an advertising agency and had talked about giving her a job. That last bit she'd said in a dull sort of voice. Though Ida still talked of herself and Freda being girls flying high in Amelia Earhart's footsteps, she'd stopped mentioning wanting to report on lady rifle shooters and rhinestone buckle shoes.

'I don't mean to be feeble, but doesn't it make you sad, Freddie,' Ida asked, 'thinking about animals that are the same shape as your dog being killed and hung like that?' Ida didn't eat meat any more. All she had in the flat were tinned pears and bread rolls for the pigeons who congregated outside and tapped the little arched window for service.

She went on, 'And then seeing all these sad things like that Italian man selling salami and cheese out of a suitcase . . . doesn't he remind you of that poor tramp from back home who slept in his five bowler hats in the limekilns?'

Freda was bemused for a moment, listening to
140

Ida rattle on. Freda's one big fear was that Ida Gaze would turn into her mother, saying things out of the blue or looking for a row where there wasn't one. The other was that Ida might take up with a man who didn't care about making her pregnant, but she'd never tell her that.

Freda said, 'That man in the bowler hats had a round, jolly face like Father Christmas. The salami man has a thin, dark face like a ferret.'

'You know what I mean,' Ida said, looking up at her, but Freda didn't want to understand. All this depressing talk unsettled her and she saw enough at work to make her feel dismal. Ida was staying in bed more, saying she was cold all the time and going on about missing the sea, and the horses in the field, and licking butter off each other's fingers after getting kippers from the fish shop on the front.

Ida said, 'I sent Aunt Bess a postcard of the Tower of London and she sent back one of the sea.'

Freda knelt and put her arm around Ida's shoulders. She felt bonier than ever, like the small bird's skeleton the two of them had once found at the bottom of the cliffs.

Freda said, 'I didn't think you'd be so homesick, on all the time about that place.'

'Don't you miss anything, Freddie, like those twisty little secret paths to the beach and lying in the caves listening to the waves, and that man throwing bread for the jackdaws on the cliff tops?'

Freda shrugged. 'Not really. I suppose the main thing I miss is my dog's snores and his paws smelling of shortcake.'

She hoped Ida would laugh, but she dropped

141

her head. The mention of Cruncher had probably made her think of that damn dripping carcass again.

'And the sea,' Ida went on. 'Don't you miss the sun on the water stretching forever and the moon in the waves at night?'

Freda looked uncomfortable. She didn't want to say, 'I told you so.'

'You've always got the Thames,' she said.

Ida sighed. 'I'm sorry to be so gloomy. It's not so much I'm missing home or that place,' she said. 'It . . . it's just that I never thought it would be this difficult. I suppose I'd like a job I really want—that's all.'

Freda was trying not to lose patience. 'Is there anything I can do to help?' she asked.

Ida shook her head in a way that suggested a new round of self-pity was coming and said in a tight little voice, 'It's all right for you, Freddie, you've got nursing.'

Freda had received top marks in a gynaecology test.

'I wouldn't go that far,' she replied, thinking of yesterday when the porters came in to Edna's ward to carry away the body of a young boy who hadn't survived a fall from a roof he'd been tiling. His cheeks were so soft and new, too young to die. It made you question who lived and why, and then you realised you ought to do some good with your life and not waste it.

Seeing Ida's pale, plaintive face as people bustled around them on a darkening February afternoon, Freda suddenly let the thoughts that shamefully dogged her rise to the surface.

'It's not Frank or anyone, is it?' she asked. 'Has

142

anything happened? Why are you feeling faint at the sight of something you saw every day of the week in the window of the butcher's back home?'

'I don't know,' Ida said, and Freda felt grateful she hadn't seen what she was getting at. It was a terrible, shocking thing to suggest, Freda knew that, but there was something childlike and unknowing about Ida for all her gobby bluster.

The longer they spent apart, the less sure Freda felt about what was going on, and not just whether Frank Shankly was on the scene. Ida was buying clothes she couldn't afford and leaving them on the floor. Then there was that so-called journalist in the flat downstairs who had a gramophone player, which meant Ida was always in his room 'listening to jazz'.

She felt how light Ida had become as she hauled her carefully up from the pavement.

'Fancy some sweets?' she asked, but Ida shook her head saying, 'I'm trying to lose a bit of my belly,' and Freda had to stop herself saying, 'What belly? Where? Let me see!' in a frantic tone.

It looked like rain. They walked in silence until the streets became less crowded and they were on a rackety old road of abandoned buildings. Freda let out a gasp.

'Just look,' she said, pointing at a filthy downstairs window. Through a gap the bird might almost have rubbed clean itself, they saw a robin looking back at them, standing boldly with his red breast but trapped all the same.

'Is there a brick we can use to break the window?' Ida said, suddenly alive and looking about.

Freda slipped out of her jacket, pulled her

sweater over her fist, and said, 'Fly back, little fellow,' before punching the pane, every last bit so there were no sharp edges, as people passed by looking.

It took a while—with the two of them standing holding their bag of rolls, cheese and two bottles of ginger ale—for the bird to fly free and when it did, they looked at each other for ages.

'Wasn't that a lovely thing to happen, Freddie, us saving a life like that?' Ida asked. 'Do you think it might be a sign things will change?'

'Wait,' Freda replied, smiling to herself as she picked up a piece of broken glass shaped remarkably like a heart.

'Here,' she said, handing it to Ida, 'but I don't expect you'll want to keep hold of something so sharp.'

Ida took it carefully and put it in the pocket of her new coat with black velvet buttons.

'Oh, but I do,' she said, and they walked off arm in arm.

Into Freda's mind came the day she'd been waiting for Ida at the lake and the kingfisher had gone from a vivid shape on the bulrush to nothing in the blink of an eye. As they went along the pavement, Freda wondered what would become of the two of them, and what each of them was waiting for, clinging to their reeds at the edge of the water. Perhaps they weren't such Wonder Girls, after all.

# CECILY 2009

When I did take that picture downstairs and lever the back off the frame with a pair of nail scissors, I felt quite terrible, the most awful traitor, as though I was opening a letter marked *Addressee Only*. But hark at me—with my past—standing on ceremony.

I think I knew I'd find something, that I was on to something, or maybe it was just I wanted there to be something, anything to stop me thinking about living and dying and things held precious being snatched away.

Old photos usually have something written on them, don't they, a clue perhaps to the girl in the bathing costume. Back then, it was such a novelty to be caught by the click of a shutter—pap, and the second you've caught is gone!—and there were no computers to make handwriting such a rare event. People were quicker to take pen to paper with no plastic keyboards to do elegant italics. It was a way of stamping our mark, something unique to us, like our own inky fingerprint. I used to get such pleasure from writing. I'd go on and on, page after page, my hand and the black lines going up and down like the pattern on a hospital monitor, and I suppose, funnily enough, it was like a heartbeat keeping me going, saying everything in those letters, and then—best of all—getting a reply.

The writing on the back of the photo was a careful curly script. *Ida Gaze Attempts to Swim the Channel,* 1928. That's interesting, I thought, a young girl wanting to swim the Channel, and the year occupied me too. There can't have been many girls with the wherewithal to do that back then, so long ago—not long after I was born in fact. There was a photographer's stamp from this town which I had my magnifying glass out for—he went a long time ago, I checked. And when I turned back to the picture, I saw the message on the bottom right corner. *To my best friend Freda, Yours forever, Ida.*

Innocent enough a thing to be hidden beneath the fancy curve of a chrome art deco frame, that's what I told myself. Girls used to talk like that back then—it was all do or die in those years—but it bothered me that I'd never seen the photo.

Freda could play her cards close to her chest, I knew that. I felt so uncomfortable having the savings she'd kept quiet. I don't know what she had planned for that money, but that's just one example of how she carried on. She had this way with her, you see. If you did something she didn't like, she'd say, 'I'm not telling you again,' and you didn't do it again. Or if you asked something she didn't want to answer, she didn't have to tell you not to ask again.

The next day, I went into the town's library. They've got copies of all the old local papers from back then. Everything that happened here is bound in red volumes and locked in a room in the corner, though there's no need for that kind of security in this town. Everyone knows everybody's business.

The first dash to the library, I remember thinking I'd save my hips by avoiding the big steps up to the doors so I took the disabled slope—an elaborate concrete spiral; it seemed to take hours, the ring Freda gave me clicking on the metal handrail as I staggered round and round to the top. What's the idea? A hamster wheel to keep the arthritic old-aged occupied?

Up I went in the lift—I like that, a lift in this little town's library—and found it difficult to be civil while I waited at the table upstairs for someone to fetch over the 1928 editions of the *Times* (not the big paper in London, the local paper here). I tried to keep a grip on myself, looking around at the usual old buggers sitting reading the day's newspapers, too tight to buy their own, but I couldn't help wondering if Freda might be in a picture, a face in a crowd, come to see Ida Gaze take to the water. That would be strange, as remarkable as seeing one of yours truly as a child, not least because I never had my picture taken.

Then I wondered if I'd recognise Freda. I hadn't known her when she was a young girl, but she was one of those that stayed much the same through life. It's to do with bones, I think, and keeping a good head of hair, though that applies mainly to men. Most people, I find, are unrecognisable when they are sixty from when they were twenty—though they, of course, can't see the difference and tell you they still feel sixteen.

'The first six months of the 1928 editions of the *Times*,' the librarian said, laying a vast volume on the table. I had to keep my hands between my knees to stop from snatching.

All those yellow, oaty-smelling pages to go through—and be careful not to rip—stories different, but not so different, from today. *Lady Baseballer to Wed*, *Dog Show Success*, adverts for three-piece suites, funeral services. The librarian brought me the second volume and left me to it. I was champing at the bit by then. If I could just find an article about the girl, it would give me

147

something to settle my mind on. I wanted at least to know if she succeeded in crossing that water.

I used my nous and thought, with her being in a costume, it would be summer, so I didn't waste time on the winter pages; and not that long in, I found two pages on Ida Gaze in the third week of August.

There she was, the same as the picture I found in Freda's drawer, standing on the beach. Ida Gaze was successful. She had swum the Bristol Channel, all that freezing water between Wales and England, and was the first ever to do it. I was taken aback by the girl's guts.

In one picture, a man had his hand on her chest. That must have been taken after the swim because Ida looked done for, sitting in a rowing boat pulled up on a beach. It was a compelling sight, all these people around her, some of them looking at Ida, some at the camera. No sign of Freda, just men in flat caps, cigarettes hanging from their mouths, hair brushed sweatily back from their faces as though it was them that had just swum the twenty-two and a half miles.

There was only the one woman in the crowd besides Ida, dark-haired and in a knitted top with a bow at the collar, looking at the girl, and I wondered if it might be her mother. She looked a bit of a sourpuss, but then wouldn't you, if someone had their hand on your daughter's front? I looked again and again at that photo, at this man with one hand holding a whisky bottle and the other right down Ida's costume. Checking her heart-rate, I don't doubt, but that wouldn't be allowed nowadays. Nowadays there'd be a bit more whatchamacallit. Nowadays he'd have had it off

148

Esther Rantzen.

I read through all there was and it turns out this girl worked as a reporter on the paper, the *Times*. She swam all that way from here to Weston when many men had failed. Fancy that at sixteen years of age, and being a reporter too. Ida must have been quite a girl at taking on the boys. I'd thought back then that newspapers, like most things, were run by men in macs. I liked her already, and when you're my age snap decisions are a bonus.

The Channel swim was called 'a meritorious triumph' and Ida was crowned the Wonder Girl. It was a proper occasion. All the town was there.

When I discovered Ida's name on some of the other old articles—well, that was it. I'd be back and forth to the library to read her stories while the old colonels around me clunked mints against their falsies. Old men and boiled sweets go together like babies and dummies, I'd think, but then I always keep a tissue up my sleeve, like a baby's comfort blanket. It's handy if your eyes run.

Once I'd started looking, I couldn't stop. I started to think I could spot what she had written without seeing her name. I fancied there was an air of naïve authority to some of the writing, as though it was done by a child becoming an adult, or one who had done so too soon in life. I read articles on everyday events written with such a contemporary archness and confident tone that I'd be sure Ida Gaze was the author. There was another little story that took my fancy about the American, Amelia Earhart, who landed on the Welsh coast, not far from here, and became the first woman to cross the Atlantic in a plane. June 1928 it was, not long before Ida did her own crossing.

'Fancy that,' I told the assistant librarian, a nice girl with black hair who collected ammonites, rode a pistachio-green moped and didn't mind striking up a conversation with us oldies. 'That American girl landing in Wales.'

'You ought to get yourself a computer,' she said. 'You'd be in your element on Google.'

'What's that then?' I asked, and when she told me, my first thought was I could use it to track down Ida Gaze.

There was a special offer on computers through the old age so I pulled out enough of Freda's savings to get it rigged up in the house plus three discount coaching sessions on how to start a Word document, write an email and suchlike. This Google business was a revelation. You typed in anything you wanted to find more about, pressed a button, and up came pages and pages relating to what you'd asked for—all sorts of information at your fingertips. It made my old copies of *Encyclopaedia Britannica* either side of the fireplace as dated as the Dead Sea Scrolls.

I'd be there for hours scanning through the references for female champion swimmers of the 1920s and 1930s in search of Ida Gaze. It's a wonder I didn't tan, the time I spent in front of that burning gas-blue glow of my DabsValue widescreen.

I hadn't realised you got pictures, and it was such a treat. I could sit in my middle room here in this little seaside town, and see a woman as old as a statue—probably not much older than me—handing out trophies at a school sports day up North.

'Don't follow the crowd,' she'd be telling

schoolgirls in Speedos. 'Follow your own star, and when you have achieved your goal you will have that with you for the rest of your life.'

I started thinking, Hark at these girls, who bared themselves for a challenge at a time when the talent and stamina and ambition of most women were kept shrouded in frocks that covered the calf. I hadn't known that when I was practically in my nappies, girls were in bathing suits winning medals. It made me feel so humble thinking of the determination and bravery, the strength and go-it-alone guts of these women. Most of them were probably six feet under, but they cheered me up no end.

Valerie Davies, who won two bronzes at the 1932 Olympics, three medals at the 1930 British Empire Games, and trained in the boating lake at a Cardiff park. Sunny Lowry, the first British woman to swim the English Channel in fifteen hours and forty-one minutes on an eight-egg omelette, covered in lanolin and chilli paste and condemned as a harlot because she bared her knees.

Perhaps it was to stop anything else bothering me that I settled on one thing, and it was this: I couldn't find anything on the internet about Ida Gaze or her meritorious swim. Oh, it didn't half niggle that this girl who'd been hidden from me for so long wasn't on show for anyone else either. She was sixteen when she swam that Channel. It has vicious currents and it's taken so many lives, and if a girl got through that, well . . . that's what I let myself think: might Ida Gaze still be alive?

I started to buy the local paper then, had an interest in what was going on, saw that this little

151

newspaper was a marker of our times and that a century from now someone might go in looking back like me—as long as the Government doesn't put the kibosh on libraries, that is.

One week, the front page was taken up with the death of a young man killed in a car accident. The road that took him is long and wide and stretches like a challenge to the town's youngsters wanting to go faster in life.

The tragedy was reported with the usual mix of fear, false concern and photo of a makeshift shrine of garage forecourt bouquets. I felt for the boy. He saw a long stretch, nobody in his way, and he thought, I'll open up. But the road is deceptive. It's got a sly little bridge squatting near the end of it, a nasty bump that sends speeding cars into the air and they don't always land butter side up.

Not that I was obsessed or anything, but it did make me think of Ida Gaze seeing her way clear and going full steam ahead. I wondered no end about this girl who swam all that way and where she ended up. There was one line in that write-up on her swim that didn't half stand out. Miss Ida Gaze was the town's Gala Princess 1928. I didn't have to be Miss Marple to suspect I was on to something.

*       *       *

I was standing in the front watching the bees gently bouncing up and down on the foxgloves in the sun, when a car drew up outside. Next thing, the dog was charging up the path as though he'd been released from a trap.

'Mungo!' Sarah called. 'Watch out, Ceci!'

152

There was nothing for it but to bend and hope he stopped. When he skidded up sharp I felt the precious sensation of warm, eager fur beneath my hands.

'You're a big handsome boy, aren't you,' I said to him. 'I might need one like you.'

I don't know if they thought I'd been telling them too much at the old age, because when I was saying this and that about Mungo and Sarah and her cakes and how I was hoping she'd get back with her husband, one woman fired up about damned dogs and how they should be kept outside in the yard on a chain. I was itching to give her what-for, not least because I'd got to like having a dog about the place again, but I laughed instead because she was one of those who take pleasure in being as miserable as sin.

'Sorry, Ceci,' Sarah said, appearing at the gate. 'I've told him about running at people but he doesn't listen. You look nice.'

I was wearing a navy quilted waistcoat I'd bought in town after my last hospital visit. Gilet, the girl in the shop was calling it. You can get them in fur too, she told me. When the winter comes, you'll have to get one in fur.

'I thought I'd better smarten myself up a bit,' I said.

'Are you coming for a ride?' Sarah asked. 'It's such a lovely day.'

We sat in her car, a blue, low-slung affair as though you're going about in a go-cart—*It's a Triumph TR5 1968, seeing as you've asked, Ceci*—and I said, 'I didn't know the roof came off.'

I should have kept my mouth shut. Leaning across me to pull the door to, Sarah started on

153

about this and that and its Michelotti lines and the front trunnions seizing if they weren't properly lubricated and how that could put a strain on the drop link on the wishbone . . . she couldn't half go on about that car.

'You're a bit of an all-rounder, aren't you?' I said, because as well as being handy in the kitchen she'd done a motor-vehicle mechanics course in London.

'I have to get my hands dirty,' she replied, 'or I couldn't afford to keep this old banger on the road.'

'I was forty-five when this car was made,' I told her, 'and you weren't even waiting to be born.'

As we took the hill down to the prom, under the curved rafters of leafy branches, past a crying child dawdling behind his mother with a pushchair on their way up, Sarah looked in her rear-view mirror. The dog was jammed sideways in the slice of a space behind our seats.

'Mungo's not happy,' she said. 'He thinks you've taken his place.'

'Mungo lives the life of Riley,' I replied. Walks by the sea, the girl to himself, and I'll bet he was having most of what she put on her plate because she looked peaky as anything despite all the cooking she was bringing round. Bean burgers, spinach and caramelised-onion quiche, tomato and basil risotto, and once a banana and coconut curry which she said brought back memories of her gap year volunteering in Indonesia. I was having a taste of it all. The place is full of food, I told her, I can't eat all this, it's enough to feed a family. Not the best example of tact. Your appetite goes as you get older, I said quickly. I'd noticed that, Ceci, she

154

replied. I'll eat up if you do.

'Any news?' I asked as we parked on the prom. Fishermen balanced rods over the pier's railings. A slow-moving boat with turquoise sails cast a zip of froth in the water.

Did you know there's still a Pier Master, Sarah told me once. Yes—and did *you* know he used to wear a navy uniform with gold stripes on his shoulder, I replied, because she liked little bits of information like that.

'Tom phoned again last night,' she said. 'He says he's been working too hard and he's sorry he's been letting his precious civil liberties take over. He wants to meet up.'

'Does he now?' I asked, looking out at the water. 'And what did you say to that?'

'I told him I was quite enjoying doing what I liked,' she replied. 'Instead of waiting for someone to come home when the rest of London has long gone to bed.'

'He works all the time, does he?' I asked, in case there was something else she wasn't saying. I was used to that, half expected it.

Sarah turned to me. She didn't look well at all.

'Do you know, Ceci, it would be so much simpler if he was seeing someone else, but I was there when the phone calls came for emergency orders to prevent another breach of human rights. He really cares about his freedom fighters. I . . . I . . . do admire him terribly for that.'

'If he's always working, then how did you two get together?'

Sarah laughed. 'I wasn't one of his clients, if that's what you mean.'

'You say you want your freedom and he's

155

prepared to fight for it. One day you two will have to meet,' I kept on.

Inclined as I was to tell her outright she should give the boy a chance, I erred on the side of equanimity. 'Are you answering one of my questions or not?' I said. 'Give and take and all that.'

I could see she wanted to talk about him, and maybe a time when she was happier and more hopeful.

'It was at a party, in the back garden, at my friend Marnie's.'

'Like the Hitchcock film?' I'd watched an awful lot of telly after Freda died.

Sarah laughed. 'You are funny, Ceci. Yes, like the Hitchcock film.'

Apparently, the talk at this do was of shoes, gadgets, holidays, what people wanted with money they wanted.

'They were talking about skiing and flying lessons and cars and stuff, and then someone asked Tom what he desired,' she went on. 'That was the word they used. *Desired.*'

I'd seen a picture of the man in a T-shirt saying *Make Waves Not War*—Sarah managed a smile when she pointed it out—and that evening he impressed her well enough by replying he had everything he needed. Desire must have come into it when their eyes met because soon enough they got themselves a flat near Hampstead Heath on account of both of them liking their space.

'All you're after is a baby and you'll be right,' I said. 'Now the two of you have had more space again.'

Bold didn't begin to describe how I was getting.

156

'We'll see,' she said. 'What about you, Ceci? Tell me about you.'

Sarah hadn't been so direct before.

'Hark at the sun on the sea,' I said, pointing at the horizon. 'I don't know why I don't come more often. I love looking at the water.'

'You and me both,' Sarah replied. 'Mungo and I are always down here, aren't we, boy? All hours of the day and night.'

## 10

Ida sat before Sir Neville in his first-floor office watching the trail of sweet-smelling smoke that came from the end of his gold-tipped cigar.

Outside, she could hear the low hum of mid-morning traffic going up and down the streets that surrounded the office. The sky was high and clear, the air had that fresh spring scent of lemon jelly. People had started wearing jackets, not coats, into the office. Back home, the lido would be a sea of ripples in the breeze off the Channel.

Her new job wasn't journalism, but at least it was something to do with words. All she had to do was think up catchy slogans that would appeal to female consumers. Sir Neville Osborne was an MP with an advertising agency hitting the buffers: he'd wanted to improve business by employing a 'Girl Friday' to tell him what made women tick.

'I've called you down to ask you a very important question,' he said.

Ida nodded. She was coming up to nineteen and had already been given her own room in the attic of the three-storey offices on a smart street of white buildings behind black railings. Always getting the garret, I'm clearly destined for the top, Ida had said, but Freda didn't laugh. They were drifting apart, Ida could tell. Freda was spending more time with her chum Edna, asking why a career girl like Ida would be bothered with a smelly nurse like her. When Ida told her Frank Shankly had phoned out of the blue to congratulate her for a mention she'd had in the public relations industry's newsletter, Freda went off, saying she had studying to do for exams.

'What would make you buy bacon?' Sir Neville asked. He'd got wind that the British Bacon account was up for grabs and was intent on pitching an idea that would appeal to housewives.

Not a dripping carcass, that was for sure. Ida thought for a moment. Sometimes it seemed so ridiculously easy she felt sure she was saying something daft and waited for the shriek of laughter after she had spoken.

'What about,' she said, 'a beautiful young woman in an apron cooking bacon with her husband in a suit and his arm around her waist and the words *Why Bringing Home the Bacon Makes a Happy Home*?'

'I like it,' said Sir Neville. He shouted out of the door to his secretary, 'Angela dear, tell the artists we're scrapping the pig's head on a plate idea.'

Once he'd got what he wanted, Sir Neville never kept Ida talking. He made a comment about her new hairstyle—longer and pinned up at the sides with orange Bakelite clips—and then said he had to get on, to his club probably. He was old and fat and hairy, but Ida liked him. Sir Neville had a wife

158

who said to call her Joan and sometimes came into the office telling the girls to keep her husband in check.

'You're dismissed,' he said to Ida and she rose, crossed the landing to the small kitchen and made herself a black coffee which she carried back up to her desk.

Ida's office, as she liked to think of it, was decorated with clients' posters. One for a skin cream showed a woman with her face up to a looking glass with the words *Don't show your age— face the future with fadeaway!* Another was a close-up of a tyre on a red Riley car with the words *a tyre to keep you ahead*. It was a play on words, she'd explained to the male board of the company; 'attire' might appeal to Bright Young Things. They'd looked at her with dull expressions on their faces though they wanted to tap into the female drivers' market, and attract women like Sir Neville's friend, Miranda Drabble, who whizzed about in open-top cars looking like something from an advert herself.

Ida was making notes on a new account for a cruise-liner company—she fancied a poster showing wispy elegant women leaning on railings looking out to sea—when there were hurried footsteps on the stairs and Miranda put her head round the door.

Miranda was funny and quick and constantly on the go. She had a husband called Ernest who owned a hosiery factory up North, but she never strayed far from the West End. Though Ida had been to nightclubs with Miranda, and once a grand hotel function where they danced together beneath vast chandeliers, Miranda was older and, Ida

159

thought, far more sophisticated. She was never entirely relaxed in Miranda's company, but then nobody would ever match up to Freda for making you feel you'd found your missing half.

'Just popped in to pick up Nevie,' said Miranda, dancing into the room. 'But do tell. It's the talk of the club.'

Ida suspected Miranda never felt as gay as she seemed. Once, when they'd had a bit to drink, she'd tearfully told her about losing a baby who was born premature.

'Tell what?' Ida asked. People seemed to do nothing but gossip. She'd been hoping for some quiet.

'The word is, sweetie, that Nicky Hobson is rather taken with you,' Miranda said. 'Is it reciprocated or are you one of these viragos wanting to get on?'

Nicholas Hobson was a tall, fair, floppy-haired journalist who worked for a weekly magazine called *Red, White and Blue* which covered topics such as travel, adventure and fox hunting. The magazine was quite a patriotic affair, a bit behind the times. It seemed to think the world was changing too quickly, what with women flying and working. The editorial page asked questions such as: *Is the country going to the dogs?*

Ida had been in several meetings with the magazine about placing clients' adverts, and the day before, after one of the bosses had instructed her to make notes of what he was saying, Nicky had taken her aside and told her a funny story about the man being mistaken for a waiter at his club.

'You told me he was nice to everyone,' Ida said,

rolling her fountain pen in her hands. Nicky had a reputation as a gentleman. He was 'too nice', one or two people said, whatever that meant. When she and Nicky had gone for a lunchtime drink, he'd told her being polite in business sometimes made one come across as a bit soft. 'I think girls prefer a bit of a brute too,' he'd said, looking into his drink.

'Though if you're a woman,' Ida told Miranda, 'I've been told it's better to seem more of what you call a virago, or else you might get walked over.'

'My, aren't you one of these new career girls?' Miranda put both thin, veined hands on Ida's desk, leaning in at her. Under the desk, Ida pushed both of her feet back into her new grey suede shoes. Though she wore two-piece navy suits with the same aplomb as the women who strode down Regent Street wrapped in fox furs, inside she still felt a podgy swimmer in a too-tight costume.

Though Miranda was amusing company, Ida sometimes wished she had a job to go to. She smiled, realising that was the kind of thing Freda would come out with—not that she'd seen her in a while.

'What is it, Iddy?' Miranda asked. 'Do tell. People are talking. There's got to be someone, surely. Are you and Nicky, you know . . .'

'Certainly not.' Ida blushed. She felt disloyal. Nicky stuck up for her. Another time, he'd very quietly but firmly told one of the old-timers at the magazine to show some respect for the female point of view.

'Oh well, it was worth a try,' Miranda said. 'I'm bored. Anyone or anything else going on?'

'Here,' Ida replied, handing Miranda a couple of jars of skin cream from her desk drawer. It was one of the perks of the jobs, getting free products from grateful clients. 'Let me know what you think. We need testimonials for a new ad.'

When Miranda departed, Ida was relieved and thoughtful. Sometimes she felt sure of things, and other times, in quiet moments, she felt a nasty little clawing inside telling her that things weren't quite right or might go wrong. All it needed was for someone like Miranda to say something like 'people have been talking'.

That afternoon, each time the phone rang, Ida picked up wondering if either of them—Freda or Frank—might be at the other end.

'Miss Gaze speaking,' she said, at around a quarter to four after leaving it to ring several times. In the offices opposite, figures flitted back and forth at the windows. Summer would be here soon enough. She thought of pink-skied evenings and leaving restaurants for walks in the park.

'Still basking in glory?' It was Frank. She thought he'd call again but Ida felt disappointment. Freda *was* being funny with her then. The last time they'd seen each other had been an outing on the Heath, and when Ida had pointed out frogs in the pond, Freda hadn't really wanted to know.

'How are you, Mr Shankly?' she said, attempting a formal note. That first time he'd called was after seeing the PR magazine headline *ad girl's lipstick triumph* with a photograph of Ida sitting on her desk in a skirt which seemed far shorter than she'd realised. Frank had been rather presumptuous, she thought, for a man who hadn't spoken to her for so long.

All the agencies had been after the cosmetics

162

account Ida won with the motto *Smart Girls Stay Fast With LippieLux*, a new long-lasting formula. It was the same brand Freda had given her way back when in their blackberry field, but Freda hadn't wanted to listen when Ida tried to tell her this, the same way she said she'd had enough of hearing about Amelia Earhart's latest adventure and that some people needed to start living with their feet on the ground.

'Oh, you know me and the limelight,' Ida replied. Frank's voice sent a shiver of excitement through her though she sat as still as anything, concentrating on being confident. He'd been made editor of his paper. When word got back from Stella on the switchboard that first time he telephoned Ida, Sir Neville looked the most impressed Ida had seen him.

'PR, you see—it's more me,' she went on. 'Something soft, thinking about nice things and imagining people enjoying themselves. I think you were probably right all that time ago when you told me I wouldn't make a reporter. I'm not cut out for the Kellogg-Briand Pact.'

'That's a shame, I was going to offer you a job,' Frank replied. Not sure if it was a joke, she laughed. She didn't need Frank Shankly.

'I'm impressed you're on top of the Kellogg-Briand Pact,' he said. 'Though that's old news now, of course. I might have to examine you on the rise of the Nazis in Weimar Germany instead.'

Ida wished she could be aloof and cool but she was enjoying herself. Her eyes rested on a poster of several girls in belted bathing costumes and stripy caps gathered round the gleaming white pillars of an outdoor pool with the words GET IN

*THE SWIM AT SOUTHPORT.* Girls love the water, she'd told the tourist people when she pitched for the account. I can't keep out of it myself.

'Now you have me,' she said, 'though I'm good on Amelia Earhart.'

'The powderpuff flier's still at it, is she?' he said. 'Didn't you meet her once or is that something I've drummed up to keep you talking?'

'No, you're right, I did.' Ida felt a rush of pleasure he should remember. 'I still follow her.'

'Perhaps you could have her as the front woman for one of your clients,' Frank said. 'Then again, judging by that rather revealing snap of yours, I wouldn't say *you'd* look out of place on a billboard.'

'Ha ha. What? Me being a woman and only fit for smiling at a camera? PR's not all namby-pamby superficial nonsense, you know, though I grant you it's a world away from your pit disasters and striking miners.'

There she was, rattling on again. Freda gave her a look sometimes now, as if to say *I wish you'd shut up*.

'I wondered if you fancied a bite to eat,' Frank said. 'From that picture—can't take my eyes off it, actually—you certainly look as though you could do with some meat on your bones.'

Ida heard herself say, 'I'd like that, thank you,' as if it was the most natural thing in the world to be going to dinner with Frank Shankly, the man she had wondered about all this time.

'Pick you up at eight then.'

When Ida put the phone down, she realised Frank didn't have her address. He'd never asked for it. Then again, Frank was one of those proper

164

journalists who ran front-page stories telling the Government what to do. He'd probably done his research, but Ida wasn't going to phone back and check. If he didn't come, he didn't come. She wasn't that fussed to go chasing after him. She had her job now.

*     *     *

'It's ridiculous,' Ida was saying, 'all the money companies spend on getting agencies like mine to come up with ways of selling things to the public. You'd think people would want to buy lipsticks and ready-made pancakes, and cars and cruise holidays without the need to be told, wouldn't you?'

Freda shrugged. She was standing at the window of Ida's flat listening to the wind in the tree outside and watching the heads of passers-by down below. An old woman lived opposite. Freda hadn't seen her coming carefully down the steps with her stick in ages. Nursing taught you to expect the worst— like the elderly coming in dehydrated or emaciated by tapeworms—but also to try and make the best of things.

Ida was relieved Freda had come round but there were too many silences, and not really looking at each other moments. She was only trying to keep the mood up.

'And then there's all the market research being done,' Ida went on, 'basically paying people oodles to ask questions they ought to know the answer to themselves. If you were a brand selling, oh I don't know, say soap-flakes, do you really need to fork out to find that housewives want some that get rid of difficult stains?'

This kind of talk was outside Freda's area of interest, but she saw Ida's eyes shining as she listed how many hundreds of pounds she was bringing in for the company. She hadn't realised what a business success Ida had wanted to become.

'I'm so proud of you,' Freda said. 'You've rallied and got there. I knew you'd do it.' Freda meant it and waited, hoping Ida would see it was a moment between them.

'Well, thank you, and you know how proud I am of *you*, but I'm not really a success, am I?' Ida replied. 'I never did become a reporter, after all. I suppose that's what I would have liked, if I'm truthful.'

'If that's what you really want,' Freda said, 'it's never too late, surely?' But she was surprised and dispirited by the idea Ida wasn't as happy as all that. Was she putting things on then?

Ida lifted her head from the pillow. She'd told Freda she did a lot of lying on the bed when she got back from the office. There were papers from work on the covers.

'Oh, but Freddie, it *is* too late. I'm practically over the hill. Do you know that at a shoot for a new oven brand, the photographer complained the girl we had for a housewife looked too old—and she was a year younger than me. Can you imagine?' Ida banged her head back down. 'And then he asked me why I wasn't hitched yet, as though I was some kind of Black Widow spinster.'

'You've always minded too much what other people think,' Freda said, but Ida didn't take so much notice any more of Freda's bold statements about doing what you wanted.

As she wittered on about face cream and

166

perfume and how women were a multi-thousand-pound industry even if they were just seen as mothers at home bringing up children, Freda's face froze in a smile. She couldn't help thinking of some of the patients in the hospital who had so little, and how many toys could be bought for the children with cancer with the kind of money Ida talked about.

'Summer's coming,' Ida said, 'and there's nowhere to swim.'

'Yes, there is,' Freda replied. 'Tooting Bec, for starters. We could go there if you like.'

But Ida was off, moaning about how it had been nearly three years since she'd been in the water and how Freda would never go in because of her golf balls and what a thing it was being in London with nowhere to wash yourself clean of the grime up your nose.

Gradually the mood in the room changed and when Ida paused, both of them felt the agitation in the air.

Freda pointed at the flowers in a silver vase on the cast-iron mantelpiece. She needn't have bothered coming, she thought, not least because the moment she walked through the door Ida had said she needed to start getting ready for a date.

'Who are they from then?' Freda asked.

Ida was silent as she slid off the bed.

'All the petals are falling off,' Freda said.

'I don't want to throw them away,' Ida replied in a firm, spiky voice. 'They're Constance Spry, she's terribly fashionable. And if you must know, they're from someone at a magazine, but it's not him I'm seeing tonight.'

Freda stared at the bouquet. She knew the

names of everything from helping her father in the garden. The display was a mix of hedgerow flowers, with grasses and pussy willows, unusual and beautiful but wilting.

Ida said, 'I might as well tell you who my date is—it's your old friend, minus ten. I've been seeing him for a while.'

Freda felt resentful. Why was Ida telling her as if it was a secret everyone was desperate to know?

'You never know,' Ida went on. 'He might finally give me a job and I'll get to be a reporter, after all.'

'That's what you really still want, is it?' Freda asked. She noticed a bottle of new scent on the tiny, crammed dressing table. The room felt suddenly sickly-sweet with perfume.

Ida bent to roll down her stockings. Freda could see she was preparing to wash and felt a bolt of jealousy and something like stupidity, that after all this time she hadn't seen what was coming. Of course, she'd known underneath.

'In any event,' Freda said. 'The flowers are dead.'

'Will you please stop going on about those flowers,' Ida replied, not looking up. 'It's not as if I might never have anyone else in my life if I threw them away, is it? Come on, we have to be honest with each other.'

Hurt, then anger, ran through Freda but she tried to stay calm. She'd learned to keep a lid on her temper, but what a thing to say, after all the time she'd spent trying to gee Ida up—and now she was all right with a job, getting rises and accolades, and Frank Shankly—here Ida was making crude hints, as though Freda had only ever been trying to keep her for herself.

'All right, I will be honest,' Freda said. 'I've had enough.' It was sickening, all this frivolity and obsession with holidays on liners and creams that kept you looking young, and food out of a packet that would give you more time to slip on a négligée and tempt your husband to bed.

Ida stood up straight. 'Don't let's argue, Freddie,' she said. 'I know you've got Edna and, well . . .'

'No, you don't know,' Freda said. 'You don't know as much as you think you do, just as I don't. Nobody knows anything really when it comes down to it. We're all going around, jawing on about this and that, and work, and getting things, and . . . and then we're not seeing what's not there, what we're *not* getting, what . . . what's going that w-w-won't be got back.'

Ida's feet were bare. One of the stockings fell from her hand and landed silently on the floorboards. She looked startled and sad.

'It's you who's always telling me not to look to the past, but to buck up and get on with life and that sort of thing,' she said quietly.

'I'm off,' Freda replied, and she made to go, waiting for Ida to say, 'Running away again,' in her teasing but conciliatory way.

'Please yourself then.' Ida sounded weary.

At the door, Freda turned back but Ida wasn't looking. She was twisting this way and that in front of the mirror, her body thinner than ever, not even catching Freda's eye through the glass. Ida seemed suddenly so much older and harder, in a black crêpe dress with a narrow black shiny belt around her tiny waist.

169

## 11

The woman had come out of an ambulance looking as though she had hours to live, if that.

It wasn't the first time a grin of mischief had been wiped in an instant off Freda Voyle's face. From her eyrie at the end of the ward, Matron watched Nurse Voyle, crouched at the woman's bed, talking softly to the patient. None of them had been able to find out what the woman had taken to try and abort her baby. If they didn't know, they couldn't help her, but women like her didn't say. They were as scared of going to prison as they were of being pregnant and bringing a baby into the world they couldn't afford to keep.

'This is how I see it,' Freda said, in a whisper to the woman. 'If I was to say what you might have taken, you might nod or blink as I said it, but if anyone asks me, I, of course, wouldn't be able to say you had told me.'

The woman was still, her eyes closed. Freda looked at the scalds on her arms. She had taken a hot bath, probably after a bottle of gin, to try and burn out what was inside her, and most likely dosed up on something from a market stall too.

Freda cleared her throat. She didn't care if the rest of her shift was looking or smirking and thinking she was wasting her time. In possibly the last hours of a patient's life, truly, nothing was a waste of time.

'You see, I have a dear, dear friend, and in truth I worry this might happen to her one of these days,' Freda said. 'It can happen to any of us—well, to lots of women—but it's not only her I care enough about to want to help.'

Getting caught was what Matron called it. Sometimes, you knew the women worked the street. There were lots of them in the doorways around where Ida lived. One with bleached hair always stood beneath the illuminated sign of a club called Rolo's, though Freda hadn't seen her in a while.

The woman gave no sign of having heard Freda or being inclined to respond. Freda knew Matron was watching her, that she would probably get a dressing-down for unorthodox methods, being overly familiar with a patient and that kind of thing, but she didn't care if it affected her final diploma grade. What she wanted, more than anything, was to save the woman's life. It was such a precious thing to be able to do. It would be a crime and a terrible shameful thing to let this woman slip away.

Freda dropped her mouth to the woman's ear again. All the signs were there, the breathing quickening, the pulse racing. Her eyelids were darker, her lips pale.

'You are a stranger to me and I am a stranger to you,' Freda said, trying to stay calm, 'but seeing you here like this, can you understand I would like to try and ease your pain? Can you see I'm not interfering or trying to cause you trouble? On pain of death, I swear that I will never, ever tell the police or anyone else in authority, anything, anything at all. Do you understand me? Am I making sense?'

The woman opened her eyes, blinked several times, closed them again and sighed.

Freda showed no impatience. 'Will you trust me?' she asked, putting her hand gently on the woman's cool arm, on a part not crisscrossed with red, flaming weals. 'It is simply that we may have it in our powers to stop the hurt and save your life.'

Whenever she told Ida about work, Ida would ask how Freda could do it. Things like seeing an old man point at a first-floor window and cry his wife's name, saying she was standing outside calling to him to cross to the other side. Or a child with cancer you had to watch growing whiter and greyer until their last breath was taken and you put the tips of your fingers on their eyelids so no more would you see the painful glint of dying staring fearfully back at you.

At the very least you must cry, Ida had said when Freda would be drawn on these things, but Freda never did. Uppermost in her mind, as clear as anything, with nothing to sway her from her course of duty, was saving life and easing pain. Edna understood, because she was the same way.

The ward was silent. Down its centre, lights hung like bells and the bodies in each row of beds either side of the room were as still as marble figures on tombs. On the chair beside the bed was the pale blue gathered dress which the woman had arrived in, with her round-toed white shoes set together on top.

Freda tried not to show her desperation. Deciding to look for clues in the small black bag the patient had come in with, she was about to stand when the woman's eyes opened.

She was looking at Freda and Freda was looking at her.

Moments later, Nurse Voyle skidded to a halt at

172

the open door of Matron's room.

'A lye douche,' she said. 'She used a lye douche.'

Matron nodded and stood—and suddenly, given something to work with, the ward became flashes of movement and hope.

Some time later, the patient's condition had stabilised, and through the window of her office Matron watched Freda pat the woman's head with a damp cloth which another nurse had brought her unbidden. It had not gone unnoticed that the other nurses looked to Freda for direction. The Ward Sister had mentioned it more than once.

Matron continued staring. She must be getting soft in her old age, but you saw this sort of thing so rarely. These girls arrived from God knows where on their first day, as cocky and flippant as they come, with no idea of how difficult training as a nurse would be. And then . . . and then, very occasionally, the ones you had down as wasters came good like this Voyle girl. She had something about her, that unknown quality that once you saw it, you knew very much what it was.

Matron had seen the kind girls, the vain ones, the cumbersome, efficient and responsible ones, and then there were girls like Freda Voyle who came in with an option before them the others didn't have—of going either way in life. The only way she could think to put it, though it was a little theatrical and Matron was not inclined to drama, was that Freda Voyle was one of those that would either end up in prison or running the country. You saw that sometimes, that fine line between the two, the loser and the leader, though hell would of course freeze over before any woman had the chance to properly run anything.

173

If she would just stop sliding about on the polished ward floors, Nurse Voyle would go all the way, to Sister and beyond.

$$*  \qquad *  \qquad *$$

'I can't believe it,' Ida said. 'Swimming after all this time. What a super idea, Freddie.'

As they headed for the long white building in the middle of a field, the sun came down like a spreading fan of gold. Ida stopped to shake out the grit caught under the soles of her new sandals which had orange, black and green flowers made of leather strips on the front.

'Who'd have thought,' she went on. 'An outdoor pool here.'

'If we ever get there,' Freda replied, looking at her watch. 'There's not much time left. My shift starts at six.'

Everything was such a rush these days. Freda couldn't explain to herself how she felt. She had woken on her nineteenth birthday wanting to make things as they had been with Ida, even though there was work that evening, and the pool was an hour's bus ride away, and then when she got to the flat, Ida was still in her pyjamas moaning about Leonard's typewriter going all hours downstairs.

'I'm sorry I took an age getting ready,' Ida said. 'I wasn't expecting this.'

The entrance to the bathing pool had curved glass brick windows either side of a tower with the word *lido* in red written down it. Shouts and screams and splashes came from within. The sound was as familiar as her father's voice, Freda thought.

174

'It's just like home,' Ida said when they saw the silvery turquoise pool with people sitting round it on towels, shading their eyes with their hands. There was a slide and a feathery fountain of water and a diving platform. Pennants flapped in the breeze above their heads, and the white wooden changing rooms had doors painted red and yellow, blue and green.

'Do you remember?' Ida asked. Looking at Freda with the strap of her khaki bag across her chest, she felt suddenly shy. All those years together and now they barely saw one another. Freda seemed half a stranger with her talk of ether and miscarriage and theatre, and the way she had taken to that hospital with its endless tiled corridors and beds of helpless people.

'I was hoping you'd like it,' Freda replied, though there was too much of a crowd for her taste.

'You've always known what I like, Freddie.'

'Only like?'

Ida looked sideways at her as she tucked her hair behind her ear. Freda kept her gaze. Ida was on about getting a new place for herself, as though the two of them would never share once Freda moved out of halls. Worse again was the possibility she saw herself marrying Frank Shankly.

'Love,' Ida said. 'I love it here. Let me at it.'

As Ida pulled her sandals off and bent to touch the water, Freda felt hope and happiness. She saw a lot of bare feet in the hospital but it was ages since she'd seen Ida's toes in the sun.

'Let's find some shade,' she said.

They passed a man wearing a white jacket and trousers like a sea captain, standing with a white cabinet on wheels with the words *Eldorado Ice Cream* on the side.

'Not here,' Freda called back to Ida, who couldn't take her eyes off the water. 'We'll get all the rabble wanting ices.'

Beneath a white arch leading into a shaded area where people sat on deck chairs reading and talking, Freda stopped and pulled out a towel to sit. Though she'd ummed and aahed over what to wear—a sailor's top with a blue bow on the collar and a white A-line skirt—Ida changed into her old costume straightaway.

'I can't wait any longer,' she said, back from the changing room. 'Are you coming in?'

Freda stuck her cigarette in her mouth and pointed both index fingers at her chest.

'Golf balls,' Ida said, and leaned to kiss her forehead. 'I can't believe I forgot your birthday. Will you ever forgive me?'

'There's not much of you to forgive,' Freda replied. 'They come malnourished into the hospital bigger than you.'

'I thought I'd never wear it again,' Ida said.

As she tugged at the loose legs of her bathing suit, Freda released a mouthful of smoke. Ida was so thin and pale and when she wasn't working she was doubtless out on the town with that insomniac hack.

'I thought Frank Shankly was taking you here, there and everywhere eating,' she said.

Ida hadn't seen Frank since a meal at Romano's eight days ago when he spent three courses with a smear of ink on his forehead arguing it was hard news and not stories about women that sold newspapers.

176

'You haven't brought me here to be nasty, have you?' Ida said.

'On the contrary, I thought it might make you feel better.'

A yell rushed through the air as someone went down the slide and ended with a splash.

'There's nothing wrong with me,' Ida replied. 'All I need is a new bathing suit.'

'Must be the only thing you haven't bought. That and a square meal.'

'Stop having a go, Freddie. I thought we were trying to get on.'

They both turned when a voice shouted, 'Fred!'

A girl in a yellow dress was walking towards them. She had a thick black fringe falling into her eyes from a strawberry-patterned turban.

'Fancy meeting you here,' the girl said.

Freda didn't get up. 'Edna,' she said. 'What the hell are you doing here?'

'And there I was, thinking it was just the two of us,' Ida said.

Edna turned her palms upwards and looked at the sky. At the side of the pool, a tanned young man wearing navy-blue trunks with a gold buckle belt did a handstand and flopped into the water.

'Why not?' Edna said. 'It's all the rage, isn't it?' She looked at Ida. 'Aren't you going to introduce me?'

'Edna, Ida,' Freda said. 'Ida, Edna.'

The two women shook hands. Ida had imagined someone thick-looking with a square face and big calves, but Edna had sparkling violet eyes and a jet choker, and white leather pumps with straps that crisscrossed up slim legs.

'You're Edna, are you?' Ida said. 'I've heard you

177

mentioned.'

'Have you?' Edna replied. That morning she'd gone early to Freda's room and caught her asking the girl opposite if she knew of an outdoor pool. Freda had thanked Edna for the birthday gift of a cigarette-lighter, put the strap of her bag over her head, and walked off down the corridor saying she was seeing her oldest best friend. Edna knew that were she to write in to one of the newspaper agony aunts, saying how things were with Freda, they would tell her to knock the friendship on the head. But things didn't work like that with Freda. Freda was different.

'Are you coming in the water?' Ida asked, trying to be polite.

Edna shook her head. She hadn't trailed halfway across London to freeze in that.

'I'll stay here,' she replied, sitting on a towel she'd laid next to Freda, who rolled her eyes.

Ida was itching to get in the water but she sat back down and listened as Edna nattered on about people at the hospital. She was looking at Freda as if she'd known her forever or they were twins or sisters, or had something more between them than anyone else in the lido.

'Your other woman,' Edna said. 'She's been asking for you.'

'She's not in trouble, is she?' Freda asked.

'Oh no, Matron's seen to that,' Edna replied. 'But I think she'll be happier when you're back at her side.'

'Aren't we all?' Ida said, though she hadn't a clue who they were on about.

'It's the patient I told you about who nearly died,' Freda told her. 'The one who tried to abort

178

her baby.'

On the top diving board, a girl stood braced for going over. The pool went quiet, waiting, but Edna carried on talking, and when everyone clapped as the girl came up from a perfectly executed dive, she said, 'What was that?'

'People applauding you pausing for breath,' Freda replied. 'I thought Ida didn't stop, but you're beyond.'

Edna gave Freda's arm a gentle punch and looked at Ida. 'We haven't said much to each other, have we?'

It was strange seeing someone else at Freda's side. Edna was very sure of herself and Freda didn't seem to mind the way she carried on.

'I think you're saying enough for the three of us,' Ida replied.

As Edna talked on, Ida watched a man in a blazer hand a woman a drink on the pavilion. When Ida had complained to Nicky Hobson that Frank was always working, he'd replied Shankly had something of a reputation for not knowing when to stop.

Edna prodded Freda's arm. 'You and me will have to get going if we're to catch the bus,' she said.

'You're working too, are you?' Ida asked.

Edna nodded as Freda stood.

'What a rotten day this has turned out to be,' Freda said. 'Will you be all right finding your own way back?'

'Don't worry about me,' Ida replied. 'Honestly, I'm in my element.'

She watched the two of them leave, picking their way through the bodies with Edna looking up at

Freda and talking and laughing away. She could cry, thinking about the way Freda had said, 'But it's my birthday,' after Ida told her she couldn't be bothered doing anything within seconds of her walking through the door.

At the turnstile, Freda turned and waved and shrugged, and Ida blew her a kiss before walking down the steps of the pool into the freezing water.

\*　　　\*　　　\*

As she climbed the stairs to Ida's room, Freda realised it would be the last time she ever did so. Now Ida was in the money, she was moving to a place where she had hot water, a fitted kitchen and a fancy chrome lift.

The first thing Ida said when Freda walked through the door to help her pack wasn't thanks for coming or what a shame you couldn't stay at the lido but, 'Do you know my new flat has a man in reception who will do things like collect your laundry and walk people's dogs?'

'That's something, isn't it?' Freda replied, looking at the boxes and bags of Ida's possessions. She hadn't realised how much stuff she had bought over the years. Each was a reminder of a moment in their lives, like the little grey velvet cape Ida had been so excited about wearing when they went for their first-ever cocktails. Or the chrome and black cigarette-holder on the dressing table that Ida had bought for Freda, giving it to her one Christmas hidden in a cracker. Freda had the sudden thought it might have hurt Ida that she had never used it, had cast it aside saying there was no need for it; she had never even taken it back with her to the

180

hospital.

'How's Edna?' Ida asked.

'Same as ever.'

'She's very keen on being your friend, isn't she?'

'At least someone is,' Freda replied.

Ida glanced up from a blouse she was folding on the bed. She seemed jittery about the move, not quite there in the room, as though she had already left the old life her flat had come to represent.

'That woman left hospital today,' Freda said. Ida preferred the happy-ending stories. If ever Freda made her laugh, Ida gave her a funny look of gratitude as though to say she knew she was trying to cheer her up.

'I don't suppose the baby survived?' Ida asked.

Freda shook her head. Seeing Ida standing before her in a lilac silk dress with a tiny black bolero cardigan and shoes with heels and black ribbon bows, Freda felt a familiar blast of jealousy and worry, thinking about Ida and Frank Shankly and what went on between them. She, Freda, wasn't really part of Ida's life any more, just good for boxing away all that had gone before.

'Oh Freddie,' Ida said. 'Let's not talk about depressing things. It's so easy to get down these days. Frank's one for doing that, talking about unemployment all the time and . . . and the possibility of war. It's almost as though he wants it to happen so the paper has something to damn well write about.'

'How are things going with him?' Freda asked but Ida pretended she hadn't heard.

'Oh, this move,' she went on. 'I didn't realise what an upheaval it would be. I . . . we . . . have been in this place for so long, haven't we—what is it now?' Ida bent to a box and started shuffling papers around.

Freda told herself this was the way things were. They were working women with different lives to lead, though they would always be friends. But Ida avoiding the question about Frank annoyed her, as though Freda was still a child who couldn't be trusted or told grown-up sorts of things when actually, it was Freda always seeing things at work, like the paraplegic airman, that could break your heart, that would have Ida in one of her faints.

'Oh look, Freddie,' Ida said, rising with a small piece of paper in her hand. Her nails were long now, and red to match her lips.

'Look, one of those old notes you used to push under my door. *Can't wait to get back to the garret, love you, Freddie.* Look at that row of kisses. Didn't you love me so very much?'

That was another thing. Ida had developed a rather false way of speaking. Everything was darling and fabulous and chic, especially if she spoke on the phone at work and Ida forgot who she was talking to. Freda turned back to the pile of magazines—*Women's this* and *Interiors that*—she was stacking in a box and her mind went to Edna.

The previous day at work, Freda had watched the consultant run his eyes over the assembled throng of nurses, waiting to hear what wisdom he would impart in his confident tones.

'You,' he'd said, pointing at Edna. 'You'll do. Come here so I may tutor all of you in the best method for examination.'

As Edna stood before them, raising her eyes to the ceiling as the doctor prodded about, Freda noticed how long he kept his hands in places and had blushed with a mixture of embarrassment, irritation and jealousy. It wasn't pleasant, having these sorts of feelings all the time and not knowing where you were with things, or letting other people know too.

That evening, the first thing Freda had done when Edna came to her room and lay, as usual, beside her on the bed, was to turn and waggle her hands at Edna's chest. She'd planned it all afternoon, as a casual joke.

'I need to demonstrate technique,' she'd said in the perfect, pompous tones of Mr Simeon, and then Edna had giggled and pulled up her mustard-coloured sweater, saying, 'Go on, then. Show me your technique, Nurse Voyle.'

Freda blushed again at the memory of Ida's salmon-pink brassière and the way her breasts, even lying down, seemed to almost topple from the cups. Freda had risen sharply from the bed saying she had studying to do.

She tuned back into Ida talking, her voice high, a kind of trill that, if Freda didn't know her and heard her talking in a shop, say, would make her head for the door.

'I'll go to Bowman's in Camden for my sofa,' Ida said. 'A black-and-white colour scheme, I think, with some chrome—a lamp say, and perhaps a cigarette stand for when you come round, though I don't see anywhere near so much of you these days. What say you, Freddie?'

It was dawning on Freda that Ida had become a kind of monster, growing thinner and shriller but amassing more and more things. She'd thought it was the satisfaction of a job well done that Ida was after, all that time she was on about becoming a reporter—just as nursing had come to mean a great deal to Freda—but Ida always seemed to be wanting.

Freda finished boxing the rest of Ida's magazines. She put a jumble of shoes in another box, not caring if she had both of each pair, which wasn't like her at all, and then said, 'I'd better get going.'

Edna had told Freda to call in at her room no matter how late she got back.

'Bye then, Freddie, thanks so much for helping.' Ida's tone was distracted or tired. It reminded Freda of how Ida used to be, before she got on in work, sounding like her mother saying there was little point to anything.

Freda looked back to wave but Ida had stopped putting her clothes in a new suitcase and was looking at fabric swatches. Freda hadn't been listening when she asked what she thought—chocolate brown or raspberry sorbet for the chiffon curtains in her new double bedroom.

Freda was shocked and a little guilty at how glad she was to be going down the stairs of the flat for the last time, but it didn't stop her worrying whether Ida was happy. Hanging by its straps from the open door of her wardrobe had been Ida's bathing suit, thin and straggly as a strand of the black seaweed they used to pop on the beach back home.

Sometimes I'd be sitting there and the thought would hit me like a brick. There I was, a former cleaner, and here was Sarah, listening to me speak as though I was the Queen.

I can't tell you what it was to have company and not be in my chair imagining Freda sitting opposite. I'd think that if I got her outline I could colour the rest of her in like a child with a picture—oh, I remember those days with the wax crayons snapping like twigs between busy little hands—but I never got further than her long fingers in a V either side of a cigarette. That was Freda more or less, I'd think to myself. Like a puff of vanishing smoke.

There were times I worried about asking after her husband in case Sarah said the marriage was kaput. It's the last few days for sowing garlic, she told me when autumn arrived, as though it was a countdown to the end of the world. I could see she was feeling things keenly and I reckoned that's why she looked so gawky. Living on her nerves, Freda would have called it. Bloody neurotic, that's what she'd have said.

One day, Sarah brought me a tin of stuffed green olives. 'What's this?' I asked. 'A jar of lizards' eyeballs?'

'They're good for the joints,' she told me, and bit her lip as though she'd been thinking about me saying my hips wouldn't hold out. I had the olives with a bit of tuna and lettuce like she suggested, and was careful ever after to take out a few here and there and drop them to the bottom of the bin. Not my cup of tea at all, though I polished off the jar of lemon curd she brought me from the Farmers' Market they have on the prom the first Saturday of the month.

Sarah loved olives, you see, they were one of her absolute *favourite* things, and when she was saying this she mentioned a game she used to play with her mother, a simple enough thing. Name your favourite this or that. So, right there, she asked me, 'Ceci, what's your favourite smell?' and without really thinking big mouth Ceci said, 'Baby breath.' She looked so surprised, then faltered and said, 'Have there been lots of babies in your life, Ceci?' I felt so damn stupid, it was all I could do to shake my head and stand to put a stop to the conversation.

'Are you OK, Ceci?'

I hadn't seen the mug on the floor. Sarah was there in a flash, cupping my elbow, as quick as she was to leave go of the girl in the photo, with that sense of hers she has, that knowing.

'It's my fault,' she said. 'I should have taken it back to the kitchen. Are you sure you're all right?'

'I'm fine, love,' I told her. 'Just old age.' It was my fault really for not seeing all along. 'Let's take that dog out before we need the Fire Brigade round to detach him from the rug.'

Though it was getting colder and I wasn't getting any stronger, I tried keeping up my walking with her and the dog. I say walking but Sarah usually left me to sit down on the cliff tops while she took Mungo for a run.

We'd park the car next to the café that Sarah said sold Chelsea buns in plastic bell jars and then

186

cross to the cliff tops slowly, her pretending to fuss the dog on the lead so I could stagger along at her side without feeling I was holding up the show. Past the shelter with wrought-iron seats and graffiti, the fancy houses with sea views, and then we were out in the open, just the sky and the sea wherever you looked.

'Isn't it great nobody can build on the water?' Sarah said one day. 'There will never be a new block of apartments in our way.'

'Don't count on it,' I replied. 'They've opened a pub called The Gull and Leek on Flat Holm Island.'

The dog would be off, bouncing like a dropped kite across the mini-golf course, and as the wind picked up for winter, everyone had their heads bowed like monks going to prayer.

When Sarah left me on the bench, I'd look over at the old lido. What a sight that was. The fence was like ripped fishnet and the concrete base had small trees growing out of the cracks. The *Times* had a campaign going to get lottery money to restore it, but it was too far gone. The old saloon doors of the changing rooms had been torn off by vandals, the dolphin in the children's paddling pool smashed. The kids used to love that dolphin.

It might have been blowing a gale but I could sit on that bench for hours. I'd close my eyes against the gaps where the pool's lush sapphire water had seeped away. I imagined its vastness, so deep, so long, so wide, so brimming with salty, shouting life. Then I'd look across at England on the other side of the Channel, and Weston a white streak of buildings on the distant shore, or at the islands in the middle of the water, and the dangerous-

187

looking patchwork of white-ruffled waves. I could listen to the ebb and flow of the tide for hours, thinking, *Ida Gaze swam all that way*.

One afternoon, Sarah took my hand and led me to the railings. I wondered about the easy way she'd done it, at first worrying she thought I needed leading—things weren't anywhere near that bad yet—and decided it was an act of closeness, not kindness. I could hardly speak at the touch of her hand. I looked out to sea, the wind like a gentle slapping on one side of my face then the other, my gaze—for what it was worth—as determined as an outstretched arm demonstrating its ability not to shake.

'Any news?' I asked, because things had gone quiet, and after years of buttoning my lip, I'd become incapable of following suit.

'Tom said he thinks I might be one of those women who end up on their own,' Sarah said brightly.

'Did he now? Why would he say that?' I didn't think the girl was a quitter but I also saw she wasn't one of those that pushes herself forward, and that made me worry she might end up lonely.

'Oh, I suppose how things have gone, and now what he's calling me "going my own way", and then when you're on your own for a while without the rows, you start to wonder . . .'

'It's that mechanics course,' I said.

Sarah laughed. 'Ceci,' she went. 'Do you think some people might be better off on their own?'

'I can only speak from experience,' I heard myself saying, 'and in my experience, two is always better than one.'

Talk about old romantic.

188

'You two being so separate when once you thought enough of each other to join yourselves up,' I went on. 'There's space and then there's remembering what's between you.'

The girl went quiet then.

'I've told you so much about me, Ceci, now you tell me something, please,' she said on our way home. Her telling me about wanting a baby with a husband I reckoned she still loved, confiding something so fragile and private, did make me wonder what I might give her in return.

If I could just hand her the gumption to get up to London with an olive branch, it would be a start, but I knew that wasn't what she meant.

\*         \*         \*

There was a time, before Sarah came along to keep me going, when I was obsessed with Ida Gaze. It was like bursting for a wee, it was all I could think of. Then again, it didn't stop me brooding on Freda and what she hadn't told me, and all the things I never dared ask.

I told myself I wanted to know what possessed a schoolgirl to step into those waxy grey waters. It seemed such a marvellous, determined thing to do.

There were no Gazes in the phone book, none anywhere on the internet, apart from one on an American 1880 Census, which set me thinking of gangplanks up passenger ships and flags waving, and docks, and families being separated. I reckon the search for Ida Gaze sent me doolally, or stopped me going doolally. Sometimes I wasn't sure what was real or not.

All the time, when I was going about the town,

through the park with its bandstand, past the old cinema now an art gallery, I'd wonder if Ida had walked the same pavements I'd walked all these years without knowing, or was this or that shop here back then and might she have seen her reflection in its window? I'd look at everyone. I'm gazing for Gazes, I'd think and laugh. Anyone passing must have thought it was Cecily's time for the funny farm.

If only Freda had answered my questions when she was here, stabbing deftly at the telly with the remote when I showed any sign of trying to start up a conversation she didn't like the sound of. There was no getting Freda Voyle to do anything she didn't want to. I'd tell her time and again about rinsing her glass and putting it on the rack after she drank her water before bed, and every day there it was standing in the sink waiting to be washed. After she'd gone, I'd go down in the morning thinking of all the years I'd wasted fretting when now all I wanted was for the glass to be there once more, the faintest blur where her lips had been.

I made notes from the newspaper article on Ida's swim. I suppose I wanted as much as I could get in black and white. I went and stood outside her address, raising my eyes to the upstairs window of an ordinary-looking terrace in the hope I'd see an old girl looking out to sea. The Gaze family may not have had the fanciest house in town but they had a view you'd pay an excess for in a Bournemouth hotel. I knocked on the door. A family called Morris lived there and looked at me stupid when I mentioned Ida Gaze.

The time I spent out on the road, people must

have thought I couldn't afford to heat the house. I'd be back and forth past Ida's old home thinking how well she'd done for herself. I didn't reckon that when she lived there everything was handed her on a plate—and that made me like her more again. I even went and stood outside her school, still in business, and imagined her running from the door beneath a Bath stone arch marked *Girls*.

I'd walk the streets, seeing snippets of modern lives too. Once a plastic wheelbarrow was set out for the recycling and that took me back. Did children still have toy wheelbarrows? I'd have thought it would be inflatable castles or French lessons these days. Another time I heard the most awful row coming from an open upstairs window, effing this and that, and it almost made me glad to be alone, shuffling off down the street, until I got back to my big, old, empty house and thought it had once been ours. *Ours*. I thought about that word a lot.

People had obviously been talking. One day, one of the GPs from the health centre caught me outside the indoor swimming baths down on the seafront—now a pub doing Sunday roasts for £4.99—and told me, 'Yes, I did say that to some extent arthritis would be helped with exercise, but there's such a thing as going too far.'

For hours, Ida was in that water, trailed by a boat of men, whisky and cameras. She was carried aloft along the prom, given a bouquet and promised a commemorative plaque at the end of the pier.

I read all the tributes that came in for 'our Welsh heroine', as the paper was calling her. And then Ida disappeared.

One letter to the paper congratulating the girl said, *Your name will never be forgotten as being the first—and no doubt the youngest there will ever be—to conquer where so many have failed.*

I sent my own little letter in after that, saying about Ida Gaze and her achievements, and that people shouldn't forget something like that, and what about the council pulling its finger out for the plaque promised all those years ago. I told myself that's what it was for, but I did wonder who might read that letter. I suppose I was hoping Ida Gaze might still be around, like one of those old lady swimmers on the internet handing out trophies.

I had my mind set on giving the girl her due. One summer evening, not long after Sarah and the dog had left, I was standing on the terrace, thinking about getting the mower out for the lawn because I couldn't have the girl doing everything. 'I like helping,' she'd tell me. 'It keeps my mind occupied, and I love your company, Ceci, so please stop telling me to go and find some friends my own age.'

The neighbours were in the back—these gardens aren't the most private of places with their short stone walls—when a helicopter flew over our terrace.

It came so low I would have seen the roofs tremble, had I been able to turn my head quickly enough. As usual, I thought about what Freda would have come out with. 'Some bugger taken out to sea on a blow-up bed.' I could hear her saying it in the way she had that suggested everyone but her was a bit of an idiot.

She used to enjoy it out here in the summer, having a lime cordial with ice, or we'd sit eating ice-cream wafers with me admiring her hard work on the borders. Freda wore filthy gear for the garden. Saying that, she might be scruffy but she didn't half have something, the way she carried herself and her bone structure. Watching her standing somehow so elegant in the garden, I'd think of a scarecrow in a fashion shop window. For so long she was strong and bony and her skin was always so pale she couldn't take the sun. In the heat, she'd get a stain on her forehead where the black rim of her baseball cap had sweated onto her skin. That's a black mark for me, she'd say. You couldn't accuse Freda of always looking on the bright side.

That evening I could hear next door's kids jumping about on the trampoline they'd set up at the bottom of the garden, and their little fair heads stopped bouncing when the helicopter came over.

'Look, Dad,' the lad said. They're brother and sister, those two next door, yet I can't tell them apart—when did it get that little boys have hair as long as girls?—but I'd taken to the girl after her mother told me she'd slid her tiny cooked pizza onto her brother's chair at teatime.

'Air-sea rescue,' I heard someone say and looked across to see the children's father squinting through the empty trellis in my direction. 'Probably someone caught in a riptide.'

'Oh yes,' I replied. I knew a bit about those tides. 'All the more amazing to think a sixteen-year-old girl swam that Channel in 1928.'

I felt so proud of Ida Gaze, I can't tell you, earning her stripes like that by swimming to another country, when nowadays girls get fame and fortune from showing their backside on the box.

'Wasn't it an American who was the first woman to swim the Channel?' he asked, puzzled. I expect he liked to know these things in case he got on that millionaire's quiz on the telly. They value their money in this square.

I bit back saying it was the Bristol Channel, the one Ida swam, that was important, and then I heard my voice again.

'It may well have been an American who first swam the English Channel, but I doubt she was sixteen, nor that the tides were as double-crossing as they are in the Bristol Channel, this channel, the one I meant. Ida Gaze was the first person to swim twenty-two and a half miles in treacherous waters.'

'Blimey, you're well up on your local history,' he said. Then he gave me a look through the trellis as if to say he'd realised I was old enough to talk about such things as though they happened yesterday.

Later I looked it up, about the American swimming that other one, the English Channel. Gertrude Ederle was the first woman to swim the *English* Channel on 6 August 1926, in the record time of fourteen hours thirty-nine minutes. She was the daughter of a German immigrant who had a butcher's shop on Amsterdam Avenue in Manhattan, and her father told her she could bob her hair if she showed an interest in swimming.

I recognised one of the women I'd seen at the start, when I'd been looking for Ida Gaze. 'Hello, Ethel "Sunny" Lowry,' I said, 'the first *British* woman to swim the English Channel in 1933.' I saw they made a point of saying Ethel wore a red-cotton twopiece swimsuit, possibly the first bikini, long before the French one made its appearance in

194

1946. Ain't that something, the first bikini? Of course there was no mention of Ida Gaze.

I never found any more on her than the story in the library, and I started keeping records. The girl with black hair in the library helped me photocopy Ida's double-page spread and a man came round and set up an Epson printer so I could keep anything off the computer about female Channel swimmers. The piles of paper on my desk got higher and I'd be sitting there wishing I could read them. My eyes would settle on the words on the printer—*Epson. Exceed your vision*—though things were becoming so much less clear.

## 12

When they stepped into the lift, the attendant asked, 'Going up, madam?' and Ida replied, 'I should say.'

Their fingers found each other as they stared ahead.

'What are you looking for?' Frank asked her when they came out of the lift and the doors were pulled together behind them.

'What are *you* looking for?' she replied, giggling.

Polished parquet pathways led to little sample rooms. There were sofas and television sets, magazine racks, sideboards, cushions and beds. Frank was buying for his white three-storey stucco, Ida for her serviced two-bedroom apartment in a redbrick mansion block.

Ida laughed. 'We must want something,' she said.

The way the shop assistant was poised reminded her of the cover of a comic she had seen on a news-stand, a shaggy purple monster stalking an unwitting victim.

'Can I help?' the man asked.

'I do hope so,' she replied.

'The lady will choose for me,' Frank said as Ida walked to a display, sat on a sofa, and settled her heel in the pile of a black-and-white rug with a spiral that went round and round to a dead end.

'Come and sit down, Frankie,' she called.

'I'm not performing in a shop display,' he replied. 'This is your show.'

Frank laughed as the salesman watched her turn her head to and fro against the back of the sofa, as though she'd be careless enough to let her lipstick leave a mark.

The man turned to Frank and said, 'Would sir like to see the colour range in that particular design?'

Ida crossed her legs and put both hands on her knee, listening.

'Or perhaps your wife has a particular scheme in mind?'

'She's the boss,' Frank replied easily. He stared at Ida, who smiled graciously at both of them.

'I was thinking of something *moderne*.' She said it the French way, the proper way, with a curly-sounding ending.

'*Moderne*, an elegant choice if I may say so, madam,' he said, practically bowing at a lounge suite as boxy as a sofa in a Hollywood film.

'That's the one,' she replied. It was as though the make-believe room gave her confidence, as though she could act as she pleased and it wouldn't

196

matter if she said something stupid. Frank grinned.

'With regard to the colour scheme?' the man asked.

'I think we'll keep it monochrome.' Ida kept her eyes on Frank's. 'White walls, very Syrie Maugham, with the odd splash of colour, a Susie Cooper vase perhaps to bring a bit of sunshine to the room.'

'Certainly,' the man said. 'We have the sofa in black, in a velvet or a damask. Would either suit your taste?'

'Velvet, I think.' She looked back at Frank who shrugged and said, 'I'm just the wallet,' and the assistant laughed and seemed to relax a little after that.

As they walked, Ida got so much pleasure from hearing the click of her heels she kept going when she would have liked to stop.

When Frank pointed at an oak veneer sideboard decorated with stiff green napkins arranged like little teepees, and glasses upturned on a silver tray, she stroked a radio cabinet as curved as the fenders of a car.

When he ran his hand down floral curtains, saying his mother had something similar, she fingered drapes with a swirly black-and-white pattern and caressed a moderne vase with stepped sides.

Ida was enjoying herself so much she doubted she'd leave the shop.

'We see things so differently we could almost be married,' Frank whispered.

'You can get everything you ever need here,' she replied, in a loud voice because the man was coming and he was behaving as though they weren't *almost* anything. He was treating Frank like the bee's knees.

'That's an Eileen Gray design,' the assistant said, when Ida's gaze fell on a circular rug with two swirly parallel lines running across each other.

'I think I'll get that for my place,' she said.

'It looks like two paths crossing,' said Frank quietly. 'Perhaps I'll have one too.'

On more or less Ida's instruction, he ordered a three-piece suite, a black-and-white rug, a black Pel table with chrome trim, white cushions, and a black lacquered cocktail cabinet. She felt down just the once, when one of the pretend sitting rooms made her think of her mother's crocheted antimacassars on the armchair for the back of her father's brilliantined hair. In all the time she'd been in London, there'd been one letter from Mr Gaze. The main thrust of it was: *Your mother says she doesn't know what you're doing up there with the life you've been given*—and sending her new address seemed a cruelty all-round.

As they walked from the shop, Frank said, 'Are you coming for something to eat? Get some meat on those bones.'

'Haven't you spent enough, Frankie?'

'What if I was to let you be the judge of that?'

He'd had another pay rise. Frank was in a good mood. He was tall and fair and she was small and dark. They stepped out into the pale sunlight and stood between the blackened buildings like a couple on a wedding cake.

\*     \*     \*

Even though she was a grown-up working woman,

198

Ida couldn't help marvelling that she had her own place, all hers, with nobody saying, 'Don't use all the hot water,' or 'Look at all the lights on, it's like Blackpool Illuminations,' or, 'What sort of time do you call this?'

It must be because she missed the sea that the best thing of all was lying in the bath, putting her toe up the tap, half to see if she wouldn't be able to get it out again, sloshing about washing off the scent of smoke and perfume and the rest of the day. Her swim seemed so far away, yet she would remember the cheer that went up from Weston when she was sighted, a black speck of a swimmer, for the rest of her days.

Ida dropped her head under the water feeling it jelly around her. She couldn't imagine where she'd found the pluck to do it. Had she grown more fearful since coming to London? Though the corporate parties and drinking sessions were fun enough, this was one of her favourite times, being on her own with her own things.

But people had started talking, keeping on about when she would marry and whom. Last time she went for a meeting at Nicky Hobson's magazine, one of the senior men had asked, 'What's the matter with you then? Working and single with no sign of wanting children?' and then he'd given Nicky a look too.

Nicky had been so kind, rolling his eyes and telling her not to worry—that the old-stagers were a bunch of women—but it had shaken her, the idea that nothing really changed, that London was like being back in that town, people thinking things about you they had no business thinking when you might be perfectly happy as you were.

199

Freda hadn't been round since they'd fallen out, and Frank hadn't telephoned since they'd gone for a meal and she'd left the restaurant afterwards on her own in a cab. He'd wanted to go on to a hotel for drinks but Ida had felt suddenly scared, as though things were getting out of control, and she might do something she hadn't had time to properly think about. Waving at him from the rear window of the taxi, her body had wanted more, and then she found herself thinking of Freda; she missed her so much, the way she used to walk through the door and make life seem worth living. At least that's how it had been until things turned sour.

What was that? The bathwater, cooler now, was trembling. Ida rose up so it swung like a wave. The doorbell went again, vibrating through the flat like an alarm. Someone was standing on the second-floor parquet landing pressing the smart chrome bell outside her door for the first time!

Ida stood, dried herself quickly with a towel and grabbed her kimono which she tied as she went down the hall. Had Freda come round to see the new place after all? Ida had a box of cream horns in the kitchen and perhaps Freda would stay the night. There was a spare bedroom with a pink-satin bedspread and a bedside chair shaped like a cloud. Sometimes Ida stood at the door, admiring her extra room where she could go and lie or sit if she pleased.

The bell went again, sounding impatient. It had to be Freddie. Oh, she couldn't wait to see her and show her all she could share. It was lovely having your own place but lonely too, really, once you'd done all your things like having a bath and a bag of potato crisps.

But it wasn't Freda. Through the spyhole in the door, she saw the figure of a man in a suit with his hands in his pockets and looking down at his feet. She watched him raise his hand so it seemed like a giant distorted fist coming towards her as he rapped at the door.

'Ida,' she heard at the keyhole. 'It's me. Come on, let me in.'

I have two options, she thought. I can duck, crawl on all fours along the hall even though I know he can't see me, and go back into the bath, top it up, and feel safe and warm between its little walls. Or I can open the door to Frank Shankly.

His voice came again, low and desperate through the tiny hole in the door.

'I have to see you,' he said. 'Please.'

Standing in the hall, staring at but not seeing the invitation to Miranda's fancy dress fortieth birthday party propped on her new bird's-eye maple console table, Ida knew she was going to open up.

'Hold on,' she said, tightening her belt.

As she turned the handle and stood back, Ida felt an awful lovely sort of hopelessness, looking into Frank's face as he sized her up, from the nail varnish on her toes, her purple cotton kimono clinging to her damp skin, and her hair as wet as if she'd come from the sea.

I want him to come to me, she thought. I want him to touch me, to kiss me, to see me naked. I want someone to want me and I want to be with someone besides myself. Isn't that what I should want?

'Come here, little mermaid,' Frank said, and she

201

felt his arms around her, his lips on hers, his breath and his hands and the graze of his stubble on her cheek.

The weight of them together on the door made it slam shut loudly, which would probably get the old woman from across the landing complaining. She lived alone in a pink velvet turban secured with a diamanté brooch shaped like a Scottie dog, and was known as Mad Phyllis.

Ida had got where she wanted, she was Frank's equal now, and she was old enough to do this and more. She had done enough waiting and wondering and worrying, and she was tired of being on her own.

*       *       *

This was awful. Neither of them would look the other in the eye though each cast quick, resentful glances across the table.

There was a time when Freda and Ida fell laughing through the door of a Lyons Corner House, desperate to get their mouths round an Eccles cake and a strong cup of tea, to hear what each other had to say and to sit, especially at the start when they got to London, on the same side of the table, so they could hold hands in a safe, warm, secret way that made you feel things would turn out all right. Now look at them, Ida thought. Like enemies, not the best of friends. She half wished she hadn't stuck a note under Freda's door at the hospital suggesting a meeting like old times.

'Is there any point in us being friends if this is how we're going to be?' Ida asked. Between them on the white linen tablecloth stood a three-tier

202

rack of cakes that she'd said would be her treat. Neither had touched them and she could see Freda thinking it a waste of money and how Ida, obsessed with her figure, wouldn't eat anything anyway, and what was she eating because she was as thin as a lath, and then Freda would get her medical face on, talking about nutrients and fainting . . .

'Are we still friends then?' Freda asked, turning her saucer round and round so the tea slopped about to the rim of the cup. She'd come to collect Ida from her new apartment block and been quizzed by the man downstairs as though she had no right to be there. Then up in the flat, she'd not said much when Ida showed her round, and made Ida feel like a show-off when all she'd really been was excited about having a proper place of her own that she'd worked for, and wanting Freda to share the thrill.

'I don't think friends have to be mutually exclusive, do they, Freddie?' Ida said. 'You know, it's not just you and me, or you and Edna.'

Freda said, 'Or you and Frank or you and that man from the magazine. What's happened to him?' She looked Ida in the eye. 'Are they friends? Or are they something else? You talk about being friends, but don't friends tell each other things instead of going all silly every time something is mentioned they don't want to talk about?'

'What do you mean?' Nicky Hobson was old news. It was Frank Ida had given herself to, as though it was always supposed to have happened. That's how it seemed more than anything, not so much the do-or-die love she tried to recreate in adverts for British Bacon.

'You know full well what I mean,' Freda replied.

Really, she was tired of it all, and if she knew Ida as well as she thought, then she too would be fed up—bored even—with all this toing and froing and not getting on. That's what seemed so strange; they knew each other so well and yet they were behaving like strangers intent on loathing each other.

'How's that for not answering a question properly?' Ida said. 'You're not exactly the world's biggest talker when it comes to saying how you feel. Remember when you used to run off? Well this is the same sort of thing. You're always avoiding things, Freddie. You never really talk about things either.'

Freda bit her lip. She could say. Despite Edna. It could all come out about how she couldn't believe it had come to this. Freda could tell Ida how long she'd hoped they'd be friends and more, about all that knowing each other, the way she'd grown up waking in the morning and going to sleep at night revelling in Ida being there—to run *to*, not from— and how it felt to have someone who completely understood you, who knew what upset you, made you laugh, who remembered without trying that you didn't like rice pudding or people standing too close. And then there was your own happiness at knowing *them* so well, so you could do things to make them happy, and you cherished every moment with them. You felt high and as though life was more than all right when she reached for your hand, and oh, how greatly you despaired if anything happened to upset her, like her baby sister dying; and you wanted her to have everything she wanted in life, but for all this being friends and all the rest of it, the truth in the end (because that's probably what it was now, the end) was that her wanting things didn't include you.

She didn't want you in the way you wanted her. Even if they were the best of friends, and so close and loyal and all those things—and she, Freda, would have been glad for them to carry on that way, even if it was like living with a part of yourself behind bars—then that was all very well, but how, *how the hell* had it come to this, that they had nothing in common any more? It seemed that friendship wasn't always about the person so much as the way things happened in life to change you— or was it that the person never had been what you thought she was . . . or was she, Freda, someone else all along too? Because this was awful, had been for a long time now. Perhaps, perhaps it would have been better never to have met and known what it was to be so in l—

*Oh, for goodness' sake,* Freda told herself. *Pull yourself together, woman.*

'There's no point,' she said aloud. 'I can feel one way and you can feel another. Then things go one way and then the other, and . . .'

Ida's eyes seemed to wobble, as though she might cry.

'Look.' Freda stood. 'It's not that I mean we haven't ever been friends and that I don't care for you or want the best for you and all those sorts of things, it's just I don't know that we can be, or even are, friends any more. There's such a thing, isn't there, as growing apart.'

Ida looked up at her. Freda was grateful, at least, that she hadn't started glancing about, seeing other customers staring, and told Freda to sit back down. That's the kind of thing she might have expected from Ida these days.

She was taken aback when Ida stood too, in tears.

'Of course we're still friends, Freddie.'

But Freda was frightened and hurt. You couldn't get too involved in friendship or whatever it was, without things—yourself, really—getting out of control, and then you ended up not knowing what might happen next. And if you opened yourself up, it only meant people could get in or out as they pleased. And then you might end up upsetting them as well as yourself. She was thinking about Edna there.

Tears were running to nothing down Ida's cheeks. Freda stuck her hands in her pockets. She couldn't stay, she couldn't, she couldn't say any more. You had to make a decision and stick to it or else you'd be all over the show.

'I'm off,' Freda said. 'Don't let's drag this out in some fearsome tragedy of tagging about after each other when we both know the score.'

'What's the score?' Ida asked, taking up her handbag and following Freda through the tables so the two of them turned here and there, one after the other, in a frantic sort of dance, until they got to the door.

'I've had enough,' Freda said. She might cry too and then it would all come out and she'd show herself to be feeble and wretched and without any sort of hope.

'I—I can't stay,' she said. 'I've got to go.'

Shading her eyes with a hand, Ida watched Freda walk off down the fiercely light street, elbows sticking out from the pockets of her tight black jacket, her ponytail tied in a piece of grey

206

Petersham braid she'd pulled off the edge of an old cardigan, bouncing on the back of her head.

Ida couldn't think how this had happened, how Freda was walking off and she was watching, the two of them moving apart for good and neither stopping it. It was a strange, awful feeling, knowing you might never see someone again. And yet you had it in your power to run up behind them, tap them on the shoulder and say something light like, 'Let's not row, we're turning into my parents. If you're hurting, please tell me and we'll make things better.'

But Ida stayed where she was in the Lyons doorway, until a couple coming out made her move aside, and soon the people on the street had hidden Freda, even the top of her head which Ida saw for quite some time. Then she went back inside the café, which smelled of tea and smoke and scent, to settle up because all the while this had been going on, she'd been aware of a waitress in her little black-and-white uniform darting agitatedly about at the window, as though Ida would ever dream of running off without paying.

13

The day after Freda qualified, she was summoned to Matron's office, but she walked the corridor to her old ward with confidence and anticipation.

When she arrived, Matron was talking to a consultant but paused to wave her in, such a picture of welcoming bonhomie it was disconcerting, like having the devil tap at your window with a fairy's wand. Matron practically herded the doctor from the room so Freda would not be kept waiting.

'I have to tell you,' she said, gesturing Freda to a chair, 'that I have put your name forward for midwifery in the hope you will follow through on the wish you expressed to me that it is an area in which you would like to specialise. Furthermore, after seeing your grades and the reports made on you, a letter has been sent to your parents saying you are a credit to the hospital.'

'Thank you,' Freda said. It was strange, sitting down in Matron's company. I think it is the first time I have done so, she thought, baffled at her own bemusement and humility. She was a fully blown nurse, and back in that town, Aunt Sylvia was probably organising a wake. Not that any of that mattered any more.

'I'm very grateful, Matron, thank you,' she said. 'It is very much an area I'd like to go into.' Freda paused, not sure whether she should say what was on her mind.

'Out with it,' said Matron. 'Have I pushed you into something you'd rather not do?'

'No, no,' Freda replied. 'On the contrary, midwifery is very much up my stree . . . I mean exactly the area in which I'd like to specialise. No, what I'd like to say, or have been thinking about wanting to say to you is . . .'

Matron looked down at the small clock-face hanging from the braid clipped to her chest.

'I haven't got all day, Voyle,' she said, and when Freda looked at her eyes, she saw she was smiling.

'I suppose we all recall things that have an impact on us,' Freda said. 'You know, from right

208

back when we started.'

Matron nodded, her mouth a straight line. Her cheeks seemed redder than ever and a few wisps of grey hair showed from under her headdress.

Freda said, 'I remember you calling me in once and giving me a talking-to, and though in one way I deserved it, in another way, perhaps with how I was, always joking and messing about, I didn't deserve your attention and advice.'

Freda brushed at her forehead. She wore her hair in a fringe which fell into her eyes when she wasn't working, but on shift it was pinned back under her hat so all you saw was her pale skin and high cheekbones.

'I'd very much like to say thank you,' Freda said. 'That's what it is. That perhaps feeling as I do today, glad to have stuck with it and become qualified and made my parents proud—well, I think that it might be very much thanks to you.' She still hadn't learned not to be awkward with gratitude. Like love, Freda thought it made her seem weak and a tad simple.

'I'm glad to have been of assistance,' Matron said, and she stood from her chair. For a moment it felt as though the two women might embrace but then Matron said, 'Must get on.'

Freda nodded. As she opened the door to leave, Matron's voice was quiet. Outside on the ward, a nurse taking a patient's pulse turned to look.

'Aren't you going to click your heels for me?' she asked, so Freda obliged with a little salute and another shaky-voiced *thank you*.

As she walked under the cloisters of the quadrangle to meet Edna, Freda was thoughtful. She'd seen a moment that was a lifetime in

Matron, those seconds that showed the woman who had spent years assisting and saving, and then there were all the others after her that would do the same again. Matron lived on her own in the hospital grounds. Wasn't it odd, the way you could spend all that time with someone at work and still know so little about them? She'd never have dreamed Matron would have a sense of humour, nor that she, Freda, would be so bloody soft to get teary. She'd made a decision. Work was what she would focus on, not losing Ida.

*     *     *

Freda and Edna were having thick pea soup in the canteen from small white bowls. Around them, rows of heads went up and down and left and right at trestle tables, eating and chatting. There was the occasional burst of steam from the long stainless-steel counter at the front of the room.

'The other night something really strange happened,' Edna was telling her. 'Do you want to hear it?'

Freda nodded, though she was thinking that she might never see Ida again. Ida used to say things like that, that she had a strange story and did Freda want to hear it, all those years ago under the bedcover when Ida's baby sister was dying and Mrs Gaze would be downstairs, as they tried to block out that awful keening noise they could hear up in Ida's room.

Edna said, 'One of the new intake said she bumped into an old man in the corridor outside Ward Ten.'

Freda's attention was drawn back to Edna. It

210

was taking Freda time to get used to phrases like the new intake, now they were the senior girls, the proper nurses. Even though people thought she had a bossy voice and that others listened when she said something, Freda had never really felt in charge in her life. Underneath, it had always been Ida who made her feel whole, Ida who understood if she needed to run off because things became too much when people were on at her.

'This old man,' Edna said, 'didn't look well at all so this girl said to him, "Excuse me, sir, can I help you?" And he looked round and said, "Yes, please, I'm a little lost."'

'So anyway,' Edna went on. She enjoyed telling a story—Freda liked that about her, getting her mouth greedily round the words so that everything she said sounded thought-out and designed to please its listener. 'This old gent takes the girl's arm and she says to him, "Where am I taking you? Is it this one here, Ward Ten?" And he says, "Oh no, I must have strayed a bit. I'm on Ward Five."'

Freda nodded. She was trying to think what the ending might be, though she wouldn't show Edna she had guessed it. Freda always got the twists of films and crime books well before anyone else. She relished having a mind like that, one step ahead, though sometimes it made you cross with others for being slow.

Edna said, 'When they got to Ward Five, there was his empty bed so she settled him in, said goodbye, and waved at the door. He was a nice old gent and waved back, and she resolved to go in the next day and see him. But the next day, when she got there, the bed was being made up for another patient who was sitting in a chair waiting.

211

'"What happened to the old man in here yesterday?" this new girl asked. "What old man?" they said. "The old fellow in a navy dressing gown, who had white hair and slippers with the backs down." "Oh him," the nurse said back. "That was Mr Trimble. He died three weeks ago and we're only now filling his bed."'

Freda hadn't really been listening, but she said, 'Crikey, that's a tall tale,' and felt a shiver run through the whole of her body. Sometimes she enjoyed complaining how irritating life could be, but how easily it might slip away too, so that all you became was the ghost of a person on a corridor looking for the way back to where you had come from.

*          *          *

Edna didn't knock when she came into Freda's room that night. She'd been talking about the two of them getting rooms together now they were moving out of hospital quarters. Lots of girls do it, Edna had said. She was quite go-ahead, Edna, if she wanted something—but then Freda wouldn't do anything she didn't want to.

Edna slipped in, wearing a rosebud-print nightdress with her dark arms bare in the warm night air. The curtain was drawn back at the window so the room was filled and not filled with the white-black shimmer of a full summer moon. The door clicked closed.

She knew Freda was awake and watching her as she came to stand at the side of her bed.

'Are you ready?' Edna asked.

Freda nodded. Her naked body lay tense under

212

a single, clean white sheet, her long limbs still with expectation and desire. She watched Edna cross her arms to lift her nightdress up her body and head. In the moment that Edna couldn't see her looking, as the light tube of material covered her face, Freda stared at Edna's body, at the curves of her bosom and hips, the slight swelling of her belly and insides of her thighs.

'Move over,' Edna whispered, as Freda lay, looking up at her, when she came to the bed. Edna smiled. Freda didn't. She went further into the bed, on her side, so her bare shoulder blades touched the cool of the wall.

'Lie flat,' Edna whispered. 'On your back.'

Freda closed her eyes as Edna straddled her. Through the open window came the sound of footsteps louder then quieter on the quadrangle path outside. Ida could never love me this way, Freda thought, and Edna is the girl I want.

The space around her was hotter again. She felt the small heaviness of Edna's breasts as she bent to kiss her. Freda felt suddenly awkward and guilty and avid. She tried thinking urgently of something to say. This was too easy, the way Edna was taking away her memories of Ida, as though Ida was being carried away on the tide.

Freda heard her own voice sound harsh and stupid in the room.

'You're not going to ask me to do Matron on about the casters, are you?' she said.

But Edna shook her head so the tips of the black bob she'd been told to tie back that first day stuck to each side of her mouth. She had the look of a woman on a route and she didn't want to turn back.

213

'No, Freda,' she said, 'I have something else on my mind altogether.' And then, as Edna's lips came towards her again, and she felt the warm, urgent pressure of her breath, Freda closed her eyes.

The moon seemed to shine directly in at them, as though something that looked over the vastness of the world had chosen to focus its attentions on a small first-floor room in London where a momentous event was taking place.

Afterwards, when Freda lay beside Edna, she felt more whole or, better again, half of a whole. She was different, new, daunted but surer. There seemed less of a fault line through her now that people could pick at to make her moody and unsure.

Night after night, they couldn't get enough of each other. They were greedy and happy and qualified, but while things had wound down, in terms of studying and working into the night to be sure you passed your exams and didn't mess up on the practicals on the wards, the great machine of war was said to be cranking up.

War or no war coming—and the word was that one *was* on its way—you had to make a life for yourself. Freda saw that, when one day a hospital bed had someone alive in it, and the next they were dead.

## 14

Ida looked at the phone on her desk. The worst bit, she told herself, would be asking Stella on reception to put her through to the hospital. She'd wonder what it was about and it would go all round the office. Or she might listen in—Ida was sure the constant clicks weren't a quirk of the local telephone exchange—and then if she did get through to Freda and Freda wouldn't talk to her, that would be awful. Ida felt herself blush with shame, that here she was worrying what Stella would think when the important thing was just getting through to Freda. She hadn't spoken to her or seen her in ages. The need to get back in touch with her had come over Ida suddenly in the office.

Ida wondered if she should nip across the road to the hotel and call from one of the booths in reception, but that wasn't any less private than here really. In any case, she couldn't wait.

She picked up the phone, waited to be connected, and when a woman's voice announced the name of the hospital—as though Ida might be calling about an accident or an emergency—she remembered just what an important job Freda was doing, how perhaps she ought not to disturb her, and almost put the phone down.

'Hello, I'm sorry to trouble you,' she said, 'but this is terribly urgent.'

Ida worried over her words. How she was speaking reminded her of the way, in those last days with Freda, she had felt as though Freda thought she was making a fuss about things, shrieking and obsessing about trivial matters. Ida felt regret at the way she had been, spoiling everything with wanting to get on, and not seeing what was truly important.

'Speak,' said a female voice. 'Give me the details.'

'Well . . .' Ida didn't know how to say she'd lost contact with her best friend and needed to get back in touch, but nor could she say, 'This is a long story . . .' and jabber on to fill space as she'd done for so long.

'It's not urgent in that way, you know, a medical emergency, but I was just trying to track someone down who works at the hospital. Freda Voyle, her name is.' Ida paused. 'Do you know her?' she asked.

'Freda Voyle?' Ida imagined the woman in earphones sitting at a switchboard, in a room with an electric heater with all four bars on, running through the faceless uniforms that strode up and down endless dark corridors or tended the sick in row upon row of beds.

She ran her wedding ring up and down her finger, wondering what Freda would say about her having married. You'd think it would make you feel a proper sort of person to have found someone to love, who said they loved you back, and then everyone would know you were two people who felt the same way when you wed and got on in life, but Ida didn't feel whole. She felt empty.

'Yes,' Ida said. 'Freda Voyle.' Her voice broke, like wireless interference, with hope. She had to pull herself together.

'Everyone knows Sister Voyle,' the woman replied. 'But she's left, I'm afraid. Just had a massive send-off with party hats and everything.'

'Left? Do you know where she's gone?' Ida was torn between shock and hope. People remembered Freda.

'Hold on a sec.' Tinny chatter she couldn't catch

216

came down the line. Ida closed her eyes and pictured Freda's face, her grey eyes flecked with yellow and that mouth that stretched across her face when she smiled.

'You sound like a nice girl,' she heard the woman say. 'I'm sure Sister Voyle won't mind me telling you her new place.'

The jury's out on both counts, Ida thought, picking up a pen, but she couldn't write as the woman gave her the address of the maternity clinic where Freda worked. It was in one of the best areas of London, Ida couldn't help noticing. She hoped Freda was happy and successful, and wondered if she might miss or think of her too, and what would happen when she got in touch, which she would, soon enough. Most definitely.

'We all miss her,' the woman was saying. 'Give her our best.'

Ida replaced the receiver in its cradle. Now she didn't need to speak or put on a show she spread her hands over her face and brushed the tips of her fingers along her eyelids. If anyone came up the stairs now, they would find her crying.

She felt worked up and let down, as though she had opened a door, braced to see the face and the body and the smile of the only person she had ever truly loved, and all there had been was a black oblong of space. Just a place with nothing there at all, so that if you stepped forward through the doorway, all that would happen is you would fall. Freda hadn't bothered to tell her she was moving—why would she when they weren't in touch?—but that detail set Ida back terribly.

\*        \*        \*

217

It must be something that happened as you got older, being mature enough to acknowledge mistakes you had made and not pretend to yourself they were other people's fault, nor that things like that didn't really matter.

Ida did enough of the superficial stuff at work, putting her mind to ways of making people want things they didn't really need, when what really mattered in life, when it came down to it, were things like kindness and truth and loyalty and friendship.

Around her, a party at Frank's boss's house was in full swing—one of those grand affairs determined on showing that war wasn't coming and it was business as usual—but Ida was sitting alone, drunkenly thinking how stupid she had been.

She had married the wrong man. Frank Shankly might have loved her once, but now he loved other women. He was blatant about it, across the room now, with his arm round a young blonde, the sister of Nicholas Hobson. Ida shouldn't have married at all, actually, she'd have managed better on her own—but the biggest error Ida Gaze had made, one that made her flush with remorse and sadness and despair when she thought of it, was losing touch with Freda Voyle.

Ida lifted her glass at Miranda Drabble who was talking to Sir Neville by the grand piano, knocked back the last of a vodka martini, and took up another from a proffered tray. Drink was something she hadn't messed up. She was quite good at drinking. She was still good at her job too. Sir Neville was taking her to America to give a talk on the Female Perspective in Advertising. Onwards and upwards and all that. Ida raised her new glass at the waiter. She really would be flying as high as Amelia Earhart.

'Ida, my favourite girl! Fancy seeing you here.'

She looked up slowly. The room had started spinning some time ago and the sound of the woman playing bright little tunes on the piano was going right through her. Now she didn't need to worry about money, or thinking she had to do this or that—like marrying or never having chipped nail varnish or smiling at policemen—Ida spent hours thinking about Freda.

'I do believe you're as squiffy as I am.' It was Nicholas Hobson.

'Don't come to me for help,' she replied. 'I'm sorry I can't do anything about him. I stopped trying a long time ago.'

Fond as she was of Nicky, she wanted to think about Freda.

He gave a scowl-smile after looking back at his sister. Annabel Hobson was Frank's type, happy to keep her head to one side.

'When power goes to a man's head,' Nicky said, 'the fool within him emerges. I stopped trying to tell my little sister about bastards a long time ago, but it seems they have a certain appeal.'

Ida wasn't listening. She was thinking about the contrast between how things used to be with Freda, and how they were now with Frank, who came home from the office in the early hours and went straight to the bathroom before sleeping in a separate bed. He said it was so he didn't wake her. Ida wasn't daft, though she couldn't tell you which young female reporter was current flavour of the week. From what got back to her, there were as many ex-flames of Frank Shankly as there were editions of his papers. Frank was in charge of the whole damn lot of them now.

Ida said, 'I chose the wrong one.'

'Easily done,' Nicky said. 'I imagine there's plenty of them—wrong ones, I mean. Budge up.'

Nicky was such a sweetheart, always talking her up, while Frank made her feel so wanting.

'You know,' Ida said, as he sat beside her on the velvet chaise longue she was smoothing, 'I don't think you can ever really tell with people, how they truly are.' Like Miranda, she thought, who could seem so sharp and funny but who was lonely and desperate for another baby, though now she was too old for even hope.

'At least *I* can't,' Ida went on. 'And life too—you know, all this,' she swung her arm round, 'seeming so glamorous and fun and all that, and yet it's a bit empty really, isn't it? Once you take away the dresses and the chandeliers and money and homes by the coast, if you haven't got something else, perhaps a sort of mission in life, like tending the sick, or someone else, someone you love more than anything else . . .'

'You sound as if you need to get away for a bit,' Nicky said gently.

'I do,' Ida replied. 'You're right. But I get away and what have I got? That's my point. I *have* nothing away from all this. I've thrown everything good away.'

Nicky turned to her. 'I'm serious,' he said. 'I've been worried about you for a while, sitting in meetings staring into space. It's not your usual style.'

'Sorry.' She didn't think she could help the way she was any more. Not even a visit to dear Aunt Bess, which she never seemed to get round to. 'I must be an awful bore.'

'You've never bored me, Ida, but I've always thought I might rather bore you.' Her head wobbled imperceptibly as she thought, He's so nice—why didn't I see that before?

Nicky pulled back to look at her and smiled. He had light eyes. He was handsome in a quiet, slender way.

'Oh, Nicky, I think I've had enough of all of it,' she said. 'Persuading clients I know what I'm talking about when I don't know myself any more. All that game-playing to make people think this or that.'

He took hold of her fingers the way Freda once did. Ida looked down at their hands on her lap. She was wearing a purple satin dress and shoes to match.

'You're not a game-player, are you?' she said. 'I had a friend once who was most certainly not a game-player. In fact, she always said exactly what she thought.'

Nicky listened. He'd always done that, heard her out. She couldn't help talking about Freda. The two of them were drunk in any case.

Ida said, 'At least I think she did—say exactly what she thought, that is. I wish I'd never lost touch with her. She never took any rubbish from anyone and you knew where you were with her.'

Nicky said, 'I suppose you're aware there used to be a bit of that sort of talk about you, but,' he rotated his hand like the introduction to a music-hall act and bowed slightly, 'Yours truly put them

221

straight.'

'Thank you, Nicky, you've always stuck up for me. And she always stood up for me too.'

Freda had always been there, when others doubted, coming round the corner saying, 'Yes, Ida *will* swim the Channel,' in that way she had of sounding as though all she said was right.

'I had to do it then, for her as much as for myself,' Ida said now, laughing. 'Yes, you couldn't tell her anything, but then later, you'd sort of know it had sunk in. She came to London with me, did you know, even though . . . even though she . . . and then I . . .'

'Don't let people get you down, Ida,' Nicky said. 'Just because a woman hasn't children and is a bit of a worker, people seem to think there must be something a bit funny about her, but you're good at what you do. The best there is, in fact.'

How did it happen? That people missed each other when they were right under each other's noses?

'And then,' Ida said, 'then, she went a bit funny with me, sort of not saying everything there was to say. She seemed to be holding back and I think she thought I was holding things back too.'

They had both started to annoy each other, Ida saw that now. The two of them had realised that life changed, and that they had to make something of themselves, aside from being the best of friends to each other.

'Girls holding back?' Nicky said. 'You'll get those old buffers going again.'

'It was my fault, wanting to get on in a job and her stories from work making me feel low. She was a nurse, still is—a Sister now. She's doing terribly well, but I never see her. I didn't even know she had changed hospitals. To think I wouldn't have known where to find her. I really do think a terrible lot of her, after all this time, and she really was the most wonderful friend and sort of got inside me and never left and . . . I've never really met anyone like her. She's the only . . .'

Frank was on the other side of the room, lifting his head back like a whinnying horse, offering his throat to Nicky's sister. She could hear her husband's confident, expectant laughter. Nicky saw her seeing him.

'In the interests of all parties,' he said, 'I feel obliged to take you away from all this. Fancy a breather?'

She nodded and rose shakily from her chair. Ida felt old and exhausted and lonely and full of regrets and wonderings at what might have been. She'd had far, far too much to drink but she was glad of the company and she could do with a breath of fresh air, even if it was a bit chilly for spring. It would be like dropping back into the water.

## 15

In the new hospital, grand women came up the curved steps from vast cars, but they were all the same once they took off their fancy clothes and put on a hospital gown ready to be wheeled to theatre to bring a new life into the world.

Freda's long legs hurried down the steps, two at a time, worried she had kept Edna waiting. A new mother-to-be had come in, the wife of the chief executive of an oil company, and she would only deal with Freda. That tall one with the air of authority, she'd said, and the nurse who'd come to fetch her had muttered it was lucky Matron was off shift. Freda knew how to handle Matron. She had only to walk in the room and Matron was putty in her hands.

Downstairs in the black-and-white tiled foyer, the girl on reception gave Freda a wave and Edna stood from the row of chairs that ran along the wall.

'Freda!' she said loudly. They both had strong voices. On a Sunday in summer, if Edna could get Freda singing to the wireless out on the precarious cast-iron balcony at her flat, London seemed terribly quiet by comparison.

'Sorry about that, Ed,' Freda said. The patient who'd kept her had high blood pressure which might cause problems for the baby. Freda had sat with her for fourteen hours on the trot. 'I won't stay out long.'

The moment they stepped outside, Edna pulled on her hand. The June sun was warm on their faces.

'I've missed you terribly, Fred. Come on, let's be brave and not care what people think. Let's have a kiss on the steps.'

'I'm all for that,' Freda replied, 'not caring what people think.'

But as Edna, her eyes closed, leaned up to kiss her, Freda looked about and nearly stalled from their lips meeting. There it was, the figure in the park opposite she'd seen yesterday from the upstairs window, getting up from the bench

224

between two palm trees, one hand to a small straw hat.

'What are you looking at, Fred?' Edna asked, as their mouths drew apart. 'They say someone doesn't love you if they don't close their eyes when they kiss you.'

Freda tried to grin but being false didn't suit her. Both halves of her felt disloyal. She couldn't look up—she wouldn't. If she'd been on her own, Freda might just have gone over there, crossed the road quickly, and said something like, 'Hello, how are you?' Just to show she still thought of her, that someone didn't go from your life just like that. But Edna was here and she kissed her forehead.

'I wouldn't listen to what "they" say,' Freda said. '"They" have always had rather too much to say for themselves. Come on.'

The two women walked quickly down the steps, close but not holding hands, Freda just ahead, setting the pace along the pavement. She couldn't stop, could she, not with Edna there.

'My mother has written to say their house is finished, right on the seafront,' Edna said. 'Though she finds it far colder than India, I think she's glad to be back, getting rid of Father each day to Millbank. They've invited us for a break—they've heard all about you. There's a swimming pool. Will you come, Fred? It might be such fun.'

'That sounds like home—I mean fun, great fun.'

Freda told herself not to look round, she wouldn't, that was all over and done with, a part of her life she wouldn't give back but wouldn't want back either. She couldn't do it to herself or Edna, let those feelings in.

'What is it, Fred? What's wrong?' Edna asked

225

when Freda stopped and turned at the sound of a car horn—her nurse's instinct, and fear too—to see a man with a briefcase raising his hand at a departing car.

Edna touched her arm. 'You're worried about leaving that woman, aren't you? Do you want to go back?'

But the figure had gone, and feeling Edna's hand on hers, hearing the love in her voice, Freda felt the guilt then relief and gratitude of her decision to push away what might bring pain. She crooked her arm, inviting Edna to put her arm through hers.

'No,' she said, 'no, I'm not worried about the woman and I'm not going back.'

Freda felt Edna's fiercely loving little elbow against her side. However much Freda's heart cracked, she meant it to stay in one piece.

*     *     *

Sometimes from nowhere something Ida had said, or a time they'd been together, would come into Freda's head.

It could be the two of them building wigwams of driftwood on the beach to burn with flames as orange as marigolds late into the night, or sitting under the graveyard yew tree counting out grass seeds they'd picked off their cardigans, or splashing their feet in the canal; and then Freda would feel low and quiet, as though nothing might ever seem worth much again.

But then Edna would come and kiss her neck, and she'd see that though Ida had meant everything to her, that was then and this was now.

Another war might be coming, and if anything taught you the need to keep up and on, then war was it. Freda knew that. She'd heard the older nurses talk of terrible injuries.

'Do you think there'll be another war, Ed?' she asked. Fred and Ed, that's how they were known to their small circle of friends. Freda was sitting at the table in her flat. She liked to keep her own notes on patients or treatments and techniques she'd read about coming over from America. Freda knew as much about Caesarean sections as the doctors, probably more in some cases.

'I don't really know,' Edna said, looking up from her nature magazine. 'We'll have to see what the men who start them have to say.'

Later, they were going for a meal with four others in an Italian restaurant that was down in a basement and had red tablecloths and candles dripping down empty green wine bottles. Edna was more sociable than Freda, who preferred it just being the two of them. Her favourite part of any outing was coming home, to either of their flats. In time, they might move in together, but not just yet. Freda had said so.

Edna rolled off the bed and came to stand behind Freda. She put her arms around her.

'I suppose,' she said, 'you have to think along the lines of . . . well, at least there hasn't been a war yet.'

And it happened again, as Freda looked at the white wallpaper in front of her, Ida coming into her head—the sun on Ida's hair as they ran to their tree in the blackberry field, or the two of them sitting in the park's navy and cream bandstand watching a lone gull bobbing on a barrel in the sea.

At least Ida isn't dead, Freda thought to herself. She could have been killed in a war, and Edna is right, at least there hasn't been another war yet. And here Edna is, with me, the two of us obliged to make the most of life.

Edna said, 'I believe you always have to think, however bad things seem, that you are always one up from something worse again. It's like there used to be a woman living in our street who'd had polio as a child, and she only had half of one of her legs. My mother used to say we should count ourselves lucky, that at least we had two arms and legs and eyes, that type of thing. I'm ashamed to say that my brother and I used to laugh about it, and it became a sort of family joke—"at least you've got two legs" et cetera—but I see what Mother meant now. It's a way of getting through life if you're not one of those who always feels up.'

Edna put her hand around Freda's long fingers, which had grown drier with being endlessly washed. Freda was silent but Edna knew she was listening hard, her hand as still as anything on the table. Freda's dog, Banjo, had not long died, and Edna knew she was trying to hide how much that hurt.

'I think that might be why I wanted to become a nurse, seeing that poor woman, and hearing my mother say it was a damn shame the doctors hadn't been able to do something about it,' Edna said.

'I had a similar thing.' Freda spoke slowly for her. 'A family I knew with a baby who died, not just the poor child, but the pain it caused them for years after.'

'You do have to live in hope, don't you, Fred? That things will get better and not worse. I mean, not just at work because there'd be no point going to the hospital if you thought you couldn't make things better, would there? But also in life—you know, going about the place and being with people and so on.'

'Sometimes I wonder if I have the energy though,' Freda replied. 'You know, to keep geeing myself up into thinking at least it isn't this and at least it isn't that.' She turned back to Edna. 'But I know what you mean. I love you for that.'

'Is that all you love me for?' said Edna, embracing her. 'There's nothing else?'

Freda felt the weight of Edna fall gently on top of her and the violet smell of her perfume as she nuzzled down into Freda's neck.

'Oh, there may be one or two other things,' Freda replied. She should count herself lucky. You could be in a low mood and then in an instant, you'd feel such a silky shot of pleasure through you, as though if this moment lasted for even a second more, you wouldn't have done too badly when it came to being happy.

*     *     *

That evening, arm in arm, they passed a news-seller shouting 'AMELIA EARHART MISS-ING!' Edna wanted to stop and buy a paper, but Freda said to keep on. You had to concentrate on what there was, not what there wasn't, otherwise life became a gap it was impossible to fill.

All the same, when a blast of air from the open door at the top of the basement restaurant's steps blew out the candle on their table, Freda caught Edna watching her, and she had to roll her eyes as though she was there with them, instead of thinking of Ida and how she was taking Amelia going down in the sea.

## 16

Ida couldn't pass a news-stand without looking at the headlines in the hope of seeing that Amelia Earhart had been found. She didn't want to miss the train but she stopped as usual, at the stand near the station.

Amelia had been missing for four months since disappearing over the sea on the last leg of her round-the-world flight. People talked about sharks in the Pacific, but you couldn't give up hope. All those years before, when Ida was training for her swim and Amelia had landed in the water, nobody had written her off then. She might have made it to an island this time.

As Ida read the words ROOSEVELT WARNS THE WORLD, a shoeshine boy blew a pink bubble of gum which grew and grew. The likelihood of war was one of Frank's favourite subjects. She walked on, into the tunnel, and the boy wiped a filthy hand across his mouth when the bubble burst.

The station was a sooty, oily place with great cast-iron arches above your head, and every so often a hoot or rush of steam went right through you. A couple stood by a pillar, cleaving to each other. A woman on a bench watched them, clutching the claws of her stole.

When Ida pulled her coat to her, the gentle spikes of fur on the collar brushed against her

230

cheeks. It was rust-coloured, expensive. She could afford it, the money she was earning. On her hands she wore the finest kid gloves, cream with black silk bows.

Standing at the end of the platform, Ida stared at the tracks watching for movement. She always dipped into her shopping for a thumbful of something if she saw mice running along the rails in the Underground—how else did they survive down there?—but today she had nothing to give. As she made her way to the train, she was holding a little case made of crocodile skin from a place in the Burlington Arcade.

Her father had said he'd be waiting. The sky was low when the train drew into the town after a journey through patchworks of bare, prickly fields and houses looking lonely in the middle of nowhere. With a mix of dread and anticipation, Ida wondered if he would be compos mentis, and what they'd look like to each other after all this time. What she was after was a new start, she'd tell them that.

'Hello, Father!' Ida called, when she saw him in the square next to the ticket office, standing in a tweed jacket and a trilby with an elbow hitched onto the roof of a car.

A girl she'd been to school with walked towards her in a purple dress and jacket, but Ida couldn't remember her name. She smiled, but the woman was looking beyond her and when Ida turned she saw a man in a suit waving back.

'Couldn't be sure I'd recognise you,' Mr Gaze said, looking her up and down. 'What's the royal visit in aid of then?'

He took her case and Ida thanked him.

'How's Mother?' she asked in the car.

'The same as ever,' Mr Gaze replied, as they drove off. Like the town, everything about him seemed smaller, apart from his nose.

In the sitting room, her mother looked up from her chair when Ida walked through the door.

'It is you, is it?' she said. 'For a moment, I wondered who he was bringing back.'

'Don't get up,' Ida replied, putting her case on the dark stained floorboards. There was the old mink-and-blue-patterned velour three-piece suite and the chair in the bay with legs of barley-twist oak. On the small round table by the fireplace stood a lamp with a painted oriental scene on its base, and the photograph of Maud in a black frame with crosses at each corner.

'What brings you here then?' Mrs Gaze asked. 'We didn't think we'd see you again.'

'How are things?' Ida asked, and then to fill the silence she told her mother how well she was doing at work.

'People say my boss, Sir Neville, thinks the world of me.'

Mrs Gaze stared at Ida's middle. She can't look me in the eye, her own daughter, Ida thought.

'I've got my own secretary called Stella who used to work on reception and runs to fetch us snacks from the Milk Bar round the corner. And I'll be going to America.' Ida clasped her hands in her lap. 'At some point.'

'America seems to think there's a war on its way,' Mr Gaze said. 'What is it you do for a living exactly?'

'I think up ways of making people want, Father. Like holidays or brands of tea or cars. I've been

232

working on the Morris Eight account. What do you say to that?'

'No future in it,' Mr Gaze replied. 'The only thing I can see people wanting is peace.'

On the road outside, a horse passed, its hooves like frenzied, hollow clapping that took ages to fade. Her parents weren't really people you could talk to, not like Stella's mother, say, who sometimes popped into the office with treats from the haberdashery department in Peter Jones because Stella was like Aunt Bess for making her own clothes.

'How's Aunt Bess?' Ida asked. She'd been meaning to get in touch. The last time she'd sent Bess fine eats from Harrods in a box tied with green ribbon and had a long letter back saying *Thank you and stop spending your money on me and when are you starting a family for me to come up there and play nanny.*

'Funny woman,' Ida's mother said. 'We stopped having much to do with her a long time ago.'

Mr Gaze sat forward, his hands dangling between his legs, looking at his wife.

'What's that Freda Voyle doing?' Mrs Gaze said.

'Freda's fine,' she replied. 'Doing very well indeed.'

Her mother's expression was the same as when Ida used to talk of swimming the Channel or becoming a reporter or going to London.

'How long are you staying for?' her father asked.

'Probably just the one night.' Ida pulled her coat to her. 'If you'll have me.'

The following morning, as she passed the chemist's, Ida raised her hand to Mrs Gates looking out of the window, but the old woman turned away and put her fingers to her neck as though she'd cricked it. In the newsagent's, where Freda used to buy their sweets, Ida stocked up on Peace Babies, gobstoppers, dolly mixtures, liquorice twists, and the strips of sugared coconut the two of them would share, both of them biting an end and chewing to the centre until their mouths met.

'I know I'm too old for this sort of thing,' Ida told the woman behind the counter, who was watching her load small brown bags into the pockets of her coat, 'but I've got a sudden craving.'

'I dare say,' the woman replied, before turning her back to move one of the glass jars a smidgen so it stood in perfect line with the rest.

What a mistake coming back had been, Ida thought as she walked over the railway bridge. She had stayed awake all night in her old room and in the morning Mrs Gaze had stood in silence at the front door as Ida walked off down the path, not long after her father had left for his garage. Never mind not being like other people's parents, her parents weren't like other people.

She went down the cobbled slope to the ticket office with her head down and the same low grey sky above. There was nothing more to be said. She hadn't even told them she'd married. Ida was leaving the sly unkindness of this small town behind. She was going back to London to make a new life.

*       *       *

Ida was trying to think how best to tell her. She hadn't seen her in such a long time and Freda

234

would be upset, she didn't doubt it. In the past, Ida had thought about herself too much and now there was this to think about and Freda as well. Especially Freda. She hadn't done enough of that.

Where did she start? With the solution or the problem? Ida thought perhaps the solution, but then she saw it wouldn't make sense without the problem, but she wanted Freda to know she had everything sorted out. She didn't want her to think she was running to her just because things had gone wrong in her life.

The city's trees were twiggy and sombre in the smoky, sharp winter air. Ida was walking to Freda's hospital, eating fairy chips from her pocket, cramming them into her mouth and chewing on the pink and white sugary strips. In the other hand she held her little crocodile case. She couldn't stay in that flat another night. It was going back home to her parents who hadn't wanted her there that did it, seeing the places she and Freda might never go to again.

She would start with what had happened with Nicky Hobson and how she'd gone to his house in a lovely quiet square in London and just as she'd got to the door, she couldn't do it. She couldn't tell him the news. They'd both been half-seas-over. It was something she had to deal with herself, that's what it was. Saying anything would show her to be nothing better than a drunk.

Ida felt a twinge, like being snipped at with scissors, and put a hand to her belly.

She would explain to Freda how gradual everything was for a while. The spiteful tightening of her skirt, then her jacket not buttoning up and then how sudden it was—going to see that doctor in his grand offices with a nameplate outside saying *Qualified Physician*, and Ida lying on cold green leather looking at the watercolour battle scene over the fireplace when he told her the news and then her almost running out down the stairs.

She would never have done what he suggested, not with what had happened to Maudie, her baby sister. You couldn't stamp on a life trying to be born. She had to follow through with it even if there was no coming to terms with the unbelievable bad luck of the whole thing. Just that once, at the bottom of the garden, at that do with Nicky.

Another jab, something not quite right, like waking in the night, walking in the dark and imagining a step on the stairs when there wasn't one. Ida felt, in one invisible footfall, far less happy.

She thought of Miranda turning up at her flat and sitting on the bed saying nothing about the state of the place, just looking round her feet as though she was on a desert island getting smaller by the second with water lapping at her toes. Ida knew how she felt. There was so much stuff— including the sweetest, tiniest little white lace outfit she hadn't been able to resist in a shop window—that there wasn't room to move.

'I know,' Miranda had said, all eye sockets and jawbone, and Ida had felt heavier again, but somehow hollow too, as though something was missing as well as being in place. 'I know, you know.'

'What am I to do, Mira?' Ida had asked.

'Who'd have thought you were playing away with Nicky Hobson?' Miranda replied. 'You didn't

236

think people wouldn't see you, did you?'

'We didn't really mean to,' Ida said, and Miranda had laughed and replied, 'Of course you didn't, Iddy.'

How could people be so hurtful? Ida thought of a sheet of paper ripping and the pain as if it were her own skin. It was so hard to bear.

'But I didn't,' she'd said, and the look Miranda had given her—how could she tell Freda this—the kind of look a judge would give a guilty criminal insisting on his innocence.

There weren't many cars now and the street was quieter. It was getting dark. Ida told herself to walk straight and to think straight. Night came quickly in November. Winter was here. Christmas was coming.

She stopped to pull a paper bag of gobstoppers from the small pocket of her coat—she couldn't stop stuffing children's sweets—and brushed at a trail of icing sugar spilled down her coat. It was sticky on her clammy hand.

Should she tell Freda how everyone was talking about them –Ida and Nicky?

'You know London is a village,' Miranda had said. 'What are you going to do?'

And then she'd patted the bed, queerly really, and told Ida to come and sit with her, and not to worry because she would help.

'I know a doctor,' she'd said, 'who will make sure everything is all right.'

Ida had stood away from the bed then, backing away so she trod against one of the shoes all higgledy-piggledy against the wall, shouting, 'No, no, no!' because she'd been thinking of Maudie and how her little curly hands used to stretch towards her and how you couldn't . . .

Oh my God. She clutched at her belly—or was it her head? The agony was beyond bearing, like being chopped with an axe. A man under a street-lamp was looking at her as though she was mad. She couldn't tell if he was disgusted or concerned. She went to speak, turned away. London was no different to that small town, people always looking with something they didn't say.

'I don't want to see anyone,' she'd told Miranda.

'No, I don't mean that,' she replied. 'I've got a plan for us, Iddy. A plan so that everything is all right.'

Ida was almost there now, at Freda's hospital, the same place Miranda Drabble had mentioned. Oh Freda, how would she take this news when for so long she had warned her . . . and Ida hadn't listened. She hadn't listened.

Walking on, she felt a step away from what was happening, trying to catch up. It was as though she was there but not there, as though she was watching herself being watched.

Miranda had said about her husband, how he was always up North with his rotten hosiery factory and how he spoke like a bumpkin but had money so he was good for that but nothing else. That she rarely saw him, but when she did she had to strap him to the bed and hold on tight, but nothing had happened, aside from once—but that hadn't turned out because the baby had d—

And Ida, seeing her distress, had come to sit on the bed with her and said, 'Don't get upset, Mira, please don't get upset.'

'Died,' she'd said and Ida was sad because Miranda was sad, and Miranda was usually so happy and full of fun—apart from when she'd lie in the bath crying about her baby and get Ida to come and fill her glass with champagne.

And then Miranda had seemed to turn a bit crafty when she said, 'I know how much you don't like being talked about. And I know everyone is talking about you carrying on with Nicky Hobson.'

'I wasn't carrying on with Nicky Hobson,' Ida had told her and Miranda put a bony hand on her arm and said, 'Everyone *knows* you were carrying on. Why the bloody hell couldn't my carry-ons have given me a baby?' That's what she said.

Ida had started to understand then and so would Freda. Freda would see what she was getting at and how everything could be sorted out and the baby would be safe and comfortable and Ida could carry on with her job in advertising and Sir Neville still speaking to her because Miranda Drabble was a good friend of his and if she, Ida, didn't do what Miranda said, well . . .

She was at the hospital now, with its grand curved steps. It all made such sense. The baby would grow up loved in a family, and Miranda was talking about money which they could give to a hospital or something, for children say.

She hoped Freda wouldn't be like Frank. She couldn't face him again. She'd told him and he'd looked hurt and she could see why, really, because he knew it couldn't be him, since they hadn't been close in such a while. And he'd been bitter, and said he'd make sure everyone knew he wasn't the father. She'd wanted him once—but had she really? If she was totally truthful, she'd wanted Freda; of course it was Freda, always had been, always would be. And now she didn't have Frank to

239

want, he'd made that clear, but it had *always* been Freda anyway. She had to tell Freda that. She never had. She had told Frank she loved him when she wasn't even sure what that meant, and he had said it back to her, like the marriage vows. *Repeat after me*. What did any of it mean in the end? The two of them marrying because that's what you did, wasn't it, that and having children . . .

Ida pulled another sweet from her pocket. Oh! Look at her coconut strips all over the ground and the gobstoppers running away from her, as red as rolling beads of blood.

Something precious was seeping away, she could feel it. She had to get to Freda quickly, to tell her. And why had that woman walking by on the pavement opposite stopped to stare? Ida looked up at the ranks of windows which seemed suddenly to rush up into the air.

'Have one of my sweeties, Freddie,' she said. 'You're always buying me sweets.'

There was a loose, wet feeling between her legs or perhaps it was hot, like sitting on the slate front step in the sun, but it was winter, not the summer, when they used to race to the sea beneath an endless blue sky.

The two of them on the pier in the sunlight, their bare feet on worn planks, Freda moving to shield her from the wind. A penny for a Wembley bar of toffee that would last a whole performance of a pierrot show. It lengthened as you bit each piece off.

'Fairy chips,' she whispered. Someone was standing on the steps, coming down towards her. Ida closed her eyes. She could still see the shape of the open doors behind the figure, fuzzy and luminous, like a cinema screen. The Kinema. *The Wonder Girl!* People were cheering from a cliff top. The smooth hardness of pebbles under her feet. She was at the water's edge and felt the water around her.

'Coconut with sugar and a crisp . . . long strips of coconut, pink and white . . . about tuppence a quarter,' she was saying.

And then what Miranda had said when she was leaving, swinging her black stole round her neck. *How curious. Fancy you carrying on with another man when we thought it might have been a woman. You are a greedy girl, Iddy.*

Ida dropped her head to her swollen chest and put her palms to her belly. It was wet but where was the water?

We can look after the baby, that's what she really wanted Freda to say. You and me. We will be three.

She moved her head from side to side to try and seesaw away the pain.

Was that Freda?

'Golf balls,' she said.

A voice speaking over her head. *Hallucinating. In a bad way.*

'Will you help me train, Freddie?'

But she was going down, she could feel it, she was being pulled down, the tide was trying to beat her. Where was Freda? Freda pulling at a liquorice shoelace . . . She wanted Freda.

A voice. *Take her quickly, please.* Freda was coming. Freda was flying towards her. Hands were on her, trying to push her down—'No, get off me, I WILL NOT GO UNDER'—or pull her up.

I can still get there, she thought, before brisk

241

hands clamped her arms and she closed her eyes. Moving now, crossing quickly a blur of tiles, her feet not touching the ground—was she really flying, was she really on her way to America? And then a long, screaming sound, like a spiky ball of metal being pulled through a tight tunnel of glass.

The little cleaning girl in the hospital, watching from the upstairs balcony with her mop and bucket, thought she made out the name *Freda* or it might have been *forever*.


## CECILY 2009

The estate agent told me a house always sells quicker if the clutter is hidden from view. Give me a couple of weeks, I replied, and the place won't look so much like a car boot sale. I couldn't read his expression when he left, but I'll bet he was preparing a speech about the property being a bit of a wreck compared to the neighbours', and the work that needed doing being reflected in the price.

I don't know why so many of those plastic charity sacks for children in war zones were coming through the door, but half an hour after he'd gone another of the damn things dropped on the tiles in the hall asking for unwanted items.

If it hadn't been for my eyes, I might have thought about hanging on here to the end, but the stairs, the steps up and down on the landing, the journey between the bedroom, the lavatory and the kitchen . . . the house had become a health and safety hazard and too big to clean to boot.

'I think I'll have an early night,' I said to Sarah

that evening in October.

'Oh, OK, Ceci,' she replied. I couldn't see her face but I heard wary concern in her voice. 'Is there anything you need?' she asked.

I shook my head. She was doing too much for me and she'd be gone soon enough, back up to London, if only because she tired of me reciting the train timetable. I wasn't letting up on making her see she shouldn't just chuck up her marriage like that, and what I had planned was a solo job in any case.

I wanted to make the house the closest I could get to what the estate agent called a blank canvas. It's best to minimise your presence or personality, he'd told me. People like to picture their own possessions in your home when they come through the door, to imagine they've already moved in and you're long gone.

Up the stairs I went, and beneath the lamp hanging dim from the ceiling rose in our bedroom, and the cool late autumn dusk beyond, I removed everything from Freda's wardrobe. Out came a pair of her boots I hadn't seen in years, an old grey hospital blanket stitched in red around the edges and, scrumpled up like a dirty towel for laundry, the white, sleeveless dress Freda wore for her sister's wedding.

The funny thing is that when I felt the little suitcase at the very back, it was Sarah I thought of. Oh, Ceci, she'd say, is that *really* crocodile skin?

I clicked open the catches and pulled everything out. A dress in black crêpe and another in lilac silk, a little cardigan and a long green dress with a cream lace collar, a black bathing suit with thick cross-over straps folded in a bundle. There was the

243

faintest whiff of perfume, like dipping your nose in a vase of roses, the old-fashioned ones that smelled so powdery and fine.

When I held up the bathing suit I had such a start when a couple of round grey pebbles—the pair of them could have come off the beach here—dropped out and gave two raps on the floor. They were as smooth as the onyx eggs I used to roll about in my hands while Freda and I watched the telly in silence. She liked gruesome thrillers, the sort that didn't credit you with the imagination to picture a severed head for yourself so there it would be, crossing the screen like a bouncing bomb. 'I've seen far worse than that,' Freda would say. And that would be it. Subject closed. Things were different then. There weren't the emotional opportunities there are nowadays.

In the gathered sleeve of this case—all the inside was done out in the prettiest rosebud-patterned lining—I found a lipstick, which had a beach scene etched on the case, row upon row of little wiggly lines like waves, and the outline of a figure throwing a ball.

More than anything, it was that little suitcase that made me see what I'd been missing all these years, the feel of it, shiny and smooth as the skin of a lady, set as it once was on the floor by a hospital bed.

After that, I had Freda's old letters out, kept for all this time in one of her father's shirtboxes. That box must be fifty years old now but still so pretty, olive green with gold writing, the name of a department store that's been turned into city apartments.

At one time, Freda and I rattled along through

244

letters—which suited her, I realise now, because though I asked questions, she didn't have to answer them. She gave me little stories instead, tales I lapped up thinking there was nothing more I needed to hear.

I went through the back bedroom then. Out came the old ice box we'd take on picnics, parking up the Morris and sitting in lay-bys munching on sandwiches with Freda, her mouth as full as though she had a fist in her cheek, saying, 'Are the Brits the only ones to eat their dinner on the motorway?' I remembered a trip to Brecon when the pair of us were getting on a bit, and coming up a hill with that ice box, dripping wet after a summer storm. There were two youngsters, fresh from the car park in waterproofs, and I heard the boy say to the girl, clear as a bell, as we passed them, 'Respect. To think Hitler thought he stood a chance.' When I told Freda afterwards she said, 'Bloody cheek,' but they had got her down to a tee. Freda did look so like a woman who would have done something strong and capable and brave in the war. I could always see her being captured behind enemy lines and refusing to buckle when questioned.

Kneeling on the floorboards by the fireplace of pine cones I'd collected over time from the square, I wasn't sure I could get back up again. My life with Freda—all that had happened between us and all that lay between us too—I wasn't sure of anything any more. She took so many answers with her.

I was with her when she died, when her pulse became so slow I wasn't sure of another beat and then her breathing so light it seemed only to come

245

from her mouth. I was holding her hand when the last of her life sighed from her. All our years together and then she was gone.

\* \* \*

Though Sarah dropped by most days—she and the dog coming down the passage like a pair of travellers glad to be home—I knew our friendship couldn't last forever.

Her parents were on their way back from Spain and she'd started talking of getting that hard-working husband down here to meet me. 'That's not what I'm after,' I told her. 'It's you and him, not me and him that need to become acquainted.' I did my best to keep up but I felt awful maudlin the moment Sarah and Mungo went out of the door.

That rocket of an exhaust on her car would fade to nothing in the winter darkness, and I'd turn back, looking down the hallway half hoping there'd be a light at the end of it, and my troubles would be over.

I had never thought I'd enjoy myself so much again that summer, being driven around in my padded gilet with the sun on our heads, but then the weather changed and the Triumph's roof went on and dead leaves blowing turned to hard, frosty ground, and the church choir started rehearsing mournful carols in the square every Thursday night. I took to standing in my bedroom looking at the illuminated stained-glass arches through the bare tree branches, thinking of years before when I'd sat in a pew praying for Freda to come home.

I had terrible difficulty sleeping. I'd lie in bed with a nose as cold as a corpse worrying that if I closed my eyes I'd open them in the morning and see nothing but the night. I couldn't take my mind off the darkness and spent hours feeling the ice patterns on the insides of the windows with the tantalising black of the early hours outside.

One morning before dawn, I rose and went to the row of white charity sacks lined up against the wall of the bedroom. I hadn't been able to put them outside the door, after all. I stuck my finger in one and ripped it. Then I went for a second and felt one of Freda's jumpers. I pulled it out, then another, and I put the two of them on, the Fair Isle on top, before I did up my slacks under my nightdress. Wearing Freda's old grey walking socks, I went slowly down the stairs. Who'd have thought putting one foot in front of the other would become such a challenge?

In the hall, I struggled into the boots I'd had on the first time I met the girl in the front, and then out of the door I went into freezing air dark enough to be midnight. I used to lie in bed a lot watching for the small black line of the clock's hands marking midnight, the difference between day and night, the gap between one day dying and the birth of another: the between time.

My cold, hollow bones cracked away along the pavements, down the hill to the sea with the moon silver on the water. The Channel was as still as anything, aside from the faintest layers of waves flattening on the pebbles.

*For David who loved to walk here, with love from Edith always at his side* was the inscription on the bench I sat on, the one I'd gone to so often to imagine Ida Gaze crossing to the other side.

Never mind it was a good few degrees below

247

zero. As I sat there, I got to wondering how the water would feel around me too. In the distance, the old lido was cracked and dry, and here the sea stretched, endlessly black. It looked filthy but it's silt, or so I've been told. It was years since I'd dipped my toe.

Dawn was fading black to grey as I made my way down the steps onto the beach. People would be about soon enough. I pulled off my boots and socks and headed for the sea like a wizened old toddler determined on paddling. I was as intent on getting to the edge of that water as I'd been on tracking down Ida Gaze.

You'd have thought I'd have my work cut out negotiating the pebbles, but my mind was overtaken with memories of Freda. The two of us walking along the prom, pushing through the gap in the hedge at the top of the hill, and going down to that lake and its stepping stones.

The water's first freezing touch wasn't shocking at all, and the further I went, I started thinking that the beauty of water is you don't have to worry about putting one foot in front of the other. You can forget about having to stand up straight.

Then the voices came.

'Call the police!'

'Don't be ridiculous. She's not a body.'

'Yet,' came another voice, and then I heard the pebbles going crazy. Someone was coming towards me though I was getting further away, back in time, lying by the lake with Freda, and the fish in the bottle-green water, and then her sitting up so suddenly. Is there someone coming, I'd asked her. No, she replied, I'm watching a bird in the reeds.

A voice said, 'You are brave going for a paddle

in this, Ceci.'

I turned. It was Sarah wading towards me in the thick white light, and the dog behind her with a small piece of driftwood sticking from one side of his mouth like Winston Churchill's cigar. She was smiling, I'd say, as she reached for my hand.

'Mind if I join you?' she asked, and a shriek came from up on the prom. It's that, I think, that caused me to lose my balance. I didn't mean to pull her down too but the pair of us went over like cabers and then Mungo weighed in and started jumping about, thinking it some sort of game.

'Get off!' Sarah said. There's a heck of a weight on that dog—a good six stone, I should say—and he's got a set of claws on him too. One time, when the three of us went to the local country park, Mungo's paws were making such a noise on the lake's wooden boardwalk that a man shouted, 'Get that dog's claws cut, will you!' Freda's right. People don't care what they say, do they?

I don't know how we made it back to the car but Sarah helped me into the passenger seat where I sat looking down at the frill of my nightdress stuck to my slacks like a trail of fancy seaweed.

'I'm all for swimming,' Sarah said, as we moved off, the heater on full blast, people still watching, 'if the water isn't battleship-grey and well below zero. It wasn't much cop, was it, Ceci. Better out than in, don't you think?'

'A girl swam that Channel,' I said, uncurling my fingers. 'Twenty-two and a half miles.'

The small circle of metal was still there in my palm. The number of times I'd run my finger over it. *Gala Princess*, it said, 1928.

As we went up the hill so steep the car rose in

low gear like a tram, I was coming back round to feeling ashamed of myself for causing such a scene, as well as wetting the seats of Sarah's treasured car.

'She's the swimmer in the picture, isn't she, Ceci?' she said quietly. 'The girl who swam the Channel.'

I nodded. 'Freda's princess,' I told her.

The December morning was frosty and dry. On the high street, people walked with scarves tied round collars up on their coats beneath fairy lights hanging in loops from the lamp-posts.

Outside the house, we sat looking through the windscreen, until the man next door in a suit had driven off to work, and I said, 'I don't mean to be rude, but that dog could do with a bath. With the roof down on this car, there's a smell in here like a rabbit hutch.'

Sarah laughed. 'Oh Ceci,' she said. 'I'm so glad we met. There I was, walking along the prom in a daze, and now you've brought everything back to life.'

I was wet and still freezing, and felt awfully foolish and guilty for dragging Sarah into the water, but I couldn't help laughing too. What people must have thought, seeing that production on the beach and then the pair of us walking up the concrete slipway outside the Yacht Club, and Mungo shaking himself by the milkman and a woman in an apron delivering baskets of vegetables to the Italian restaurant where we'd been three times for pizza.

'I'm so sorry,' I said. 'It won't happen again.'

Mungo put his great bear head between us. I could never get over the size of him. Sarah claimed he was half Labrador but he always looked whole polar bear to me.

'Come on,' I said. 'Let's have a cup of tea.'

'And some cake,' she replied, pulling up the handbrake. 'Even if it is barely nine.'

'Down the hatch,' I said, and put my hand on hers. 'Thank you, Sarah.'

'Ceci, thank *you*,' she replied.

What I liked very much about this girl was she didn't once tell me *What were you thinking of* or *You shouldn't be doing things like that at your time of life*. Perhaps she suspected it was exactly the type of thing someone in my position might do.

That gap in years between us and yet so much she understood.

We sat in the cosy middle room, me in Freda's dressing gown which I'd never taken off the back of the bedroom door, and Sarah in towels and blankets, her hair loose and curling and the same red as mine used to be, and I said to her, 'It's about time I told you about mad, old Ceci.'

She laughed carefully, and when she flattened her hand on the radiator, I heard the chink of her wedding ring.

'And the girl in the old-fashioned bathing suit?' she asked.

'And the girl in the old-fashioned bathing suit,' I replied. 'She was Freda's friend.'

'Go on then, Ceci,' Sarah told me. 'Dive in.'

I remember once telling Freda she was a little blunt for some people's tastes.

'Life's too short to pussyfoot about,' she said. 'You should always tell it as it is.'

Not that Freda ever did that—Do as I say, not as I do, she'd tell me, only half joking—but here it is,

251

me telling it as it is, my story, and Freda's too. Ours.

# PART TWO

# 1

It sounds so rum, doesn't it, taking a baby from a hospital, and the years passing don't make it any easier to say.

Nowadays I might get a grainy image on *News at Ten* with a *Crimewatch* reconstruction three weeks later, but back then there weren't cameras on corners or endless forms to fill in or fancy electronic systems to stop you getting in or out of places.

When the hospital door closed behind me, a voice called my name as though an alarm had gone off—'Ceci, Ceci, Ceci'—and down those cast-iron stairs I went, terrified of dropping a lady's baby.

'Here, over here,' the voice was going. 'Come. Quickly.'

I like to think I wasn't a complete stooge when I crossed the space where the surgeons parked their cars and two hands reached out.

'Want to give me the baby?'

It was bitter that November night, everything frozen a little smaller than itself, like water turned all to ice in a bucket. I hoped the baby was warm in its woollen shawl, bonnet and blanket. There was darkness and buildings all around the narrow alley, where who knew what was coming.

'No,' I said. 'Where's Sissie?'

'She's with Matron. She'll be along later.'

It was the woman from upstairs, looking dark-eyed and awkward and suspicious in her little black veil. I can picture her now. You'd think after all this time, and with reading endless newspapers and books and the internet, and years of me looking at people's faces and learning new things and listening to conversations in the post office queue, that what happened back then would have been pushed from my mind. But that night so long ago, when Sister was Sissie and the baby a stranger, is as clear as anything, as clear as my sight once was before it started to feel as though I had Vaseline in each eye. You may find, my consultant chappy told me, that as your sight fails, other senses come into play to compensate. Yes, I told him. Things are sounding better already, aren't they? Now doesn't macular degeneration seem so much fancier than going blind? They tell you this grand name as if it's a title, as though it will improve things, like saying lavatory instead of privy and passed on instead of dead.

'Best get on,' the woman said. 'Come with me.'

'Who are you?' I asked. 'And what about the mother?'

'Shush,' she said, breath rolling from her mouth like smoke. 'Keep your voice down.'

She cleared her throat. The baby felt warm and important against me but so helpless too. On the wall behind, a cat stood with its tail curved like a tiny arm in a ballet.

'You ask a lot of questions,' she said, and I had the sense this was something she'd already been told. 'Look, we need to get going. Come on.'

I felt suddenly uneasy, as though people had stopped talking the moment I walked in a room. A car went by in the distance.

'I'm not going anywhere without Sissie's say-so,' I said.

It didn't seem right, a baby in the alley where

the slops wagon came. I headed for the stairs, hoping the door hadn't locked against me. The first step had a dangerous sheen to it.

'The baby will die in this cold,' she called after me. 'They'll come looking. They'll find you and you'll be thrown into prison.'

I turned round. She stepped forward, I stood back. The woman had the look of the teacher who came across the playground at school to tell me my mother was dead—sad but determined—and she said, 'Look, the baby's mother is dying. We are doing the best for the baby. Sister says so. Sissie, you like Sissie, don't you? Ceci and Sissie?'

I nodded and she knew she had me.

'Well, Sissie says this is for the best, else the baby will go to a home it would hate.'

*A home it would hate.* I thought of my father back home, my brothers blaming me for everything.

'You can give me the baby, stay here with Matron and keep your mouth shut for the rest of your life,' she whispered. 'Or you can come with me now, both of you.'

I saw her catch my second-hand coat, the old boots, the thin skin on my cheeks.

She said, 'You have somewhere to go, somewhere safe, for good. Nothing bad will happen, you'll see. Sissie says so.'

It was strange hearing a woman so dark sound so soft. It felt wrong—like warm water from a cold tap—but an unexpected comfort too. I saw then there were lights in windows at the backs of the houses, like giant flaring matches to mark our way.

'Besides,' she said, 'any more of your backchat and that new baby will freeze to death.'

The baby stirred and twisted one foot onto another like a twirl of chunky rope.

'Are you in or out?' she asked.

I thought of the baby with no mother going to a home it would hate, of Sissie and Ceci, and my father waiting to give me what-for. There seemed little to lose.

'In,' I said.

'Then let's get on.'

We walked quickly on the pavement side by side, me checking for the faintest puff of breath from the baby's nostrils, and the woman humming a tune. I could tell she wasn't humming for me to join in. She was humming to herself to keep me and the cold and perhaps the thought of what she was doing out of her head.

Once or twice I peeped at the baby's head to check it really was a baby and not a roll of blanket. It scared and thrilled me to see that little fragile bulb of blue-white flesh and bone. When the woman stopped, I knew we had arrived at the start of something else.

'Go on,' she said, pointing to an ordinary-looking house, and up the garden path I went.

\*     \*     \*

In a first-floor room at the back of the house with no fire in the grate, I sat on the bed as I was told and held the baby as though I would never let go.

I listened to the muffled thrum and pause of music and laughter from somewhere down below and tried to take my mind off things by imagining the worst that could come through the door—and that was the devil with red eyes, and horns, and a

258

black, smoking cloak.

I remember a pair of pyjamas on the pillow, a pile of books in the circle of light from the lamp by the bed. There was a brown wardrobe with a curved top, a small table, a chair in the corner, and two pairs of boots and shoes along the wall. I can see it now on the television in my mind as clearly as I took it all in then with my fourteen-year-old eyes. There were no pictures on the walls.

'Not long now,' the woman said, pointing at the baby and putting a finger to her lips. She took off her hat and I saw she had dark hair pulled back to the nape of her neck and lips so red and shiny I wondered I hadn't noticed before.

When there were footsteps on the stairs and Sissie pushed through the door it somehow fitted—that the room was just a room and belonged to her. Though Sister could be sharp, she was a relief from the devil. She had a cigarette in one hand and in the other a big white hospital bag which she put on the floor before closing the door.

'Good girl, Ceci,' was the first thing she said.

I didn't know what the hell was going on, but good was more than one up from being at home with my father, who came a very close second to the devil. I liked hearing that word good. The teacher told my father I was good enough to stay on at school and he'd been quick to get me out working after that.

Sissie nodded at the woman in a chair in the corner, took a drag on her cigarette and turned her mouth sideways to blow out a mouthful of smoke. I saw her profile, all bony curves and handsome slopes, and I suddenly felt less fear and more shyness. I looked down at the baby's pale, quiet

259

crumple of a face, and all my questions vanished. I think I knew then that something would happen, that my life would change. The baby gave a murmur that added to the little awakening inside me.

Sissie stubbed out her cigarette in a tin lid on the table.

'Let me have her,' she said softly.

'Her?' I said.

'She's a girl, Ceci. But she hasn't a name yet.'

'A girl,' I said, marvelling, when I had been so sure it was a boy, and though the baby wasn't mine to admire, a little seed of hope settled in me that she would grow up and see all this behind her.

'The mother?' I asked, handing the baby over. I could hear my voice tiptoeing in fear. 'Has she . . . ?'

'Ceci, you are not to worry about the child's mother, but I need to ask you a very important question.'

Sissie's voice was so serious it was like something off the wireless talking about whether war was coming. I halfwondered if I should stand.

'The baby has a home waiting—a good, safe home,' she said. 'Now, the baby needs a friend to go with her, someone who can feed her and stroke her and love her, someone who might be having a sorry sort of time and who wants a good, safe, new life too.'

She told me, 'You must remember that what you do next is up to you. That's true of anything in your life, Ceci, and I am grateful to you for carrying the baby this far.'

Sister looked at the other woman and back at me.

'What I am asking is this, Ceci. Would you like to keep the baby safe in her new life? Would you like it to be you and her on a train to the baby's family, or will you stay here with what you have now?'

Sissie looked at me steadily though her voice seemed broken with emotion. It was all so strange I couldn't order my thoughts or words. If the baby had a family, why hadn't they come to fetch her? I imagined a grand house with more rooms than London had streets. There would be a stern man with a moustache and a watch on a chain, and a great long winding driveway and maids in starched white aprons with a butler who told everyone off.

'The baby's family is waiting and they are happy for you to go too.'

She went on, 'I do know how you live. You've told me about scrubbing shirts and no money for the meter, and I've seen that sometimes you sleep at the hospital to stay away from home.'

I remember feeling embarrassed by that and looking across at the woman in the corner, wishing I had a veil for myself, but Sister's head moved, like a tic of impatience, and I turned back to her.

'What I am saying is this, Ceci. If you stay here tonight with me and the baby, you will never go back to your father and brothers or Matron again. You will go on a train to a place with fields and trees and the sea as big as the city, though you will be far from the smoke and the noise.'

'On a train?' I said.

She nodded, jigging the baby, speaking so softly instead of her usual way that the new life sounded so gentle and kind and caring, and I longed for my mother. The baby needed someone to love her.

261

'The baby's home is a place where you will be cared for as much as you care for the baby, Ceci,' she said, handing her back.

'Will you come?' I asked, and though I had started to move my toes about to get the warmth back into them, I blushed red and hot when I caught her gaze, and I looked back down at the baby in my arms.

'No, Ceci, I must stay here for now, but it is such a special place I shall come there for a holiday.'

'Think of it as one big holiday,' said the woman in the corner, so suddenly, I started. I had forgotten there was anyone in the room but me and Sissie and the baby.

'And what with talk of another war,' she went on, 'it's the safest place to be.'

'Yes,' said Sissie, 'that's a good way of looking at it.' Then: 'Well, Ceci, what do you say?'

I'd never had anyone, least of all Sister, ask my opinion. It was intoxicating. I thought I knew what I wanted and I nodded that yes, I would go with the baby to a new warm milky life.

Sissie was brisk then.

'You wait here for a moment,' she told me, 'and think of a name.'

The woman stood when Sister flicked her eyes at her and then they were gone.

*     *     *

I sat there I don't know how long with the baby, as though we were practising being a painting of *Mother and Child*, until Sissie returned alone.

'You're so cold,' she said softly, putting one hand to the baby's cheek and another round my own hand. 'In bed with the pair of you.'

Sissie seemed so much older, so when she took the child from me, set her on the bed, then turned to push off my coat, I must have felt I'd found the mother I'd lost.

I remember feeling horror at the heavy noise the coat made falling to the floor as she undid the front buttons on my old knitted dress. Everything was quiet in the house. The room was dark but I could see the baby, a white bundle on the white bedcover, and I stared at it, my eyes unable to meet hers. I knew Sissie was looking directly in my eyes for the longest time that night. I didn't feel cold then, only the warmth and sound of her breath.

She took her pyjama bottoms, held them for me, in my thick wool stockings, to step into and then she waited with the top until I saw I was to lift my arms so she could pull it over my head. I was a child and I had made a promise to a baby.

We lay in the bed, me against the wall, Sissie on the outside, hitched up on our elbows looking at the baby between us. I took quick glances at Sissie's long, straight eyelashes as she stared down at the child. She wore a slip as pale as her skin, so it seemed almost as though she was naked. Then I closed my eyes and slid down into the bed.

There was a smell that night, of Sissie, her hair and her pyjamas and the pillow with its coating of cigarette smoke. There was the scent of something hidden and dangerous, something unknown and exciting. I didn't know what lay ahead but I felt a tingling, a shiver, a sense of myself trickling out of myself or into myself, and a new kind of life. I wasn't frightened any more. I felt something unfolding, opening. I felt the gentle promise of a baby's yawn.

We woke the next morning to the baby crying and the new day grey through the window at the end of the bed.

'What will happen at the hospital?' I asked, holding the baby while Sissie came back and forth bringing in a kettle, a bowl and a baby's bottle, and setting them on the table.

'They know the baby is to start a good new life away from any war that might come,' she said to me. 'They know the baby is going home.'

Nowadays a child might know better to ask more questions but I was a timid thing, used to being told what to do—*or else*—and Sister had a way with her of making sure people knew to listen. She had spoken and that was good enough for me.

The next night we slept again in the bed with the baby between us. In the morning I woke knowing I would leave Sissie that day. I put the tear in my heart down to leaving London and my family, or perhaps it was the safety of that little room at the end of the corridor. It had been a room with a bed in it and not much else, and then it became so much more.

## 2

When the train pulled to a halt, a face right up at the window mouthed, 'Are you Ceci?' Then the girl saw the baby and put a hand to her lips. I could tell what she was saying through her fingers.

'Just call me daft,' she said, and laughed, and

264

that put me more at ease.

This girl didn't care one bit for the stationmaster telling her to keep off the train if she wasn't going anywhere, and on she came in her red crêpe dress and a matching band in her yellow hair with a silk flower just above her ear.

'No, you keep hold of that,' she told me when I went to hand her the baby. 'They terrify me and Mother's had her fill of them too.'

She held out a hand I couldn't shake because I was holding the child.

'I'm Dotty and you're to come with me.' She looked as though she'd come off the stage.

It was late afternoon, the darkness coming over this small town with its station the size of a shoebox. I didn't know where I was going or if there would be a man with a moustache and a watch on an albert chain. I sat in the taxi with the baby.

We drove past a row of shops, up a hill and then right and right again till we stopped outside a redbrick house on the corner with its own garden. It wasn't a country manor, but while Dot was paying the driver, I gaped at this place with its lawn and all different shapes of bare trees, and then up at the sky and around for the sea. I must have looked as if I'd come down on the milk train.

I couldn't get over the way the baby had been so quiet on the journey. Sometimes I held her a little tighter, just to feel the give of her body as she took breath, a new life celebrating its few days on this earth by going to the seaside.

I'd never been on a train before. I had a few looks here and there but mostly people were passing our carriage and tapping gently on the window to point and smile. Talk of war seemed to have made babies extra-precious, though for a while I feared a policeman would come knocking with his baton. I had no clothes or food, and a roll of money as thin as a cigarette from Sister. I kept my hand on the pocket of my coat and an eye on the bag of baby things, and thought of Sissie kissing her fingers and blowing them to me as the train drew off. That set me up for the journey, thinking of lying side by side with Sissie.

'We can be Sissie and Ceci,' she'd said, 'our little secret.'

'Do what the guard tells you,' she told me at the station. 'You will be met at the end of the line.' As I say, I didn't ask questions back then, and that was enough for me. The end of the line.

Nancy, I suggested for the baby. 'Then Nancy it will be,' she agreed.

'Are you sure now, Ceci?' Sissie asked, as we queued for my ticket, in such a voice that even if I had had doubt as big as a balloon in my head I would have nodded. By then I was thinking of the back of my father's hand too. Young girls were always vanishing after getting themselves into trouble one way or another. If they fell pregnant, they might die having an abortion or else they'd run away with the baby. Some were killed, like they are today, and never found. I could see my father writing me off one of those ways. I did him a favour by vanishing. One less mouth to feed, though there would be nobody to light the fire or put out plates of food.

'You are a good, brave girl,' Sister told me, not caring for the glances from people around us in the station. 'God bless you.' She could be quite distant,

266

but that was the nicest thing anyone had ever said to me, aside from a teacher who told me that if I'd been given another sort of life I could have been anything I wanted.

There were five of them in the house, mother, father, two children, and a terrier puppy called Cruncher who had the freedom of the place. Dot was four years older than me, and her brother, Josh, two years my senior. The baby and I had our own room upstairs with a bed and a wooden cot brought down from the attic.

'What do you say, Ceci?' Dot's mother asked the second night in the sitting room with all of them listening. 'Will you stay?'

I stared at her, the baby in my arms. It hadn't occurred to me to have an opinion. I was still waiting for Sister's instructions.

'Are you the baby's family?' I asked.

I hadn't stopped wondering about the woman in the hospital, but there was an awful long wait after my question, as though I'd dropped a stone into a well so dark and deep I'd never catch it hitting the water.

'I'm sorry,' I said, thinking it must have been a relative in that la-di-dah clinic after all, though they all seemed rather easy-going for mourners, and when they dropped the bombshell they were quite jaunty with it.

'Your Sister is my daughter,' the woman said. 'We call her Freda. She's asked for you and the baby to come back here and stay with her family.'

'My sister too,' Dot said kindly. She had green eyes that seemed to vibrate when they looked at you. 'Like you, Ceci. All of us sisters.'

'Steady on,' said Josh lightly. 'Two is enough for

me.'

'Quiet, Joshua,' his father said, but in a voice so mild it wasn't like anything I'd known before.

I looked down at the dark polished floorboards, then up at the wooden cabinet with plates standing on its shelves, and then at all of their encouraging faces, and I felt the black and cold of the night outside. I saw they spoke quickly as though hurrying for decency's sake to pull a shroud over a body, or something else just as final.

'Freda,' I said. 'Your daughter.'

'We are your family too if you'll have us, Ceci,' Freda's mother replied.

They said I might call them Aunt and Uncle but I told them I'd stick with Mr and Mrs Voyle as they weren't really my aunt and uncle, though I didn't say that. Soon enough they became Beatrice and Herbert because they put me at ease in so many ways.

I went to bed that night wondering what kind of Sister took a baby from a hospital without saying it was going to her family, and what had happened that had to be kept hidden. I never called Freda Sissie again. It sounded a bit babyish and I was trying so hard to be a mother to the baby.

\*       \*       \*

Not that long after Nancy and I arrived at the Voyles', Freda sent a flatteringly chatty letter saying I'd never guess where she was. She was right. She was in the middle of the Atlantic Ocean working as a Sister on a cruise ship which had its own operating theatre and a guest-list of aristocrats and film stars.

*You should see the way they carry on*, she wrote, *clothes strewn all over their cabins, and the language!* Freda was never one for letting a Lord and Lady get in the way of her opinion.

I read the letter sitting on a bench overlooking the Channel. She wrote she had to buy white dresses and shoes and stockings as uniform, that she intended going everywhere she could, and that she'd already been up seventy-one floors of the Chrysler Building in New York.

What the heck, I thought, building up a head of steam to stop myself crying from shock and disappointment. There's me coming here like she wanted and now she's waltzing off around the world. *I didn't want to stay in London any longer*, she wrote, and I tried my damnedest to think it was her way of saying she missed me. I sent a letter back asking when she'd come on that holiday she mentioned, and why had the baby been brought here to her family, and what had happened to the mother, and who was she . . . and then another when Freda replied without answering any of my questions, and by then I just liked getting her letters and starting a reply the same day.

If I wasn't lying in bed at night imagining a giant globe being spun round to show me Freda's boat in a raging sea or sitting in a dock with skyscrapers and the noise of hooting cars, I'd be thinking, What am I doing here, and when might they tell me to leave?

Sometimes, if Nancy was having a tantrum, I'd think, Who is this baby to me? Then I'd feel guilty and entranced when she caught hold of my finger and wouldn't let go. Quite quickly, I stopped handing her to Beatrice when she didn't stop

269

crying, and began to think the world of her and more.

'Are you one of us?' a girl who was a nanny for a big house in the town asked me as we sat with the other nannies, our perambulators lined up on the prom. When people wanted to know about me and the baby, I was told to say we were cousins from London, and when Nancy was older she called me Ceci, not Mammy, which is what the children called the other women at the school gates.

One afternoon, a woman called Mrs Sterne, who wore a flat cap to fish for her own supper off the pier, saw me staring at the waves while holding Nancy, and she said, 'Like her big city mother for the water, is she?' and I said, 'Oh no, she's not—' but she interrupted and told me sharply, 'It's no secret, you know. Sad, mind.'

When I told Dot, she looked away and said that's how people were when it came to babies; there was no knowing what they'd come out with. She told me about a girl in the town who'd stopped letting visitors in the house when her belly got huge because all they wanted to do was to touch it. People were odd, she said, best ignore them, and I laughed because Freda said much the same thing in her letters.

At first I was shy of the family and joining them downstairs in the evenings, but soon enough, with the shouting and laughing and pushing and shoving that went on between Dot and Josh, I joined in.

When Christmas came, I walked into the sitting room to show Nancy the tree with its clip-on candles, and there were presents for the two of us in among the other wrapped gifts beneath its branches.

270

On Sundays we went to a church which had little stained-glass pictures of the saints and the Virgin Mary, and I was very taken with the Voyles' garden with its borders of flowers and herbs, a magnolia, and a tree with yellow flowers whose name I forget. I'd sit out there for hours in warm weather, Nancy in her pram in the shade of the apple tree, the sun hot on my scratchy blanket, and Cruncher's curly coat smelling of lavender he'd brushed against as he made his way around the garden.

That first summer I stood in the garden and heard Beatrice in the kitchen saying, 'The girl seems happy enough.'

Then Freda's sister said, 'Josh has a bit of a thing for her but I think she might be—'

'That's enough, Dot,' Beatrice said. Then, 'I doubt Freda will come back. She's on about going to Russia and all sorts.'

I stood by the door biting the inside corner of my mouth, wondering about never seeing Freda again. Every time I thought of her, I got a nice sick feeling in my stomach. I barely knew her but I missed her. I didn't know then that might become the story of my life.

'She this, she that,' they were going. In I went, intent on getting some answers, as though I had a right to know.

'Where is she at the moment?' Dot was saying. 'The West Indies, isn't it?'

'You know why she's done a flit, don't you?' Beatrice said. 'To get—'

They didn't see me and I blurted out, 'When will I be going?'

Both of them gave me an odd look as though I wasn't all there. I sometimes wish I'd asked more questions from the get-go and then they mightn't have thought me such a pushover.

'Going?' Dot said. 'You can't go with her. Freda's working.'

'Where?' Beatrice said.

'Back to London,' I asked, my voice breaking. I'd seen other girls crying but it didn't come easy to me.

'You don't have to go, Ceci,' Beatrice said, looking at Dot. 'Do you want to then?'

'No,' I replied. 'But why am I here?'

'To be with Nancy,' Dot said, looking at her mother. Both of them seemed quite unfamiliar now I really looked at them, the way I'd imagine meeting famous people might be.

'Yes, but why?' I asked.

I took a look at myself, as though I was outside my body, and saw a girl with red hair in one of Dot's old Paisley dresses and I began to cry.

I started on about it not being fair because Freda had said she would come back and now she wasn't going to, and that here I was with the baby, and why wasn't I told anything, and if it was true I was never going to see Freda again and I was made to leave, I'd have nowhere to go and then I didn't in truth know what I would do, not least with there being more talk of war. What a little drama queen I was.

Soon enough, I saw they were silent and I was making them uncomfortable raking up things they didn't want mentioning, and I suddenly thought they might send me on my way, and then never mind Freda, I wouldn't see Nancy again. Besides, I'd come to like this town, and the Voyles, and the room I shared with the child that once belonged to

272

Freda.

'I'm grateful to you for having me,' I told them. 'And I'm sorry if I've spoken out of turn because I'm very happy here, and the baby too.'

I didn't miss my father or brothers one bit. I used to lie in bed thinking of London as endless up-and-down lines in smoke, and there I was riding on the cliff tops with Josh on his old motorbike, my arms around his middle as we rode into a space as vast as the sky. There was something up with that bike and one time, he got it going and it wouldn't stop so we rode round and round the block until it ran out of fuel with Nancy standing on the corner waving on each lap. But I'm jumping ahead.

'I imagine it's been very difficult for you, Ceci,' Beatrice said, 'but you're here to start afresh and take care of Nancy, and we won't be telling you to go.'

It was the softest I'd seen her in a while because Dot said her mother was going through the Change and could turn like a weather vane in a blizzard.

From then on, wanting to make sure they knew I wasn't ignorant took over from any questions. Though I didn't know if I was guest or staff, I was keen they saw I was thankful for my new life, even if it was born of another woman's sorrow. I started wondering then if Freda had told them I'd had a miserable time of it before, and thought they might be a wonderfully kind family who wanted to help me as well as the mother and baby, and that made me more grateful and useful and quieter again. As it turns out, I wasn't far from the truth, only I didn't know then there was another girl they all wanted to do well by too.

Not long after my little outburst, the knocker banged again and again, and Beatrice went to the door. A woman shouted over her about 'gone on too long' and 'everyone knowing', and when I heard Freda's name, I came from my room and stood on the landing. Nancy was asleep in her crib which had two wooden panels top and bottom with painted pictures of a baby holding itself up by the bars of a cot. Up the stairs came words—*baby* and *daughter* and *my, my, my*—which I couldn't make any sense of, not until much later that is, a long time after Beatrice had told the caller she was surprised she'd left the house because look at the state of her, and everyone knew she wasn't all there and if she tried anything at all, she, Beatrice, would make it her business to tell the town and the church that whoever it was on the path wasn't fit for purpose. I'd never heard Freda's mother talk like that or slam the door—people in the town thought her such a lady—yet when she went into the sitting room to Herbert straight afterwards, she didn't sound anywhere near so fierce and started crying, which made me sure not to ask any more.

Next morning, when Herbert told me that a new flower on a border was cause for comment in this town, I nodded and tried not to care so much for people's questions or looks.

As time went on, I'd catch myself staring at Dot and Beatrice, searching for a resemblance to the child. One time I asked Josh if Nancy's mother was his sister and he told me not to be so daft. No, I said, I meant did he have another sister, and he said no it wasn't that, and that I should leave it because it would get the gossips going and upset Freda. That shut me up, not least because I had no

274

desire to hurt anyone, though I didn't realise my holding back then might cause such pain in later years.

Freda's brother took a shine to me from the start, and when the hot weather came he asked if I wanted to go for a swim in the river, just me and him. I loved Nancy like a mother or sister or cousin or even a complete stranger might end up doing, but I was glad for a break from her, though I didn't like staying away too long.

'Come on, Ceci,' he said.

'Get off,' I said to him. I was a city girl more used to a wrapping of wall around me. 'Anyway, I ain't got nothing to wear.'

'Go starkers,' he replied. With his wide mouth and grey eyes, Josh looked a little like Freda. They both had that way with them that made you think things you thought you shouldn't.

With the Voyles, nothing was ever a problem—they didn't flinch when a soldier knocked during the war and said nobody was to panic but there was a very large bomb unexploded on the lawn—and when Josh ran into the house shouting, 'Ceci's threatening to go naked,' out came one of Dot's bathing suits.

'Get it on, girl,' he said when we got to the river. 'I won't look.'

Josh was down to his black trunks.

'You're looking,' I said.

'So are you,' he replied, and then he did a mad little dance on the spot.

'Oh Ceci,' he sang. 'Let me see you. You and me. We . . . we . . . we . . .'

He was long and thin and half-feral and all the girls liked him. He had a scar on his cheek which everyone thought was from fighting, but he told me he got it as a child when he'd jumped up and down on his mother's bed one morning and gone over the edge onto a smashed teacup he took down with him off the bedside cabinet.

I thought of my own mother, how she had died without ever having gone for a swim in a river in the sun, and I felt obliged to run into the green and freezing water as the cows with their big bodies on thin legs came over to watch.

'Swim,' he said.

'I can't.'

So he caught hold of my arm and taught me, supporting me on my back to start with, and holding my head as gently as the water. I'd tell him I was floating and he could leave go, but he'd keep his hands around my head. 'Let go!' I'd shout, 'or I'll never learn to do it on my own.' I always felt relieved when Josh's fingers fell from my ears into the water though he kept them there long enough to show he didn't take no for an answer as easily as all that. The trouble was, in the same way some are quick to point out a dress or a three-piece suite or a house they've fallen for, I always knew what I wanted when it came to the other half of me.

Later, when Nancy was old enough, the three of us went to the lido on the cliff tops, which was the thing to do when it was hot.

Josh had fits and was never called up when the war came, but once when Nancy saw him shake and his eyes go up into his head—it only ever lasted a few seconds but he wasn't really supposed to drive—she was inconsolable. I saw then that if I was the closest she had to a mother, Josh might be her idea of a father.

The three of us spent hours on the beach. We'd hire a rowing boat and laugh ourselves silly going back and forth with Nancy trailing her hand in the water. Once we put the girl on a donkey, which tried bolting, and when Josh whipped her from the saddle, she had her arms out crying my name.

Every one of our outings ended the same way, with me wondering if there'd be a letter from Freda.

## 3

We learned about the war from a little note on the Voyles' hall table one Sunday morning coming back from church. The Prime Minister was speaking on the wireless at eleven o'clock and that was it.

The war gave me plenty to think about. Soldiers dying and girls in saucepan factories suddenly making weapons. And there I was, wanting for nothing but Freda to come home. I'd blush at my selfishness, and desire too.

The sky would be hanging with barrage balloons and patrolling planes. Road signs were taken down, streetlights and house windows blacked out at night, car headlamps shielded so they were dim, glimmering circles coming at you out of nowhere, all of it so much about not knowing what was round the corner.

The worst thing I saw in the war was a hole in the road after a bomb came down and people putting pieces of bodies in baskets. Nancy was with me and said Herbert had told her lots of brave fathers were killed in another war, and that might be where her daddy had gone. As we walked on, she took hold of my hand. The questions that girl must have had, but she only started asking in earnest when she was older, when she saw what she'd taken as normal was anything but.

At one time she was obsessed with trains, and rain or shine we'd go to sit and watch them. The stationmaster got to know us—he let her hold his flag and put his cap on. One day, she was lifted into the cabin with the driver and he held her up so she could see down the track. I felt such a nasty little pinch at my heart that she seemed so happy to be there, looking down the line, as though searching for where she had come from or where she might go.

I tried to keep my face in a smile but I didn't like leaving her there too long in case the train should go.

'Mammy's not happy,' said Mr Higgins the stationmaster, rubbing his nose. 'Give the little girl back to her mammy.'

I must have been coming up eighteen and didn't know what to be more embarrassed about, him seeing my fear of losing Nancy or him thinking I'd given birth. We walked off, my face as red as the bands of ribbon on our matching straw hats.

Not long after starting school, Nancy came back one afternoon asking where her mother was.

'Let's go and see Beatrice,' I said, hearing myself sound shifty. The more I grew to love the girl, the more I realised she wasn't mine to love.

I took her hand and we found Freda's mother on a deck chair in the garden, stretching her bare leg and curving her foot as though she was trying on

278

stockings. She had the same long legs as Freda and made me think of a beautiful horse. Dot said she came from a good family that funnily enough had kept horses, and met Herbert through his father's saddler's; apparently, her parents had been furious. Beatrice had arched eyebrows and a wardrobe of expensive clothes. One time, Josh came back with a gramophone player he'd been given as payment for building a wall and he put on a record in the sitting room. He and Dot laughed when their parents caught hold of each other and danced and smiled and locked eyes, but it made me sad watching them, the same way I felt when Cruncher grew old and Beatrice said, 'He's still got his appetite,' while he lay waiting for his food to be mixed in his bowl, instead of showing his teeth and ramming your leg.

'Nancy has a question,' I said, grimly pushing my little Trojan Horse forward.

'Where's my mother?' the girl asked.

Beatrice put both feet on the ground.

'Your mother is . . . has . . . gone away.' She gave me a look that said she wasn't impressed with me pulling such a stunt, and a few days later I did tell her I was sorry and hadn't meant harm, and she replied that she knew I was doing my best.

'That's why Ceci is here,' she told Nancy. 'To look after you, for good. This is a very difficult time, with the war and everything. So neither of you need worry, or ask me such questions again.'

Then she told the girl her mother was a very good, clever, beautiful woman far away, which made me think of Freda tending elegant women in their first-class cabins, though the war had put a stop to her gallivanting on cruise ships and by that time she was nursing war casualties in a London hospital.

All these invisible women, I thought, listening to Beatrice spin her fairy tale in the garden with Nancy listening as hard as if she was being told the truth. I remembered that day in the park when my mother had played Find the Lady and hadn't been able to put her finger on it either. I wondered no end why they wouldn't say more.

\*     \*     \*

As the war went on, I'd write over and over to Freda asking if I'd ever see her again, and she'd reply with such sad stories about her work at the hospital I'd feel ashamed and useless.

There was one woman, she wrote, who was saved from a bomb's rubble because she had a white towel wrapped round her head from washing her hair, but her baby didn't survive. I'd picture the little boy who called Freda 'Nurse Lanky'. He'd lost both his legs chasing a convoy of American lorries because the troops used to throw children chocolate bars, but his nerve was still there. *The cheeky beggar tells me he doesn't like tall nurses*, she wrote, but she let slip he'd have a cuddle each night because nobody came to visit.

I felt Nancy and I were blessed to be out of London for the war, especially when Herbert came back from the saddlery with stories about people fighting for space in the Underground to shelter from bombs. I didn't miss my family but I hoped well enough they were surviving.

People in this little town got used to spending the night in a shelter of strangers resentful at being tipped out of their homes, and next morning seeing houses with no roofs or windows and sunlight bouncing off ankle-deep shattered glass. We had our fair share of blasts here. Sometimes they blew the back door open. One night, after a landmine dropped nearby, the marble washstand slab from the house opposite came down the stairs and I thought, Nancy isn't staying in bed if the siren goes off again, I'll take her down to the shelter.

But even then, sometimes it was so cold that death seemed better than getting backsides like ice cubes on the stone seats, so when the siren started up, me and Josh and the girl would sit under the stairs and hope the planes couldn't see us. One night Herbert said he was grateful to Nancy for keeping all of us going. 'A child's high spirits while all around all hell is breaking loose,' he said. I loved hearing my little girl praised. Herbert was very dry and could calm things down with a joke. Freda adored him and so did I.

I counted the weeks, then months, then years since I'd last seen Freda. She was like a character from a book, at once vivid and nothing, but I kept on writing in my head the ending I wanted to our story.

'Fancy coming to the pictures?' Josh asked me one afternoon after he came up behind me sitting on the swing on the willow tree at the bottom of the garden. There'd been talk that stopped whenever I came in, something to do with Freda and a friend and dying and the name Edna and 'won't get over another one', but when I thought about what I'd heard, I wasn't sure I'd heard anything at all.

'If you like,' I said, because we were three years

into the fighting, and while we all carried on going, there were times when hoping came to a stop.

'No need to go overboard with the enthusiasm,' Josh replied.

One of his friends, Michael Rogers, had taken to coming round, and whenever he asked me to dance on the lawn, Josh would put his hands either side of his mouth and shout from the back step where he often sat, 'He's after you!' and I'd think to myself, That's true enough because he ain't ever going to get on top.

I kept on pushing my foot on the ground, swinging back and forth, but Josh came round to the front and put his hands at the bottom of each rope, stilling me and standing so I was looking at his chest in the lime-green sweater he wore with cream trousers so baggy he might almost have borrowed them from Freda. He had the same things I liked about her—long neck, thin wrists and a mouth as wide as anything when he smiled. He was left-handed, which had always appealed to me, and you didn't always know what he'd come out with, and I liked that too.

Josh was looking at my mouth. His body was so still I knew he wanted to move closer.

'I'll be performing a public service,' he said. 'It's dark in the Kinema so you won't depress anyone with that face you've got on.'

I hadn't seen Freda in five years but I lived my life as though she was in it. Sometimes in her letters, she talked as if I was still a child like Nancy. Freda was so much in my mind, I felt she was there in the room and I was spying on her, waiting to tap her on the shoulder and say, 'I'm nineteen, you know. I'm not a baby.' I could blush thinking of

282

what I wrote in those letters. *I'm going to sleep now*, I'd put, *in your bed, imagining you are still in it.* People seem to know how to behave, especially as they get older, but sophistication has never been one of my strong points. At one time, I wondered if it was on account of me being treated for so long like a child, not being told things, but that would be making excuses.

Josh and I went and queued right round the block to see *Night Train to Munich* in the Kinema, and five minutes into the picture, all this firing started. The giant screen shivered, the building was shaking, and the double doors at the back kept flying open, making everyone jump again.

'There you are,' Josh whispered to me as he put his arm round my shoulders. 'I take you out and the fireworks start.'

When they eventually let us out, Josh followed as I ran up the hill to check on Nancy and the rest of them. I used to worry so after hearing of one girl who was fire-watching from the roof of a department store in Cardiff. She saw the bombs drop into the furtive blackness of the city, and in the morning back she went to find her family and home burned and gone. Seeing my relief at the house still in one piece, Josh offered his arm and suggested a walk to the beach.

That night, we stood on the prom and watched the sky across the Channel in Weston alight with wave after wave of blasts like a giant firework display. It was shocking to think of mothers whisking babies from baths too late to get to the air-raid shelter. That's what I thought of always, children—and Nancy—being safe, and Freda, of course.

'You and me,' Josh said, 'we come out and set the place on fire.'

If you drop any bigger hints they'll be as obvious as those damn bombs, I thought to myself, but when Josh said he couldn't bear to go back to the house, and he wouldn't sleep, and could we just lie on the beach nicely and stare at the sky, I said I would. He was always watching out for me, walking into a room to break things up with Nancy who did as she was told if he spoke.

'Had we better get back for Nancy?' I asked.

'Nancy gets enough of your attention,' Josh said. 'She's becoming spoiled.'

We lay awkwardly on the pebbles, listening for planes, ready to run if they dropped anything. That was the war, always being ready to run. I was poised to sit up sharpish too, if he tried anything.

'If a bomb took me out now I'd have known this happiness,' he said. 'Lying here with you.'

He was so still beside me. Usually Josh was jumpy, like Dot, and up for anything. I felt his hand take mine. I didn't want to upset him but I pulled it away. Josh raised himself up on his elbow so the pebbles shifted under him and made the most awful racket settling back down. I turned my face from his.

'Don't tell me tough little Ceci is crying,' he said. 'My big sister would be very upset.'

Then, quieter, he told me, 'Sorry, I had an idea but I wasn't sure.'

'Ain't no need to apologise,' I whispered. 'Your heart is as good as any.'

*    *    *

Dot stood in the kitchen in a pale grey cotton dress and lemon-coloured shoes with square heels looking down the hall at me when I came through the door with Nancy one summer evening, back from a walk in the woods. I used to tell the girl all sorts of stories about trolls living in the holes in the tree trunks as we went under the arches of leaves collecting bunches of flowers for Beatrice and Dot.

Nancy was six or so. I was twenty and didn't mix much with others my age. I liked staying round the house, talking to Herbert and Beatrice and listening to Dot's tales about trying to catch the eye of Andrew Baker, the town's much sought-after junior policeman who had a sister called Gladys. Dot used to go and stand at the police station windows and put her hand to her nose and waggle her fingers when Andrew looked up from his desk. Her strategy seemed to be working. They'd already gone for a walk in the park and he'd picked her a huge apple off a tree which turned out to be a cooker and as bitter as anything.

My evenings were spent in the sitting room listening to the Voyles or reading in my chair in the bay, always with an ear out for Freda's name. Then I'd go up to my room with Nancy lying sleeping, bursting at the seams with desire to talk about Freda and how I longed to see her pale, bony face. On the Voyles' chiffonier, there was a school photo next to the oil lamp that saw some service in the war, but you couldn't make out Freda because she was sitting on the end of a row, turned away from the camera, ready to run. That's Freda, Dot had told me once, and that's her best friend, Ida, and then she'd put a hand to her mouth with an expression as though she was sniffing a horrible smell on the ends of her fingers.

'What's up?' I asked Dot, because she was coming down the hall to me and Nancy with a funny look on her face.

'Go and see the oracle,' she said, pointing to the sitting room. 'He's got some news.'

'Freda?' I replied.

After work, Herbert always went for a sit-down in his chair with an arm over the side, stretching his fingers to the dog. Cruncher loved it if you rubbed your finger up and down where his ears met his head. It was the silkiest bit of him. The rest felt as coarse as the wire wool I used to help Freda's father take rust off stirrups.

'Here,' Nancy said, handing Dot the posy we'd picked. I could feel my little girl coming behind, her breath sensing something bothering me. By then, Nancy was as high as my elbows with dark silky curls, and eyes and lashes like the centres of exotic black flowers.

Dot stood at the door, looking at her mother on the sofa opposite Herbert while Nancy and I were in the centre looking round. Josh was out seeing a girl called Helen Reynolds, but none of his courting lasted longer than five minutes.

'Don't fret, Ceci,' Dot said. 'It's nothing catastrophic. At least you won't think so.'

'Here comes trouble,' Herbert said, without looking up from his newspaper which he folded into a quarter so he could read it with one hand.

'What's wrong with Freda?' I asked.

'Where do you want me to start?' he replied, knocking his head back against the chair with his eyes to the ceiling. Then, laughing, 'Nothing's happened to her, kid. She's home this weekend and said to tell you she's looking forward to catching up.'

'Who's she?' Nancy asked.

'She is the cat's mother,' Herbert replied. At least the cat knows who its mother is, then, I thought, looking at the girl so curious and trusting, and yet here we were like a circle of secrets around her. But what filled my head to bursting was the idea of seeing Freda after all this time.

'I can see you're going to be another one who goes looking for it,' Herbert told Nancy. 'Just like Freda.'

'What was she like when she was younger?' I asked.

One time I'd asked Dot more about Freda's friends—we used to lie on her bed on Sunday afternoons while Nancy played in the garden with Josh—and she said there was just the one who was always in the water, and then Beatrice had come into the room, without me hearing her on the stairs, singing a tune I didn't recognise which sounded like la-la-la for the sake of it.

'Far worse than she is now,' Dot said from the doorway. 'If you can imagine that.'

I remember when I first arrived, Dot cleaning out Freda's wardrobe for me to store the clothes I'd had from her. 'That is so DISGUSTING!' she shouted as she reversed out of the bottom and stood with a long hank of dusty dark hair trailing from her hand. That's Freda for you, she'd said, throwing it into the box for rubbish.

'What do you mean?' I asked. 'Far worse?'

Herbert looked at his wife, who had started helping at a clinic for unmarried mothers and their babies, and mentioned a couple of times how well-behaved they all were.

'She was a damn nuisance,' he replied.

Beatrice raised her eyebrows. It was clear they all thought the world of Freda and would do anything she asked and more.

'That's not fair, Father,' Dot said. 'You told me all of us were a damn nuisance, not just Freda.'

'You still are,' he replied, though Dot spent less time at the house now things were getting serious with Andrew Baker.

'All over the world Freda ended up going,' Herbert said, 'tending the rich on boats, and now she's back in London helping the poor devils bombed in the war. Important work. Yes,' he said, winking at Nancy whose huge eyes were listening hard. 'We had terrible trouble with her but she's done all right.'

In fact, Freda worked like a trouper during the war and once, when a bomb came down next door while they were delivering a baby in the hospital, a hail of bricks fell on her shoulder but she carried on going.

One time, she told me, a doodlebug took out all the glass in the theatre but not the little round windows in the doors people are forever looking through. *You'll know the ones I mean*, she wrote, *you nosed through them often enough*. Over time, I had it in my mind that was the closest Freda would come to being close.

I assumed she found it difficult to be easy with feeling, but she was no slouch when it came to hard work. Unless it came down direct on her Sister's cap, she'd be there, handing over instruments to the surgeon as though they were knives and forks at a picnic.

*　　*　　*

The weekend she came home, all I could think of as she and Josh sparred—he was the only one who dared take her on—was how I'd get Freda to myself. I'd forgotten how distant she was. She had a little ring about her like Saturn, and people knew to keep away, though Nancy had been worse than me for asking, 'What time is she coming?'

'Look at you, little girl,' Freda said, bending to Nancy who turned away with her hand to her mouth. I hadn't thought of the girl as shy until then, though I'd noticed the way she'd look before laughing, which I took to be a mark of the war. I hadn't thought of Freda as soft either until I saw her expression. What must have gone through her mind as she studied the girl? The last time she'd seen her she'd been a baby wrapped in white.

'Who are you?' Nancy asked.

'I'm Freda—and you are?'

What a look of disappointment Nancy had then, as though she assumed Freda knew very much who she was without needing to ask, and was going to say something else altogether.

'Nancy Voyle,' she said. I held my hand out to her but she went to stand by Josh, watching Freda like a mouse spotting a cat.

'The girl will stay here,' Beatrice told us, seeing Freda and me looking at each other. 'You two go off for a catch-up.'

'Catch-up, is it?' Josh replied. 'Surprised they haven't had everything covered, with all the letters coming and going.' He was another one with a gag for any hint of an atmosphere.

289

I'd spent so long with Nancy I worried I might have forgotten how to behave like an adult, but the first thing Freda said when we got outside was hadn't I grown. My hair was down beyond my shoulders and I had a dab of red on each cheek where my pale skin was catching the sun. Sometimes I'd think about myself and not be sure I was me. I'd grown up in a flat with shared washing lines strung across alleys thick with smog, and now here I was weeding the garden for Herbert and helping Josh round up seventy-five cattle for milking. I felt I had half a new life.

'Let's walk, Ceci,' Freda said, and she offered her arm so dashingly my heart did a cartwheel. Freda was a looker though she was never vain. She ate what she liked—sherry trifle was a favourite—and was never out of trousers, but when she went along the street, even later in life, people would look at her as if thinking they ought to recognise her.

If I'd sat too long brooding on what was the big secret about the girl's mother or why I was here and whether I'd be sent away and who I'd miss most of the lot of them, walking through the town arm in arm with Freda Voyle made me feel like one of these film stars in heels on red carpets. I came to see Freda as looking a little like Lauren Bacall, though when I eventually told her that, she went the shyest I'd seen her and said I wasn't to say such things or people would think I was simple.

'I suppose we'd better get our priorities right,' Freda said, pulling out Nancy's sweet coupons and pointing at Ball's the newsagent's, which had the best selection.

'She'll have coloured fish or pear drops,' I

290

replied as Freda flicked through a comic on the counter while waiting to be served.

'I used to love Josh's *Champion*,' she replied, 'but you've got to wonder why it's always the boys who get to be the heroes as though girls can't do brave things too.'

I started when the man next to us turned round.

'You and your talk of girls being brave,' he said. 'I don't need to be a comic-book hero to know what's gone on.' It was the same man who'd shouted after me and Nancy one time on the pavement—I know who you are, he'd said, in the girl's face—and he put his face right up at Freda too.

'Do you know him?' I asked, as she caught hold of my arm saying Nancy could wait for her fish. 'What's he on about?'

Out in the sun on the pavement with the smell of Jeyes strong from the newly washed front of Jenning's the grocer's next door, Freda lifted her hand to her mouth as though she was holding a glass and shook it.

'The resident wino,' she said. 'Ignore.'

We walked down to the prom, with rowing boats on the sea, and women grabbing children trying to reach the water, and old men stretched out on the sand with hats on their faces, passing people who seemed not to see us though I don't know if that was me not seeing them.

'Where are we going?' I asked, when she led me up a hill and through a gap in a hedge so I scratched my bare arms.

'You'll see.'

Her fair hair was pulled back into a ponytail high on her head. I thought that if she looked at

291

me like that again, I'd have to turn away.

'How are things?' she asked. 'You're not to worry about ever having to go, you know. They think the world of you, not least because Sylvia doesn't drop round anywhere near so much since you arrived. Mother just wishes you wouldn't skivvy so.'

'Aunt Sylvia's the one who doesn't have much to do with Nancy, isn't she?' I said, and Freda's smile went and she shook her head as though I'd brought up the Black Death.

'I suppose I should be grateful to her, really,' she replied.

Freda asked about my new job, three days a week at the florist's, helping the owner, Ceridwen—who hated her name and only answered to C—put together arrangements from whatever we could lay our hands on. 'You'd think working with flowers would be very different from mopping floors in a hospital,' I told Freda, 'but they're not that far apart. You still hear about people dying and babies being born too.'

I was itching to know where Nancy had come from, but Freda was silent and looking straight ahead. I told her I wanted the war to be over and for her to come home, but she didn't say anything to that either. I said Nancy would like her back too and then I wondered at myself for being so ready to leave the girl at the house. I went on about Nancy, telling Freda about one of her drawings, of houses on fire and a horse rearing and a policeman being knocked flat in a hail of shrapnel. This town did suffer because the Germans knew the Americans were bringing stores into the Docks and their planes followed the river to drop bomb after

292

bomb.

'Crikey,' Freda said. 'I didn't think you'd have it so bad here.'

But I could see she'd taken it all in about Nancy and was pleased the girl was doing all right.

'I've been meaning to ask,' I said. 'Who is her mother? And her father? Might you tell me after all this time why the baby and I came to your family? I'm very glad we did, but I just wondered . . .'

We were going down a hill, sideways because it was steep, and ahead—oh, I never knew it was there and it was very beautiful—was a lake with an island in the middle, and beyond it an old house the size of a castle with windows that had no curtains.

'Don't say anything,' Freda whispered. 'Come with me.'

She wore pale trousers and a polka-dot blouse with short sleeves and little pleats high up to her neck. Her arms were so long, thin and white— paler again than mine—that when she held them out to me at the side of the lake and said, 'Come and say hello properly,' all I could think to reply was, 'Well, you ain't seen much of the sun.'

'Ain't seen much of you either,' she said. Freda seemed half happy, half sad, half with me, half not. I'd noticed the war made people like that, one minute glad to be alive, the next fearful who'd be the next to die.

'I take it you've missed me,' she said, putting her hands on my hips.

Freda was what you might call a cool customer and she had a habit of making me forget what I was trying to remember.

293

'I have missed you,' I whispered, thinking about the number of times I'd imagined seeing her, and wondering when I might sniff her ashy scent again. The water on the lake was still and glinting like foil.

'Come on,' she said suddenly, and I followed her across huge stepping stones over the water to an island in the middle and a hut she called the Bathing House.

We lay on the floor of this big shack with its broken glass ceiling. Freda was silent beside me, and I went over in my mind how distant she'd been when I mentioned Nancy's mother, and then what my little girl was doing back home without me and how she hadn't come out to wave us off down the street. I thought too how brave and wonderful Freda was being in the war, and how I couldn't believe she was at my side. Then she asked if I'd care to join her for a swim.

'I can swim,' I said brightly, trying so hard to sound worthwhile I must have come over as dim.

Freda gave me a funny look and for a moment, as daft as it seemed, I thought she was going to cry. Beatrice sometimes did that, burst into tears out of the blue, if she heard about someone's son being killed, or one time, a hedge she'd passed the day before all clipped nice, and the next morning blown to nothing.

'Glad to hear it,' Freda said.

'What I mean is, well, I've learned lots of things,' I said, reddening. 'I'm older, I've got a job, I'm not who I was in London . . . It's hot, isn't it?'

It was quiet but I felt sure she could hear my body shuddering with want as she told me the old house in the distance was empty. Freda asked me

294

to undo the buttons on the back of her blouse and I fingered each one from its hole, shaking as though I had St Vitus' Dance. My mouth was dry and thirsty. Her cream silk vest was edged with lace so fine I thought it would tear if I touched it.

*Dear Freda,*

*It was so good to see you. I wish you'd had more time but I know you have a job to do.*

*I think Nancy regrets not coming to see you off. She's like you with her passion for travel and usually doesn't miss an opportunity to see the trains. If we go and sit in the station again, I'll imagine you might appear out of the steam!*

*Josh is making her a train of her own. It's coming on beautifully, from a piece of a flagpole, and boxes, and cartridge cases for wheels, and he's painting it too. Your brother is so good with his hands. You might have guessed who her Number One Favourite is!*

*Beatrice is taking me to join the library because I've used up all her books, so any time I have, I'll be reading if not writing to you.*

*I wish the war would end so people stopped dying and you could come home for good.*
*Yours,*

*Ceci*

4

One early evening, Beatrice and I were seated

opposite each other at the kitchen table, our heads propped in our hands, looking at this little plate of fairy cakes we'd made as if they were the Crown Jewels. Sponges were at a premium in the war.

From above came a thundering on the stairs as Nancy hurtled down, grabbed one of the cakes, bit into it then tipped her head forward and dropped the mouthful on the floor. There was a scramble of claws on the tiles and a snuffling sound from the dog.

'Where has she learned that?' Beatrice asked.

Cruncher wagged his stump. The girl took another bite and dropped that too. The dog scared me at the start because he'd take your fingers off if you lingered too long giving him the tail-end of a sausage, but Nancy loved him from the off.

'Not from me,' I said. 'I always eat mine.'

One of Nancy's teachers had told Beatrice the girl was able but incapable of concentrating. She was, according to Miss Hinton, becoming a disruptive influence in class. I'd noticed she wouldn't always look at me when I was talking to her, as though she was listening to another voice saying something else.

'I've tried telling her,' I went on. 'She doesn't listen.'

Nancy carried on spitting bits of sponge on the floor with Cruncher scooping them up as though they were a double act down on the pier. Beatrice gave me a look.

'What can I do?' I asked. 'I'm not her mother.'

'What was that?' Nancy said.

'Nothing,' I replied.

Beatrice turned to Nancy and said, 'Miss Hinton says you're always asking questions instead of

296

getting on with your work.'

Herbert put his head round the door, probably on account of our voices going up. Whenever any shouting started, he usually came round the corner saying we were loud enough to alert the Germans.

'I don't see there's anything wrong with asking questions,' Nancy replied. 'If you ask questions you get answers.'

'She's got a point,' I said. The girl would have been coming up to eight and was quick off the mark.

'Do you want to come for a walk?' I asked. She used to love our hikes in the woods, glimpsing a stoat or a greenfinch and, once, a water vole sitting up on its back legs looking thoughtfully at the stream. If it rained, we'd be out the moment it stopped, watching the newly washed stillness all around us until a nettle leaf shimmied with a big fat drop of water that came so suddenly out of nowhere.

'No,' Nancy replied. 'Why don't you go with Freda?'

'Because Freda isn't here.' I stood up, my chair making a horrible scraping noise. 'And this war is never going to end.'

'That reminds me so much of Freda,' Herbert was saying as I went out into the garden, 'the girl answering back like that. Remember how she used to be with Sylvia?'

The May sky had a cold white look to it. I sat on the swing that Nancy rarely used any more, lifting my feet and feeling how it was to sit in the air.

From inside the house came shrieking and for a moment I thought Beatrice had lost patience with Nancy. Then I heard laughter and was ready to go back inside but Josh was standing in front of me, appearing out of thin air as he so often did.

'Guess what?' he said.

'Freda's coming home?'

He shook his head. 'Far more to celebrate than that. The Baker halfwit has been fool enough to ask Dot to get wed. They've a date set and everything. She'll be off our hands soon enough and we'll have the place to ourselves. Nancy's bagged her room.'

Oh, I thought to myself, good for Nancy, and Dot too. Andrew Baker was a bit of a drip but probably just what she needed, not some hulk of a thing telling her off for not stopping.

'That's the best joke I've heard in ages,' Josh went on. 'The loony marrying the strong arm of the law.'

Then he crouched so his face was looking up at mine.

'Don't fret, Ceci,' he said. 'You only have to say the word.'

A week or so later, I had another letter from Freda.

*Dear Ceci,*

*Your last letter was almost a book in itself! Still a lot about Josh. Am I missing something? (I think I am but I wish I wasn't, if you understand me.) Whatever did you mean, that time you said he was good with his hands?!*

*I wouldn't have thought I was Number One on Nancy's Christmas card list but if you say she's waiting for my train to come in, I should be very happy to be on it.*

*I've been doing a lot of thinking, not least about all those stars I met on the cruisers. I tell people here I met Hedy Lamarr and they think I'm joshing them. Everything was perfect about her but that doesn't mean I don't think other women aren't beautiful too.*

*Freda*

Dot married a week or so before we heard the country was no longer at war, and Beatrice came into the florist's to put in an order for the prettiest bouquet of pink and purple and white nigellas for her daughter, and a bunch of lily of the valley tied with silver satin ribbon for Nancy as bridesmaid.

The eve of her wedding, Dot had her mother's wardrobe out and the girl and I sat on the bed watching her go through it for a dress for her honeymoon day-trip to Weston.

'I wonder when Freda will come back,' I said, hoping Dot might have heard more.

'Filling my shoes before the ink is dry, is it?' she replied, and laughed.

I shook my head, horrified that was how she'd taken it. The house wouldn't be the same without Dot in her brightly coloured knitted tops and tight skirts with a split that showed a little black mole she had on the back of her knee. During the war she'd scrub and soak bits of old torn parachutes to make cream silk bloomers that had seams in funny places.

I was biting the inside of my mouth, thinking about things coming out wrong and never knowing what was round the corner. Nancy was quiet beside me.

'Don't worry about Misery Guts,' Dot said. 'She's forever going through the Change.'

Beatrice had been on about Nancy behaving herself at the wedding.

'Who's she?' Nancy asked, watching Dot pull on a long pink glove with a little row of pearl buttons. 'And what change?'

The girl grabbed the other glove and Dot helped pull it up her arm. I could see Nancy was going to be what Josh called a looker.

'Am I beautiful?' Nancy asked, waving her arm about. 'Like my mother?'

I had nothing of my own mother and Nancy had less than that. Would a name or a photo help her imagine a life with parents she chattered on through the night about having?

'Do you know who she is?' I asked, as though Nancy wasn't there, though the girl nodded at me when I glanced at her.

'Just call me daft,' Dot replied, which was the response she'd started giving whenever I tried tapping her.

'Sorry, Ceci,' she said then. 'You know how the old man is forever telling us to say as little as possible, so that drunk and his depressive wife can't make trouble for the g—' Dot raised an imaginary glass and said, 'As if the Voyles are anyone to talk!'

'Who? Who is?' Nancy asked. 'Do you mean my mother?'

'A mother is a very good thing to have,' I said, though I've since seen some that fight like cats with their daughters.

'Until she goes through the Change,' Dot replied, and then we started laughing on the bed,

300

until Nancy jumped in with us and hugged me and everything was as it used to be.

The girl cried when Dot moved in with Andrew, though she soon enough settled into Dot's room, with me staying in the boxroom—the *twll*, they all called it, which is Welsh for hole—we'd shared for so long. I found a box under Nancy's old bed and one of the things inside was a large piece of paper with a man and a woman cut from Dot's old sewing patterns stuck either side of the fold so that when it closed you might think they were kissing.

One night, Freda phoned and told her father she wasn't coming back here nursing after all. Though I was half used to thinking I'd never know what the heck was going on, I got myself into a bit of a state. I thought she could at least have spoken to me.

'She's doing very important work, Ceci,' Beatrice told me. 'In London.'

'Very clever,' Herbert said. 'Helping a surgeon called Mr Mountjoy repair soldiers' faces. It's a very skilled thing to be doing, using bone from their hips and shins, rather a privilege to be part of it. The things they can do nowadays.'

Josh was out on his motorbike or in the pub or under the pier with one of his five-minute girls, Dot was living with Andrew, Nancy was up in her room and there I was, sitting with Herbert and Beatrice like the backward spinster, listening to them singing Freda's praises for staying away.

'I could always go and visit,' I said, though I was reluctant to leave the girl and had little saved from my job. Nancy didn't have a mother but she was the first in town to have a little red-and-cream record player which didn't stop the moment she got in from school. My pay didn't last the length of the high street, because even through rationing there was usually something to buy for the family.

'You should keep hold of your money,' Beatrice said, 'not go spending it on trains. You'll have a better use for it one day.'

'Poor buggers,' Herbert went on. 'Freda says some of the wives have been turning their disfigured husbands away because they can't stand to look at them.'

'I will say for her,' Beatrice said, 'she's inherited my desire for helping other people and not always thinking of herself.'

Herbert said, 'To think, if it wasn't for that smashing girl I . . . da . . .'

'Now then, Ceci,' Beatrice told me. 'Work tomorrow. I think it's time we all turned in, don't you?'

I was tired of turning in. I was twenty-two. I wanted to stay up all night with Freda.

As I rose from my chair in the bay, Beatrice gave me a challenging look and I went up to my room thinking everything had seemed on the verge of something and now there was nothing, and Freda didn't think anything of me after all. I was fed up with the lot of it, feeling like I was the last to know.

I went into the *twll* and found Nancy back in her old bed with her head hanging over the edge. She didn't wake when I set her back on the pillow, and holding the warm weight of her, I felt such a proud, protective love. The nights we'd spent, me embellishing Freda's tales from her cruise-ship days about actresses and ice-skaters and politicians travelling the high seas, and Nancy always wanting one more story and then, I promise, Ceci, she'd say, we'll go to sleep. I thought to myself that

302

Freda might be breaking my heart by stringing me along in her letters, but Nancy was still there for me to cherish.

For a time the girl once more slept in my room as though things were as they had been, though we didn't half miss Dot walking about the house in her silky dressing gown on the heels of her feet with lavatory paper stuffed between her toes whenever she varnished her nails.

'Where does the day come from?' Nancy asked early one morning, as the room lightened to the sound of birdsong that always stopped so abruptly, though sometimes there'd be one extra little solo before the new silence of a day.

'It's the night opening its eyes,' I said, wondering if Freda was alone when she woke, and who might be keeping her from me. Though I tried hiding it, Nancy must have known I was unhappy.

I'd walk to work imagining Freda coming towards me on the pavement. We'd embrace outside the chemist's to give Mrs Gates—looking out of her window—reason for knocking back another tablet, and then I'd stick my head round the door of the florist's and say I was taking a day off.

When it came to Nancy starting at the County School, I'd given up on Freda coming home. I thought the Voyles knew things I didn't, and Beatrice had told me to save my money because I'd need it for a new life. I started bitterly staring at the paper for a place to rent for me and Nancy.

'She loves her work,' Beatrice said one day in the kitchen, 'but I think she's had enough now. There's only so long you can do that sort of thing.'

I heard my voice saying, 'Why have you kept me

here so long?'

'I beg your pardon, Ceci?'

Freda must have got her way of asking you to repeat things that made you wish you'd never said them from her mother. But I kept on. I was more or less spoiling for a fight.

'I just wondered why I came here with Nancy. And why you've been so . . . kind to let me stay.'

'You're one of the family, Ceci,' she said.

'Yes, but that's what I mean. I'm not, am I . . . and Nancy . . .'

'Oh!' Beatrice went, as though I'd delivered an insult. I couldn't tell if the charade had gone on so long she believed I was her own flesh and blood or if she was being deliberately obtuse. I didn't see that I was in no position to be querulous either.

'I don't suppose,' she said, 'when others were quick to put my daughter down . . . there was a girl who stood by Fre—'

The front door slammed. Freda's mother looked horrified, as though she'd done something impolite, and ran her fingers over her forehead. It was mid-September, the air was cooler, though Beatrice only needed a shaft of sunlight through the window on the floral-patterned tablecloth and she'd be patting her neck saying how hot it was and what a blessed relief that the war had come to an end.

'Nancy,' I said, as she walked into the kitchen. 'Speak of the devil!'

'What do you mean?' the girl snapped. The mothers at the school gates had warned me she might change once she began at 'big school'.

'You're always waiting to start on me,' Nancy said. 'Why can't you leave me alone and live your

304

own life?'

'Because I like hearing what you're up to,' I said, but she was right. I didn't have my own life.

'Up to?' Nancy said. 'Up to? What's that supposed to mean? That's another thing,' she went on. 'You're always trying to make out there's something going on.'

It was my turn to ask, 'What do you mean?' I looked at Freda's mother. *A girl who stood by Freda.* How many of us were there then?

'Oh, stop going on at me with the questions all the time,' Nancy said.

'I know how she feels,' Beatrice murmured as the girl went rushing from the room, the dog looking down the hall after her, too stiff to follow.

As I told myself often enough, one war was over but a smaller one was starting.

Beatrice clanked the lid back down on the bread tin and said, 'That's me done with the questions too.'

Not long after that, Cruncher died in his sleep and Nancy didn't speak for a week.

*　　　*　　　*

The day Freda wrote saying she'd got a job in the hospital here and wanted to buy a place, I thought, I shouldn't count my chickens but at least I've got something in writing. *Do you really think you need to ask?* I wrote back, when she raised the idea of me moving out of the boxroom and coming in with her.

When I told Beatrice our plans, she said, 'Where will the girl go?'

'With us, of course,' I replied.

'I expect you'll be glad to move somewhere with space for the three of you,' Beatrice said.

'Not half as glad as you'll be to see the back of us, I don't wonder.' I didn't intend to be cheeky, I just meant we could all have a new start.

Nancy didn't come with me to the station. She had her own friends and Beatrice said it was no bad thing, her not hanging off me all the time, that perhaps it was unhealthy, the way I'd been at her beck and call. I knew where she'd be, sitting under the yew tree in the churchyard not feeling the cold, with her best friend, Fflur Mason, the two of them plaiting each other's hair.

While I waited to leave, I ran up and down the stairs checking my face in the mirror of the little curved dressing table jammed between Nancy's old bed and mine.

Every time I rose from the sofa, Josh looked up. I wore a red-and-green patterned dress with stockings, and brown T-bar shoes, and red lipstick with a green pillbox hat on my smoothed hair curled overnight with rags at the ends. I thought a coat would spoil it, but Dot, who was round talking to Beatrice in the kitchen, made me take hers because it was November and the puddles from three days of rain were slippery with ice.

'Go on,' she said to me. 'She's waiting for you.'

But I was early, and I stamped my feet and touched my hair and tested my lipstick with my fingers as though they could see it didn't go over the edges, and when Freda got off the train she did an exaggerated double take as though she hadn't recognised me, and then both of us laughed. Oh, I felt happy walking back from the station, my eyes and then my head swivelling to look at her and then turning back straight ahead when I'd stared too long. Big ideas and dreams I had, and, Better late than never, was what I was thinking.

Freda's hair was tucked into a brown beret so what you mainly saw was her long pale neck coming out of a short black overcoat with large brown buttons, and her legs as long as anything in grey woollen trousers over black lace-up boots that made no sound on the pavement.

While the house purchase was coming through—they wanted this and that to prove a single woman had the deposit—Freda slept on a bed made up in the sitting room because she said my little room—her old one—was too small for the two of us. Nobody dared try winching Nancy from Dot's old roost.

A couple of times Freda mentioned that lying on the sofa was making the shoulder she'd injured in the war play up, and sometimes when I stayed down late with her, giggling and getting excited about having a home of our own, she'd give me a look in the pinky light from the fringed standard lamp as if to say it was a crime to be happy. It's that damned war, not you, she said once, when I got upset thinking there was something she wasn't saying, so I went back to stabbing at the fire with a poker because I liked seeing the sparks fizz just when you thought it was dying.

'You can tell me, you know,' I said, which is the closest I dared get to the subject of Nancy or anything else, especially when Freda was down. I didn't want to spoil things, but I see now I should have pushed more on the girl's behalf.

One night, Nancy came down in her nightdress poking me with her freezing feet and asking when I was coming up to bed. 'I thought you liked having your own room,' I told her, 'but you're welcome to stay down here with us.'

'Why are you always with *her*?' she asked, not calling Freda by name. We had a game of Ludo then, with Nancy looking at Freda as she kept on that Beatrice would go up the wall if she knew she was up so late with school the next day. After that, Nancy didn't come down again, and Freda and I started going for walks. The stars might have been points of ice in the sky but I didn't feel the cold when we stood on the prom, our hands on the railings, looking out at the sea.

'It's a wonder it doesn't freeze,' I said, the first night, and Freda put her hand on mine, then turned me to her and pulled me close, as the waves came over and over, and all there was in the darkness were white lines sinking into rattling pebbles.

The morning we left the Voyles', Nancy didn't want to go. She made an awful scene.

'I hadn't known she cared that much for us,' Beatrice remarked.

'I'll stay here with Josh,' Nancy said, while he and Freda were loading the van.

'No, you won't,' Beatrice told her, though I had an idea she'd miss us. When I touched her arm and said, 'Thank you for everything,' Freda's mother replied, 'It's us who should be telling you that.'

\*     \*     \*

'It's me who should be telling *you* that,' I heard myself saying.

I gave Sarah a look from my chair, the same one

308

I used to give Freda, to see if I should carry on talking or stop, not that I could make out her expression all that well.

'Oh Ceci,' she said. 'All this inside you not coming out. How have you lasted so long, seeing people like me make a fuss about nothing when all this has happened to you?'

'We've all got our situations,' I said, and she was quiet then.

'Well,' I told her, 'I don't know about you, but I've always thought things seem better with a fire,' and that's what the two of us did: we laid a fire in the hearth. Sarah scrunched the newspaper into balls then tipped on coals from the scuttle and I set a little teepee of kindling on top.

'Thank you for showing me,' she said. 'I've never made a fire before.'

'Go on,' I said, handing her the matchbox. 'Do the honours.'

I like a grate of real flames. That was one of the few things I stood fast on with Freda. No pretend coals in an electric fire in my middle room and that's final, I'd tell her. She gave me such a funny look when I spoke like that; perhaps I should have done it more often.

'Go on, Ceci,' Sarah told me. 'I'm listening.'

I worried my voice would be full of holes—as you get older, your voice starts to go and others stop hearing—but I'd seen well enough that Sarah, with all her marvelling at art deco cinemas and lidos, Bakelite switches and biscuit barrels, had a regard for the past and a taste for not letting go. I say that, but there was still her and that husband that needed sorting.

The dog was flat out in front of the fire, paws

twitching with dreaming, as he soaked up the warmth. The place reeked of wet fur, but that's another thing I see makes a house a home—a dog, though the estate agent had pointed at Mungo's rug saying it might be an idea to get in professional cleaners if sprucing the place up a bit was beyond me at my time of life. The truth is, the girl was giving me the will to go on.

## 5

The first night I left Nancy in the attic room of our new home, I thought of that moment years before, when I had carried her down a fire escape without a clue where we were going.

She had a blue bear night-light on her side-table which she kept on in the dark even when she was older and thought herself anything but a baby. She would have been thirteen or so at that time.

'Sweet dreams,' I told her. She lay still beneath the steeply sloping ceiling in a bed the Voyles had given us.

I was at the door when the girl said to me, 'I know, you know.'

'Know what?' I heard the break in my voice as I turned.

Nancy sat up and folded her arms. It was the first time she'd spoken all day. At one point, I thought she'd gone back to Josh, but I eventually found her in the cupboard under the stairs. She must have liked small, dark, fenced-in places because she did the same at the Voyles', Cruncher beside her, right up until he died.

310

'I know Freda is my mother. That's why you've made me come here. Beatrice told me.'

'Beatrice?'

Josh and Dot used to laugh, claiming Beatrice was growing more like Freda and saying whatever she pleased, but this was beyond a joke.

Nancy said, 'She told me my mother was a clever, beautiful woman far away and Herbert said too, about Freda working far away.'

'Oh,' I replied, coming back into the room. Nancy's little attic window was a black square between the eaves with the bare trees beyond, and then the church which always looked so forbidding if you didn't know it was supposed to be welcoming and good.

'Let's see what Freda says in the morning,' I said.

'Why hasn't she told me?' Nancy asked.

I went to kiss her cheek before she pulled away, and I caught the peachy scent she'd been given for Christmas by Dot and Andrew—*L'Aimant* by Coty, advertised by a woman in a long red dress twice Nancy's age. I thought it far too old for her but Dot gave the girl all sorts of things. At eleven, Nancy was parading up and down the high street in shoes with heels and tops in black. I don't say they should be wearing pink all the time but black isn't right for young girls, at least I don't think so.

'Is it always what Freda says?' Nancy asked. 'Will she tell me about my father?'

Standing on the landing, I thought of Freda saying nothing all this time and I went to the bathroom to wash and then into the front bedroom to crouch by the mattress on the floor and pull my nightdress from the old case she'd given me in

311

London to carry the baby's things. The January cold was shrinking me into myself while Harvey, Cruncher's successor, would be back at the Voyles' stretched out in front of their green-tiled fireplace with the small, worn leather bellows on the hearth that Josh used to aim at his rear. That dog loved the fire as much as he did scavenging for food.

Freda's voice came coolly from the doorway.

'I expect we'll sleep well tonight,' she said. 'Even without a proper bed.'

'Nancy's asking about her parents,' I whispered. Then louder, because Freda didn't seem to have heard, 'Even if you won't tell me, might you say something to her? Who was Nancy's mother?' My voice was going up. 'She died, didn't she?'

Freda shook her head. 'I can't say,' she said.

'Why not? Shouldn't you say something so at least she has . . . some idea? She's old enough now.'

'Please . . . leave it.' Freda paused. 'The war's done this to a lot of children. She's not alone.'

Though the landing light was on, her face was dark in the doorway. Once, during the war, when Freda's Aunt Sylvia came to the house, Beatrice had pushed her into the kitchen when she saw me coming down the hall. I was always catching things on the other side of the door. *The girl's parents*, I heard that time and *stop* and *gaze* as well. Funny, isn't it? The first time I read that poem—*What is this life if, full of care, We have no time to stand and stare* . . . I remembered Sylvia jawing away in the kitchen about stopping and gazing. *No time to wait till her mouth can, Enrich that smile her eyes began*. That's the line that always brings to mind Freda.

'Though I know that doesn't make it any easier,'

312

she said.

'She thinks you're her mother,' I told her.

'Me? Where did she get *that* idea? That's ridiculous. Bloody people. What have they been saying now?'

There was a little gasp from behind Freda and a flick of bare feet on the stairs as Nancy went back up to her room. 'Who *is* my mother then?' the girl shouted, when I ran up after her. 'And why did Beatrice tell me it was Freda?' She pushed at me as she told me to stop lying and go away and leave her alone. I called downstairs.

'Shove off,' Freda muttered as she came up, and for a moment I thought she meant me until she pointed at the wall and I heard thumping. The house had been empty for ages and with all our performing, the neighbours must have wondered what hit them. Talk about a baptism of fire.

I waited, doubtless with my mouth open, thinking me and the girl might finally hear the truth.

'I'm not lucky enough to be your mother,' Freda told Nancy. 'And I don't deserve to be, either. But I'd like to be your friend.'

I watched the two of them looking at each other. Freda's voice was flat and her face set the way I imagined she'd have had it at work for the worst things that happened during the war.

'Beatrice told you the truth,' she went on, 'about your mother being good, kind, clever and beautiful, and there is nothing more I can tell you aside from you being very much her daughter, and a special girl we want to care for.'

When Nancy climbed back into bed, Freda kissed her own fingers and put them to the girl's forehead. I did use to wonder what gripped her so when she stared at the girl's face as though she'd seen a ghost.

'Your home is here if you'll have us,' Freda said, and I had to will myself not to cry hearing that and remembering Beatrice telling me near enough the same when the baby and I came from London all those years before.

'Shush now,' Freda said at the door, 'and be strong and happy and successful for your mother. Sweet dreams.'

Back in the bedroom, we lay in silence until I said, 'That woman in the hospital, her mother, she d—?'

Freda put a hand on my leg and what she said shook me as much as her tone. 'Best to leave it,' she told me, her voice far firmer now. 'If it comes out who her family is, Nancy might be taken from us by law.'

That night there was only the noise of the house—the creak of an invisible tread on the stairs, a sigh from a stray breath of air in a pipe—showing me the way it would be. I felt there was something deep and sad and dangerous between us and I didn't know what to do. Then I felt Freda's breath on my cheek as she said, 'I'm so sorry.'

She was silent then. Through the night, each of us went and checked on the girl who was sleeping. I couldn't get warm. As dawn came through the bare windows, I felt Freda's fingers in my hair and turned to the white curves of her face. When her lips touched mine, all going round in my mind went to nothing, though minutes later when Nancy tapped on the door and came to lie between us in bed, hope and happiness filled the space and the

314

three of us stopped shivering in time.

Nancy never mentioned me and Freda sleeping in the same bed. She didn't come in again, too old for that kind of thing really by the time we were living together as a family, if that isn't an optimistic description of the way things were, for a while at least.

The end of the spring term, I answered the door to Nancy, a gerbil and a tortoise because the school caretaker was creating about feeding them in the holidays. One sunny Sunday morning Nancy put the gerbil on Freda's chest as she lay on the back lawn, and though Freda liked nature she balked at opening her eyes to see scratty little things with claws and whippy tails staring back at her. She chased Nancy twice round the square as the Eucharist crowd was leaving church.

The three of us laughed well enough about that, perhaps with our eyes looking between each other a little too often, but laughing all the same, though the gerbil and the tortoise went missing in the garden, and when we couldn't find replacements, Nancy went back in with two ten-shilling notes instead.

Freda insisted on both our names on the deeds of the house. In case something happens to me, she'd say, and then I'd feel sad and wary.

'Are you happy?' Josh asked, taking my hand the first time he came round, looking me in the eyes, and I nodded and smiled. You do know he holds a candle for you, don't you, Freda would tell me, and when she tried joking like that, I saw she wasn't anywhere near as haughty as people thought.

'Are you happy?' I'd ask Nancy, and she'd tell me, 'I liked it best when it was the three of us,

Ceci. You, me and Josh.'

Several times I'd think to tell the girl about that night in London and then I'd remember Freda's talk of the law and Nancy not being ours to keep. I'd wonder whether her mother died, after all, and why Freda stayed away so long after the war. In winter, when the trees were bare in the square outside, and Freda was on nights, all kinds of things went through my mind as I stared at the ceiling rose in our bedroom, a circle of acorns and oak leaves, still there, stuck fast, no cracks, after all this time, though Nancy went a long time ago.

\*　　　\*　　　\*

Nancy was sitting on her towel beside Freda who lay out in the gentle September sun. Their latest set-tos were about the girl's new friend, Sandra Martin, who Freda thought as thick as two short planks. 'Who are *you* to say that about my friend?' Nancy would start up. Poor Sandra had lost her mother and was being reared by an older sister who had stopped her coming on a picnic to the beach with us, which had made Nancy go quieter again.

'I wonder if there are still rabbits on that island,' Freda said.

Nancy and I looked at the patch of land that rose like dough out of the water. It had a lighthouse and low buildings as white as anything in the sun. The warm salty wind blew strips of hair across our faces.

'When I was a child,' she went on, 'that island's rabbits had white spots on their lungs and nobody could eat them. There was a cholera hospital on

316

the island at one time. They put them there off the ships.'

'What's a cholera hospital?' Nancy asked.

'A hospital for people with cholera.'

'What's that?'

Though her job made her touchier than ever—a cottage hospital's idea of clinical excellence was never going to match up to Sister Voyle's—Freda could always be drawn on pathology.

'Not being able to keep anything down or it coming out the other end like water,' Freda said. 'It spreads like wildfire through contaminated water and can be fatal,' she went on. 'That's why they used that island, to keep the poor buggers isolated.'

The two of them shared a fascination with grim sorts of things. I think this made Freda think Nancy could easily become a doctor, though I'd have liked the girl to read more. As Nancy grew older, she'd ask about my books: 'Who's in this one that you don't like, Ceci?' And when Freda noticed it was bad characters the girl liked hearing about, she started coming through the door saying, 'Mrs Danvers was buying two pounds of potatoes in Jenning's,' or, 'Bill Sykes just staggered out of the Con Club tanked up on whisky.' That's why it's so harrowing living in a small town, she'd tell Nancy, because they're all here, all those characters, every last one of them, and sometimes, with the tone Freda used, the girl didn't know whether to laugh or not. I used to like C. S. Lewis too, and coconut strips from the newsagent's, until Freda said it was the White Witch behind the counter and I couldn't go in again keeping a straight face. Get Freda in the right mood and she was wicked for impressions of people.

'Without a boat, nobody could get there, without a boat, nobody could leave,' Freda went on. 'This Channel's currents make San Francisco Bay look like a paddling pool, so the cholera crew were well and truly on their own. Escaping Alcatraz is a holiday camp in comparison, and yet a—a girl swam these waters once, beyond the island, all the way to Weston.'

'What's Alcatraz?' Nancy asked.

'Alcatraz?' Freda said. 'It's a prison where they put children who don't do as they're told.'

When Nancy went to splash awkwardly in the water, I saw how long and thin she was in her bathing suit.

'Stop staring,' Nancy shouted so I raised my hand and made a point of looking down, knowing the girl was becoming self-conscious. She'd stopped having meals with us at the table and I'd started taking a tray up to her room. Pandering, Freda called it. It's her age, Beatrice would say, Freda was just the same, and if Nancy was there to hear it, she'd look, as if still puzzling what link there was between her and Freda. Join the club, I used to think, looking across the table at the girl every Sunday, which is when we went to the Voyles' for lunch.

'Did you do much swimming?' I asked Freda. Her effusion had made me curious. Verbal diarrhoea was her phrase for it, if anyone said much more than a yes or a no.

'Tell me about you growing up,' I said.

'Remember, only paddling!' Freda bellowed. 'The tide's on its way out.'

'I'm too old for paddling,' Nancy yelled back.

318

'Who were they then?' I kept on. 'Your friends. Are they still in the town?'

'I had just the one, really,' Freda replied. She turned onto her side, her back to me. 'This sun,' she said. 'It's burning me already.'

I started telling her I wished she would be more open about her past, and why wasn't she, and had it something to do with Nancy's mother, and why had the Voyles taken us in, and how close were the two of us really if she wasn't prepared to say. I said I was grateful to her family for having me, but I'd looked after the girl all these years, and while I thought I could see there was something very serious behind it all, would it be so terribly illegal to tell me, because didn't I deserve to be told—and more so, didn't the girl deserve to know, especially if her mother had a link with the town?

Freda had seen such shocking tragedy in the war, I said, so I wondered what could be so dreadful she couldn't say? And I went on about it being easy to doubt how much she thought of me and Nancy.

When Freda shot up I thought it was due to me going too far—until I heard Nancy's screams.

'Holy Moses,' Freda said. 'She's gone in too deep.'

Freda ran so fast she had the girl out of the water as I got to them with a towel.

I heard Nancy say, 'You said a girl swam it and I wanted to say hello to the poor buggers.'

'There aren't any,' Freda replied. 'They went a long time ago.'

'Died?'

Freda gave her an awfully long look before she said, 'Yes, dead.'

Freda was so strong and gentle that day. No mention was made of Nancy not doing as she was told, or going out of her depth, or even of Freda's damp clothes sticking to her body. She made a fire from driftwood and got it going with her lighter. We sat and ate in dusky, orange silence. I felt so much to blame, I couldn't look at either of them.

'I don't understand,' Nancy said. 'Why don't we fall through the sand when it's made of all these tiny pieces?'

'They're grains,' Freda replied, as we watched sand run from Nancy's hand, and when I looked again at Freda she was rubbing her eyes. 'Damn wind,' she said, 'it's blown it in my face.'

Back at the house I helped the girl with homework she was always leaving until the last minute.

'Work hard and you'll become someone important,' I used to tell her, because I had such a respect for education. I should have told her she was important anyway, but we were never that sort of family.

In the bedroom, Freda was lying in her white cotton pyjamas on top of the covers with a fire in the grate sending warmth into the cool summer evening air. I sat and took her hand. I couldn't have been happier and sadder at the same time.

'Nancy's in bed,' I said. 'I'm so sorry about going on. Are you all right?'

Freda shook her head. 'She went out too far,' she replied. 'We could have lost our brave, strong girl to the sea.' Then she put a long white finger to her lips and closed her eyes.

I looked at the fire crackling away. From every chimney we'd pulled out carpet someone had shoved up to block draughts. We've given the house back its lungs, I'd told Freda, and she'd replied that I had a way with words. For a while after, I'd wonder how that was meant—if she might be saying she didn't have the words herself.

I enjoyed bringing those hearths to life but it's a sad sort of thing, a fire, giving out all that warmth while burning itself to nothing. Funny to think something can make you feel so glad and despairing at once, a little like learning to count one's blessings. I find church bells the same, and birdsong at dusk, or watching white fluffy clouds move quickly across a blue sky. Another thing I used to wonder about no end was the sea and its endlessness, and whether that made me happy or sad.

\*     \*     \*

'I've a question for you,' Nancy said, putting her satchel on the breakfast-room table—which Freda had told her not to.

'Nobody's stopping you,' Freda said, her eyes on the medical magazine she had delivered each month. 'Take that bag off the table.'

I'd spend hours wondering where Nancy came from, before that night in London, and what it was that attached her to Freda, and whether she wouldn't or couldn't tell me why she had taken a baby from that hospital room.

'They might not stop you but they may not answer,' I said, putting the bag on the floor.

'You told me,' Nancy told Freda, 'that you are not my mother.'

Freda didn't look up. The breakfast-room

window looked onto next door's wall only a few feet away, which could come over very claustrophobic.

'And you said about her being good, kind, clever and beautiful.'

I was looking straight ahead, counting down to another of their rows.

'If you know that,' the girl went on, 'you must know who my mother is and who my father is too.'

Freda looked up. As Nancy became less malleable, Freda became tetchier.

'That's the kind of cock-eyed rationale that won't get you anywhere near medical school,' she said.

The girl seemed on the verge of tears. She was struggling with Freda's precious science subjects and had joined the town's amateur dramatics group where she and Sandra were the youngest-ever members. I liked hearing Nancy's stories about rails of outfits in the basement, and the smell of the dust in the spotlights, and how it felt standing on stage looking into the blackness trying to make out a face.

I said, 'But she has a point.'

Freda turned to me. 'And that would be?'

'That she doesn't know and you do.'

Sometimes I'd think how little I knew of Freda, the dark, wet streets she might have walked, the films she'd seen, the parks she'd sat in and meals she'd eaten, and who she was with each time, and then I'd wonder if that's what she thought of when she sat in one of her silences. For a long time I lived, I see now, waiting for a knock on the door and the sound of heels tapping determinedly into our home.

322

Nancy said, 'Just tell me. What's the big secret? Why won't you say?'

Freda's face was still, her lips slightly apart. She looked between us as though it was dawning she was trapped. Nancy was running a little red bead bracelet Sandra had given her up and down her wrist.

'Are you two going to keep on?' Freda rose from the table. 'Because I've told you. Please, both of you, it's difficult . . .'

I looked down the hall but Sandra wasn't waiting. She was round all the time since her sister had got herself a boyfriend and her father was out all hours, visiting his lady friends who didn't know about each other though the rest of the town did. The camp bed we set up the first weekend Sandra stayed was a permanent fixture and her toothbrush with a head shaped like a pig never left the glass in the bathroom.

Freda was barely out of the room when Nancy said to me, 'Josh says she talks to you like a child.'

'Go and do your homework,' Freda shouted from the hall.

*       *       *

She didn't speak to us for three days and then only cracked when Nancy, who couldn't stand it any more, asked if she'd go with her looking for glow worms.

'I didn't mean to upset you, Ceci,' the girl told me. 'I only wanted to know about my mother . . . and . . . and my father.'

'I'm sure Freda would tell you if she could,' I replied for the umpteenth time.

The first I knew of any amnesty was Freda making a show of rifling through the kitchen drawer for the torch.

I stood in the doorway and said, 'It wouldn't hurt to tell her what you know, would it?'

Freda didn't turn round. Like me, she didn't cry readily, though in time I was able to tell when her head was as heavy with tears as mine. Mostly though, she gave a good impression of being one of those who could close down in an instant, as though a blink was a full stop to emotion.

'It would,' Freda said. 'Please, it would, and besides, it's very . . . Ceci, I'm sorry.'

I started to doubt myself then. I questioned how much it was about Nancy and how much I was using her mother to look for a row. I wasn't sure what Freda felt for me and whether I might make trouble for the girl. I didn't want to rock the boat and risk losing what I wasn't sure I had. If Freda told me it was best to leave it, who was I to keep on? And I couldn't bear upsetting Freda.

That was wrong. I let the girl down.


6


On Nancy's fifteenth birthday, there was silence as she opened the gift from Freda and pulled out a huge book. Freda had a reverential expression on her face, as though it was the Holy Bible.

'*Gray's Anatomy*,' Nancy read out. There was a diagram of a human torso on the cover showing internal organs including a purple heart.

Her school reports always said she could do

anything she wanted, though increasingly there were caveats (*easily distracted*, *lacking confidence*, and *spending lunchtimes talking to boys*). Much later, I'd think we'd taken the teachers' comments to mean the girl could do anything, when perhaps their intended emphasis was on it being what she wanted.

'It's a medical textbook,' Freda said. 'The best there is.'

Nancy looked at me as if Freda was trying to be funny and then said, 'Very nice, thank you.'

'A doctor saving lives,' Freda went on. 'I can't imagine anything more important.'

'*You* can't imagine,' Nancy replied. 'What about me? Perhaps I don't want to be a good, clever woman.'

She stood up from the table as though squaring up for another fight about her mother.

'In any case,' she said, 'I'm going to be an actress.'

'No security in it,' Freda said. 'You'll be signing yourself up to the back end of a pantomime horse.'

Nancy turned to me. 'I'm the Virgin Mary in the am dram Christmas tableaux,' she said. 'Will you come and see me?'

'Of course we will,' I replied, though Freda was staring at the table as though she'd been asked to applaud animal cruelty.

\*     \*     \*

The evening of Nancy's debut at the Salter Rooms, Freda and I ran through the streets in coats and berets and boots beneath bare, frosty branches but we were still late. Freda preferred arriving at the last minute to minimise the risk of having anything to do with people either side. Nancy watched from the wings as we pushed along the row of tip-up seats to Josh. She ignored my smile but waved so ferociously at him, the coat-hanger shaped like a halo on her head wobbled. Before lights out, I sensed Freda's eyes bolting back and forth. She got terribly agitated about being waylaid by one of the garrulous women from the hospital who asked after Nancy.

'Why are you always late for everything?' the girl asked us afterwards.

'I couldn't keep up,' Freda said. 'With all you were saying.'

'Very funny,' Nancy replied. She had been given the prized finale role of sitting with a small blond boy, *Mother and Child*, as the church choir sang.

'You looked so beautiful,' I told her. 'And "Jesu, Joy of Man's Desiring", I love that.' They'd put a gold-painted board with an oval cut into it around her so she looked like a cameo. I felt so grateful and peaceful and proud after all that had gone on.

'Its correct title,' Freda said in her Sister's voice, 'is the tenth movement of the cantata *Herz und Mund und Tat und Leben BMV* 147.'

Freda enjoyed listening to concerts on the wireless and had picked up a few bits of languages on her travels. From the start she encouraged my reading. *Animal Farm* she came back with one day. It's not rustic whimsy, it's political comment, she said. I know who George Orwell is, I replied, thank you very much.

'Well, I'm glad the words were in English so I could understand it,' I said. 'Every word.' And I started singing *Striving still to truth unknown . . .*

326

until Nancy said, 'Ceci!' so loudly that everyone looked round and I realised I was spoiling our girl's moment with my smart alec ways.

Freda didn't let up assuring Nancy know she thought her acting ambitions were a pipe dream. I knew she was disappointed when it became obvious the girl wasn't going to be the next Marie Curie, but what can you do, I'd tell her, it's Nancy's life, not yours.

'Didn't you ever have dreams?' I asked.

Freda gave me one of her looks.

'No, not like that.'

'Like what then? How did you go to London to train as a nurse? You must have had some ambition.'

I imagined it was Freda's humility that made her say no more. She loathed boastfulness or people being overly forward. I can't abide that girl's appalling sense of entitlement, she'd say about Sandra Martin, who wasn't at all sure of herself underneath that face of full make-up. But Freda did see that Sandra thought the world of Nancy, and there were times when the girls loved being with Freda because she could be very witty and good company.

One Saturday, we took the two of them to an audition in Bristol for a dance troupe, and Freda was brooding in the driver's seat. She regarded kicking your legs in sequins on a provincial stage as completely unacceptable. Anything to do with stage schools and ballrooms in Blackpool and men with snake hips in trousers with folds down the front, and she'd be off about how showy and trashy it all was.

'Nothing more than a line-up of tarts,' was the

327

way she put it before we left the house to pick up Sandra. 'Next thing,' she went on, striding down the hall, 'we'll be watching the pair of them in bathing suits in a beauty contest.'

'That's an idea,' said Nancy, who knew how to get her going. She handed me the flask I'd forgotten to put in the bag for Freda, who maintained civilisation was being in spitting distance of a cup of tea, a lavatory and Marks & Spencer.

On these outings with the girls—we took them to see a few plays and one or two day trips to Weston, and once to an ice rink which we all enjoyed—I was braced for a bust-up, but Nancy was so much calmer with a friend at her side. I loved seeing her and Sandra together, rolling their eyes at each other as Freda held forth in the front. It was clear the girl liked having someone she could call her own. My friend, Sandra, she'd say in a proud, possessive voice.

We were going along in the Morris and a van came towards us with the words *always available for hire* above its windscreen.

'How can it be always available,' Freda asked, 'if someone's driving about in it right now?'

I enjoyed that sort of carry-on—if people's grammar had been as bad back then, she'd have been one of those writing letters to the papers about apostrophes in wrong places—but it annoyed and embarrassed Nancy, who let out a terrific sigh in the back. You're always having a go about something, she'd said in a spat the night before, and yet if I ask you anything, you tell me to shove off. Why don't we just leave each other alone?

328

'This girl is going out half-dressed again,' I heard one evening not long after the Bristol jaunt, and went to see Freda in the hall with Nancy on the stairs wearing a sleeveless yellow polka dot dress with a fashionable full skirt—an outfit I'd bought her with my money from the florist.

'You may as well have the words *always available for hire* tattooed on your forehead,' Freda said, which made Nancy crosser again because she hadn't a clue what she was on about.

'Why do you always have to comment on me when I never say anything about you?' Nancy asked. 'Though I could.'

'I beg your pardon,' Freda said.

'I said—'

'I know what you damn well said.'

'I said,' Nancy went on, 'I can't believe I ever thought you were my mother.'

Freda headed for the front door and Nancy followed, on her way to rehearsal. She was Lottie in J.B. Priestley's *When We Are Married*, and Sandra was the maid.

Nancy turned back to me. 'Tell her, Ceci,' she said.

'I'm not saying anything,' I replied, as the front door slammed so the sash windows jumped on their cords. Like Freda, I thought to myself, I won't say anything. I'd had enough of the rowing. We were getting like those families you see nowadays on morning television shows where bouncers are poised either side of the stage to break up any fights.

\*     \*     \*

329

One evening I was surprised when Freda agreed to come and see Nancy off on a school trip to the theatre. I wasn't sure if Freda noticed people looking at us as we waved off the bus. The other parents stood talking but she wanted to leave.

'Don't you feel as though someone should be here to meet us with a suitcase of clean clothes?' Freda asked, as we walked off.

'What do you mean?' I hadn't seen her so breezy in ages.

'Well, it's like getting out of prison, isn't it?' she said, then saw my look of surprise.

'That's not a very nice thing to say,' I told her.

'Who wants to be nice?' she replied, taking my hand.

It was a weekday with nobody about. On the high street, Freda put her arms around me and kissed my lips. When I looked across the road, a man was standing in a shop doorway with a cigarette halfway from his mouth, blowing out smoke and watching us through narrowed eyes.

\*        \*        \*

The following summer, Freda and I were sitting in the garden on stripy deck chairs I'd bought from a new shop in town called the Golden Opportunity, when we heard running footsteps and then Dot shouting from the other side of the back wall.

'Freda!' she called. 'Quickly! Come to the door!'

Freda didn't have to be told twice.

'Nancy!' she shrieked as she ran down the hall, no doubt thinking something had happened to the girl—but Nancy came to the top of the stairs and shouted, 'What?' So the three of us were in earshot when Dot caught her breath at the front door and told us Josh had been in an accident. He was going into Cardiff on his motorbike and he'd been hit by a lorry turning right into the main road out of town.

'You'd better come up the house,' Dot said. 'Mother and Dad have blacked out.'

Freda paused. 'Is he . . .'

Dot said, 'He was doing sixty miles an hour, Freda. Andrew said he'd have gone out like a light.'

She began to cry, huge heaving sobs that made it seem as though she was lifting herself off the doorstep, and Nancy started up too behind us.

When the girl ran up to her room, saying everything was awful and she couldn't bear it, I didn't want to leave, but Dot said please, could we all just come, because Herbert and Beatrice would want Nancy there too. 'I will then,' she said from the top of the stairs, because the girl loved Freda's parents even though they weren't always impressed by her behaviour.

At the house, Freda's parents were sitting in two separate chairs, with Dot and Freda on the sofa and me in the dark wooden chair in the bay where I'd sat so often, and Nancy standing beside me saying, 'I want Josh.' I couldn't take in him dying. All I could think of was us chasing cows or him holding my head in the river, or me, him and the girl sitting under the stairs during an air raid.

'This is the end,' Freda said, as though her parents weren't in the room. 'They won't come back from this. I've seen it happen.'

Dot shook her head fiercely and Nancy started sobbing again. There was an awful sort of feel in

331

the room, as though all the laughter and singing and atmospheres there'd ever been—and once, Josh and Dot and Nancy doing a conga round the sitting room because Herbert had won a whack on the horses and had never bet a penny in his life—had gone to nothing.

Nancy didn't come to Josh's funeral. She said she had an upset stomach and couldn't keep anything down, though I hadn't seen her eat since the night he died.

Sitting in the church I thought of the first thing Josh had said the last time he was round.

'This place is a cattery,' he told me, kissing me on the forehead as he came through the door. 'You need a man round every so often to break things up a bit.'

I resolved then I wouldn't get involved in any more of the shouting. I'd never been one for brawls in any case. I remembered one morning a man coming into the florist saying he wanted a bouquet for his wife who'd made him sleep in his car, and it depressed me all day thinking of couples warring, and how I used to try to come between my mother and father, and then my mother with her hand to her face.

Freda said later she thought Josh's fits were epilepsy and we wondered if he'd had a turn on his bike. The coroner ruled death by misadventure so nobody thought it was deliberate, though I know there was talk about him drinking too much and being wayward and not having a purpose in life, but then people had always said that kind of thing about one or other of the Voyle children.

Our house in the square was quiet after dear, gentle Josh died, and when Harvey went not long

332

after, having choked on a chicken bone, it became quieter still.

We barely saw Nancy and she never spoke about Josh or anything else. I'm all right, she'd say, shaking herself down, as though I'd tried to take hold of her, and then I'd go down the stairs tearful at that sad scowl of hers that always seemed like a smile given up.

After a poor show in her exams, Nancy got a job in a jeweller's in town. It was the same every night then. In she came and out she went. Though she'd been offered a place in the dance troupe, Sandra Martin hadn't. Sandra was a little thick in the leg, I always thought, but Nancy had long thin limbs like Freda. If Freda wasn't so fair and Nancy so dark, you might think they were mother and daughter, and someone once did, outside a cinema in Cardiff, which stopped the two of them quarrelling for all of five minutes.

'Why did we go through the performance of taking them over to Bristol if Nancy never had any intention of joining that outfit?' Freda asked.

'Because she doesn't want to leave Sandra,' I said. 'They're best friends. They do everything together.'

Freda gave me such a funny look. Since she never fought shy of saying her piece, I felt uneasy whenever she kept her mouth shut, not least because silences in our house were always so loud with unanswered questions.

I could give you any number of examples of her being quick off the draw.

When we first moved into the house, we all had bikes. One Sunday, we were going along Broad Street, the three of us on the pavement because

Freda didn't want Nancy on the road, and two girls coming towards us didn't go single file so we could pass.

'You shouldn't be on here,' the girl told Nancy, who was first, then me in the middle.

'And you shouldn't be so fat,' Freda replied, bringing up the rear.

The girl was a tub—Bethan Elias her name was. Nancy told us she had to have the belts on her school tunic let out, but that still didn't make it right, Freda telling her to lose weight.

The following week I listened to Bethan's father, the vicar, talk about goodwill to all men— the gist was don't say anything unless it's pleasant—though of course Freda wasn't there to hear it. She was back at the house with a cigarette and the Sunday papers. She didn't believe in church or God or heaven or hell or anything else like that. 'When you die, that's it,' she said. 'The End.'

Whenever she said that, it made me think sad thoughts, like how it would be to hold the hand of a loved one dying. I went through a stage of being awfully mawkish, what with Nancy growing away from me, and then there was the way Freda was too.

\*　　　\*　　　\*

Freda did her best with Nancy, I know she did, but the girl seemed to run away, with us forever in her wake telling her to calm down.

One afternoon the phone went and it was Dot's husband saying it was lucky he was the town's policeman or Nancy, who had been caught

334

pocketing a lipstick and an eyelash-curler from the chemist's, would be in Cardiff police station needing a solicitor. Could we come and collect her and never let her out of the house again, as he'd started receiving complaints about the crowd she was keeping down on the seafront.

Freda was quietly furious and told me she would deal with it. I remember thinking her anger a little perfunctory, as though she'd had enough of not being in control. That, or there was a streak of nervousness about Nancy's brush with the law.

'She'll only make you feel in the wrong for not having bought her everything she asks for,' Freda told me.

'Don't shout at her,' I said. 'I can't stand much more of it.'

Andrew Baker must have wished he'd never met the Voyles. By then, Dot was on Valium and all sorts of other things, and I was so fed up with the lot of them I was this close to going up to their house and clearing out Dot's bathroom cabinet for myself.

That evening, Freda, who'd been watching the hall from her chair in the sitting room, discovered the girl had gone from her room even though she was grounded for a week.

'She must have gone down the damn drainpipe,' she said.

'She's sixteen years of age,' I replied. 'She's trying to find out who she is.'

'She's going off the rails, Ceci.'

'How old were you when you left for London?'

'That's different. I had a reason.'

'Which was?'

'I'm going out to fetch the girl back in.'

'I'm coming.' Then: 'Freda,' I said, as though she'd listen, when we saw Nancy and Sandra sitting laughing between two boys on a bench on the prom. I must say the boys looked trouble, with big thick hair in points and all in black, like something from a fairground, and quite a bit older too.

'Back to the house *now*,' Freda said.

Nancy's kohl-rimmed eyes looked back at her. Behind the girl, pale egg-shaped faces in the Italian café watched through the window. A small child in a ribbon-edged tartan frock ran by holding an ice cream and squealing when she stopped and turned to see her parents making long arms and hurrying to catch her. Nancy used to do that—run from me and enjoy being caught.

'You're not my mother,' Nancy said. 'Apparently. So I don't have to do anything you tell me.'

I was waiting for Freda to tell her to stop showing off, which Nancy always loathed.

'You will while you're under my roof,' Freda replied.

'I'm not under your roof. I'm under the sky.'

One of the boys sniggered but when Freda turned to him, making asterisks of her eyes, he pulled at the collar of his jacket and looked away. Beneath the low grey sky, she looked fierce and beautiful in a pale blue halterneck top and cream cotton trousers so wide you could hear them flapping when she walked.

'I'm so angry I can't speak,' she said. Freda's face went red very quickly when she was cross.

'Well, don't then,' Nancy replied so loudly, a man in a white overall paused from lifting a pole to the red-and-white canopy over the shop where we

336

used to buy off-cuts of rock in small plastic bags as a treat on Sunday-afternoon walks.

'Home,' I chipped in, though the girl had stopped listening or talking to me a long time ago. 'Now. It's going to rain, in any case.'

Freda noticed a couple promenading turn to look back at us. I put my hand on her bare arm. She was fond of saying the town should have kept its stocks in the marketplace to give the gossips something to do with their hands.

'That's all, folks,' she shouted, stepping back and bowing. 'But same time tomorrow, we'll all be here.'

'I bloody well won't,' Nancy said, standing up. 'This is beyond embarrassing. Bye, you lot.'

As we followed the girl back to the house a roundabout way, up the steps that ran alongside the black park railings and past a grand terrace of houses with huge white buttons for bells and gardens of wilting hydrangeas, it started to rain.

'Listen to that,' Freda said, when a round of thunder shook the air. 'That'll clear the decks down on the prom.'

The dotted lines of rain fell so surely it was a wonder they gave when they hit us. I thought of the people sitting at the outdoor tables on the seafront and the little candles in white glass lanterns they lit every evening, and a story someone had told me about an open-topped bus in Weston-super-Mare getting caught in a deluge and the bedlam as passengers rushed below deck on a roundabout.

'There on a bench with boys like that,' Freda was saying as we crossed the square.

Nancy turned round. Her wet hair was darker again, her eyelashes clotted with rain.

337

'It wasn't just me,' she said. 'Sandra was there. And anyway, is it such a crime, sitting on a bench with *boys*?'

'Shouting and screaming like hooligans,' Freda went on. 'They might just as well have been on the front at Porthcawl with a bottle of cider.'

'Chance would be a fine thing.' Nancy's voice rose.

We stood as though it wasn't raining hard and I've noticed that—that once you stop running from a soaking, you start not to care.

'Tell me,' the girl said at the gate. 'What's so wrong with boys? Or wouldn't you know?'

'That's enough,' Freda said. 'Go to your room.'

'Why is it enough?' Nancy asked. 'Because you say so? Everything's always what you say.'

She pouted at us with red shiny lips, her hair as wet as if she'd been swimming. Freda was staring at Nancy as though her mind was running for a connection it couldn't make.

'Why don't we talk about what you're *not* saying?' Nancy flicked her hand at the hair on her shoulders.

'That's enough,' I repeated. 'People will be wondering what we're doing, standing in the rain shouting.'

I'd come from a home I couldn't wait to escape, and Freda had seen children lose their parents day in, day out during the war. The pair of us must have seemed so very hard to Nancy.

'But it's *not* enough, is it?' Nancy said. 'I'm sixteen. I can do as I please. I haven't any parents to stop me.'

Freda watched her march up the path. For the strangest moment I thought she was going to tell

338

the girl about her mother, and that night I felt the closest I had to her in a while. She made it clear she needed someone to hold, and whether it was right or wrong, I was always ready to put my arms around Freda, whatever she might not be telling me or the girl.

## 7

'That's smart,' I said. Nancy was wearing a new jacket, navy suede with what looked like a real fur collar. I rarely remarked on her appearance. She could go off like a ship's flare.

There was a time when the girl used to like me telling her about her most famous tantrum. One summer's day when she was around six, Nancy refused to come in from the garden when a plane appeared overhead dropping bombs. One, two, three, I could see them coming down, and I was pleading with her as she ran up and down on the sand pit screaming as though she was guiding the blessed plane in.

Was I really that naughty, Ceci, she'd ask, and then as she got older she stopped asking and started saying that she could never do anything right with Freda. I think Nancy's biggest mistake was growing up and not staying jumping in the waves with Freda sitting on the beach as alert as a lifeguard.

'I can see you looking,' Nancy replied. 'It's a present. From my boyfriend.'

'Boyfriend?' Freda asked, from her chair in the living room. That's what she'd started doing when she got back from work, even in summer with the garden to do, sitting staring into space. I knew she was unhappy. There'd been another falling-out at the hospital. All Freda would tell me was she'd put someone straight about Nancy.

I gave Nancy one of the looks we'd use between us when Freda was being touchy. It signalled we should clear the decks and regroup later. Freda saw it, her head swinging between the two of us, as though she felt out of the picture.

Over time it came out, as most things do in this town, that Nancy had hooked up with a married man, the manager of the bank opposite the public conveniences up by the roundabout and a big noise in amateur dramatics. I went in for a look at him one day and there he was, shooting his cuffs behind the glass screens with dark combed-back hair and a pair of blue braces.

'What do you like about him then?' I asked her, because she wouldn't tell us who her 'boyfriend' was, though this town being the way it is, we probably knew before she did.

'He's an actor,' Nancy replied. 'He always gets the lead.'

Freda started calling him Romeo after that, though she thought it anything but a love story. Have some pride, she'd tell Nancy, which made the girl run upstairs crying, because Freda could sound very cold. We never saw the man whose wife was from one of the big families in the town, but I know he used to wait in the car for Nancy round the corner because someone in one of the houses complained about him keeping the engine running in the foggy winter air.

Nancy became so secretive, her expression like a

340

boy I remembered way back from school, who would shield his work with his hand. The girl would come in late and stand briefly in the doorway of the living room, looking at me waiting up, her face pink with the pleasure of being wanted. I saw she was after something she could call her own, though I did wonder at her taking up with a man who belonged to another woman.

Nancy grew so thin. I knew she wasn't eating the breakfast I took upstairs to her, because one morning I came back from work with a shocking migraine and found a beagle on the pavement eating a rasher of bacon she must have thrown from the window. I was hoping the dog was a stray but when I tried coaxing him up the path, he ran off quite as though he'd heard about us and didn't want to get involved.

'You'll be ill if you don't eat properly,' I told Nancy one evening when she came in looking drained, and the moment I said it, she started to cry.

'What is it, love?' I asked, touching her shoulder because we'd long ago stopped hugging. She pointed at her belly. How I wished she was saying she was hungry, but Nancy was seventeen and pregnant.

My first thought was that this house was big enough for the four of us—if the father was who I thought, he wasn't going to leave his wife, whose family owned half the town—and my second was, Here we go.

Ten minutes later, I stood at the door to the sitting room, Nancy beside me as though I was her solicitor and she was wrongly accused of a crime.

'I've got some wonderful news,' I said. Freda,

always wary of superlatives, looked up at us.

'What's that then?' she replied.

When I told her, Freda was so quiet Nancy asked what was wrong.

'Nothing,' she replied, staring at the floor.

But there was something terribly wrong, in so many ways, and Freda saying nothing was worse than Freda letting rip. I looked at Nancy watching Freda, and me watching the two of them, with Freda not looking at either of us, and I felt what a rum thing it was, not knowing your place in the world.

\* \* \*

Nancy seemed such a child while she was expecting, watchful and fearful and walking about the house with a hand on her swelling belly as though she was trying to push it back down. She'd sit with us, listening to a play on the wireless, barely holding her nerve when Freda stared across at her for minutes at a time.

The baby was a girl—Harriet, Nancy called her—born without a hitch in the cottage hospital despite Freda saying the midwives there couldn't run a bath. Though she wasn't on shift, Freda robed up to keep an eye on them in the delivery room, which I don't think went down too well. I sat on the bench outside.

'It's got to be,' I remember a nurse saying as she and another woman walked towards me in the corridor. 'You have a look now and tell me if I'm wrong.'

When they pushed through the doors into the room where Nancy was becoming a mother, I couldn't help myself. I stood and went to the little round window and watched and listened as a new one was born. I do remember seeing something else through that window—the one nurse looking at my girl on the table and nodding at the other as if to say, 'You're right.' I thought about that a lot, wondering what they were on about, and how I always seemed to be on the outside looking in.

I saw a beautiful crib in the expensive baby shop in town. Freda said it was ridiculous, the way people spent a fortune on children, but I bought it, and lots of other bits besides. I went my own way on quite a few things to do with the baby, and enjoyed letting Freda see I regarded it as a new start, a proper child who knew where she'd come from—well, more or less. (Though Nancy would never say, my money was on that fly-by-night in the bank.)

At first it bothered me that the girl wasn't inclined to seek out the father and then I saw she was trying to manage by herself. I say manage by herself, but I was happy to support her, to try and make up for everything else. I didn't really see it was closing the stable door after the horse had bolted. Nor did I know another bolt was coming too.

Freda once told me she went into midwifery because working with babies was preferable to nursing people made sour by life, but she didn't go out of her way with the child.

'You're not turning into one of those miserable old buggers you used to complain about, are you?' I asked her one afternoon, and she said nothing, just smiled, because despite everything it did lift the mood having a baby about the place. We used

343

to take Harriet round to the Voyles', who welcomed us as though it gave them new life too.

Though I knew people were talking, Freda always told Nancy and me not to give a stuff. Once, not long after Harriet arrived, Nancy came back in tears saying a woman in a café had said, 'The girl's old enough to know,' as she passed her table.

'People haven't anything better to do than peddle tittle-tattle,' Freda told us, 'and that's their look-out, not yours.' Her dismissing the town's gossips as simpletons used to cheer Nancy up no end.

We enjoyed the calm of Nancy being out all day. I don't know what drove her back to work more—earning money, or getting away from us and the baby, who liked a good bawl until you picked her up and then she'd go quiet.

One day, I was standing at the sink and I said to Freda, 'I feel as though I brought this about.'

'Whatever do you mean?'

I described a time I told Nancy to be careful with boys. I felt so crude doing it but I did worry terribly about her wanting to find a role in life. Of course, she'd run out of the room saying she didn't want to be a doctor and just wanted to be left alone. Whenever she said that last bit, I wondered if she was pressing a point home.

'I know what you mean,' Freda said.

I turned.

'Do you? ' I asked.

She looked beyond me into the garden, where there was an empty bowl we put food in every evening for the fox—it ate well, since Freda would clean up on the reduced pork pies at the Co-op until the vermin man told us we were drawing

344

rats—and a row of baby outfits blowing in the wind so gaily it seemed they were laughing.

'Thinking or saying something,' she said, 'and then it happening.'

Funny that. One of our closest moments was over the baby, when Nancy on her own so often came between us.

The girl wasn't much for work, and Sandra was round most evenings staring at me and Freda as Nancy talked over the baby about the two of them saving for a trip abroad.

Nancy wanted something she wasn't getting, I think even Freda saw that.

'We must try and help,' I said, wringing a little towelling outfit in my hands. I didn't have any of my own mother's phrases to say as I got older so I'd started sounding like Freda's mother instead.

*    *    *

Sometimes Nancy would come back from wherever she'd been after work and give me a look that made me put Harriet straight back in her cot.

One night, Freda was waiting to tell her she shouldn't stay out so late because the baby hadn't stopped all evening.

'She's always crying,' Nancy said.

Freda said, 'You should have thought about that before you had her.'

'Don't you see?' Nancy replied. 'I don't want to be here.'

'Think of all Ceci has done for you,' Freda said. 'And you leave her holding the baby.'

I was too worried about things blowing up and waking the child, and next door banging on the wall, to laugh about that one, and besides, I could feel the air in the room springing as though preparing me to leap.

'You're Harriet's mother,' Freda said.

'At least Harriet has one.'

'Has she?' Freda asked. 'You're never damn well here.'

'Like mother like daughter then,' Nancy replied. She could be as quick as Freda.

I heard myself saying, 'Freda, couldn't you tell the girl something of her mother now she has a child of her own?'

'How many times do I have to say it?' Freda said. 'I—can't—tell you.'

It was always strange, seeing her go from being so capable.

'Why not?' Nancy asked.

Freda said, 'This town . . . There was a girl . . .'

I waited, listening hard, Nancy too. A girl who stood by Freda.

'I can't really say any more,' Freda went on. 'Not yet. Please—we don't want trouble.'

'I brought you here from London,' I said to Nancy. 'There was a woman in a bed at the hospital. They told me she was a very important lady. You were hers. They said she was d-dying . . . but I don't know if she d-did . . . ' I heard my words sound like gasping breaths.

'Ceci,' Freda said.

'No.' I felt a rush of hot blood in my head and I couldn't stop. 'Freda was the Sister at the hospital. About your father, I don't know. A man came once—old though—and then another woman, and then a woman with dark hair who I went with—'

Ceci, *please*,' Freda said. 'Nancy's mother . . .

She . . .'

I turned on her. 'How can you not have told us all this time? How can you have seen the girl struggling to keep her head above water? Not knowing where she came from? And where she's going? The pain you've caused her by not saying because it's "so damn difficult". What's so damn difficult that you can't say? Tell the girl, *for goodness' sake!*'

'Ceci.' Nancy put a hand on my arm but I elbowed at her. Once the baby came, she was less keen than she had been on kitchen sink drama.

'No,' I said. 'I *will* speak.'

But the moment I'd spoken, I lost any more words as Freda ran from the room. Ever afterwards, when I thought of her face, I felt so ashamed of wanting for Nancy or myself at her expense. I think I always hoped she never meant to hurt us.

'Perhaps it's best to leave it,' I said then, suddenly doubtful about raking up what was long gone.

Harriet started grizzling and Nancy took her from the cot.

'I will,' she replied. 'I will leave it.'

The girl went from the room without looking at me, her eyes to the baby, mother and child. I felt such guilt and shame and hopelessness when she turned back at the door, crying.

'All these bloody secrets,' she said. 'Why can't anybody tell me who I am?'

'I'm so sorry,' I replied, but she'd gone, and I was left apologising to myself.

*       *       *

347

A month or so of silence followed, and I came down one morning to a note from Nancy on the table, saying she had to go away. *With Harriet, so the baby at least has a mother.* That's what she'd written. *AND YOU HAVEN'T BEEN LEFT HOLDING THE BABY,* she put in capital letters.

Sandra's sister phoned an hour or so later to tell me Sandra was gone too. From the notes they'd left, we gathered they were intent on seeing the world, on being clever, beautiful women far away.

While Karen Martin was on the phone, Freda stood in the background and walked away before the call ended. I never showed her Nancy's goodbye letter because of the postscript. *I'll miss you, Ceci,* she'd written, *but Freda can't wait to get shot of me.* I knew that wasn't true and that it would upset Freda terribly.

At night, I'd lie thinking what a mess it all was, and wondering when the girl would return. Some of the things I worried about were so daft, like how Nancy would carry the baby and her belongings, though she left the mink-collared jacket on her bed where it stayed for some time.

'Can't you tell me?' I asked Freda one day, but she shook her head even before I'd added, 'Now the girl's gone.'

I couldn't keep the resentment from my voice though I felt to blame for not being more of a support, a friend if not a mother, to Nancy. Freda hated all that sort of talk, the newfangled 'nonsense' of parents being chums with their children.

Damn nuisance, that's what she called the little ones who moved in next door, though once or twice not long before she died she'd be standing chatting to them over the wall, telling them about a little girl's tortoise said to still be living in one of the gardens, or the rabbits that roamed on an island in the middle of the sea. I'd be poised waiting to stop her if she started on the symptoms of cholera. Children seemed to like Freda, probably because she told them things other people thought she shouldn't. That was Freda. Saying things she shouldn't, and not what I'd have given anything to hear.

*  *  *

Freda was pensioned off early from the hospital, which wasn't her style of doing things at all. She had spent her working life being indispensable. It came out later that one of the doctors had wanted to change her working methods, though there was also talk in the florist's of her tearing a strip off a nurse who was always on about Nancy.

'I'm not having it,' she said.

Sheer cussedness she'd call it, if someone didn't see things her way. I could understand how her ways might jar in a place where people chose to interpret her craving for efficiency as despotic, and her straight speaking as arrogance. I wept, seeing Freda go downhill, and I stopped working at the florist's. I didn't like the idea of her being at home on her own, the way she was brooding.

In time, she got herself back out in the garden, but sometimes, if people came to fix things in the house, they'd get a scare when they came across her sitting in a chair reading.

'She was nursing, a Sister, you know, saving lives

and rebuilding soldiers' faces in the war,' I'd say to these men who came round with a screwdriver and a sneer on their faces, but one time, she emerged from the sitting room as I closed the door on an electrician and said, 'What's the matter with you? Telling people all our business. It'll be all over the town in'—she looked at the large-faced wristwatch she'd always worn—'oh, all of five minutes.'

Soon enough I shut up. I never asked about the girl who stood by Freda again, though I rarely stopped thinking of Nancy and the baby.

For a long while I'd wait in, expecting to hear the girl's footsteps on the path or the phone going with a brusque demand to be picked up from the station. Then, well into the 1960s, when time crossed the line that said she wasn't coming back, I took up Freda's idea of evening classes. That first night, standing outside the leisure centre, seeing chairs and desks bleached by strip lighting, I almost didn't go in for fear of showing my ignorance. But when I saw there were others as timid as me, I looked forward to two hours out of the house. I took an O level in English literature first off, then an A level. In time, the thick sweet smell of a new book's pages and the whiff of chlorine from the pool next door became a comfort and delight, and the shelves either side of the fireplace filled up with Hardy, Austen and Shakespeare.

When they handed out the certificates, there Freda was, a few rows back, clapping, and in her chair five minutes early. That, of course, meant more than any qualification, but try telling Freda that sort of thing and she'd bat you away with, 'Stop your waste talk.'

Sunday nights in the house were my favourite. Freda didn't tend to go on one of her walks then. I think she liked the smell that came from the ironing—a hot crisping of damp cotton that would fill the sitting room when I brought the ironing board through. Then it was up to bed, but not before she'd had her water biscuit and cheese. 'Make you dream,' I used to tell her, and she'd look at me in such a way I didn't know if she thought that a good or a bad way to spend a night.

She never mentioned Nancy. I tried taking solace from that, because I'd come to equate Freda not talking with emotion words couldn't say. I kept the loss of the girl, and the way we had failed her, to myself.

## CECILY 2009

The air was a darker grey again outside the window of my middle room, which looked onto next door's wall—beyond which was a fancy new kitchen extension with decking that 'brought the outside of the house in', or so the estate agent had said when he stuck his head over and told me, 'That's probably what someone will do here. Knock through.'

Sarah was upset when I got to the end—well, I hoped it would be a beginning of sorts, but I didn't say as much—and we sat sniffing dimly in the light from the fire with the faint scent of soot that sometimes came down the chimney.

'I thought we were supposed to be holding each other up?' I said, feeling for the tissue that had dropped from the sleeve of Freda's dressing gown.

'Oh, Ceci,' she told me. 'You're so strong. There's me going on and on about Tom and babies and things, and all along you had all this you weren't saying. It's so sad, losing Freda and Nancy and . . .'

'Well,' I said, 'neither of them was really mine to lose.'

'Oh, but, Ceci, they were. And are. Nancy must still be around.'

Nobody had ever said that to me before, that Nancy was mine to lose. Cold, hopeful fingertips played over my skin. I was getting a chill, I could see it coming off.

'We have to find her,' Sarah said, a determined set to her jaw. The girl seemed to take it as a duty not to notice I was so much older and frailer. I felt such fondness.

'How on earth do we do that?' I asked, because it always played on my mind that Nancy knew where to find me but never came home. That was another thing going through my mind on the beach before I went for a paddle.

'Ceci, it's really not on,' Sarah said. 'There's you telling me to get back with Tom and now you sound as though you're having second thoughts about Nancy.'

'You should be thinking about getting back to London,' I said. 'Not chasing after long-lost girls for me.'

Suddenly I felt the most awful gap of years gone by, the Christmases me and Freda sat with the turkey wishbone slippery between us—you don't believe in this silliness, do you, she'd say, but she'd still go along with it—and then another year

352

starting with no sign of Nancy.

'It's too late, anyway,' I told her. 'There's nowhere for her to come. I'm putting the house on the market. Keeping it warm and everything, it's too much really. The cost and the size and . . . memories.'

The dog must have heard something in my voice because he lifted his head from the floor, but Sarah, love her, wasn't listening to my performing. She had an idea, she said, about how to get started, but she needed to speak to Tom first.

'I hope you won't think I'm being thoughtless, Ceci, after all you've told me,' she said, 'but before I go, because you must want a hot bath and more to eat, I've got something to quickly get from the car.'

'You haven't been keeping him there all this time, have you?' I asked, because I've always thought a joke is a nice way of trying to keep up.

'A Christmas tree that connects to your USB socket,' she said on her return, holding up what looked like a frayed pipe cleaner about six inches tall.

'A what?' I must have looked as though I'd thought she was going to bring something else altogether in from outside.

'Sorry it's not a real one, Ceci,' she replied, 'but I thought it would light the place up a bit.'

'Plug her in then,' I said when she explained how it worked.

'Come and watch, Ceci, so you can do it on your own.'

'You know me and computers.' I wasn't moving from the fire. 'Google's about my limit.'

Well, I could barely believe how pretty this scrap

353

of a thing looked, changing from red to green to blue and yellow and purple and pink on my desk. Ta da, Sarah went, splaying her hands showily like one of those girls in mini-dresses they used to have indicating prizes on quiz shows. I was glad enough to be sitting in darkness because I could feel my eyes more watery again.

'One thing, Ceci,' Sarah said, once she'd checked over and over if I was *really* OK and would I get an early night because I'd need plenty of energy for all she had planned.

'If Ida was a local girl, wouldn't the paper have covered her . . . her dying as well? I wonder what they said about the baby.'

I couldn't keep my eyes off the colours fading and strengthening on this little Christmas tree sitting on the pile of papers I'd collected in the past year or so.

'I haven't looked,' I replied, because the truth was, I'd been trying to keep Ida Gaze alive.

The following day, Sarah came with me to the library, the two of us arm in arm up the old-age ramp, puffing breath into the cold morning air.

When I asked for the bound copies of the *Times* from 1937, the librarian looked at me, and then at Sarah, as though for her to confirm over my head that I was losing my grip.

'Where's my black-haired girl who likes fossils,' I asked. 'Taking a sabbatical in the States,' he replied. 'Isn't it usually 1928, Miss Stirling?' he went on, because they all knew me in there, the number of times I'd been in.

'Yes,' I said. 'But not today. We'd like the second half of 1937, if you can spare the time. November 1937 we're after.'

354

The dust was thick in the winter sunlight a week before Christmas. Regulars sucking their sweets didn't stir. It didn't take Sarah long to find what we knew would be there. That didn't stop the tears when her clear, lovely voice read it aloud, and I felt eyes around us lift from their pages to hear her speak.

The girl got a couple of pages for her swim and a couple of sentences for her death. That was my first thought. The second was that after all this time, the name of Ida Gaze had finally been said out loud in this whispery old seaside town.

### CHANNEL SWIMMER DIES

Miss Ida Gaze, 25, has died giving birth in a London clinic. She was the first person to swim from this town to Weston in 1928 at the age of sixteen, and was married to the newspaperman, Frank Shankly. She is buried in Golders Green Crematorium in London.

When Sarah left me in my chair, her little tree was flashing on my desk, the fire was dying, a quiet honeycomb of orange and black sinking into the hearth, and the room was cooling in the silvery darkness of a December evening. The staircase was all shadow and stillness and echoes of those who had trodden it in years gone by, and the air in the house seemed green with the smell of a pine tree we used to have in our sitting room. It was always my little treat every year, a Christmas tree in the bay. I'd sit with Freda, pointing out how pretty the fairy-lights were and looking to see if her stare reached that far.

Best leave it until after Christmas to put the house on the market, the estate agent had told me, or else the decorations will date the particulars if it doesn't fly off the shelf.

I remembered Freda's last kisses, dry and quick and regretful.

'I can't tell you how I feel,' she said, and I think I finally understood what she meant. When I'd pulled out that silver disc to take to the beach, I'd found Freda's diary in the sideboard, but I didn't read it. I already suspected I'd spent my life loving a woman who belonged somewhere else. But that evening, I took it out and put more coal on the fire.

When I reached the last blank page—which stopped on 13 November 1937—and saw an envelope on which she had written my name, I wasn't sure what to do. All those letters that had gone between us, to and fro, for all that time, with me left so unwitting . . . Well, I thought, is this another missive telling lies by omission or something she'd have me read to smooth over the cracks once she's gone?

And then something happened, as I sat by the flames so ready to eat up empty words and leave things be. I held the envelope, knowing it was one of the last things Freda would have touched, and I remembered how much I loved her. A great surge of sorrowful joy—if that doesn't sound as daft as it might—ran through me. Whether I opened the damn letter or not, I knew no matter what else, nothing—not one of her looks or words, or her walks and wanting to be alone, nor the contents of a letter not saying what I wanted to hear—none of them could change my feelings. I loved that woman beyond any power I have to express. And I felt such strength I can't tell you, realising that though I had felt in thrall to Freda, and though I had come to think she had denied me answers, it was me, Cecily Stirling, who had been given the power of loving. I loved Freda and Nancy and Harriet, and no matter what I got in return, that—even if it was less than nothing—couldn't take away my love.

Suddenly, for all her reluctance to speak in life, Freda had given me such strength of happiness and hope. No matter what was inside the letter, she could not break my heart with what her final words did or didn't say. I had loved Freda enough that she couldn't break my heart. That was love, I realised, something powerful and enduring and invincible, and what a joy it was to feel such a thing.

*Dearest Ceci,*

*This is the last letter I will write to you, and I hope you will forgive my cowardice in not having the wherewithal and sheer decency to say face to face what I will put down on these pages.*

*You might think it unlike me not to tell it as it is, when for so long I have seemed like a woman who doesn't hold back. But I have no appetite, not least as I am now, for revelation and confrontation. Forgive me, for I should have told you long ago how much you mean to me but the truth is, brave as you have always called me, I have run away from things. I have in my heart so much I wanted to tell you, and to my shame there is so little I have said.*

*I know we've had our differences. I*

357

*understand that being with me may have seemed like living in a jigsaw where only half the pieces were pressed into place. The truth is, dear Ceci, without you and with you, I felt half of a whole, and yet I never told you more about myself and what happened. Will you believe it seemed like an intrusion in the new life we were starting together? That it was not an attempt to keep secret in my heart something I felt you should have no part in? Rather, I worried I might destroy what we had together, that if you were to find I had hoarded bits of my old existence in my mind as well as the wardrobe, you might question if my life with you was the one I—or you, more to the point—wanted to continue. But I am making excuses for my failings, there is no other way to put it, and I am fearful that what I say here may seem the less for not having been said in life.*

*I knew a girl called Ida Gaze who grew into the mother who gave birth to the baby you selflessly reared into a beautiful, courageous young woman. I wanted to share my life with Ida, in that way young girls do when they grow from little ones holding their best friend's hand in the belief it will be forever. But then real life comes in and the need to survive and work and build something for oneself, and then the days when a best friend is all one lives for start to seem very far away.*

*When Ida came to me, giving birth and dying in the hospital—our hospital, yours and mine, where we met, though I didn't know then what you would become to me—it seemed such a terrible loss and joy in one. And that is how life is, of course.*

*At the sight of Ida, I felt such gladness she had come to me, that I might help her, but such terrible sadness for how things were and had been. I saw I had abandoned her, run from her yet again, and the pain and guilt of her dying were truthfully almost too much to bear. Many times I visited her grave on which the words* friends forever *were inscribed.*

*Ida died not long after giving birth to the baby you—good, dear, kind Cecily—brought back to her home town, my home town, the place where Ida and I grew into young women who thought we could take on the world, and the place you and I eventually made our home.*

*I won't detail the way things went, but it's enough to say that she fell unlucky and what I had most feared might happen did. For that I have never forgiven myself, that somehow I may have offered into the air a self-fulfilling prophecy that grew from the feelings of despair I nurtured when I thought I was losing Ida to another sort of life. I stood holding her hand while the surgeon cut Nancy from her, but Ida didn't survive the Caesarean. She lost too much blood.*

*I should have given what I saw as Ida's failings the same understanding she gave what were truly mine. The same as you and me, Ceci, I think. For that is surely what friendship, like love, is about, giving the space for the other to be, but staying put like a damn ten-foot iron pole in the earth for when they return to your side. You have stood by me, Ceci, but I failed Ida. In these, my final days, I have looked at her photograph time and again, asking her image for forgiveness.*

*For a time I made a life with a dear girl called Edna. She was the woman who helped you and me take the baby to safety. When she died in the war after a bomb hit her ambulance, I found it difficult to continue living, but you gave me hope that weekend I came home and we lay by the lake. Do you remember it, Ceci? That hot day in the middle of the war?*

*I feel blessed to have met such giving and loyal women who I have no doubts I have not deserved, but none more so than you, Ceci.*

*Please, dear, dear Cecily, I want you to know that it is you who became everything to me, and yet there was so much I did to make you despair.*

*I have no doubts I contributed to Nancy's departure—and your loss of both her and Harriet—and that is also to my eternal shame. I feel such remorse at what was taken from you when it was your unquestioning goodness that saw Ida's child grow into a young woman I felt proud to know. I cannot express the disgrace I feel over the way I behaved towards Nancy, not being able to say what a brave and beautiful woman her mother was, and the way I was over Harriet too, how something in me couldn't stand to see what I felt was history repeating itself. I suppose I imagined that if I rejected that truth it would somehow become a lie and I could persuade myself I had not completely failed Ida or my mission to give her child a good new life.*

*You are no failure, Cecily. It is I who has let*

*you and Nancy and Harriet down more than I can bear to say.*

*I didn't see with Nancy what was there in myself, the need to not always be told—though there were things I should have told her—but the desire to get on in life. You tell me I have spent a lifetime helping others, yet I believe myself to be rather more self-centred. Perhaps what you called my selfless altruism has been nothing more than an attempt to escape myself.*

*I should have seen that Nancy needed to know where she came from so she might know where to go, and that, like me, she was a girl who'd do better with a freer rein, not a rod of iron. It's funny the lessons you think you've learned and haven't. When I started in nursing, Matron told me I was similar to her—meaning, I believe, that she didn't like being told what to do either—but I went away thinking she felt I might become as accomplished as she was. Her careful way with me meant I owed my success to that woman, as much as to Ida who encouraged me to make the best of myself from the very start.*

*How much people do for us without us realising, and how easy it is to do too little for them. How much you have done for me, Ceci, and how little I have given of myself to you.*

*I never properly thanked my parents for giving you and the baby a home—do you know how much they thought of the two of you?—or for their determination Nancy would not be taken away. Ida's parents were still in this small town and my talk of law courts was not a smokescreen. We did in truth worry terribly they*

361

*might make trouble for their grandchild, but here is no place to list the reasons why I feel little guilt Nancy was kept from them. There were times my mother was in tears because Winifred Gaze came to the house taunting her about Nancy being born out of death and cursed to damnation. It was a sad state of affairs. Ida's father was a drunk who did nothing to help his desperately ill wife. Neither of them could ever be bothered with Ida. I fear I didn't behave much better towards Nancy.*

*Most of all, dear Ceci, I must thank you for coming here so bravely with the baby, and creating a new life for us. If only we could live it again so I might tell you from the start how I felt. What would you say to that? Would you give me another chance?*

*I didn't think there were any tears left in me, the times I cried on those walks of mine you wished I wouldn't do. It wasn't space from you I craved when I told you to stop following me here and there. It was everything I am saying now and more. But how self-indulgent it felt, how crude and uncaring to you it would have been, to reveal the child you had reared as your own was the daughter of a woman I once loved.*

*It is your great sweetness and generosity that gave the two of us a life together. Yet I never gave you the respect and dignity of learning what had gone before, and that is why I go racked with guilt.*

*But, and here is what I have most need to say, I am also leaving with the greatest love of my life for you, dear Ceci. You were no crutch to get me beyond unbearable sadness or to save*

362

*a baby from an uncertain future. You were the*
*girl in the distance to whom I was running*
*(even if I didn't yet know it and you were always*
*complaining I didn't write enough).*

*You will always be the girl to whom I am*
*running.*

*How greatly I wish I had told you how much*
*I loved you and love you and love you. My lungs*
*are giving out, this thing is taking over, but it*
*cannot destroy my love for you, which will*
*continue until I take my last breath and beyond*
*for evermore. I know you, Ceci, I know you will*
*understand that I couldn't do this any other*
*way. I trust you to think the worst and the best*
*of me, the least and the most of me, and to*
*know that when I write now, it is because there*
*was no other way.*

*Yours from then until now and forever more,*

*Your Freda*

It was lucky I was able to read with a magnifying glass because I went over that letter so many times I could soon recite it as surely as if it were the Lord's Prayer. I counted myself blessed on that score too, because when I lost the power of sight, I gained the treasure of memory. Remembering is like loving, see. Neither can be taken from you no matter how much they hurt.

# EPILOGUE

## CECILY 2010

Sarah agreed there should be a plaque on the pier to recognise Ida Gaze's swim and I was after finding Nancy, of course I was. I couldn't let things drop. Freda used to say that.—*Let it drop, Ceci*—if I asked too many questions.

You see despite and because of everything, I felt strongly about a young woman who swam to another country getting written off in a couple of sentences and her baby being airbrushed from the obituary. I knew Ida Gaze gave birth to a child that lived. Like her mother, that baby grew into a beautiful young woman with the world at her feet.

I had a Google of Ida's husband, Frank Shankly. He was dead but one of the greatest newspapermen who ever lived, apparently, a man who mixed with heads of state, and changed the course of newspaper history with his challenging editorials and pictures of topless women. I ordered his biography from the library. *Playing God*, it was called, its title in the red and black writing of a tabloid newspaper. *A journey through the world of newspapers and some of the biggest political clashes of the twentieth century*, according to the blurb. *The private animosities, sometimes harsh, invariably torrid. This book is the story of what happens behind the headlines.* When I checked the index, there was one page reference, and when I turned to that I found one sentence describing his marriage to Ida Gaze as *ill-advised*. There he was, making a name

364

for himself, and the Wonder Girl became a throwaway line.

I can't say I enjoyed reading the rest of his book, with all its talk of politicians, boardroom rumbles and girls in knickers. He talked more about them than he did about his wives, five in all. Who did the man think he was? Henry the bloody Eighth? I went in to the city library to look at *Who's Who*, and found there was no mention of Ida in Frank Shankly's entry. Married four times and all of their names. Wrong. Married five times and you've missed out Ida Gaze! I found endless obituaries of the man, lovingly written by macho hacks holding him up as an icon of old-school journalism. He was spoken of admiringly as a womaniser. I'd read those hagiographies, then reread them. Every single one, gushing about the man's revolutionary approach to journalism, claimed the woman journalist he must have married after Ida was his first wife. Ida Gaze the go-ahead girl had vanished.

It was Sarah who suggested letters to the newspapers mentioning I was looking for Nancy Voyle, the daughter of Ida Gaze, a woman who deserved the town's recognition and more, for her meritorious swim. Though I felt beyond embarrassed at the idea of spouting off in print, Tom had told Sarah in one of their daily phone calls that it was the best way of making waves. If we had any hope of finding Nancy, we needed to make waves.

Sarah composed a masterpiece at my computer and then the phone calls started. The local paper was quickest off the mark, then one of the London journalists offered me the money for the plaque. Apparently the editor was taken with the idea of

365

an old girl searching for her baby—who was of course by now well into her seventies, only fourteen years younger than me—if she was still alive and wanting to get in touch. As a precaution, I didn't put the house on the market.

The morning of the interview, I had a hospital appointment, and nerves and all sorts of other feelings were making me chopsy. Besides, I felt sorry for having been abrupt with my consultant. He was a nice enough young man and I hadn't been the easiest of customers.

I said to him, 'This business about me losing my sight . . .'

'Yes?' he said.

'There you were, saying about only seeing round the edges . . .'

I could picture Freda's face watching me jawing away like this, as though the cork had come off the pop.

'Well,' I told him, 'I've seen so much more in a way.'

Usually, he's patient and tells me a little bit about his family—how his wife is a teacher and they're trying for a baby—and I ask him a bit about IVF, what chance there is for a couple giving it a fourth go, say.

'That's something for you to think about, Miss Stirling,' he said, very straight, and I thought then, These people haven't got the time for you, Ceci. Get yourself back out to that waiting room and save Sarah having to read another magazine.

'I've spent most of my life on the edges,' I went on, enjoying myself. 'But now I feel so much more at the heart of things.'

Oh, I wanted to laugh out loud in the silence.

366

When an old woman speaks, what do people think? My ability to make out faces may have been going, but I could see a referral to the mental health department on the cards as clear as you like.

'Miss Stirling, I have to ask,' he said, as stern as they come. 'This condition of yours—do you fully understand your situation?'

'Yes,' I replied, standing up. 'Yes, thank you, I do.'

Then I told him I couldn't stop, that like him I had another appointment. These doctors aren't the only ones with important business to attend to, and out I went to Sarah with her nose in one of those magazines that ring sweat patches on celebrities. 'Only time I get to read them,' she said.

'Don't worry about it,' I told her. 'At least you can,' and she offered her arm before we went down the corridor.

On the way home, Sarah stopped at the florist's and came out with a bouquet of roses and tulips and all sorts of greenery.

'I know you don't much like clutter,' she said, 'but I thought these would be nice in a bowl on the dresser.'

We drove home with me behind this giant bunch of flowers. Last time I saw one that size was on a coffin at a big swish funeral, car after car, going into the church in the square. A bouquet for Ida Gaze, for Freda's girl, the Wonder Girl. This is what it's like, I thought, what the doctor said about only being able to see around the edges.

'Now, Ceci, you will answer all her questions,' Sarah told me, while we waited for the journalist. 'You won't be like you were with me, will you?'

'You're not going, are you?' I asked when the

door bell went, the dog barked, and Sarah grabbed her bag. She had a little knitted mohair corsage pinned to the strap, a flower sprouting from green felt leaves, purple, a favourite of bees.

'I can't stay, Ceci. This is private.'

She looked at her watch, a big-faced one, like Freda used to wear. It's a piece of luck she wasn't wearing it when I took her down in the water.

'Where are you off to in such a hurry?' I asked.

'Do you want me to go or not?'

'Really?' I hadn't stopped telling her the trains ran every hour to London.

She nodded. 'To work at it,' she said, coming towards me. 'You've taught me that, Ceci, not to let go of love.'

Sarah let the journalist in as she was leaving and I was wiping my eyes. Soft, that's what Freda would have called the pair of us. Too soft for our own good.

\*       \*       \*

They did us proud with a double-page spread like Ida's swim, except the heading was CECI THE WONDER GIRL so large even I didn't need any help reading it.

It was all in there, me working at the hospital, taking the baby, setting up with Freda, finding the photograph, my search for Ida Gaze. They took my picture standing in the back, brown needles of branches around me and bruised apples at my feet.

'Will you mention about Sarah?' I asked. 'I don't think I'd be here if it wasn't for her.'

When the journalist asked me why I thought Freda hadn't told me about Ida Gaze, I didn't

368

hesitate. 'She loved her more than she could say,' I told her, because I couldn't say more than that.

There were other things I kept to myself, like Freda writing in her diary how a Sir came to visit Ida in the hospital and how a woman called Miranda Drabble wanted the child, but they had me talking away about the photo of Ida I hoped Nancy might see, and how I had a letter the girl might like to take a look at. I wanted Nancy to know how much Freda cared.

I felt Sarah and I had given Ida a voice all the town and beyond would hear. The paper put in about Nancy and Harriet leaving for the other side of the globe, which brought to mind that American flier. After reading in the *Times* about Amelia Earhart landing in Wales, I'd had a book out on her. She went missing close to becoming the first woman to fly around the world. Her plane went down over the Pacific on 2 July 1937, a few months before Ida was lost, and the baby and I came here.

It won't just be in the paper in this country, it'll be on the internet, the journalist told me, it will go all over the world. Then I had a call from her.

'Ceci,' she said. She was like Sarah with her first names. When she came to do the interview she asked if she could get one thing straight. 'I hope you don't mind me saying,' she told me, 'but you don't seem like an old lady, so would you mind if I called you Ceci?'

'What?' I said back to her. 'I don't seem old or I don't seem a lady?' and she saw I didn't mind at all her calling me Ceci, and we both laughed. *Find the Lady*, I thought to myself. That could have been their headline.

'Anyway, Ceci,' she said, 'I've got some news.'

369

'Oh yes?' I replied.

She told me that in these circumstances where family—I can't tell you how much that word meant—have been separated for years, the experts advise you don't rush in with a reunion.

'It can be too much, seeing people face to face after all this time,' she said.

I suppose she meant it could be awkward, that we could get off on the wrong foot and beat merry hell out of each other. That would probably be true if she was on about my first family, that mob off the Old Kent Road, but it wasn't them, though I often wonder what became of my brothers when I see these youths in baseball caps flicking fingers at the television cameras outside crown courts.

'Would you like Nancy's number or shall I give her yours?' the reporter asked. 'She's very keen to speak to you.'

'Let's do both,' I replied, and when my phone went within seconds of me putting it down after calling and it being engaged, I knew who it was. Nancy, my other little Wonder Girl.

Sarah had already called to say she'd be back at the weekend with Tom, and that they were thinking of going on a break somewhere, just the two of them. I'll take Mungo, I said, because I knew that was what was stopping them going—that dog being too darn spoiled to go in kennels. I can't say I didn't fancy having a dog about the place. You can get these ones now, trained, so the hospital says, to see you onto buses, stop at traffic lights and no doubt boil the kettle. Mungo will pull you over, Ceci, Sarah told me. No he won't, I told her. I ain't going down yet.

# A NOTE FROM THE AUTHOR

Though *Wonder Girls* was inspired by the 'lady swimmers' who swam the Bristol Channel in the 1920s, from Penarth to Weston-super-Mare, it is a work of fiction and I have played fast and loose with dates.

The first person to swim from Wales to England was Kathleen Thomas in 1927—see the note on the real-life Wonder Girls. In Ida's world, it is a year later when she strikes out for the other side after seeing Amelia Earhart land in Burry Port on 17 June 1928.

It thrilled me to read newspaper coverage of these events occurring at a time when most girls were expected to aim for marriage and motherhood, and Wales was regarded more for heavy industry and less for female derring-do.

Though a product of my imagination, I hope *Wonder Girls* shows the go-getting guts and stamina of the young women who swam such a dangerous stretch of water.

Crossing from Penarth to Weston, they would have battled a number of currents as well as the most powerful part of the tide.

The Bristol Channel is regarded as especially treacherous, not least because of the vast volumes of tidal water being funnelled through narrow spaces caused by headlands such as those at Portishead on the English side and Lavernock Point in South Wales.

Travelling at around three to five knots—or just over three to five miles an hour—the water is pushed around by these prominences, as well as by sandbars and islands, creating 'overfalls' or turbulent sections of water. This means the movement of the tides is always changing. In summer, the water temperature is unlikely to reach more than 13.5 degrees Celsius.

The seaside location in the novel is loosely based on the South Wales town of Penarth, a popular holiday resort during the Victorian and Edwardian periods, which became known as 'The Garden by the Sea' on account of its elegant parks. Five miles south-west of Cardiff, the Welsh capital, it lies on the northern shores of the Bristol Channel and boasts one of the last remaining Victorian piers in Wales. Each summer it berths the world's last sea-going paddle steamer, *Waverley*, which takes passengers to destinations such as Ilfracombe and Lundy Island.

At the entrance to Penarth Pier stands the Grade II listed pavilion which is undergoing a £4m restoration project after 10,000 people signed a petition to save the art deco building. The refurbishment, which recently received a £1.68m grant from the Heritage Lottery Fund, will create a cinema, café, and an observatory to view the estuary's wildlife, which includes shelduck, rock pipits and oystercatchers. Clearly the future for Penarth and its 24,000 residents is far brighter than Ceci's vision of her home town where everything is 'on its last legs'.

Like the fictional town in *Wonder Girls*, Penarth does have streets of Victorian Blue Lias houses, a library with a clock-tower and a seafront restaurant selling pizza, though it has never had a lido. That privilege belonged to the neighbouring town of

372

Barry which boasted one of the largest outdoor pools in Britain until its closure in 1997.

Built in 1926 by men employed on the 'docket system' and paid in vouchers which could be exchanged for goods at local shops, the Knap Bathing Pool was 120 yards long, 30 yards wide and held one million gallons of filtered seawater. Two concrete arcs of flat-roofed chalets and changing rooms with brightly coloured saloon doors were added to the lido in 1937, designed by the Borough Architect and Surveyor, Major E.R. Hinchsliff, who was said to be an admirer of Le Corbusier, a pioneer of the modernist movement.

From the start, many events, including swimming galas, water polo matches and diving displays, were held at Cold Knap, as it was known, and guests included Channel swimmers Kathleen Thomas and E.H. Temme.

Having enjoyed many freezing swims at the Knap lido, I attended a public meeting where three generations of Barry residents turned out to try and save the decaying pool. Victoria Perry of the Twentieth Century Society called it a 'wonderful asset to the town' but in August 1997, CADW, the Welsh equivalent of English Heritage, refused to list it saying it lacked 'the quality we would look for in a building of this type and period'.

As the lido fell into further disrepair, the council cited the expense of maintenance and in 2004 it was demolished. Now landscaped over, it is a place where people sit or skateboard and when it rains heavily, a spreading puddle forms in the dip where the pool once glistened in the sun.

The photograph on the last page of Janet Smith's wonderful book, *Liquid Assets*—a history of the lidos and open-air swimming pools of Britain—is the broken dolphin statue in the children's pool at Barry lido. How I regret not pushing through the old rusting turnstile one last time and taking what was left of it before the bulldozers did their worst.

Catherine Jones, Penarth, December 2011

# THE REAL-LIFE WONDER GIRLS

## Kathleen Thomas

In 1927, when Kathleen Thomas mooted her plan to swim the Bristol Channel, such was the disbelief that anyone—least of all a woman—should attempt so perfidious a stretch of water, the local newspaper in Wales was obliged to issue the following statement:

### Miss Thomas Confirms Echo Report

*Miss Kathleen Thomas, the Penarth lady swimmer, whose decision to attempt the Bristol Channel was exclusively reported in yesterday's* South Wales Echo, *reaffirmed in an interview today that our report was correct in its entirety.*

The Suffragettes were fighting for women's rights and the first total eclipse of the sun for more than two hundred years foretold great things. But the stretch of water which separates South Wales from the south-west of England was known to have a cruel appetite for taking lives.

Undaunted, twenty-one-year-old Kathleen stepped into the chill and dangerous channel at 4.15 on the morning of 5 September 1927. The event took place in great secrecy, with a Welsh Amateur Swimming Association representative in one of the boats that accompanied the swimmer as she battled seven currents.

375

Fortified by Bovril, Kathleen made the crossing from Penarth to Weston-super-Mare, a distance of more than twenty miles, in seven hours and twenty minutes, coming ashore at 11.35 a.m. The first woman and the first person to swim the Bristol Channel, she had a hot and cold bath in a Weston hotel before half an hour's rest and a good fish lunch.

Generous praise followed. Numerous plaudits stressed the achievement's importance for a 'mere woman'. Kathleen received fan mail from the Cardiff Women Citizen's Association, the Cardiff Union, the Red Cross, and from one woman who apologised for her delay in writing on account of 'such a lot of business to do and a lot of worry with maids'.

Another letter of congratulation—marked *via Siberia* and stamped and dated 6 September 1927—was sent by a 3rd officer on *SS Rompoe*, a steamer positioned about 1,600 miles east of Yokohama, about 4,000 west of San Francisco and about 1,800 north-west of Honolulu. You are famous *to the uttermost parts of the earth*, he wrote, including a copy of the radio report the ship had received. *Good old Penarth, we'll show the world. Congrats, old girl!*

A growing celebrity, Kathleen was the subject of newspaper cartoons and guest of honour at civic receptions. At one swimming gala, she made her entrance to 'Men of Harlech' and the audience rose to their feet to applaud.

In 1927 interest in travel and speed was growing thanks to Malcolm Campbell's world land speed record at Pendine Sands and Charles Lindbergh's solo flight over the Atlantic in the *Spirit of St Louis*.

A year later, in 1928, Amelia Earhart became the first woman to fly the Atlantic when she landed in Burry Port, West Wales. Twelve months after that, Welsh schoolgirl Edith Parnell decided she too would swim the Bristol Channel.

Edith Parnell

Only E.H. Temme, a world-famous male swimmer who also conquered the English Channel, had matched Kathleen Thomas's feat between Penarth and Weston, but on 15 August 1929 Edith was snapped on the beach in her swimming costume by a doubtful paparazzo. Her first attempt, two weeks previously, had been postponed due to rough weather. *Miss Parnell only wants tide and weather luck to achieve her difficult object*, said the town's newspaper, the *News*, on the day of her attempt.

Suitable tides for such a swim were rare, and tides around the Holm Islands—Flat Holm and Steep Holm—were notorious for turning over boats. The mood was one of valiant optimism, but at sixteen, Edith's ambition was thought to wildly outstrip her chances of swimming the so-called Severn Sea—or *Môr Hafren* as it is known in Welsh.

It took her ten hours, seventeen minutes and ten seconds to make the crossing and when she arrived back in the Welsh seaside town of Penarth, a police constable escorted her through cheering crowds to the tune of 'See the Conquering Hero Comes'. *There was a feeling of relief throughout the town when the news came in, confirmed afterwards by a record sale of evening papers*, reported the *News*

377

which headlined her as *The Girl of the Moment.*

At a reception in the Pier Pavilion, Edith was presented with a silver cake stand and a bouquet of roses. The chairman of the Penarth Council told the audience the Bristol Channel had only been conquered three times, and two of the great swimmers were Penarth girls. They were especially proud of Miss Parnell *who had displayed amazing pluck in enduring for over ten hours one of the biggest trials that could be demanded of any athlete, man or woman.*

What became of these go-ahead girls? Both moved to London and married journalists. Kathleen taught swimming and raised a family, before her death in 1987. Edith, a talented writer who sold short stories to magazines while still at school, died in 1938 of heart failure after giving birth to a baby boy who lived for twelve hours.

Until the early 1990s, Kathleen's Channel crossing was included in *The Guinness Book of World Records* and in 2007, thanks to the efforts of her relatives and eighty years after her triumph, a plaque was finally unveiled on Penarth Pier.

Edith's achievement remains unrecognised by the town though there is a Gaumont Graphic clip of her swim in the archives of ITN Source (see link) :

http://www.itnsource.com/shotlist//BHC_RTV/1929/
01/01/BGT407141115/?s=edith+parnell&st=0&pn=1

With the second highest tidal range in the world, the Bristol Channel remains as dangerous as ever. Looking at its clashing waves, it is impossible not to marvel at these girls in their swimming caps and long-legged bathing suits, poised at the edge of a new era of opportunity for women.

*Never do things others can do and will do,* said Amelia Earhart, who in 1932 became the first woman to fly the Atlantic solo, *if there are things others cannot do or will not do.*

For their strength and bravery, determination and ambition, here's to the real-life Wonder Girls.

# ACKNOWLEDGEMENTS

Many interesting books helped with the writing of *Wonder Girls* and they include *History of Penarth* by Roy Thorne, *The 1930s Home* by Greg Stevenson, and Mary S. Lovell's biography, *Amelia Earhart: The Sound of Wings*.

I would like to thank Paul Evans for putting ideas in my head; Nic Lanagan, Clive Hosken and Clive Wilton for their knowledge of trains and all things marine; Mike Kingston for telling me about the Bristol Channel; and the late Judy Smith for her curiosity, wisdom and kindness.

The staff at Penarth Library were always so willing to help and show why libraries are best treasured not closed.

A sea of wonder girls helped this book cross from one shore to another and they include Maxine Hitchcock for wading in near the start; pacers Susannah Godman, Daisy Parente, Jane Finigan; copy-editor Joan Deitch and proofreader Mary Tomlinson in the pilot boat, and designer Lizzie Gardiner who has created a beautiful lido on the cover and given 1920s' movie stars Dorothy Sebastian and Anita Page twenty-first century roles as wonder girls.

Those I haven't mentioned by name will have had their head under the water at the time of writing, but thank you to everyone who helped me reach my goal.

Ladies—and Gentlemen—I give you the fleeting-and-not-forgotten Francesca Main for setting this book afloat, the brilliant Jessica Leeke

for showing it how to swim, and gala princess
Sarah Lutyens for catching sight of it under the
surface, giving it the kiss of life, and never leaving
its side.

382